the TIME KEY

PRAISE FOR MELANIE BATEMAN AND *THE TIME KEY*

"To change the past . . . to know the future . . . these ideas are not unusual in stories of time travel, but Melanie Bateman's book breathes new life into these concepts through intriguing characters and compelling storytelling. The connections between people in the story are blended with the ideal amount of mystery and adventure, tragedy and triumph, that the novel is nearly impossible to put down. *The Time Key* is certain to resonate with and inspire readers everywhere."

–Brett Jensen, author of the Relegated Trilogy

⚉

"Time travel is a fascinating yet confusing subject, but *The Time Key* weaves a brilliant and exciting story in such a simple way that instead of being confused you're left wishing you were a time traveler yourself. Stanley Becker's tear-jerker of a story has it all: tender family moments, exhilarating time travel, mysteries to be solved, strange creatures from other worlds, child-like imaginings, and a personal journey like no other. It's like *Gulliver's Travels* for a new age. I wish I had a Time Key!"

–C. Louis S., author of *Pizza Planet*

⚉

"Melanie Bateman weaves fantasy and mystery into a fusion of adventure. Her attention to detail and setting brings this new world to life. It's a clever and heartwarming book that will arouse your life-after-death curiosity and have you eager to read about the possibilities. The classic tale and beauty of life and death springs out of the pages and into your imagination. *The Time Key* will have you wondering if the unseen can truly help us."

–Erin Nelson, author of *So You Got Boys, Do Ya?*

⚉

"Melanie Bateman's new novel, *The Time Key*, is an entertaining, fantasy-infused romp through space and time. She has artfully created compelling characters woven into an intriguing plot and storyline. I highly recommend this enjoyable read for anyone partial to the sci-fi/fantasy genres."

–Kevin C. Scholz, architect, artist, and educator

the
TIME KEY
Melanie Bateman

SWEETWATER
BOOKS

An imprint of Cedar Fort, Inc.
Springville, Utah

ISBN 13: 978-1-4621-1856-4

Published by Sweetwater Books, an imprint of Cedar Fort, Inc.
2373 W. 700 S., Springville, UT, 84663
Distributed by Cedar Fort, Inc., www.cedarfort.com

LIBRARY OF CONGRESS CATALOGING-IN-PUBLICATION DATA

Names: Bateman, Melanie, 1992- author.
Title: The time key / Melanie Bateman.
Description: Springville, Utah : Sweetwater Books, an imprint of Cedar Fort, Inc., [2016] | ©2016
Identifiers: LCCN 2016003637 | ISBN 9781462118564 (perfect bound : alk. paper)
Subjects: LCSH: Widowers--Fiction. | Time travel--Fiction. | LCGFT: Science fiction.
Classification: LCC PS3602.A8536 T56 2016 | DDC 813/.6--dc23
LC record available at http://lccn.loc.gov/2016003637

Cover design by Michelle May Ledezma
Cover design © 2016 by Cedar Fort, Inc.
Edited and typeset by Justin Greer

Printed in the United States of America

10 9 8 7 6 5 4 3 2 1

Printed on acid-free paper

For Chance,
who begged for more

Part One

I

There couldn't be a better time to begin Stanley Becker's story than at the moment he stood on the frozen stone wall of Kingston Bridge overlooking the river Thames, breathing in the winter night and pressing the icy metal barrel of a pistol to his jaw.

I have often wondered where it would be most appropriate to begin. A few other moments come to mind, but despite the significance they play, I choose to begin Stanley Becker's story at the approaching end of his life.

Before he found himself standing on the bridge, Stanley hadn't contemplated what the best approach to ending his life would be, but he had assumed that a bullet to his head would be the quickest. What did he know about suicide? All he knew was that it would be rather unfortunate if he missed.

Through his misty breath, he looked down at the black waters that seemed so calm and knew it would be the perfect resting place for his worn-down body. The moment he blew his brains out, his corpse would crash down into the dark waters and conceal him from the world he was so determined to leave. Few things could be more poetic. Stanley Becker smiled. Soon he would see Jane again, holding little Maisie's hand and grinning, just as the last time he had seen them alive.

Although Stanley Becker was about to take his life on this particular night, his thoughts lingered elsewhere, remembering the tragic event that had taken his entire reason to live. He remembered it quite vividly. Six years ago, Stanley had refused to attend the opera despite Jane's pleading. He had stayed home to write a story that he would never finish. Unbeknownst to him then, on the same bridge where he now stood, his wife and daughter had lain sprawled in the crimson-stained snow, lifeless.

Perhaps the fact that Mr. Miller had not driven that night, but one of the drivers employed by Jane's father, could have been the single event that sealed his family's fate. There were other incidents that only I had been able to see as I revisited the night when everything changed, and although unclear, they nevertheless deserve some mention. Perhaps the cause had been that Jane's father had insisted on sending his own driver, that the driver himself had had a drink too many and had failed to see the incoming collision. Or, possibly, that a street cat had darted across the street and consequently startled the horse of a carriage whose driver had had recent late nights looking for a runaway daughter, losing control only moments before the accident.

I only observed the minor events of that night, but the matter of life and death could have been the result of numerous decisions by unknowing players and (as Stanley's mother always told him) could not have been stopped and can never be changed. I can't help but feel sympathetic when I am reminded of this truth, however insignificant it renders us, but it would be a long time before Stanley understood the fragility of our human existence, and how crucial our resolve to ignore such realities impacts the way we play our set role.

As he presently stood on the bridge, yearning for the end to come, Stanley was comforted by the thought that he would no longer need to worry about what he could have done differently. Soon, the long, numbing, excruciating life he had led for six years would be over. He was ready for whatever awaited him in the next life, if there was anything waiting for him at all.

The pistol felt heavy and the cold embraced him. He wondered if attempting a suicide could be any less pleasant. As Stanley passed a hand over his eyes, he steadied himself for the big moment. The barrel pressing on his jaw was aimed straight to his brain. For a split second he wondered if it would hurt.

His gloved hand gripped the gun. His finger touched the trigger. Stanley Becker held his breath and felt the end draw near. He squeezed the trigger.

Click.

For a moment Stanley stood on the bridge, holding his breath. He sloppily looked down the barrel and cursed. For the love of heaven, had he forgotten to load the bloody thing? He quickly checked the chamber. All were full.

Of all the bad luck in the world—

In frustration, Stanley pressed the pistol to his temple and gritted his teeth.

Click.

Crying out in defeat, Stanley dropped the pistol. It clattered on the cobblestones. Apparently, there were powers higher than his own stopping him from putting an end to his misery, and instead wished to inflict as much anguish on him as possible. Perhaps freezing in the river wouldn't be so painful. He had once heard that in the end one only felt pleasantly comfortable.

Stanley felt the heaviness of exhaustion settle on his shoulders. He sat down on the stone wall and hoped that it would crumble under his weight and deposit him into the river below. In a good poem he would embrace the cold water and let the current carry him into the tranquil abyss of wonder that would grant him passage into the next world, peaceful and untroubled, or some rot like it.

At that moment, when a loaded pistol would not take his life, Stanley remained a defeated man, wishing he possessed the strength and willpower to end it by merely hoping for it.

It is possible that the beginnings of stories are best when they reflect the happy events of life, simple moments that Stanley Becker missed. Or they might observe critical events that can alter and change the path of life. Throughout my travels, I have seen many things and met many people, but none of their stories have impacted me as much as Stanley's. I often find myself returning to this particular night, where I see Stanley's hunched figure motionless in the cold December night of 1897.

What Stanley didn't know was that powers higher than his own, or perhaps merely *fate*, had led him to that exact spot at that moment for a reason. What he was about to witness would push him into a world of wonders and terrors and, according to his decisions, would finally lead him to the simple peace he had sought for six years. For that, at least in the boundaries of Stanley Becker's life, is what follows a failed suicide on a misty winter night.

The anger that Stanley no doubt felt rushed loudly in his head. He didn't hear the commotion in the alley south of him. He did sense, however, an unexpected chill up his spine. The moment he turned to look over his shoulder, he saw unnatural shadows that stretched behind him. They were a dark mist, dancing over the dimly lit streets. They moved of their own will and dashed past him like eels underwater to disappear into the dark alley.

It is an unnerving sensation being in the presence of the shadows that Stanley saw, unnatural creatures that roam the depths of dreams and stories. The terrible vision of shadows lurking the streets of the night stirred a dormant memory in Stanley that he had never imagined as a possibility in his reality. He had forgotten why he was even on the bridge. Stanley dropped down to retrieve his useless pistol and fixed his gaze on the dark alley where they had gone. He couldn't say what urged him to follow them, but he was hardly aware of his echoing steps. As he walked down the street he briefly questioned his sanity, but shrugged it off when he reminded himself that committing suicide did not necessarily describe stability.

He followed the direction that the strangely animated shadows had taken. No sooner did he hear the sounds of a struggle than he saw the hidden scene of a merciless mugging. As Stanley got closer, he saw two figures beating on a lone man, while four others stood back to watch. The largeness of the group intimidated him, but he raised his arm and pointed the pistol at them.

"Hey!" Stanley's voice sounded hoarse in his ears. "Leave him be!"

The figures paused to look back at the ungainly man. At first, Stanley readied himself for the approaching group to turn on him, but was horrified when they began to vanish before his eyes. Their shapes seemed to melt into the ground, creating the moving shadows he had seen on the bridge, dissolving where they stood. Stanley's pistol fired. The bullet hit the rising fog. Silence followed.

The figures continued to melt into shadows. Fearing they would come after him, Stanley kept his pistol pointed and could not help cursing at the convenience of his firearm working at that moment. But the shadows remained shadows, and Stanley felt the coldness they had brought disappear with them. He panted heavily as adrenaline lingered in his veins.

"Easy there, fellow."

Stanley's attention turned to the mugged victim, who rose to his feet shakily and stumbled to where Stanley stood.

"You could put that down," the man said, motioning to Stanley's pistol. "I'd wager they're gone now."

Still uneasy, Stanley stood his ground and slowly lowered the weapon. The man was shadowed by the tall buildings around them as he leaned against the wall in pain. He glanced at Stanley with clear eyes that betrayed a playful light filled with mockery.

Stanley assumed he was in no danger and cleared his throat.

"Are you hurt?"

"Not badly," the stranger mumbled, shifting his attention to the ground. From his pocket he brought out a handkerchief and dropped it on the wet cobblestones. Stanley wondered whether that had some meaning he should be aware of, but his attention was elsewhere. Already the dark windows in the buildings were lighting up as people peeked out, curious and alarmed.

The stranger spoke again as he straightened up and slipped the handkerchief back inside his pocket. "I suppose I should thank you for not blowing my brains out."

Stanley ignored the call on his aim when he saw the man limping. "Wh-what were those?" he asked.

At last the stranger's bloodied face became clear to Stanley, who in turn attempted to conceal his own to avoid being recognized. If his association to a higher class were to be revealed it might end badly for him. Around these parts, one couldn't be too careful. Thankfully, the stranger hadn't noticed or had chosen to ignore Stanley's impeccable clothing.

Regarding Stanley's question, the stranger shrugged and approached him slowly, wiping a bloodied lip with his sleeve.

"They're gone. And that's all that matters now."

Stanley couldn't shake the uneasy feeling he had. He gripped his pistol tightly until his leather glove crunched. The stranger eyed him curiously.

"Don't fret. They won't come back for you."

It was possible that Stanley had imagined the shadows. Besides, the stranger didn't seem the least bit concerned. Stanley decided he had only been seeing things. When the stranger reached him, he paused to take a shaky breath but kept his curious eyes on Stanley, as though he recognized him from somewhere. Stanley had never seen the man before.

"What's your name?"

Stanley felt a gnawing sensation in his gut. Unwilling to give the stranger any more information than was necessary, he replied, "Stanley."

The stranger nodded and continued past Stanley, bumping into his shoulder as he limped. "Thanks again, Stanley. Perhaps I can repay you in the future."

I feel the urge to draw your attention to the stranger, who, upon bumping against Stanley in an effort to leave the alley, was betrayed by his injuries as he walked. The stranger, a grin plastered on his lips, maneuvered his hand in a most skilled fashion that only a careful observer could see. His left hand held a metal object, small and seemingly insignificant, that he carefully slipped it into Stanley's pocket, who, unaware of the stranger's actions, seemed annoyed by the wounded man's clumsiness.

Stanley watched the man stumble down the street and disappear into the rising fog. The events of that night kept Stanley's mind occupied as he returned to his spot on the bridge and, mounting his bicycle, rode away from his attempted suicide. It would be a long ride home. He decided it would probably not be worth the trouble to attempt ending his life again.

That night of December 3, 1897, chilled his bones, but he could not help wonder if he had come across something in which he should not have intervened. Somehow, he thought, his miserable excuse for a life had been altered by his decision to shoot himself that night, of all nights.

❧

Mrs. Miller howled like a hound the moment Stanley rode through the gates just minutes before sunrise. Her thick frame waited at the door, impatient but concerned. When Stanley dismounted, she smothered him in a flurry of questions. During the long twenty-nine years of being mothered by Mrs. Miller, Stanley had learned not only to obey the bossy housekeeper, but also to alter the truth of his answers to avoid a scolding. If Mrs. Miller's wrath was aimed at you, you'd never hear the end of it.

Her warm embrace, however, felt soothing as she led him inside the house where Russell Gilmore waited. To Stanley's dismay, his tall brother-in-law smoked his pipe and wore that all-business look Stanley knew so well. Gilmore seemed to suspect what Stanley had tried to do and was quite displeased about it. Stanley nodded to him. He handed Mrs. Miller his coat and removed his shoes at the door. One thing Mrs. Miller despised, among many, was muddy floorboards.

"Now sit down, Dr. Gilmore," Mrs. Miller said and motioned to the library. "I'll put on some tea."

"I'm quite all right, Mrs. Miller," Gilmore replied, but obeyed.

Stanley sat in his usual armchair that faced the window. After a moment, Gilmore approached Stanley, who stared fixedly at the patterned rug beneath his feet, musing over the reality that the morning brought. He had returned to his pitiful existence.

"Please tell me you didn't go where I think you went," Gilmore said, puffing out a cloud of smoke.

Stanley sighed.

"Don't you realize how worried we've been? Mrs. Miller came to my house at midnight, *hysterical.* She sent Mr. Miller out to find you, but he hasn't returned. I haven't slept a wink all night just to keep her from running out into the streets after you. So after all that, I do think I deserve an explanation."

"Where do you think I've been, Russell?" Stanley muttered. "It's been six years."

Thoughtful, Gilmore stuffed his hand in his pocket and placed the pipe back in his mouth.

"Don't think I don't miss them too, Stanley."

Mrs. Miller came in and set down the tray, filling the room with a sweet aroma. Stanley scrunched up his face when she handed him the cup of tea.

"And my scotch?" he asked sourly.

Mrs. Miller shot him a glare. "No more drinkin' for ye, Mr. Becker. Not after last night. That drunken frenzy would 'ave ye waking up in some Whitechapel ditch."

He took a sip.

"I wasn't drunk."

Gilmore thanked her for the tea and took a seat next to Stanley. After a moment, he asked, "Did you go to the bridge?"

Stanley wouldn't meet his eyes. Instead, he kept them glued to his cup and tried his best to ignore his brother-in-law.

Unmoved, Gilmore pressed on. "You took the pistol, didn't you? Mrs. Miller said it was missing."

Stanley cursed. "The useless thing didn't work when I most needed it."

"Thankfully," Gilmore said with a sigh, running a weary hand through his dark-red hair. "Stanley, what can I do to dissuade you from trying that again? I'm not the only one that's concerned for you—Mary, the children, Mr. and Mrs. Miller . . . What would I tell little Mark if something were to happen to his dear uncle?"

Stanley didn't answer and struggled to pretend to be unaffected.

"It's been six years," Gilmore continued, fingering his pipe wearily. "It's time to let them go."

It took Stanley all he had not to burst out in anger. "Don't ask me to do that," he said quietly.

"You must let Jane and Maisie rest."

"Then it's time for me to join them."

Before Gilmore could reply, Mrs. Miller returned to offer them more tea, but Stanley shook his head and waved her off.

"Dr. Gilmore was just leaving. Weren't you, Dr. Gilmore?"

After giving Stanley a defeated look, Gilmore nodded and thanked Mrs. Miller. Without looking back, Gilmore left Stanley in his drunken stupor that lacked the alcohol he so craved. Mrs. Miller stood back uncertainly. Draped over her arm was Stanley's damp coat that she patted like she would her cat, Brutus, and waited for Stanley to take notice of her. Stanley stared out the window, watching the outside world come to life with little interest.

"Mr. Becker," Mrs. Miller said softly, but getting no reaction, she approached him. "Mr. Becker, there's something in yer coat that I'd rather not touch."

Stanley nodded. His blue eyes didn't waver from their fixed gaze on the window as Mrs. Miller placed his coat on the armchair next to him. She patted his arm before leaving him to his thoughts. At the door, she turned.

"He only worries, Mr. Becker. Don't condemn 'im for caring."

Stanley brushed his damp, dark hair away from his forehead and leaned back in exhaustion. He had not slept all night, and the lack of rest made his head spin. He took the coat and reached into the pocket where the useless pistol rested, cold and heavy. Stanley unloaded the pistol and scowled as he remembered. He wondered why it had not worked. It had been loaded and ready. He had even tried it the day before. Why had his attempt failed so miserably? And then he recalled the shadows he had shot at. Stanley had been sure he had imagined them. In the light of day, the memory seemed like a disturbing dream.

Something about them chilled his skin, but he tried to convince himself that they had not been real.

Stanley rose, straightened out his coat, and heard a thud by his feet. He looked down.

It was a pocket watch, lying on the carpet with an air of indifference. Its bronze surface winked under the light of morning. As Stanley examined the unexpected contraption, he felt a cold shiver run up his spine. His awkward fingers picked up the pocket watch to study it. The old thing was rusted, but its intricate design showed glimpses of incredible craftsmanship. The front side of the pocket watch had an elaborate symbol made of iron that resembled a rose, kept closed like a window through which he could barely make out the quivering hands of the mechanism. Stanley flipped it over as he straightened up. The back revealed a snake, coiled and wrapped around itself in a circular design, biting its own tail with fierce aggression.

When he opened the little rose window, Stanley was surprised to see that despite resembling an ordinary pocket watch, this contraption appeared to be far more complex. There were four hands, instead of the common three, each of different lengths that pointed at three circular sections around the axis. The sections were lined with symbols that Stanley's inadequate knowledge failed to decipher. Strangely, the three smaller hands pointed at a marker where the number twelve should have been, motionless, while the longest hand swung slowly around in a counterclockwise manner. At the other end of this hand, a tiny arrow attached to it circled in its own way, both slowly spinning for no apparent reason.

Where had this contraption come from and how had it come to be in his pocket? In his tired mind, Stanley could not make sense of things, much less of how and why this pocket watch had come to be in his possession.

In any case, Stanley's usual disinterest resurfaced. He took a long swig from the flask he carried in his trousers, deeming the curious contraption and its sudden appearance in his pocket well below his regard, as he was unwilling to induce any effort on his part. The repeated struggle of ignoring the world around him had trained him to avoid most natural feelings. Other than depression and a common surge of anger, Stanley felt nothing.

In the dawn of the new day, Stanley remained trapped in his library, immersed in the scotch contained in his flask, exhausted by the events of one night six years ago. And although he had tried to end it, his life waited mindlessly for the approaching consequences of an attempted suicide made on the same night that a stranger had slipped a pocket watch into his coat.

II

It wasn't the frozen air stiffening his limbs and causing his nose to run that irritated Tom Miller, but the slowly drifting hours as he waited for his employer to return. Despite the shivering fits that frequently overtook him, the coachman kept his thoughts occupied on his assignment.

"Wait in the carriage," Mr. Becker had instructed him before disappearing into the crowd.

It had been hours since his employer had left him in the busy streets of Kingston by the river Thames without any indication of where he would go. But the coachman knew this to be another one of his visits to the pub, where Stanley often went in search of solitude. It wasn't uncommon for Tom to take Mr. Becker on weekly trips to various pubs, but tonight's visit seemed different. Tom should have expected this would be a lengthy wait after the second hour had dawdled by without even a sign of Mr. Becker's return.

A shove at his back startled Tom, who patted the horse nuzzling his coat. Perhaps it was time to find Mr. Becker.

Tom could still hear his wife's shrill voice from earlier that day, distressed as she had been to learn of Stanley's intended trip to Kingston despite the hectic events of the night before. Tom had his suspicions about his employer's midnight bicycle ride, but who was he to question what the man did? Mr. Becker was a generous man—even after the terrible accident, Stanley had allowed for the Millers to keep their jobs and residence in the Becker home. While other servants lived in the cramped quarters of attics and basements, the Millers were given their own space and privacy in a little building apart from the main house, which they had called home for numerous years.

Walking through the dispersing crowd, Tom abandoned the carriage in search of Mr. Becker. As his thoughts recollected the events of that day, his lips turned into a tired smile.

"That blasted man!" Norah Miller had exclaimed, throwing her hands. "Thinks he can outdrink the devil 'imself, he does!"

Mr. Miller had chuckled.

"Oh, Tom, do watch 'im. He doesn't know when to say no more till his heid drops on 'is lap from spinning!"

Presently, Tom approached a brightly lit building where people of all types streamed in and out, grinning in merriment and stumbling on unstable feet. Tom shied away from a woman with gaps between her teeth that fluttered her fingers at him, and entered the tavern. The clink of glasses, the sounds of laughter, and poor drunkards moaning in misery welcomed the coachman inside, where he scanned the room in search of Mr. Becker. Several more women flashed alluring smiles at him, but Tom brushed them aside politely, visibly uncomfortable in the atmosphere he found repelling.

"Looking for someone?"

Tom was surprised to see the man leaning against the wall behind him, studying the coachman with sparkling eyes shaded by unruly waves of hair.

"I am, sir," Tom answered. "Have you—"

The man interrupted with a tilt of the head, gesturing to the far corner of the room.

"Might be that poor devil there."

A lone man, hunched over, rested his dark-haired head by a glass of scotch. Tom immediately recognized Stanley. Before he could thank the stranger, Tom saw he had walked out of the building, placing a top hat on his head without a trace of interest.

Stanley mumbled curses when Tom shook his shoulder.

"Wake up, sir."

"Tom," Stanley said, his tongue heavy from liquor. "I s'pose it'd be time ta head home . . ."

"It is, Mr. Becker."

"Norah'll be cross . . ."

Tom faithfully helped his employer to his feet and led him back to the carriage, nodding in agreement at all the nonsense that the man mumbled. The coachman was glad to have found Stanley, but his condition never ceased to be cause for concern. Mr. Becker wasn't a bad man, only a broken soul. Tom couldn't help him out of the hole he had dug for himself, as badly as he wished to, but he certainly hoped someone else could.

"Thank you, Tom," Stanley muttered, taking a seat in the carriage. The coachman nodded, closed the door, and leapt up to his perch.

Thoughts of a failed suicide had sent Stanley to a tavern in Kingston that night, thoughts that seemed infinitely abundant inside his mind. He had been close to death only the night before. So close had been his reach that he had been able to taste it. All he could savor now was the bitter trace of scotch on his tongue.

Unseen and undetected, a stranger watched the carriage drive off into the busy streets. Only a careful observer would have noticed the man with lively eyes wearing a top hat, who, highly skilled in stealth, had remained unnoticed in the shadow of an alley. He emerged only when he knew that the man in the carriage could not see him and mounted a horse he had borrowed. He held the reins tightly in one hand as he made himself comfortable on the saddle and secured a bottle of brandy in his pack.

"Aye," the stranger said to himself, nodding. "He'll do."

The stranger kicked his mount to a run.

❧

Back home, Stanley brushed off Mr. Miller, convinced he could get himself inside. Already his head ached terribly, but he was aware of something not quite right when he stumbled into his own house.

It was quiet and cold. Mrs. Miller was probably asleep in her own house. Stanley shed his boots and coat and stood in the hallway near the library, listening to the wind seep into the house through a cracked window. It was unheard of for Mrs. Miller to leave any windows open. This was not her doing.

Stanley's feet dragged as he walked down the narrow hallway. Leaning against a wall for support, he shuffled his way to the library in hopes of finding a bit of scotch to finish off the night. He sniffed when his cold nose began to run, and caught a whiff of smoke.

The uncanny feeling returned as Stanley became aware of a figure in the darkness at the far corner of his library when he entered it. If the figure had not moved, Stanley would not have seen it. The intruder half turned. The cigar in his mouth lit up part of his face. Stanley's alarm cleared his head enough to realize the danger.

"Who is there?" Stanley demanded, and wished his speech wouldn't slur. "What are you doing in my house?"

The figure chuckled and let out a puff of smoke, clearly unconcerned about being caught intruding on private property. Motioning with his hand to the armchair next to the window, the figure turned to face him at last, smiling good-naturedly as if nothing pleased him more than to visit with Stanley.

"Make yourself at home, Stanley. It is your home, after all."

It took Stanley a moment to realize that somehow the stranger knew him. He puffed out his chest and demanded in a hoarse voice, "How do you know my name?"

Something about the man was so familiar, but Stanley could not seem to remember where they had met, if they had met at all. Nevertheless, he had enough clarity of mind to know that the stranger did not belong there. To his surprise, the stranger chuckled again.

"You've been drinking late tonight, Stanley. We've met before, whether you remember it or not, and I thought I'd drop in for a visit."

Stanley felt dizzy, but he managed to reach the armchair before he collapsed. Feeling secure, he studied the man closer and began to remember.

The stranger sucked his brown cigar slowly and faced Stanley. Other than the arrogant look he wore on his face, the stranger seemed very ordinary, although the high-class coat and hat he wore most likely did not belong to him. The unruly hair that fell over his forehead made him seem younger and less threatening, but one look into those gleaming eyes gave Stanley a sense of distrust.

Stanley remembered the mugged victim from the dark alley.

The intruder blew out smoke.

"Now, don't look so worried," he said with a chuckle. "I've only come for one thing."

Stanley glanced around the man's darkened figure to his work desk. He had hidden the contraption in one of the drawers. He caught a glimpse of a familiar shape on top of the desk. The stranger must have brought a bottle of liquor. Seeing that Stanley had spotted the bottle, the stranger cleared his throat.

"A peace offering. For your troubles."

Stanley glanced at him with unease.

"I never introduced myself, Stanley. But I suppose it doesn't matter much, since you probably won't like to see me again after tonight. My name's Louis Vargas."

The oddness of the situation dissuaded Stanley from offering the stranger his hand, but Louis didn't seem to mind and continued his one-sided conversation.

"I promise to be brief," he said, blowing out more smoke. "I hope you can recall the events of last night. After our unusual meeting, I took the liberty of slipping something into your pocket, something that I thought would be kept safe with you while I cleared my tracks."

Stanley nodded. He remembered the moment Louis had "clumsily" bumped into him just before leaving the dark alley. The sneaky scoundrel must have slipped the contraption inside his pocket then. Resentful of having been included in whatever trouble Louis was trying to escape, Stanley spat out in anger, "Safe from what—thieves?"

"If only it were that simple," Louis said with a shrug. "No, I'm afraid the creatures after me are much more barbaric than mere thieves."

When Louis paused, Stanley looked up to study a sudden sparkle in his eyes that hinted at the man's mischievous nature.

"And for some reason, they seemed wary of you."

"What were those things . . . ? I . . . ." Stanley rubbed his temples. "*No!* It—it was all in my head . . ."

"Believe what you'd like. I won't argue," Louis replied.

A cold wind blew in from the window behind Louis, much to Stanley's annoyance. It had been the intruder's way inside the house. Louis continued with an outstretched hand.

"I'm only after the Time Key."

Stanley's nose wrinkled. "Time Key? That's a fancy word for a broken pocket watch. The bloody thing doesn't even tell the time."

"It's not the contraption I want. It's what's inside."

The statement caught Stanley's interest, and supposing that the intruder would leave as soon as he got what he came for, Stanley showed him the drawer in the desk where the bronze contraption was hidden. Louis let out an involuntary sigh and picked up the pocket watch with eager fingers. Stanley watched closely as Louis pulled a tiny knob on the curved side, which split the contraption in half to reveal a snug compartment inside. Louis removed a glass vial and, before Stanley could study it, slipped it into his coat pocket. Appearing to have no further need of the pocket watch that had so faithfully carried his hidden treasure, Louis set it down on the desk.

"Thanks for your time," Louis said with an air of finality. "And for the scotch. I had a glass or two."

Stanley frowned and shot a glance at the bar in the back corner of the library. The bloody sod had broken into his house and drank his scotch. At least he had left Stanley an entire bottle.

"And your pocket watch?"

At the hallway, Louis glanced back and shrugged.

"Keep it for now. I may return for it later, once things quiet down."

Stanley groaned and dropped down on his desk chair. "Get out," he mumbled.

"Oh, and Stanley . . ." Louis gave him an innocent smile. "If you find yourself in any difficulty, you can always come to us. The Roma won't turn down a brother Traveler in need."

"You're a sodding Gypsy!"

"Take a drink and forget your troubles," Louis advised.

Stanley shook his head. "Take it. I don't think I can afford another one."

Louis paused for a moment and then turned. As he left, he called back, "Only open it when you're ready."

The floorboards creaked as Louis walked down the hallway, opened the front door, and left the house with the flimsy promise of vanishing from Stanley's life, at least for the time being.

Offering little comfort, the moon's light shined down through Stanley's library window to illuminate the hunched-over figure. Despite his splitting headache, Stanley pondered over the recent events with overwhelming distress. Louis had mentioned the shadows—creatures that Stanley had pushed to the back of his mind because of what memories they brought.

He couldn't stop them. The images rushed through his mind.

"Papa?"

"Yes, love."

Maisie's little hand gripped his tightly as her fearful eyes looked up at him.

"I had the dream again."

Stanley shook his head to cast away the memory.

"There were shadows, and they came after me, Papa."

A chill ran up Stanley's back as he stared straight ahead. Those shadows, the ones that had tortured his daughter's dreams over six years ago, were the same ones he had seen in the dark alley. But that couldn't be possible. However much terror the memory of the black shapes slithering around gave him, it hardly compared to the horrifying thought that his sweet daughter had been tormented by the same creatures during countless nights, and to discover that they were real—the nature of nightmares—was all too much for him. And apparently Louis Vargas was fleeing from them.

The mere thought of the man made Stanley's blood boil. Something about the sneaky sod did not seem right. That friendly smile belied wicked intentions. It had not been a coincidence that Stanley had happened to be in the same alley to come to his aid, that they had met, and that Stanley had been the chosen caretaker of a treasure he had not even known about. Recalling the glass vial, Stanley looked down to study the contraption that had been used to carry it.

The metal surface reflected off the moonlight delicately, and beneath the rose window the long hand of the mechanism moved slightly from side to side. Intrigued, Stanley opened it and saw that the little hand attached to the long one was spinning out of control. Meanwhile, the long hand pointed away from Stanley, twitching ever so slightly. He followed that direction and saw the bottle of brandy. He could only guess it was brandy; the bottle was wrapped up in a patterned cloth. Despite the massive headache that threatened to split his head, Stanley became suddenly very eager to drink down a glass or two of whatever was in that bottle. Silently, he thanked that vagrant Louis for leaving the peace offering and picked it up by its neck.

Instead of the familiar *glug* of liquid in a glass bottle, Stanley was perplexed that he heard and felt an odd thump. Something solid was in it. Stanley shook the bottle and felt whatever was inside knock against the glass walls. He heard a tiny squeak.

Well, wasn't this his lucky day? That impudent man had thought it amusing to play a joke on him, a desperate alcoholic. Stanley muttered curses while he untied the strings around the bottle. He feared there was a mouse inside. Stanley hated mice.

I must mention that there was scarcely anything that could have prepared Stanley for what he saw inside the glass bottle, and very little crossed his mind as impulsive emotions took over common sense. He rose instantly in an attempt to run away. His hands shook. His legs trembled. A dry sound formed in his throat. His mind could make no sense of what he saw through his widening eyes, terrified, as those of the creature that stared back from inside the glass bottle.

Little else followed. Stanley's vision blurred and he stumbled backward. His hand dropped the bottle. He heard it hit the desk. The room grew dark around him and Stanley saw nothing more as he passed out on the cold floor of his library.

III

Apologies to the reader for the break in our story, but as fate has it, we must leave the unconscious Stanley to recover from the shock of seeing whatever creature was trapped inside the glass bottle. Some of you may be wondering what hideous little monster could exist to frighten a drunk man enough for him to lose consciousness, but that will be answered the moment Stanley wakes up. For now we watch from outside the Becker home, where the main door opens and a slight figure hurries down the steps, treading over the stone path to the gates with an air of accomplishment.

Finally, Louis Vargas had what he had spent numerous months seeking, transporting, and at last retrieving from Stanley, the host he had known would keep it safe until the right time. It had all worked out the way he had planned it, disregarding the troubling fact that the shadow-shifters had followed him, just as Sibyl had warned. But that had been only a slight setback. Now he was back on track and the vial safe in his coat pocket.

Louis's hand touched the gate to push it open, but he looked back over his shoulder, aware of what could be happening inside the house at that moment. Louis felt guilty. He had had no other choice. It had been his fault that the vaelie was even here, but it wouldn't be safe to keep the creature. The vaelie, as Louis had discovered the day before, had some peculiarities that would no doubt attract the shadow-shifters, and Louis could not afford to have them at his heels again. Not now that he was so close. No, the vaelie would be safe with Stanley, whom the shadow-shifters apparently feared. Louis would return some other time to take the creature back to where she belonged.

Yes, Louis felt content. Things were going the way he had planned them, and soon he would get home to his Saira with the cure. Everything would be all right.

Before Louis even had the chance to close the gate behind him, something heavy clubbed the back of his head.

"Oh, *shh*—"

Louis's vision blurred as he felt the wet ground against his cheek.

They had found him.

❧

Was he sleeping? Stanley could not remember ever climbing into bed. Certainly he was prone to forget a lot of things, even something as simple as getting ready for the night or whether or not he drank his afternoon tea. Still, Stanley was nearly convinced he had not. Then what could he be doing lying down?

Something furry brushed against his nose. The tickling sensation made Stanley sneeze. Brutus the Cat merely glanced at Stanley when he walked by, leapt onto the desk next to the open window, and looked out.

"You bloody cat," Stanley grumbled with the ill temper that comes with a hangover. "Off my desk."

It took Stanley a few tries to finally stand up and lean on his desk for support, looking about him in confusion. The back of his head ached terribly, and as hard as he tried to think, he could not remember why he had fainted. He remembered Louis, their conversation, even the pocket watch with the glass vial. Yes, he recalled the whole matter.

Brutus stared out the window and scurried outside when Stanley swatted at him. He hated that cat.

"Brutus, get back here! If you get lost, Mrs. Miller will kill us both!"

Stanley stuck his head out the window and saw the falling snow gather on the ground. He saw Brutus on the stones by the garden, eyes fixed on something. Stanley remembered.

He had dropped the glass bottle with a creature inside. When Stanley saw glass shards scattered on the stones, he realized the bottle must have rolled off his desk and fallen out the open window. But in the midst of them he spotted the tiny figure that had frightened him so much. Stanley swooned but forced himself to stay awake. It hadn't been a dream, as he had hoped.

Below, Brutus stiffened, ready to pounce, and Stanley was hit with the realization that whatever creature was down there was about to be devoured by his maid's cat.

"Get away from there!" Stanley shouted. He swung his legs over the window, dropped down to the other side, and shooed the cat away before looking down at the broken pieces of glass.

There it was—the unbelievable cause for Stanley's terror, unmoving and harmless. Stanley seemed unbothered by the cold as he slowly crouched down to study the creature. Stanley made out the shape of a familiar form partly buried beneath the snow, the likeness of which was that of a young girl, very small and seemingly human. Her exposed skin was pale but oddly hued. Long, wild hair fell over her face, hiding it from the large world around her. Her arms and legs were scratched and bruised, no doubt from the fall and shattering of the bottle.

Perhaps it was dead. Stanley couldn't be sure. He couldn't be sure of anything. He felt quite agitated. The mere existence of this tiny being fractured Stanley's entire reality.

How could he and this creature occupy the same space, breathe the same air, and not cause the universe to crumble? He looked around him, contemplating the calm world that slept despite the events in the Becker home. Stanley didn't know what to do, but he knew it was cold, and if there was anything human about this creature then it would be cold as well. Stanley wondered how to go about it as he extended clumsy fingers toward the tiny girl and touched her.

She was surprisingly solid and warm. Stanley felt his unreasonable fear be replaced by what seemed like curiosity, even wonder, but it was short lived when he saw the jagged shard embedded in the girl's torso. It was a grave and bloody wound. Stanley understood the need to act quickly.

Without thinking about the strangeness of what he was doing, Stanley carefully placed the girl on his palm and climbed back inside, shutting the window behind him. His mind raced. He spotted a wooden cigar box and emptied it out. Inside it, he placed the patterned cloth that had covered the glass bottle. Stanley looked down at the girl. Her hair had parted, revealing her young face filled with pain. Stanley set her down inside the box, where she remained unconscious.

"I must get help," Stanley muttered, hoping an answer would come to him if he vocalized his thoughts. Receiving none, he threw on his coat and stepped inside his shoes. Before he closed the lid, Stanley gazed once more at the small girl with unease. Girl—it was a girl. Merely a child.

Stanley sighed. "This is mad."

After a half hour of snowing, the streets were covered with a blanket of white fluff, making it difficult for Stanley's bike to slice through as he raced down the dark street. With one hand he steered and with the other he held onto the cigar box. If he knew of anyone who could help, it was Russell Gilmore, even this late at night. Of course, Stanley had his doubts. How would his brother-in-law react? Even if he didn't drop in a heap the moment he saw the creature, as Stanley had, would he even try to help? Stanley had never been so unsure.

Something in the back of his mind nagged at him, something he had not thought about for a very long time. Stories—that was all they had been. Curious how something he had been so certain about minutes before had kept the world in peaceful balance, but now the existence of this creature made Stanley question the durability of his fabric of reality.

As he neared the Gilmore household, Stanley grew incredibly unsettled, but he tried his best to appear composed when he knocked on the door. There was nothing unusual about his visit, he repeated to himself, attempting to keep calm.

It took three more knocks before he heard footsteps and the door finally creaked open. Winston, the butler, poked his head out with a most disagreeable frown.

"Mr. Becker—"

"There's no time, Winston," Stanley said hurriedly, pushing past him. "I need to see Dr. Gilmore."

"But he and the missus—"

"I don't care—wake him up! This is urgent!"

Before the bewildered butler could even turn to go up the stairs, Gilmore was already making his way down, red-faced and alarmed by the sudden appearance of his brother-in-law. He hurried to greet him, clutched Stanley's arm, and demanded to know what Stanley was doing out at this infernal hour.

Stanley suddenly could not find the words. "I need your help," he stuttered, pressing the box to his chest. "I—uh—I think . . . I don't . . ."

"Are you all right?" Gilmore asked as he looked Stanley over. "Are you hurt?"

Stanley glanced at the butler, who eyed him curiously. "I-I think that in private would be best."

Gilmore nodded. He instructed Winston to wait in the kitchen and start up some tea to warm up Mr. Becker, then motioned to his library and led Stanley inside.

"You'd best close the doors," Stanley said, setting the cigar box on the center table.

"What's this all about?" Gilmore shut the doors softly. "Are you hurt in any way?"

"It's not me," Stanley answered, without meeting his concerned gaze. "There's no time to explain."

"Then what is it?"

This was it. This was the moment that would confirm his insanity. What would happen when he opened the box? If they were both fortunate, there would be nothing but cold, empty space, a manifest to Stanley's wild imagination.

"Stanley?" Gilmore whispered. "What's happened? You're quite pale."

Stanley shook his head. Without another word, he clicked the box open and lifted the lid.

Oh, how Stanley wished it were empty. Instead, the same figure was at the bottom corner of the box, unconscious and bleeding. Stanley managed to tear his eyes away to witness Gilmore's expression, which, surprisingly, was blank. The two men held their breath for several long minutes before Gilmore cleared his throat.

"W-what," he began with a grimace, and Stanley saw a quick flash of the same fear he had felt. "What is that?"

Stanley clenched his fists. "I don't know," he replied. "But it's hurt."

Gilmore nodded and swooned.

"Can you help?"

Stanley was afraid that Gilmore was about to pass out, but suddenly the doctor straightened up and with pursed lips became the man that Stanley was familiar with—assertive and confident. He turned back to the doors and called Winston to give him new instructions. When he returned, Stanley saw fire in his eyes.

"I sent Winston to fetch my instruments," he said. "We need to set her on a clean cloth and remove the clothes she has on to clean the wound. Now, tell me exactly what happened."

The new tone in Gilmore's voice took Stanley by surprise, but he helped clear out the table to make space.

"It was caught in a glass bottle," he began uncertainly. "It must have rolled out the window, because I found it outside and the bottle in shards."

"Nothing else?"

Stanley shook his head.

"Lift her out, now. This will do nicely."

Pausing, Stanley wondered how Gilmore could be so composed. It was with shaky fingers that Stanley lifted up the corners of the patterned cloth and slid her off onto the table as gently as he could. She looked like a limp doll.

At a sudden knock, both men jumped. When Gilmore went to answer, Stanley sat down on the nearest chair in exhaustion. In the comfortable warmth of Gilmore's house, Stanley gradually felt the heaviness of the night's events settle on his shoulders. This was all so strange. It was draining his energy.

Gilmore gave a sharp command for Winston to go to bed and stop worrying, then returned with a tray of surgical instruments and cleaning supplies.

"Come, help me with this," he said, handing Stanley the tray.

They rinsed their hands in a bowl filled with water. Instantly, Gilmore took a pair of small scissors and, without giving it much thought, sliced up the girl's clothes around the jagged glass. They could see that the glass went in deep and covered a great part of the girl's torso from below the ribs to the abdomen. By the look on Gilmore's face, Stanley suspected it was a lethal wound.

"When I pull out the glass," Gilmore began, cleaning around the wound, "it will tear, but there is no other way. She may hemorrhage."

Stanley nodded and lowered a magnifying glass over the girl for Gilmore to see through.

"When I pull it out, be quick to dry the blood straight from the wound. Are you all right?"

Stanley felt dizzy. "I don't much like blood."

"Keep your mind off it."

With the tweezers, Gilmore pinched the glass. Stanley held a ball of cotton, which he pressed gently against the girl. Gilmore glanced at Stanley one last time, as though wondering if this was a dream, and then took a deep breath and tugged at the glass.

The girl's eyes flashed open. Stanley's heart jumped to his throat. She stared straight up at them, eyes wide and filled with terror, and then her mouth opened to let out an agonized scream. Gilmore took the cotton ball from Stanley and held the girl down with his fingers, afraid the struggle would cause more damage. Holding his breath, Stanley listened to her screams and became aware of the lamps around them growing brighter, large flames that threatened to set fire to the house—dancing, licking their containers, growing. Even the fireplace, which had not been lit, suddenly began to smoke. The veil of haze stung Stanley's eyes.

Gritting his teeth, Gilmore gave one last tug and the glass came out. The girl's voice choked, her eyes glazed, and she was unconscious again. With her, the lamps burned out.

"What in blazes?" Gilmore asked in bewilderment. "What was that?"

Stanley didn't answer. He handed Gilmore more balls of cotton and went to light the lamps again. He wondered about the phenomenon that had made them go out.

"This is mad."

Stanley agreed.

Returning to Gilmore's side, Stanley held the magnifying glass for the doctor again as he looked for any stray shards he could have missed. Very gently, with the sure fingers of an experienced physician, Gilmore cleaned the wound and soaked it in antibiotic to avoid infection. With a needle and thread in hand he stared down uneasily.

"I can't stitch it up," he told Stanley. "It would only tear the skin."

They decided it was enough to bandage her up. Once she was clean and ready, Gilmore bundled her up warmly and set her back inside the box.

"Incredible," he whispered. "So very small, but she seems so human."

Stanley stared out the window as he tapped his lower lip impatiently. Gilmore gave him a look of concern.

"Are you sure you're feeling well?"

Stanley nodded.

"Well, you certainly need some rest," Gilmore pressed on. "You are welcome to take the spare room."

"No," Stanley said with finality. "I've my mind set on my glass of scotch and warm bed."

"I really must insist. The weather—"

"I'll be all right."

Gilmore pursed his lips. "In that case, be sure to keep her warm. Her constitution's weakened from blood loss. And keep yourself safe."

Stanley rose and put on his coat, nodding slowly.

"You must change her bandages every few hours," Gilmore instructed. "If you see any sign of infection, be sure to send for me."

Stanley did not answer.

It was Gilmore's turn to take a seat. "Where did she come from?"

"I don't know," Stanley said with a sigh but remained standing.

Gilmore's fingers stroked his mustache.

"It *is* a girl," Stanley said. "Isn't it?"

"It appears that way."

"Yes . . . yes, I think that's what troubles me most."

Gilmore did not know how to reply and didn't interrupt Stanley's thoughts by prying; instead, he studied his hands uneasily. Next to him, Stanley could not seem to clear his head enough to make sense of everything. What was he to do next? He could leave the girl here and forget about her, forget about Louis, forget about the whole mess.

"I know what you're thinking," Gilmore said. "I can see it in your eyes. But you can't entrust her to me."

"Why not?"

"I have three children, a-and I am never home. How can I keep her a secret?"

"And why must she be kept secret?" Stanley complained. "I did not ask for this."

Gilmore stroked his mustache again. "Can you imagine how people would react? People can be very superstitious. They would make her out to be some sort of spirit, or sprite, or . . . demon, even."

"What makes you think she isn't?"

They were silent for a long minute, listening to the sounds of the night. In the calm, Stanley's mind refused to make sense of what they had just witnessed.

Gilmore gave a sigh of defeat.

Stanley approached the table and closed the box, placed it under his arm, and nodded to Gilmore in thanks. On the way out, Gilmore repeated his instructions and promised to stop by the next day to check on the girl. Stanley consented and stepped into the night. It had stopped snowing, but the chill left behind penetrated his bones. He said good-bye to Gilmore and mounted his bike in the cold winter night.

∞

As expected, the quick snowfall had not stuck to the busy streets, even at this time of night. It was easier for Stanley to ride back home, unconcerned about the bicycle slipping and dumping him on the side of the street. A few houses down from his, Stanley stopped and dismounted. He had a sudden impulse. Stanley held the cigar box tightly with both hands, as if to choke the life out of it, and placed it at his feet.

This was simple enough. He would turn around, head home, and forget the entire mess. This thing would not need to be his problem. It was as simple as leaving it on the streets, hopefully to never wake up. This creature did not belong here, and even less with Stanley. It would probably never recover from its wounds.

Her life would end, and no one would know about her incredible existence. This little, vulnerable girl. Her life was in Stanley's hands.

Stanley cursed at himself.

As an observer I have seen all aspects of human nature, whether that includes a kind deed for a stranger or the horrors that man will do in a raging fit. I find it curious how human one can become, even a drunkard surfacing from the sea of indifference, when one feels any type of intense emotion. It's all part of our journey in this world of many, creating dark tragedies or hopeful fairytales, and although black at times, the colorful array of stories needs darkness to allow for light.

As Stanley stared at the box by his feet, he began to see something in himself that he found frightening; a creeping darkness had settled inside him that manipulated him like a puppet. He had seen it happening slowly over the course of six years, but he had numbed his spirit with enough liquor to drown out his conscience. Suddenly, Stanley did not recognize himself. Who was this coward that saw ending a life, whether it was this girl's or his own, as an acceptable solution? Jane would be ashamed of him. From wherever she was looking down, she would turn away in disgust.

All these thoughts raced through Stanley's mind, and he was unaware of the shapes that formed from dark corners. They watched him from behind bushes, next to unlit street lamps, shielded in shadows, until their familiar coldness touched him with frozen fingers. Startled, Stanley looked up and saw the figures. They appeared human, but to

Stanley they were the terrible origins of the nightmares he wished to forget.

Motionless, they watched with yellow eyes. Terror began to form in Stanley's chest, but he forced himself to appear unmoved. He trusted his instincts enough to gather up the box under his arm, hoping that in his indifference the beasts would leave. He led the bicycle next to him with his free hand all the way to his house.

The shadowed figures' intense, hollow eyes followed him. They reminded Stanley of hungry cats watching their vulnerable prey. As soon as he reached the gates to his house, he felt safe, almost untouchable. When he locked the gates behind him he wondered whether Louis was right about the creatures, that they were afraid of him. How could this ungainly man cause them fear? Stanley did not know and did not want to ask them. He did not look back as he closed the front door behind him.

Stanley listened to his heartbeat as he climbed the stairs to the attic, slightly out of breath and agitated. His mind struggled to understand why the shadows from Kingston Bridge had come here, to his home. Perhaps Louis was hiding in Stanley's house like a coward. The thought infuriated Stanley, but he found no trace of the insolent man.

In the past, Stanley had often found refuge in his attic from unwanted situations, but he had not set foot in it for six years. Mrs. Miller seldom came up to dust around, but Stanley had always avoided this part of the house. As he walked around stacks of boxes and old furniture, Stanley thought of what this attic held, what memories it stored, what Stanley had inexcusably ignored for so long. Atop the stairs, at the end of the room, he found the hidden door embellished by drawings of curious and faraway lands created by his imaginative daughter. This had been Jane's workplace and the room Maisie had adapted as her safe haven from terrible nightmares.

Stanley did not want to open it, for he knew what awaited him in the next room, but he also knew this was the only place he could keep the girl safely hidden from prying eyes. He had thought of telling Mrs. Miller about her, but he did not know how she would react. No, it was not the right time yet; he would wait to see if she even recovered from her wounds.

Without another thought, Stanley opened the door and was greeted by the cold air of the unused room. A tall window covered the opposite wall, facing the gardens from the back of the main house. Its high ceiling made it appear spacious, despite the lack of width in the room itself. Tall cabinets stored Jane's many unfinished projects and forgotten treasures, but what gave Stanley a sense of deep longing were the countless birdhouses.

Jane had had a weakness for building and designing tiny dwellings for birds of all shapes and sizes. There were tall houses, short and stocky houses, wooden and brick houses; houses made of twine, twigs, and even grass; round, square, angular houses with tiny openings; houses with little doors and windows. It wasn't a wonder why the family had adopted the name Bird Room for this part of the attic. The birdhouses had been one of Jane's last obsessions that Stanley still did not understand, but even now it brought a smile to his lips. He felt guilty that he had not come to visit them in six years, leaving them to gather dust alone, but Stanley could not help think that Jane had left a part of her inside each of the birdhouses. If they were there to watch him, or simply left by accident, he didn't know, but their presence was painful all the same.

On the table against the wall adjacent to the door, Stanley set down the box, wedged it in between two birdhouses, and went to light the fireplace. He needed to warm up the room if the girl was to stay here. If Mrs. Miller were ever to ask about it, Stanley would give her the simple reason that he wished to spend some time alone in the attic, undisturbed.

Once he had a decent fire, he cautiously returned to the back table and opened the box. She was still unconscious, but breathing. Stanley passed a hand over his eyes in exhaustion. He wanted to sleep, to forget.

But Stanley had had another reason for coming to the attic. He retrieved an old chest from storage and brought it next to a chair that creaked under his weight. Inside the box sat volumes of the unfinished stories and memories that Stanley had recorded for years until the accident. He leafed through a stack of them mindlessly, scanning words and small sketches. The stories were familiar but seemed foreign to him, as though they came from another storyteller, another world. A few excerpts and cutouts stood out to Stanley, until he found the ones he had been searching for.

Dream Lurkers, he had called them. Creatures that invaded the dreams of children during the night, when they were the most vulnerable. According to his story, the Dream Lurkers were mere figments of a child's imagination, simple nightmares driven off by the light of day. This first explanation had not been enough to chase away Maisie's nightmares, and consequently, Stanley had created a creature of hope. He described it as being a wolf-like animal, big as a horse, with golden eyes that sparkled like fireflies at night. Maisie had called the gentle beast Bright-eyes. The short story he had created about the Lurkers and the Bright-eyes that vanquished the fear they caused had never been finished, but it wasn't the story he had wanted to read. This had confirmed his fear and brought up more questions.

The story was mere fantasy, a way to recognize the fear that children's dreams could bring, but giving a small light of hope that the sun would always rise the next the day. It had been intended only as a fairytale, but the same dark creatures from this story were somehow real.

He spotted another stack of unfinished manuscripts. The untitled tale of the underwater city of Merr with its beautiful inhabitants, the ethereal water nymphs, was one of Maisie's favorite stories. "The Travels of Gordon Bleu and the Island of the Young People" . . . "The Singing Jay" . . . Stanley traced his eyes over other titles, until he saw his scribbled notes over a single sheet.

"The Aspen Folk." It had been a short story that he had wanted to finish before Maisie's fifth birthday, and had stayed up many late nights trying to find the right words. It was a single page. His eyes scanned the words and sighed. He saw the half-finished sentence at the end and closed his eyes. Before writing the last words on the sheet, he had been interrupted by a messenger with news of the accident.

Stanley tossed aside the paper and stared into the flames. These stories, these fairytales from his imagination, were somehow coming to life. Yes, the moving shadows were the first to catch his attention, but the girl—she was a story as well, an unnamed character in "The Aspen Folk." His own creation. She was a creature of the trees, hidden from humanity, living a life of leisure and security, oblivious to the wide world that surrounded her home. And now she was here with the man who apparently had envisioned people of her kind and given them life. Could he have created her? Could he have somehow brought her to his own reality, along with the living Dream Lurkers?

IV

Mrs. Miller's loud voice awoke Stanley the next day. Her heavy footsteps climbed the attic steps with incredible quickness. Just as she entered the room, Stanley opened his eyes to find that he had fallen asleep facing the fireplace with a manuscript on his lap. Mrs. Miller's head poked in from the cracked doorway. She wore a curious smile.

"What is it, Mrs. Miller?"

"Oh, Mr. Becker," she replied, clicking her tongue. "Ye look a mess, all wrinkled and bent over. What, 'as the bed got bedbugs?"

Stanley didn't reply, but his scowl urged her to reveal why she had called him.

"It's Dr. Gilmore. Come to check up on things, he says. I left 'im at the door, for the library's gone up over backw'rds this morning when I came to make breakfast. I don't know what sorts of drinkin' ye've been doing down there but it's driven me quite mad these few days. It cannae be good for yer health, Mr. Becker!"

"Thanks, Mrs. Miller," Stanley said, and waved her off. "I'm sorry for the mess. I'll get right to it once Dr. Gilmore leaves. Send him up."

"All right, Mr. Becker."

She cast the room one last look and left.

Stanley sighed. The noisy chair had not offered the rest that he needed, and he could feel the heaviness of sleep pushing down on his bony shoulders. His slender fingers ran through messy dark locks of hair, for once aware of how unkempt he was. The first business of the day would have to be a good shave and a haircut. That is, if Gilmore didn't take up much of his morning.

While Stanley unwrinkled his clothes as best as he could, Gilmore entered the room with a medical bag in one hand and a hat in the other. The shadows under his eyes reminded Stanley of what had taken place the night before, but still he asked, "What are you doing here, Dr. Gilmore?"

"And a good morning to you, as well," Gilmore said with a slight grin. "I promised to stop by and check up on . . . you know . . ."

Stanley sighed, nodding, and gestured to the table.

Clearing some space, Gilmore set down the suitcase to have his instruments in hand. He carefully lifted the still sleeping girl out of the box and set her on a clean padded cloth to begin the inspection. Stanley did not approach Gilmore or his work, unwilling to witness what he had yet again hoped to have been a dream.

"Has she woken up at all?" Gilmore asked, holding the magnifying glass over the girl.

"Not that I've noticed," Stanley replied, standing by the far window to look at the busy life outside. "How do you know she ever will wake up?"

"I've checked her vitals and it seems she's merely on a heavy sleep, on account of her wound perhaps. Must be the reason she's healed so quickly. It's incredible! Stanley, come take a look."

Stanley did not want to look, but obeyed so as not to spoil Gilmore's excitement. It was strange to see the girl under the light of day where she appeared real but very unreal all at once. Like a giddy child, Gilmore smiled widely when Stanley stood by him. He had parted the girl's cut clothing and removed the bloody bandages to reveal a scabbing wound, still open at the center but clearly healing at the edges. The scratches on her face were healing quickly as well, but the paleness of her skin still remained. They could see that her skin was unlike theirs; it had a pastel-like hue of straw, a pale gold. Her dark hair shone lighter under the sunlight, and beneath the thick mass of it Stanley made out tiny beaded strands, one behind each ear.

"This is incredible," Gilmore repeated, plugging his ears with a stethoscope. The bell-shaped end covered the girl's entire chest and belly. "Her heart rate is fast, but constant. Must be normal for her size. Her eyes react to light, and her body is rather warm. I don't suppose she'll sleep much longer, seeing how quickly she's healing. When was the last time she had anything to eat?"

Stanley rolled his eyes. "How would I know that?"

Gilmore chuckled as he brought out more clean bandages and cut strips of them. "There doesn't seem to be any sign of infection, but I still need you to change her bandages every few hours and clean the wound. A bit of soap and water will do."

Stanley watched as Gilmore gently patted the girl with a wet rag.

"When she wakes," Gilmore continued, "give her light foods. Soups and such. Keep her drinking water and don't let her exert herself, else the wound might open up."

"Assuming she does wake up," Stanley said, "how do you suppose she'll react to me? Will I even be able to communicate with her?"

Gilmore's eyes gleamed. "You'll have to tell me about it."

The statement did little to calm Stanley's anxiousness, but he knew that resistance would not disburden him from the situation.

"Come, take this," Gilmore said suddenly, handing Stanley the bandaged scraps. "Wrap up the wound firmly, not too tightly."

"W-why can't you?"

"It's for you to learn. I'll fetch more water."

Stanley stood back and stared at the girl. A gripping sense of uneasiness took hold of him. She was so minute. Stanley lowered his hands slowly, measuring each movement carefully. If his clumsy fingers made a wrong move, would she break under his touch?

With one hand he gently lifted her upper body and with the other he wrapped the bandages slowly around her torso. He bit his lip nervously. The girl's head bent back over his finger, limp, but an exhausted expression formed on her brow. Could she feel him? Could she hear the things happening around her? Could she even understand? Stanley felt an unexpected sensation. Perhaps it was sympathy, compassion, and Stanley realized that this was only a child. It didn't matter what she was or wasn't—she had been abandoned and now Stanley was responsible for her well-being.

Stanley chuckled to himself, slightly relieved. To think that he had almost left the poor girl out in the cold to rid himself of the responsibility was sickening. But now he felt a strong urge to protect her. He knew he would do anything to keep her from harm.

Perhaps alerted by his chuckle, the girl's eyes fluttered open. They stared at Stanley, who didn't dare breathe in fear of startling her. The girl seemed confused, and she muttered something incomprehensible before she closed her eyes again. Stanley finished his work and set her on her back once more.

"You're safe here," he whispered soothingly.

He cleaned up the area around the girl before he heard Gilmore at the door.

"Does Mrs. Miller know about her?" he asked Stanley as he came in. When Stanley shook his head, he continued, "I suppose it's up to you to tell her, but it'll be difficult keeping secrets from a housekeeper."

"She'll have a fit," Stanley said, imagining the day he would find Mrs. Miller passed out on the floor.

Gilmore used a spoon-like instrument with a pointed end to scoop up water. He brought it down to the sleeping girl's lips with the help of the magnifying glass. Both men held their breath. After a moment, the girl's lips parted slightly to receive the water from the spoon. Gilmore smiled and Stanley blew out a long sigh.

"Seems that our girl is recovering quickly."

It was a small victory that highly pleased Gilmore, and to his own surprise, Stanley was more relieved than he could have imagined. With an air of cheerful triumph, the two men took leave of the attic, thoroughly convinced that the girl would recover. They said good-bye and went their separate ways. It was time for Stanley to pay a visit to the barber's.

Stanley was dressed and ready in a matter of minutes, much to his housekeeper's surprise, who, at the mere sight of him coming down to the kitchen, gave her a start. Of course, Stanley would now and then dress up to pay his visits to the pub, but it had been years since he had shown such eagerness for anything other than for liquor.

"I'm off, Mrs. Miller," Stanley said with a serene smile. "Would you be as kind as to tell Mr. Miller to ready the horses?"

"Dear me, Mr. Becker! Where could ye be off to at this hour? Surely the messenger boy's delivered the package in time—"

"It's not about work, Mrs. Miller. Tim's done a fine job. I only thought to stretch my legs this beautiful day."

Mrs. Miller wiped her hands on her apron and nodded. "Lucky for ye Mr. Miller's tendin' to the beasts this minute. I'll be out to tell 'im the news."

"Thank you, Mrs. Miller," Stanley said, and helped himself to a biscuit that the housekeeper had prepared.

It was in minutes that the coach was ready and Mr. Miller held the door open for Stanley to climb in. Soon, they were off to Kingston. Stanley knew the barber he was to see that day, but his intentions included getting information from the man that knew the latest news in the streets of London. If anyone knew a street vagrant's whereabouts, it was Mr. Bates.

❧

It took about an hour's time to arrive at the barbershop near the marketplace. The looks that Stanley received from the few customers inside made him chuckle. Yes, Stanley Becker felt like a new man, and apparently others could tell something was different about him. Even Mr. Bates appeared surprised, and when Stanley entered the shop, the barber gave an exclamatory guffaw.

"What a surprise, Mr. Becker!"

"Hello, Mr. Bates. I've come for a trim and a clean shave." Stanley ran a hand over his unkempt chin with slight embarrassment.

Stanley's matter-of-fact tone made Mr. Bates smile. The barber ushered him to an open seat to begin his work. They struck up a pleasant conversation that included everything from the terrible weather to the latest news in politics. Stanley cared little for small talk, but he knew this to be the quickest way to get Mr. Bates to share any gossip he had from the streets.

"It's a true devastation, that is. While the rich get richer, the poor get poorer," Stanley said.

"Aye, most unfortunate, that is."

"Ever been to Whitechapel, Mr. Bates?"

"Few times."

"I recall the whole mess of the Whitechapel murders. Mrs. Miller held us captive for a month!"

Mr. Bates chuckled.

"Those poor devils, stacked up on top of one another, stuffed into dwellings straining their capacity. How ill structured is our society that the beneficiaries of our highest classes build their fortune on the backs of the less fortunate. Stomping on their misery. Reminds me of that novel by Mr. Wells—*The Time Machine*. Do you know it, Bates?"

"Can't say I do, Mr. Becker."

"It's brilliant, Bates. Of course, it's a rant against the leisure of the high class and the underground working class structure. You really must read it, Bates." Stanley was growing tired of the conversation. Of course, he hadn't spoken this much to another human being in six years, and so willingly.

"Very interesting," Mr. Bates said, finishing Stanley's head and preparing for the shave. "The wife's read some of Mr. Wells's novels, although she always reads about that Sherlock Holmes fellow. Every month she sends her maid to fetch a magazine to read the latest about him."

Mr. Bates scoffed, and Stanley wondered if he had led the man into the right conversation.

"As if he were a real person!"

Stanley smiled slightly. He remembered Jane's passion for literature, and the work of Mr. Doyle had been one of her most treasured.

"The silly girl was mugged two days ago," Mr. Bates continued. "She carries her coin purse under her arm, the girl does. Out in the open for all to see."

"Is she all right?" Stanley asked, shocked at the news.

"Only got a fright," the barber said with a shrug. "They were two Gypsy dippers. Wrestled the purse from under her arm and took off like petty thieves."

Stanley resisted the urge to nod as Mr. Bates ran the blade down his neck.

"Seems that a new group of them set up camp near Canbury Gardens."

"You don't say."

"It's a big group this time."

There was the answer for which Stanley had been searching. A new group of Gypsy Travelers held the promise of revealing Louis Vargas's tracks, and Stanley was not about to waste any time. He had come for answers and would not rest until he found Louis.

Canbury Gardens was near Mr. Bates's barbershop, and Stanley wouldn't have to travel far to find them. Despite Mr. Miller's protests, Stanley had him wait with the carriage. Stanley strolled down the path to the gardens without looking back.

He couldn't shake the uneasy feeling that he was about to step into something outside the bounds of his comfort, to witness events he would never fully understand. With a mind of their own, his shoes trudged on. In his heedless, unsuspecting manner, Stanley followed a path away from the benches and peaceful landscapes. The park was eerily empty, a suggestion that betrayed the presence of unwanted strangers.

Stanley entered a small clearing shielded by tall bushes, where a few trees served as bare canopies over the resting tents and caravans of the dwelling Travelers in the gardens. The murmur of the mass of people busy running about, standing around steaming pots, and women yelling after naughty boys filled Stanley's ears. He marveled at the foreign world he had stepped into.

At first, Stanley drew intent glances from people that noticed him. Not many in their right mind would take a voluntary stroll through a Romani campsite. Soon, however, curiosity lured a more menacing crowd, and Stanley was forced to reevaluate his intentions. Just as uneasiness began to settle in, a group of robust men with puffed out chests and flaring nostrils approached Stanley. Their lips turned into grimaces when Stanley took an involuntary step back. The largest of them was a thickly bearded man with a protruding beer gut, whose dark skin looked bronze in the afternoon sun.

"What brings a *payo* to our settlement?" asked the big man in a thick accent. "It's very rude to come uninvited to someone's home without a proper offering."

Stanley thought it odd that the men hadn't assaulted him by now and shrugged his shoulders recklessly.

"It's a public park."

Another man chuckled. "The *payo* doesn't know about us."

Meanwhile, the big man studied him. "Why are you here?"

Stanley cleared his throat. "As a matter of fact, I was invited by a man called Louis Vargas. Do you know him?"

The mention of the name took the group of men by surprise, all except the big man, who watched Stanley curiously.

"If that's true, why would he invite a *payo* to come to us?"

It took all that Stanley had for his eyes to remain fixed on the big man. "He mentioned that a man would always be welcomed among fellow travelers . . ."

Stanley realized he must have said the right thing when the big man grunted his approval and sent the other men away with a foreign command. He ushered Stanley to follow him.

"I know Louis," the big man said. "His family is with us, though he likes to come and go as it pleases him. Haven't seen him in three months."

"Then he's not here?" Stanley asked, slightly confused. "I assumed he would be—"

The big man raised his hand for silence. "Don't tell me. I don't want to know what mess he's got himself into this time."

The hint at other occasions of Louis's mischief made Stanley uneasy.

"How did you even meet Louis?" the man wondered. "No, wait—I said don't tell me. I don't care."

"He owes me some answers."

"Louis owes everyone something."

The two made their way through a pair of parked caravans where three women were hanging up laundry. Stanley had seen few Roma in his trips through London, but he had never seen any of this sort. The women's exotic and extravagant beauty struck him. As he passed the three women, they did not veil their faces, as he had heard some would do. They met his eyes, theirs as black and deep as night. They watched him, almost as though to lure him to an unseen trap. The big man's voice awoke him from the trance.

"*Fátima!*" he roared. "Stop your flirting and go inside! I want to see those clothes packed by tonight."

One of the girls stuck her tongue out, and the women fled to a caravan in a flurry of giggles, chanting, "Yes, Toma!"

"Don't trust any of them," the big man told Stanley. "They only like to look pretty and break hearts. Romani women are no good for a *payo*."

Stanley realized his heart was racing, and, embarrassed, he cleared his throat. "I take it you're leaving."

"Always on the move. The people here don't like us much, and there's been some talk about us picking pockets. Once the uniforms come, we go."

Stanley nodded as though he understood, but wasn't about to tell Toma that the mugging of Bates's maid was the reason he was here.

Stanley followed Toma past running boys and yelling women, until they reached a colorful tent that stood under the shade of two trees apart from the rest. There was a bundle of clothes next to a bucket of water near the tent opening, and a small pot filled with dirt. Before Stanley had time to study the humble dwelling, the big man's voice called, and a woman emerged from the tent a moment later.

"What do you want, *Tomás*?" The woman eyed Stanley but kept her attention on the big man. "I'm busy."

Toma wasted no time. "This man knows Louis. Wants to know where he is."

The woman's black eyes drilled into Stanley.

"As do I."

"I told him," Toma said, slapping Stanley's back roughly before walking away. "Good luck, *payo*."

"How do you know Louis?"

Stanley was startled by the question and, feeling suddenly abandoned, met the woman's sharp gaze. Her hand leaned impatiently on her hip.

"I met him two nights ago," Stanley answered. "Near the bridge."

"Does he owe you money?"

The question sounded slightly sardonic, but the woman's hard eyes demanded at least a reply. He shook his head like a rebuked child.

"He owes me answers."

From behind the woman, a slender figure appeared and looked out curiously, but a soft command from her sent the figure back inside. Nodding once, the woman opened the tent flap and motioned to Stanley.

"Want to come in?"

Stanley did not feel comfortable with the offer, but he forced himself to remember why he was here at all, as daft as the thought suddenly seemed.

"I-I don't want to intrude—" he stammered.

"Come get out of the cold," she insisted, giving him a soft smile. It made her seem less threatening. Once inside, she offered to take his coat. "Take a seat. I'll bring tea."

Stanley held his hat in both hands and thanked her, eyeing the cushions on the ground. He was taken aback when he found no chairs to sit on, but felt obligated to ignore such an inconvenience as he didn't wish to insult his stern host. As he sat awkwardly, the same figure from before, a young woman, came carrying a tray with two tiny china cups. She set the tray at his feet and took a seat across from him. Her eyes never wavered from Stanley. Inside the cup was water, and to be polite, he sipped from it slowly, nodding to the girl in thanks. He quickly cast aside the fear that he did not know where this water came from, and that its promise of cleanliness was bleak. As a nervous habit, he cleared his throat again.

"Maybe you'd rather have some spirits," the girl said with a shrug and glanced at the bottles in a corner of the tent.

The offer took Stanley by surprise, but her devious smile made him laugh suddenly.

"I'm quite all right with water, miss."

The thought appealed to him, of course.

She shrugged again in a careless fashion and Stanley felt more at ease to study the girl. Like the people he had seen around the caravans, the girl's skin was bronze and glowing. Black, thick curls fell over bare shoulders in masses, creating a sort of halo that cradled her rounded face. She was a small thing, petite and slight, but her colorful garments shaped womanly features. Stanley frowned at the thought as he reminded himself that this was just a girl, no older than sixteen. What struck him were her eyes. They seemed to be a strange hue of green, but a second later they turned somewhat golden. However, Stanley dismissed the oddity to being his own crazed imagination.

Stanley had difficulty reeling himself back from the alluring vision facing him when the woman's voice startled him.

"Sugar or lemon?" the woman asked as she set down another tray in front of him and took a seat by the girl. By the striking resemblance between the two, Stanley knew they must be mother and daughter.

"Thank you, madam . . . I'm sorry, I didn't catch your names."

"You can call me Naomi," she said curtly. Like Stanley, the woman wasn't accustomed to small talk, but unlike him, she was comfortable interacting with other human beings. "And this is my daughter, Nuri."

Stanley nodded, introducing himself.

"How did you come by Louis, Mr. Becker?"

Nuri's head perked up. "You seen him, sir?"

Stanley nodded. "As I've told you, we met for the first time two nights ago. But I saw him again last night." To Stanley, it seemed as if an entire lifetime had passed since Louis's unsettling visit. He pulled out the pocket watch from his waistcoat and showed them. "He gave me this."

MELANIE BATEMAN

Recognition, to Stanley's relief, sparked in both Naomi's and Nuri's faces.

"He gave the impression that he was coming here. He invited me—"

"Oh, this bloody thing!" Naomi snatched the contraption from Stanley's hand. "It's not worth all the misfortune it's caused us. You'd do well to toss it in the Thames."

"What does it do?" Stanley asked in alarm.

Nuri rolled her eyes as her mother answered. "The fewer questions you ask, the better off you'll be, Mr. Becker."

"But Mr. Vargas—"

At this, Nuri giggled and Naomi scoffed. "Just Louis. He doesn't deserve the title of a gentleman."

Stanley detected scorn in her voice and continued cautiously.

"I take it you know him well."

"He's my husband."

Stanley had assumed as much, but her confirmation did little to reveal who Louis Vargas really was. What he remembered of Louis's appearance resembled very little to the bronze-skinned Roma. He continued his interrogation. "Louis called it a Time Key."

Naomi studied the pocket watch for a few moments before blowing the air from her cheeks and giving her reply, "No, Mr. Becker. I don't know how it works or what it does, and you won't get answers from anyone here."

Her hands shook slightly when she picked up the kettle and poured more tea.

"Would you like more, Mr. Becker?"

"No, thank you," he said. He had hardly drunk any in his persistence to get answers from Naomi. "But there must be someone who knows . . ."

"The only one who does is Louis, and heaven knows when he'll be coming around."

Stanley suspected this was the only answer he would get from her, but an unrelenting thought reminded him that this was not the only reason he had come in search of Louis. For some reason, the vagrant had left a mysterious child in Stanley's care, setting aside the question of how on earth she had ended up in his possession. Stanley deserved an explanation, at least a suggestion of what she might be and from where she had come. However, something told him that Naomi would not know either, even if she somehow believed Stanley's unbelievable account. For now, the girl would remain a secret.

The three sat in silence for a few minutes, searching for the next words at a dead end, when Nuri spoke in a hushed voice.

"Sibyl would know."

The comment startled Naomi, who gave her daughter a menacing look and whispered, "Saira Nuri, *hush!*"

"Who is Sibyl?" Stanley asked Nuri, who crossed her arms, wrinkled her nose defiantly, and faced away from her mother.

Naomi coughed softly. "Did you say you saw Louis last night, Mr. Becker?"

Stanley regarded Nuri, stunned to see the hue of her eyes flickered red, and wondered if it had not been his imagination after all.

"Umm . . . yes."

"Did he give any mention of heading this way, to the gardens?"

Stanley had difficulty remembering; unfortunately, such is one of the many drawbacks to liquor, especially when a man drinks like the world is at an end.

"I couldn't say, Mrs. Vargas," Stanley replied after a thoughtful pause. "But he took something from inside the Time Key. It was stored in a little chamber."

The sudden surprise from Naomi caused Stanley to pause again. She exchanged excited looks with her daughter.

"It can't be."

"He must have . . . ," Nuri said, her eyes wide and golden. " . . . must have found the Fountain."

Stanley began to feel left out. "What fountain?"

But the women paid no attention to him, when suddenly Naomi's excitement turned into concern. "If that's true," she said, "then they are tracking him."

"But he would come here." Nuri refused to feel pessimistic about the news. "Maybe he's only waiting—"

"He would be here by now if everything was all right."

Stanley cleared his throat, drawing irritated looks from both women. "If it's any consolation, Mrs. Vargas, Louis mentioned he had cleared his tracks, just to be safe."

"You must leave, Mr. Becker," she replied coldly. "The *bohemians* don't much like strangers."

"Mrs. Vargas, I mean no disrespect, but I came here for answers and I do not intend to leave—"

Naomi stood up. "*Good-bye*, Mr. Becker."

A moment later, Stanley found himself outside the tent, facing the flap, dumbfounded.

❧

Apparently this was a dead end, and having no other reason to remain in the Romani camp, Stanley placed the hat back on his head. This couldn't be it. He was supposed to find Louis, to get his answers.

He could not be at a dead end.

The looks he received were not as curious, and Stanley knew he would be able to leave unbothered. At least he was still alive and unharmed. As he walked he saw the big man, Toma, among a group of people speaking to a bald man with various piercings along the outline of his ear. The man held his left hand, which Stanley could clearly see was made of wood. Before the group left Stanley's line of vision, the bald man peered at him with interest, giving Stanley an eerie sense of paranoia. But he couldn't think too much on it when a handful of boys ran past him, and the last of them bumped into Stanley. The boy apologized with a smirk.

When Mr. Miller, who was pacing around the coach nervously, came into view, Stanley heard a voice behind him.

"Mr. Becker!"

He turned to see Nuri running toward him. She grinned when she showed him his wallet in her hand. Stanley checked his pockets and found it missing.

"How?"

Nuri shrugged. "Pierre couldn't help himself."

Of course, the boy who had bumped into him had actually picked his pocket. Stanley felt humiliated for being taken advantage of once again. He placed his wallet in his trousers and thanked her. The girl smiled and opened her other hand to reveal the Time Key.

"I think you'll need this."

Stanley shook his head. "It won't do me any good," he replied. "I don't even know what it does, miss."

"Call me Nuri," she said. Her eyes sparkled with a calming hazel color. "It's a Time Key. It manipulates time."

At Stanley's confusion, she opened the contraption and showed him the hands. "The outer symbols represent years. Move the hand clockwise and it will take you forward. Move it the other way and it will take you back."

Stanley struggled to understand while the girl twisted tiny knobs to move each hand.

"The symbols below them represent months. Well, seasons really. The symbol on the top right means winter, and the one opposite to it is midsummer. The other two are obviously autumn and spring."

"All right, but what does this—"

"Wait, I'm not finished," she said, looking over her shoulder. "You wanted answers and I'm giving them to you."

Stanley nodded.

"The smallest hand sets the days. There are seven, one for each day. The seasons and days settings work together, but the Time Key will not work without setting the years hand."

"And what of this hand?" Stanley wondered. "It's constantly moving."

"My father said it works like a compass. When certain energies are near, it will lead you to them. The smaller arrow at the end of the hand will spin faster the closer you get. But the most important thing to remember is to turn all the hands to this position, where the neutral markers are, if you want to get back to the time you left."

"I'm sorry. I don't think—I don't understand—"

"You will," Nuri assured him. "You can find Sibyl if you turn the big hand clockwise one hundred and fifteen clicks. She can answer your questions."

At times I wonder how things would have gone differently if Stanley had followed the girl's suggestion to visit Sibyl immediately after their conversation, but, alas, I only observe, as I have mentioned before, and I retell the events truthfully. I leave it to my own fancy to think up possible results from different choices that could have followed.

Nuri seemed to be in a hurry. Stanley accepted the Time Key and nodded to her, still confused.

"Thank you . . . a-and I'm certain your father will turn up."

Already heading back, the girl turned to smile again. "He always does."

❧

Tom Miller wondered where his employer had gone and to whom

he had been talking. The girl looked like one of those extravagant bohemians he sometimes saw in the streets. The thought that perhaps Mr. Becker had gone to meet a Gypsy girl in the gardens was a bit unnerving for poor Tom, but he chose to avoid asking about it. What did he care if his employer found solace in meeting Gypsies in gardens? At least he seemed to be in a good mood.

"Thank you, Mr. Miller," Mr. Becker said as the coachman held the door open for him to step out once they arrived home. The man hurried through the gates and down the cobblestone path to the main entrance of his house, where he tipped his hat in greeting as Mrs. Miller opened the door. She cast him an odd look as he ran inside with the giddiness of a child.

"What's with 'im?" she asked her husband, drying her hands in her apron.

Mr. Miller didn't answer right away when something on the ground caught his attention. When he bent down he saw a small glass object caught between two stones on the little path, glimmering as the setting sun shone on it. Curious, Tom picked it up as his wife reached him. It was a glass vial filled with clear water.

"What's that?" she asked, and when Tom shrugged, she said, "He seems to be in a good mood."

"He does."

"Where'd ye take 'im?"

Tom wasn't sure that he should tell her, but her look of impatience dissolved any doubt.

❧

Within seconds, Stanley had made it to the attic, eager to see if the girl was awake. His mind was busy with all that he had learned that day. He stood dumbly in the Bird Room, suddenly confused. The girl wasn't in the box. Stanley searched with his eyes but found no hint of her presence.

"Hullo?" he whispered. "Come out. I won't hurt you."

Stanley couldn't blame the girl for distrusting his intentions. She was probably frightened of the strange place she had woken up in and was hiding. For a moment, Stanley listened and hoped to catch a glimpse of her, but when silence persisted, he chose to let her be and returned to the library to drink and think.

Recalling Naomi's resistance to reveal any information about Louis,

Stanley felt impatient. Instead of getting the answers he had headed out to find, he was stuck with more questions. What could Naomi possibly be hiding? It seemed odd that the Roma were waiting for a man who apparently liked to disappear now and then without any explanation. If Louis's intentions had been to find the group of Romani Travelers, why had he not come around yet? Something that Nuri had said to her mother came back to Stanley. They had mentioned a fountain. He wondered what fountain could be so important to create such mystery. Apparently, Louis had been after this fountain, and now the shadows were tracking him down.

None of these questions would apparently be answered, but Stanley had another one in mind when he brought out the Time Key to study it. This contraption was what captured his curiosity, and even more since Nuri's strange instructions. Her voice came back to him.

It manipulates time . . .

Time—Louis had called him a traveler. Certainly he had not meant *time traveler*.

Stanley chuckled. Time traveler—he must be mad. But Nuri had seemed so sincere. Surely she wouldn't have given him false instructions about the Time Key. She was Louis's daughter, however. Perhaps deception was a common trait in the family.

And what if she had been telling the truth?

Setting down his glass, Stanley looked out the window cautiously and saw Mr. and Mrs. Miller arguing about something he could not hear. Mr. Miller had picked up something from the ground. Stanley looked down again. All hands pointed to where the twelve should have been, at the neutral markers that the girl had pointed out. Nuri had not told him how to trigger the contraption, but Stanley put his thumb on the most obvious place—the crown.

His thumb pressed down.

Nothing happened, and Stanley blushed when he realized that he had been holding his breath. Of course, he should have expected that it had all been a hoax. Stanley scoffed and let go.

Suddenly, the library vanished before his eyes.

V

If Stanley were to explain in his own words the sensations that overcame him the moment he traveled—that is to say, if he could somehow sort through his bewildered mind—some words might include
flying, weightless, ethereal, out-of-body, and even detachment from
reality, in which he felt that the laws of gravity did not apply to him.
The idea of floating through a limitless world might appeal to some, but
if Stanley could share his opinion, he would suggest that it is actually
quite nauseating. By the time his spirit, as it seemed to Stanley, returned
to the bounds of his body, the room was spinning around him and he
was sick all over the floor of his library.

Stanley gasped. Unsteady on his feet, he leaned on his desk and
wiped the sweat from his brow, feeling utterly empty in his stomach.

"Wh-what's happened?"

When he was certain that the floor under him would not crumble,
he made his way to the opposite window to look outside, surprised that
the day was radiant. There was no sign of the Millers, who had been
arguing outside moments before. Through the haze in his mind, he distinctly remembered that he and Mr. Miller had arrived home with the
setting sun, but now it seemed as if it was still morning. Stanley glanced
at the grandfather clock in the library and shook his head. *Eleven o'clock.*
Surely only two glasses of scotch could not cause him to be delusional—
but insane? There was only one explanation.

The Time Key had taken him five hours into the past.

But how could he possibly be certain? Stanley staggered out of the
library and bounced from wall to wall down the hallway like a drunk; he

made it to the kitchen when an idea popped into his head. If he really was five hours in the past, then perhaps the girl in the attic was still unconscious, and it would prove he had indeed traveled through time.

It all seemed to be a troubling dream as he flew up the stairs; at the door to the Bird Room, Stanley paused. If the incredible truth of time travel was possible, then that made him a time traveler. Time could be controlled. Time was in the palm of his hand.

He parted the door to peer inside the room, and Stanley saw the girl lying where he had left her, still asleep. Stanley let out a long breath. He was uncertain about how he should feel. The rushing of his blood was loud in his ears and his feet weighed down on the floor, but at once, a heavy load lifted off his shoulders. Euphoria danced in the pit of his stomach. It was true. Time travel was possible, and he, Stanley Becker, had the key to unlock its secrets. Stanley, the man who was lost in the labyrinth of his miserable life, suddenly saw a piece of the puzzle unfold before him. Oh, the possibilities that were now laid out before him seemed endless, and all Stanley had to do was push a button to attain them.

Movement in the Bird Room caught Stanley's eye. He waited in silence as he remembered the unimaginable presence of the girl in the room. Her small figure sat up slowly. She studied her surroundings, then reached down to remove her bandages.

"Oh, I wouldn't do that," Stanley said, opening the door. "You might still be bleeding."

The girl's eyes widened in alarm the moment Stanley entered, but when she attempted to get on her feet, she stumbled to her knees and crawled away. Seeing her fright, Stanley stood back and watched as her figure disappeared inside the nearest birdhouse. He must be a terrible sight to her. Stanley stepped back uncertainly. He didn't wish to frighten her more.

As Stanley walked to the far window on the opposite side of the room to examine the Time Key, his attention returned to what the girl's presence proved. Nuri's voice echoed in his head:

Move the hand clockwise and it will take you forward. Move it the other way and it will take you back.

Stanley frowned. All the hands were aligned together. They pointed straight to the neutral marker where the twelve should have been. He had not moved any of the hands before pressing the crown, and had still traveled through time without a specified destination. Perhaps it was defective, selecting random times in which to dump its user. Stanley found the concept of time travel too thrilling to be concerned over minor setbacks. Surely if Nuri had known about any risks, she would have warned him.

But the most important thing to remember is to turn all the hands to this position . . . if you want to get back to the time you left.

Stanley could not say what triggered the impulse to press the crown again, but before he realized what he had done the room disappeared in a flashing white light, a bright, soundless explosion. His spirit was suspended in the air. Every molecule, every atom of his being, dispersed, whirled around, then came back to him. The blinding light deposited him into a reality where the walls of the Bird Room spun and threatened to collapse on top of him. Stanley had kept his eyes open, but the force had been too great. In a daze, he fell back against the wall behind him. He sat gasping for air; his lungs struggled to expand in his chest. He thanked heaven for having survived such a disconcerting experience once more.

On the table across the room, a curious head poked out from inside a birdhouse, mouth open, eyes gaping. The girl regarded Stanley with incredulity.

"How did you do that?"

When Stanley felt sure the floor would not give away beneath him, he sighed weakly, unable to answer the girl's question at the moment.

❧

"It's called a Time Key."

The girl studied the contraption curiously from the safety of the birdhouse. Stanley had opened it and placed it face up next to the birdhouse so that she could see it. Presently, the large hand pointed straight at her, with the little hand spinning wildly. Stanley remembered that Nuri had said the contraption acted like a compass attracted to certain energies, and he knew that whatever energy the small girl contained was connected to the Time Key. But he could not guess what it all meant.

Apparently, the name of the contraption meant nothing to the girl, who looked up at Stanley in confusion and shook her head.

Stanley sat on his noisy chair, facing the table, and kept his distance.

"I can use it to travel through time."

"Time?" she said dubiously. "You appeared out of nowhere!"

Stanley smiled. He found reassurance in the girl's smooth voice and was amazed that it gave her incredible existence believability. He tried to think of a way to explain his recent journey into the past without sounding insane. With his hands, he motioned to an imaginary line.

"Pretend we are here, our time now," he said. The girl gave him a nod to continue. "I used the Time Key and suddenly found myself here"— he pointed to the start of the imaginary line—"five hours *earlier*."

The girl bit her lip, uneasy.

"While I was in the past, I came here to see you. You had just woken up. Do you remember that?"

She nodded.

"I stood by that window when I decided to return to the time I had left, our time now. That's why it seemed that I had appeared from nowhere."

The girl considered his explanation for a moment and then pointed toward the door. "You walked through that door, then you appeared by the window. How?"

Stanley felt his stomach flip at the thought that he had almost run into his past self. "Before I used the Time Key the first time, I came here to check on you, but I did not see you. I suppose the Time Key brought me back a few moments before I actually left."

The girl seemed uneasy by Stanley's incredible story. "It is strange," she said.

Stanley agreed that discussing time travel with a small being such as her was quite unbelievable.

"Quite," he added.

The silence that followed was tense, but Stanley did not want to ask the obvious question at the tip of his tongue, not now that he had gained a small ounce of the girl's trust. A sudden growl interrupted the silence.

The girl's cheeks flushed when she looked up in embarrassment.

"You're hungry!" Stanley realized her stomach was crying out for food. "Russell said to only feed you fluids."

At the mention of another human being besides Stanley, the girl became visibly fearful. Behind him, he heard the fireplace crackle louder, and he remembered what the girl's terror in Gilmore's library had done to the flames in the lamps.

"How about some milk?" he asked quickly, to take her mind off whatever had upset her.

Eager but cautious, the girl nodded. Stanley went to the kitchen as fast as his unsteady legs could carry him, poured milk in a teacup, and returned to the Bird Room in a matter of seconds. It seemed that the girl would not take a sip while Stanley was still in the room, but she thanked him. She appeared uncomfortable, and Stanley remembered her wound. When he asked to take a look at it, the girl accepted grudgingly and stepped out of the birdhouse with vigilance.

A dark pool of blood soaked through the bandages, and her pale face hinted that she had lost a considerable amount. Stanley retrieved the clean bandages that Gilmore had left before helping the girl to remove the bloody ones. Stanley bit his lip at the sight of the oozing wound, suddenly dizzy, but noticed that it did not look worse than it had that morning. The girl winced when Stanley touched her side with a wet rag.

"I'm sorry," he apologized. "I'll be gentle."

She nodded and closed her eyes. It was strange to have her out, exposed to scrutiny, and Stanley took advantage of it to study her in detail. The girl could not be much taller than five inches, and appeared to be merely ten years of age. He wondered briefly how a full-grown adult would compare. Once Stanley finished his work, he instructed her to avoid exerting herself and to rest as much as possible.

"It's a miracle you survived, you know," he said hesitantly. "The glass cut you up very badly."

Still, the girl didn't answer.

"It must hurt you."

Her nose wrinkled in defiance. "It was worse before."

Stanley recalled the night before in Gilmore's library. If fear caused the fire to grow in the hearth, then Stanley could only guess what anger would do. He wondered about the girl's peculiarities with fire and whether her emotions really controlled the phenomenon.

Without another word, and hardly a glance, the girl retreated inside the birdhouse. From a drawer, Stanley retrieved two handkerchiefs and placed them in front of the little entrance, promising to return with more food once Mrs. Miller finished cooking. The girl didn't peek from inside, and Stanley suspected she would not come out again. It had been enough to see her, to speak to her.

Stanley smiled to himself.

He allowed the girl privacy, and with thoughts of all that he had done and seen, Stanley rushed downstairs. What seemed to matter at the moment was what Stanley would do next, knowing what he did about the Time Key and its capabilities. The rest of that night he limited himself to drinking only one glass of scotch after dinner, confined to the library, as he began to plan.

∞

Mrs. Miller didn't know what to make of this new Mr. Becker, thoughtful as usual but far from solemn. When she asked him if he had been sick in the library, he apologized profusely and immediately went to clean it up. She chuckled to herself. What could have possibly happened to cause this change? It must have something to do with his trip earlier that day. Mrs. Miller hoped that, if Mr. Becker was seeing someone, he would stay away from those brothels that seemed popular among the men of higher class, but she knew such degradation was below a respectable man like her employer.

Returning from the gardens, Mrs. Miller paid one last visit to the library before she headed off to bed. She found Mr. Becker scribbling angrily on his desk.

"I'll be off now, Mr. Becker," she said. "It's no use lookin' for Brutus at this time of night."

The man barely looked up from his work. "I'm sorry about your cat, Mrs. Miller."

"S'alright, Mr. Becker." After a pause, the maid continued, "Mr. Becker?"

"Hmm . . ."

"What business had you t'day in Kingston?"

Stanley's hand stopped its scribbling for a moment. "Personal business, Mrs. Miller."

"Mr. Miller says ye went fer a stroll through Canbury Gardens—"

"That's all it was, Mrs. Miller," Stanley interrupted and returned to work. "A stroll."

She wasn't convinced. "Will ye be needin' anything else, Mr. Becker?"

"No, thank you."

"G'night, Mr. Becker."

"Good night."

That was all Mrs. Miller would get from her employer. It sufficed for the moment, and it allowed the housekeeper to retire to bed somewhat peacefully, although her cat was still missing.

∞

Tom Miller sighed in exhaustion from a day filled with satisfying work. But it was done, and he yearned to close his eyes.

"That man concerns me, Tom," Norah mumbled, although her loud voice was perfectly audible. "And it isn't as though I can give 'im a skelping to set 'im straight, as badly as I wish it!"

"He's no boy, Norah," Tom replied with a yawn.

"He certainly acts like it at times," she said, shaking her head. "Although he has been in a better mood today. First time in a while."

Tom nodded and picked at a stray thread from his trousers.

"Ye will nae believe what the messenger lad said today, Tom!" she cried with renewed irritation. "He overheard those big-headed, no-good, overbearing—"

"Now, Norah . . ."

Her cheeks were bright red. "Those *gentlemen* at *The Strand*. The lad heard 'em talking. Apparently as of late, Mr. Becker's work is not far above what they consider as adequate for a magazine. *Adequate*, they said, for a man who spends his nights in pubs till the sun comes up. Of all the self-righteous . . . shoving their noses up another man's business . . ."

Tom grunted and held back a smile.

"And that's not the worst of it," Norah continued. "The lad says they only use Mr. Becker's work, his little stories and such, to fill in the gaps. He says they widnae print them if it were nae for Frank Becker."

Tom sat up in his seat.

"Norah . . ."

"Oh, I did nae believe it, Tom! I gave the lad such a scolding for even thinking it. He writes such wonderful stories . . ."

Tom ran a hand over his eyes. "They're only rumors. Don't you mention it to him."

"I widnae think of it," Norah replied. "Mentioning his father is bad enough."

Tom was convinced it was only a rumor, but at times rumors had some truth to them. It wouldn't surprise Tom, however, the way things had turned out after six years.

Norah was ironing his clothes for the next day while she continued to grumble under her breath, wishing that her cat would soon turn up. Tom directed his thoughts elsewhere as he picked up a small tin box where he kept little treasures they had gathered over the years. The label was faded, and he had long forgotten what it had previously contained. His hand reached inside his trousers pocket to retrieve an odd little treasure he had found that day, and although he didn't know its purpose or its reason for being in the street where he had found it, Tom fancied that it was of some great importance. The glass vial appeared small and insignificant in the coachman's large fingers, and the slight tremble of his pulse created little ripples in the water inside.

Giving the vial a brief study, Tom placed it inside the tin box and closed the lid. He set the box back in a compartment beneath the floor under his bed. The coachman fitted the loose floorboard in place as he yearned to close his eyes.

VI

Mrs. Miller had retired to bed not two hours ago, and the sounds of a quill scratching a papery surface could still be heard coming from the library. There was a pause, and Stanley's hunched figure straightened up to look over his work. He had always found it helpful to sketch out ideas on paper to organize his thoughts, which at that moment regarded all he knew about the Time Key and the possibilities it offered. If he could perfect a way to safely travel from one time to the other, swallowing much of the discomfort it brought, then he would be able to control his past and future. The idea made him tremble. If he could go back five hours into the past, what would stop him from going back five days, even five years?

A scrawled note jumped out of the page. *December 3, 1891.* What could possibly stop him from going back six years?

The Time Key's glassy face winked at him in the candlelight. Stanley grinned as he picked up the contraption. He believed he understood the general idea of its functions, but he had yet to test it.

Stanley scanned his notes. His experiment was simple: travel back two days, to December 3, 1897. Setting the Time Key, however, was a bit tricky. Nuri had said that the middle section represented seasons, but there were twelve markers and only four symbols. The markers didn't seem to point to any specific symbol, yet the four symbols separated the ring of markers into four sections. Stanley assumed that the twelve markers represented months of the year. He knew the top right symbol meant winter, so Stanley set the hand to the middle marker of that section.

The smallest hand would set the day he wished to travel to. These markers circumvented the southernmost side of the section, and moving the hand clockwise, Stanley set it to the third marker.

He remembered Nuri's instructions that the largest section would specify the years in which to travel forward or back. As he moved the hand to the first marker counterclockwise, the Time Key vibrated slightly. Stanley raised the contraption to his ear. Five tiny ticks rang inside before the hand even reached the first marker. An idea formed in his mind. Perhaps the years section had been designed similarly to the seasons, in which each symbol represented more time than it was apparent. Perhaps the five clicks leading up to the first marker signified years, and Stanley certainly didn't want to travel so far back, yet. He only needed to direct the Time Key to the past. Returning the hand to the neutral marker, he moved it ever so slightly without it ticking. It should be enough.

Feeling a bit giddy, Stanley stepped away from his desk and readied to travel. As his thumb repressed the crown, he hoped the journey wouldn't be as unsettling as before.

He shouldn't have expected anything less.

As Stanley's body materialized into the past, he stumbled backward, but caught himself on the desk. Refusing to lose his dinner this time, Stanley kept his eyes closed until the sickness died away. The library was dark and still. The grandfather clock read 10:56, the same time he had left. Stanley grinned. Certainly it had worked, but how could he be sure?

He rummaged through the mess of papers on the desk before he spotted a newspaper.

"Thank you, Norah," he murmured, praising his maid's ever-faithful gesture of putting the morning paper on his desk each day.

With shaking hands, Stanley held it up and found the date. His heart sank.

Sunday, January 24, 1897.

He shuffled through the rest of the mess. Failing to find another newspaper, he let drop the one in his hand.

He had traveled farther back than he had hoped, which meant that despite his efforts, he still had no idea how to use the Time Key. Double-checking the settings, Stanley's mind raced. If this was January, then he had mistakenly placed the hand on the winter season's second marker.

He distinctly remembered that Nuri had called the symbol winter, which should have taken him to December.

Stanley paused.

"*Of course!*" he whispered excitedly.

If the symbol meant winter, then the first marker, not the marker he had set it to, would represent the beginning of the season. Each of the four symbols belonged to a section with three markers, counting twelve months. Three markers for each. *Beginning, middle, and end.* Stanley cursed himself. That meant that the first marker signified December 21, the first day of winter, and the middle marker was Jan 21. By setting the days hand to the third day he had actually traveled to three days past it—January 24.

If his theory was correct, he would need to set the seasons hand to the end of autumn, and the days hand to the third day. Leaving the years hand where it was, the Time Key ought to take him to December 3, 1897.

❧

The newspaper certainly wasn't cooperating.

Sunday, December 5, 1897. He had returned to the moment he had left. A few minutes later, to be exact.

Stanley didn't understand. He thought he had done everything correctly this time. What was he missing? The seasons hand had taken him to December, and the year was the same, but the day was the *fifth*, not the third. Unless . . .

Stanley placed the newspaper on the desk by the candle and frowned in thought. The day was Sunday. Perhaps Nuri had not meant that the markers counted days in numbers, but each symbol represented a day of the week. January 24 had been a Sunday, and he had traveled back to the Sunday he had originally left. That specific symbol must mean Sunday, and because the markers weren't in any order he could decipher, he supposed he would have to try each symbol to find which day they represented.

Going clockwise, Stanley set the days hand to the next marker and activated the Time Key.

Once the dizziness subsided, Stanley spotted a newspaper by his feet, still folded and unread. When he reached down, his fingertips brushed against a little mound of ash. Stanley frowned, smearing soot on the paper as he wiped his hand clean. There were spots of cigar residue on the floor leading to the fireplace. It was clear that the Time Key had taken him to the night Louis Vargas had paid him an unsuspecting visit.

Saturday, December 4, 1897.

He looked around him for a moment. The air was cold. Papers lay scattered about the floor, and the window behind the desk showed snow gathering outside on the sill, leaving icy traces on the glass where it touched. Louis had already visited him, and he had probably gone to Gilmore's house with a wounded girl in a little box.

Stanley shook away the unease and looked at the Time Key again. Now he knew that the third marker, going clockwise, represented Sunday, and the next one, the southernmost marker, represented Saturday. December 3 had been a Friday, and he supposed the next marker in the sequence would take him to his goal.

❧

Stanley only had time to glance at the grandfather clock when he heard footsteps climb down the stairs toward the library. In a dazed panic, Stanley opened the window and climbed out, nearly falling in a heap on the stones outside. He took refuge behind a thorn bush and pressed back against the wall as he heard someone shuffling about and slamming drawers inside. After several minutes, Stanley heard a man curse irritably and saw him look out the open window.

With a lump in his throat, Stanley stared at the other man. This could not be real. Stanley had almost blindly believed he could travel through time, had trusted in what his thrilled imagination had told him to be possible, but his eyes couldn't believe. Now he saw it. Before him was a man identical to himself, a past version of him, living and breathing in the same space at the same time, and his logic could no longer deny it.

Stanley Becker was a time traveler.

His past version closed the window at last, and Stanley let out his breath. He allowed himself to regain some calm before he stole around the house and knelt in the grass to wait as his body grew accustomed to the past.

The night was as silent as he remembered it, but the somberness that had dominated Stanley then now lacked the same persistence that had previously drove him to the bridge at Kingston-on-Thames. This really was December 3, 1897. The irony wasn't lost on Stanley that he had chosen to return to the night that had changed his life, allowing him to travel to it again. Briefly, he wondered what would happen if he somehow stopped his past self from going to the bridge, assuming he could interact with him. It would mean that he would never have tried to blow his brains out, never would have met Louis, and never would have known about the Time Key. If he stopped Past Stanley from leaving the house, would he disappear? The thought made Stanley's stomach churn. It was an upsetting idea, and for the moment, Stanley did not encourage it.

While Stanley mused in hiding, the front door opened. The shock of seeing himself had not dissolved, and he found it quite disturbing to see his past self sneak through the gardens, experiencing the memory as an outsider. He wondered how it could be possible to relive his life outside of himself. But he wasn't reliving it. He was merely observing, still bound by his own present. He was still Stanley Becker. It was all quite puzzling, but Stanley forced himself to remain the observer he believed to be. He would have no interactions with the past.

Past Stanley reached the gates, gave one look around before mounting his bicycle, and sped off into the night. Behind the bush, Stanley took a deep breath and opened the Time Key. After all that traveling, he finally acknowledged the sudden exhaustion weighing on him. The sickness that came from using the Time Key was as unpleasant as a hangover, but Stanley was willing to endure the side effects. At least it did not last long. Not for a man familiar with hangovers. But he still did not feel quite right. Nevertheless, staring at the set hands of the Time Key, giddiness returned.

Noticing a pair of eyes glowing in the dark, Stanley chuckled to himself and leaned forward.

"There you are, you little beast," Stanley said. "I wish you'd tell me where you'll run off to. Mrs. Miller's quite beside herself."

The cat only stared.

Stanley rose at last and set the hands of the Time Key to target the time he had left, and with a boyish grin on his lips, he pressed the crown.

∞

He was quite unsteady on his legs. He had had enough traveling for one night. Leaning against one of the posts of the portico, Stanley paused to catch his breath. He should have returned to the time he had originally left, but the sickness seemed to have made a turn of the worst. At least, it had never lasted this long.

Stanley closed his eyes. The dizziness and nausea had left him, and he supposed his shaking hands only betrayed how tired he was, despite however much adrenaline he still had running through him. Something certainly felt odd.

On the icy ground, with thorny bushes pricking at his coat, Stanley pressed his hands to his head.

But the most important thing to remember . . .

He recalled Nuri's instructions as he inspected the Time Key.

". . . if you want to get back to the time you left," Stanley muttered, "all hands to the neutral markers."

Nuri had emphasized the importance of this, and Stanley supposed that was the reason for the worsening sickness. But he was exhausted, and his mind refused to think further as his fingers turned the tiny knobs. All the hands returned to their neutral positions. Stanley sighed when he traveled once again.

VII

Once the blinding light subsided and delivered Stanley back to his own time, he found it was a painfully bright day.

He groaned.

"Lord!" Mrs. Miller cried.

Stanley saw the housekeeper gawking down at him. She dropped her laundry basket.

"Mr. Becker! Ye nearly made me jump out me knickers! What in blazes are ye doin' sleepin' in the garden?"

"Good day, Mrs. Miller," Stanley said, rubbing his temples. "Would you happen to know the date and time?"

"The s-sixth. It's half past noon. What, ye slept here all night?"

"I don't remember, Mrs. Miller. I suppose I'll go inside."

Mrs. Miller seemed to want to demand a reasonable answer, but she kept her lips pursed and Stanley took the opportunity to scurry off, cursing himself for his carelessness. He hadn't expected to return *hours* after he had originally left his present, but he couldn't complain. The sickness that moments before had overwhelmed him seemed to be vanishing quickly. He would have to be more cautious next time, at least until he fully understood how to work the Time Key.

As he shed his coat inside, a small smile formed on his lips.

Who would have guessed that Stanley Becker, the pitiful drunkard by day, became a time traveler by night?

"I don't suppose you gave her an explanation," Russell Gilmore's voice said from the library.

Stanley jumped in surprise. Feeling as though he had been caught misbehaving, Stanley entered the library to meet Gilmore's curious scowl. With his pipe pinched between his lips, the doctor's impatient pose demanded an immediate answer.

"Explain what?" Stanley asked, warily approaching the bar at the corner of the room.

Gilmore cupped the pipe and removed it from his lips. "I've only just arrived. Mrs. Miller said she'd not seen you all morning, and suddenly there you are, sleeping outside."

Stanley poured himself a glass, mostly out of habit, as he looked through the window. Mrs. Miller was on her knees picking up laundry from the ground, looking quite vexed.

"What were you doing?" Gilmore pressed on.

Stanley felt the lump in his waistcoat pocket. "You wouldn't believe me if I told you," he replied, turning back to Gilmore, unable to hide a grin. "In any case, why are you here?"

Casting a quick look behind him, Gilmore asked in a hushed voice, "Has she awakened yet?"

It took Stanley a moment to realize who Gilmore was referring to, and the boyish delight melted away. He had not seen the girl since dinner the night before. Such had been his eagerness over the wondrous adventures that the Time Key introduced into his life that he had neglected the mysterious child in the attic altogether. He quickly led Gilmore to the attic, making a side trip to the kitchen where Stanley grabbed a cup of milk. The two men climbed the stairs to the attic in silence.

Stanley knocked twice before they entered. He hoped that this sign of encouraged privacy would appear submissive to the girl hiding in the birdhouse, and therefore invite some sort of trust to be reached between the three. He could practically feel Gilmore's excitement, but tried to remain calm and passive. Stanley could only imagine how terrible a sight they must be to a tiny creature like her.

Instructing Gilmore to stand at a distance, Stanley sat facing the birdhouse that she had claimed as her home and waited. Nothing happened and no one spoke for at least a minute, when at last Stanley saw her slender figure approach the entrance. Her wide eyes sparkled with interest when she spotted the milk.

"Will you come out for a moment?" Stanley whispered.

The girl glanced around Stanley when she noticed Gilmore, and shook her head.

"That's Russell Gilmore," Stanley said. "He's a doctor. He's come to check your wound."

Again, the girl shook her head. Stanley smiled sympathetically, remembering their conversation the night before. It was hard to believe that it had only been a short time since he had first heard the girl speak.

"Come," he urged. "It will only take a minute."

Much to their surprise the girl stepped out cautiously. She watched them with suspicion as she clutched her ripped-up garment to her chest. It was time for Gilmore to take over. His delight was obvious, but he brushed it aside to make room for the professionalism the task at hand required. His serene smile seemed to vanquish the girl's fear.

"Hullo, darling," Gilmore said, taking a seat where Stanley had been. "Looks to me as if you're feeling much better."

Gilmore's friendliness allowed the girl to feel secure. She nodded and obeyed Gilmore's instructions to unwrap the bloody bandages, despite the evident discomfort it caused. Stanley was glad to be in the background for this. The blood made him queasy.

"That's a significant difference in the amount of blood loss from before," Gilmore said approvingly.

Hesitantly, the girl nodded.

"And I see Stanley's done his best to change the bandages frequently," he added, glancing at the unused roll of bandages. Stanley blushed.

"I changed them last night . . ."

"No matter," Gilmore said. "It's healing quite well."

The girl slipped the garment over her head once Gilmore had finished. Stanley nudged the cup of milk toward the girl, and she looked up.

"You're Stanley?"

Nodding, Stanley grinned. "And what's your name?"

"Lena."

Gilmore was at the edge of his seat. "It's a pleasure to meet you, Lena."

Uncertain, and a bit impatient, the girl gave a simple shrug and retreated to the birdhouse, leaving behind a trail of mystery. Having no other motive for staying in the attic, the men left for the library to give the girl the solitude that she apparently wanted.

From the lingering thrill that was visible on Gilmore's expression, and the giddiness that reminded Stanley of a child, it was clear that speaking with Lena had roused a dormant sense of curiosity. Stanley, on the other hand, remembered something that continued to trouble him about the entire situation.

"How did—wh-when did—" Gilmore began.

Stanley took a seat behind his desk to finger through the stack of manuscripts he had brought from the attic.

"She woke up yesterday."

"Incredible! *Remarkable!* And she appeared to trust you."

Stanley cast the library entrance a wary look, wishing there were doors to offer them privacy, and spoke softly enough to not be heard by prying ears.

"Russell, I've something important to tell you."

The secrecy alarmed Gilmore.

"I-I think . . . I think that I created her," Stanley began.

"Created her—what do you mean?"

Stanley picked up a single sheet of notes and showed Gilmore.

"Look here, Russell. I wrote it six years ago."

"Aspen folk, eh? Like the trees?"

Nodding, Stanley continued, "How could it be possible to imagine people of her sort, and then *she* appears? What other explanation is there?"

Stanley purposely omitted from his explanation the meeting he had had with Louis and the Lurkers chasing him.

"I don't see why it couldn't be possible," Gilmore said, eyes still scanning the paper. "She's here. She exists, doesn't she? If I can believe in her, I can believe anything."

Stanley nodded but hesitated before he continued with the subject he had been struggling to put into words. The familiar excitement resurfaced.

"I found a way to save them, Russell."

"Who?"

"Jane and Maisie. I can change what happened to them."

Gilmore sat up in his chair.

"What are you talking about?"

Stanley brought out the Time Key from his pocket. Gilmore hesitated before he accepted it.

"It's this—this contraption."

"What is it?" Gilmore asked, fingering the intricate designs on the front and back, awed by its beauty.

"It's called a Time Key. I can control time with it."

"Control time . . ."

Stanley took a deep breath. "I can travel to any date in history." He pointed to the crown of the Time Key. "One click of that button and I can go whenever I please. It's incredible, Russell!"

Gilmore's brow was furrowed.

"Of course, there are still a few things I've yet to figure out, but once I know exactly how it all works I'll be able to go back to the accident. I could stop it. I could *save* them. It would be as if they never left!"

"Stanley, I-I don't think—"

"If you can believe in tiny pygmies, then you can believe in this. You said so yourself."

"I don't doubt it's possible, Stanley. But changing the past—I don't know if anyone could do that."

Stanley recalled observing his past self on December 3, and grew slightly unsettled as he remembered toying with the idea of stopping himself from ever going to Kingston Bridge. The doubt encouraged further unease, but he quickly cast it aside.

"Why couldn't it be possible? If I can go back and stop them from ever leaving the house, the accident could not have ever happened."

It was all too much for Gilmore, who could only stare at the Time Key and shake his head.

"Is that why you were missing all morning?" Gilmore wondered, skepticism in his voice.

Stanley nodded. "I was in *time*, Russell."

If he truly believed him or not, Gilmore didn't show it as he muttered, "I don't know, Stanley. I suppose I would have to see it for myself."

"You'll see it is possible. Once I've perfected it, I'll go back to save them. It is possible. It *has* to be."

❧

Mrs. Miller had not said a word to Stanley about finding him sprawled behind a bush that morning, nor did she object when he poured her broccoli bisque in a teacup and locked himself in the Bird Room for the remainder of the night. However, Stanley wasn't about to explain himself anytime soon. There was still much he didn't understand about the situation he had stumbled into, and the strange occurrences of the last couple of days didn't seem as though they would explain themselves, but Stanley had decided to make the best of it. At least he had found a new purpose in the Time Key.

Despite his unease in regards to her, it was impossible to forget his very crucial role of caretaker to a vulnerable child that had taken refuge in the attic, although Stanley found himself wishing to know more about her and the reason she had been left to him. She was an extraordinary creature, Stanley couldn't deny it, but that hardly resolved his concern.

Lena was still visibly apprehensive toward him as she had been on their first meeting. When he entered the Bird Room that evening, Stanley suspected she was watching from the birdhouse. He closed the door behind him and stepped slowly toward her house. He left the teacup with a bread roll near it. From the corner of his eye, Stanley saw her peer out timidly but curiously.

"You must be famished," Stanley said quietly. "I suppose you'd like something other than milk for a change."

When the girl didn't answer, Stanley backed away to feed the dying fire. It was cold in the Bird Room, but at least he could keep the worst of it at bay with a good fire.

Stanley's thoughts wandered as he poked at the coals, inviting the flames to grow and devour the fresh firewood. He remembered a time when he would spend long hours in the Bird Room, conversing and laughing with the love of his life after chasing away his frightened daughter's nightmares. From his pocket he retrieved the Time Key and opened it. He had not used it since returning that day, and the lingering excitement of his travels was still present. He studied the strange symbols and noticed the longest hand, like the day before, had abandoned its counterclockwise trail to point Stanley's direction.

Following the hand's new target, Stanley looked back at the stacked birdhouses and saw the girl studying him from behind the teacup. In her hand was a piece of bread, which she had dipped in the soup and munched on hungrily. Seeing she had been spotted, the girl looked away in embarrassment, but she didn't leave. Stanley chuckled to himself and closed the Time Key.

"How did you make it?"

Her question was unexpected, and Stanley turned to address her properly. From the few times they had spoken, Stanley had been able to detect a slight accent. Although her English seemed flawless, Stanley could hear foreignness in her words, and she spoke like a child who spent a great deal of time with adults.

At his surprise, she gestured to his hands. "Your Time Key, I mean. How did you make it?"

"I didn't," he replied. "A man left it here."

Lena's brows furrowed.

"Surely you remember," Stanley continued. "It was the man who brought you here."

A crackling pop interrupted him, and a stray spark jumped from the fire, landing only inches from him. Stanley leapt to his feet and stomped out the flame that was already stretching hungry fingers across the hardwood. A lump formed in his throat as he remembered the night at Gilmore's house and what Lena's terror had done to the lamps.

"It's all right," he said quickly. "There's no need to be afraid. You're safe here."

But when he looked up, the girl had already gone. Half the bread was left, and she had been able to drink some of the soup, at least. Shuffling the toe of his shoe over the remaining ashes, Stanley sighed.

"I'll come in the morning," he promised. "Call for me, in case . . ."

No answer came.

Stanley retreated slowly. He wondered about the girl and the fire, and he tried to shake away the anxiety that returned. He would have to show her that she needn't be frightened. Perhaps, he thought, she would like to shed those rags and soak in a warm bath. He would try again tomorrow.

As he made his way to the library, Stanley felt the Time Key inside his pocket. For now, there was the matter of perfecting his newly found skills.

VIII

Her steps were quick and nearly silent, all except for the clicking of her heels. With pockets full of treasures, the young Romani girl made her way through the streets of Kingston, a serene smile on her face. Her childhood friend and fellow conman, Pierre, caught up to her, flashing his roguish smirk. They couldn't help give in to the common stereotype that these Londoners gave her people. At least for Nuri, it gave her a sort of overpowering sense to connive and deceive the fools, and picking their pockets was a little reward that they could claim.

The two crossed the gardens to the little clearing where the clan had set up camp before they separated, agreeing to a later time when they could count and evenly divide their spoils. Nuri removed her heels and ran to her tent, where she wasted no time shedding the uncomfortable dress that women in London considered to be the latest in fashion. In order to blend in, she often wore the dress, even though the corset cut off her breath in a most excruciating way.

It was most crucial for Naomi to remain unaware of the fact that Nuri's daily strolls were actually spent palm reading in obscured alleyways and acting as a luring distraction to passersby while Pierre emptied their pockets from behind. If Nuri's mother were to find out—well, Nuri feared her mother's temper.

In contrast, her father would find it amusing. Wherever he was, Nuri hoped he would come back soon.

"*Mare!*" she called. "Mother!"

In her graceful manner, Nuri went to the back of the tent where her mother usually cooked outside. On her way she touched a few of the many blankets and beaded curtains that her mother weaved, feeling each thread and individual yarn between her fingers. She respected the painstaking effort her mother had made with each, but Nuri felt that such menial hobbies were beneath her. Arranged alongside the tent walls were little statuettes made of wood, copper, stone, and some of gold. She smiled at these. Her father had brought them from the foreign cultures and peoples of a world unknown to her. The little tent held a variety of treasures from the many places they had lived, but it reminded her most of Andalusia, what she could call her birthplace.

"*Mare!*" she called again, growing impatient. "*Mare*, where—"

And then she saw him, waiting with his greasy smile and beady eyes on the other side of the tent flap. Nuri faced Naomi's back, and tried to remain hidden, but the bald man had spotted her. His wink sent chills up her spine.

"Thank you for your time, Naomi," the bald man said, waving his good hand at them. His wooden hand remained concealed inside the left sleeve. He nodded to Nuri. "Always a pleasure to see you, Saira."

She gritted her teeth and called out as he left. "My name is Nuri!"

Naomi turned to look at her.

"Dirty old man," Nuri spat.

"Nuri." Naomi rebuked her with stern eyes. "Where have you been? You know I need help with the packing."

"We're leaving, then? But we agreed that we'd give Da a few more days—"

"The authorities are coming. Or so Mà de Fusta claims."

Mà de Fusta. In Catalan it literally meant *wooden hand*, the name that the clan called the mysterious bald man, partly because they suspected he had come from somewhere in northern Spain. No one knew his real name, and no one really cared to ask.

Nuri scoffed. "What did that man want, anyway?"

Naomi didn't seem to want to tell her daughter, but the girl's impatient posture dismissed any possibility of letting up.

"Come inside."

"Does Toma know he's here?" Nuri wondered as she held the flap open for her mother, who was carrying a load of clean laundry in her arms.

The big man, Toma—acting clan leader, and Naomi's oldest brother—did not like the merchant Mà de Fusta, and with good reason.

While the clan had still been situated in Andalusia, the bald man, who often liked to trade with the *Calé*—Spanish Gypsies—had asked Louis for Nuri's hand in marriage. At that time, Nuri had only been twelve years old. Of course, Louis had refused, but upon hearing about it, Toma had become infuriated and ran the merchant out of town, threatening to slit his throat if he ever saw him again.

"Toma wouldn't allow him to stay the night. He'll be leaving soon. And no, he's not here to marry you."

"What does he want?"

Naomi let the clothes drop at her feet but did not meet Nuri's eyes.

"He's been asking for your father."

"Everyone's looking for him lately," Nuri said, dropping down next to her mother to fold the laundry.

Something seemed to bother Naomi's thoughts. She still didn't meet her daughter's gaze.

"Your father," Naomi began slowly. "Before he left, he went to see him."

Nuri could not believe her ears. "Why would he go see Mà de Fusta?"

"Your father never told me. But I don't believe Mà de Fusta is really here looking for him."

"You think he had something to do with Da's disappearance?" Sudden anger began to boil in her chest. Why hadn't her mother told her this before?

After a long pause, Naomi sighed and finally looked up. "You've seen Mr. Becker since he came yesterday, haven't you?"

Nuri was caught off guard by the change in subject. "I-I spoke to him before he left—"

"If you see him again, you must warn him against coming back here."

"Why?"

Naomi was thoughtful as she said, "Mà de Fusta asked about him too."

❧

Allow me to direct your attention to a darkened alley where, past strolling crowds and horse-pulled carriages, we see a man looking up from under a tilted bowler hat, chewing on straw as he watched the busy streets with boredom. This was a street that Nuri and Pierre often visited to perfect their pickpocketing hobby, but unbeknownst to them, this was also where the man often observed them silently from the shadows. Only very few people could sense the coldness that accompanied his presence, and even fewer could see the yellow eyes that gleamed hungrily.

I understand the reader's confusion, but I am only allowed to reveal certain details about the man and his dark nature, although one can feel the palpable terror that his gaze brings, the cold that penetrates the bones, and the shock of seeing his figure suddenly melt into the shadows that shield him. For now, the man watched the lively streets, retaining the shape of a dark-skinned man with a bowler hat whose identity he had taken. He had been waiting, and now he saw the bald-headed man emerge from the crowd, holding his wooden hand as though wounded, and give him a simple nod. The dark-skinned man followed behind Mà de Fusta.

"They say Louis is missing. They don't know what happened."

The dark-skinned man had no expression, and his deep-throated voice sounded hoarse and unused.

"And what of the other man?" he said.

"Naomi claims she doesn't know him, but I saw Nuri speak with him. He may have given away your presence here."

The dark-skinned man said nothing.

"I don't see why you lot are afraid of him," Mà de Fusta scoffed. "The man looks about as threatening as a *child*."

"He has a strange energy to him."

Mà de Fusta grunted his annoyance. "You useless dolt," he muttered. "No matter. We'll get the answers we need from Louis. It'll only be a matter of time."

The dark alley deposited the men to a desolate street, eerily lonely. Their figures walked to an abandoned house and entered, but we don't follow them.

At least, not now.

IX

Despite the fact that Stanley Becker had used the Time Key a few times and was confident in his ability to time travel, the man was a long way from deserving the title of time traveler. He was clumsy, overly excited, and far too arrogant for his own good. It was to be expected from a novice traveler, and we cannot blame him for succumbing to the thrill of controlling time and ignoring the obvious risks and consequences unbeknownst to him for now. For the sake of our story, I won't get ahead of myself and spare the reader from matters that will, no doubt, unveil in time.

It was tricky business, time traveling, and Stanley assumed that the Time Key had limited functions, but he accepted that he still had much to learn. While experimenting, he found that when jumping from one time to another, he would arrive at the hour that he had left with the difference of only a few minutes at most, and since the Time Key didn't give him the option of traveling in hours or minutes, he took it as good fortune. However, a few peculiarities came to his attention each time he traveled. There were times when Stanley would leave the hands at neutral when activating the contraption, but to his confusion, the Time Key wouldn't take him anywhere. This complied with Nuri's instructions, but it didn't explain his experience of the first time he had traveled. That time, he hadn't specified a destination and had still traveled back five hours. Only once, however, during Stanley's experimenting did it happen again, and he was taken an hour forward. Pressing the crown a second time had returned him to the time he had left. Stanley considered that perhaps this wasn't an intended function, but simply an irregularity. Needless to say, he was careful to avoid triggering the contraption in this manner.

It was less than predictable coming home, as he had experienced during the first few journeys. Twice, Stanley came back to find he had been absent for several hours. Once, he had skipped an entire night.

As he had done on the night of December 5, Stanley tried several times to return to his present by manually setting the date on the Time Key, as he assumed it would be the most obvious solution for the unpredictable time lapse, but he soon found that each time he tried it, the same sickness overtook him to the point of near madness. Stanley found the sensation difficult to understand, and I will do my best to put it in simple terms:

While in "time," as Stanley calls it, he is in a constant state of distress, in which his body is aware that it doesn't belong to the world around him.

It was impossible to rid himself of this persistent rejection from *time*, but as Stanley continued to travel, his body unwillingly grew used to the sensation. He considered it a lower dose of the original sickness after a jump, which would only get stronger the longer he was in time or in his attempt to return home by deliberately setting the date himself. For this sickness to leave, Stanley had to follow Nuri's instructions and set all hands to the neutral position. In doing so, the nagging heaviness in his stomach, the droning distress that clung to him would suddenly disappear in his return home. That was how Stanley knew he was no longer in time.

Unfortunately, there was nothing he could do about the hours he missed, but on his return from a quick visit to November 17 he found, to his shock, that the time lapse also applied in reverse. The Time Key had returned him several hours prior to his leaving. Stanley had never tried to contact anyone while traveling, and wasn't quite sure what would happen if he did. The fear of running into himself kept him hidden in the shed behind the house. Only when Mr. Miller opened the shed, quite surprised to see him there, did Stanley come back to the house.

Despite all the care he took to avoid such complications, the unexpected still occurred. Coming home once, he saw, in horror, a fading figure across the room, which vanished a second later. It took Stanley several minutes to recover from his fright. His greatest fear was to be caught by the past.

Even so, it hardly mattered that time travel was unpredictable and filled with discomforts. The thrill of it was worth it to Stanley. He could manipulate time.

Stanley had limited himself to going to the past only a few weeks, each time going farther back, until he knew he was ready to travel in years. It seemed that the sickness that came with it was also stronger the longer in time he traveled, but practice made it tolerable. At last, on December 8, he went farther.

It was August 20, 1892. The attic became the dusty, cold room he had once left abandoned. It always took Stanley a minute or two to regain his composure after the spinning washed over. Once he felt well enough, he opened the door and snuck down. Ghosting through the hallways as silently as he was able, he peered inside each room with caution. The last thing he wanted was to be mistaken for a burglar. But the night was silent, and the house empty.

This was a time that had been etched deeply in him, cutting and stripping away what remained of his spirit. For six years he had attempted to forget and somehow ease the pain, but he had only been able to numb it with liquor. This specific date marked the beginning of the alcoholic, an outcome that still bound him to a bottle of scotch. With careful steps, Stanley reached the entrance to the library.

There was hardly any light, but Stanley was able to make out the figure hunched over the desk, one hand used as a pillow, and the other still gripping the neck of a bottle of brandy. Stanley remembered—or rather, he could not recall a single event of that night due to the drinking. August 20 of 1892 had been his first birthday without Jane and Maisie. It had made for quite a depressing date, to say the least, despite Mrs. Miller's numerous attempts to cheer him up.

"You poor devil," Stanley whispered.

He stepped inside the library and regarded his past self with pity. Stanley stood over the man, stared at the bottom of his empty glass, and wished he could take away the pain and sorrow. It would take five more years to drink himself numb, but he would never achieve what he so terribly wanted.

One night it would all change. Stanley wondered what would become of him now. Not the drunk man before him, but his present self. Where would this path of time traveling lead him? With a smile, his thoughts turned to the past once again, to the date that caused all the pain.

"It will get better," he promised.

⟨⟩

The sun set behind a pool of clouds in the scarlet horizon of December 8, 1897, shining intensely through the windows of the Bird Room where Stanley's body appeared out of thin air. He staggered to his chair.

"Where did you go this time?"

It was a wonder how Stanley could even hear Lena's small voice above his labored breathing. Through the dizziness, he managed to see the girl sitting by the window.

"A very dark place," he said.

Lena didn't reply. When Stanley glanced back he saw the girl prop her chin on her knees, as she sat at the edge of the table facing the window. Uncertainly, he said, "You must miss your family."

Lena gave no answer.

"Don't you have a family?"

"Of course I do," she said, irritated.

"Do you know where they are?"

The small flame in the fireplace suddenly crackled and jumped in size. Stanley stepped away, wary of catching fire. But her obvious frustration seemed controlled, and Lena acknowledged Stanley's concern.

"I came here by accident," she began. "And I don't know how to get back."

Stanley thought he saw a tiny tear sneak from her eye, but it disappeared under her fist the moment he came closer.

"What is it like, where you live?"

The girl's eyes didn't waver from the window.

"It's very green there. Always green . . . There are a lot of trees—so old and ancient. We live in them, you know."

It was fascinatingly familiar, and it gave Stanley a sensation of déjà vu, as though he had once seen the place Lena came from. But it hardly confirmed what he suspected about Lena's origins.

"We live secluded from humans," she continued. "We don't trust them, you see. Not all of them are like you."

She paused, remembering.

"My mother had a garden. It was full of flowers . . . She made a ceiling of vines that used to glow during the night. I could see it from my bed. She was gifted, my mother."

"And your father?"

At this, Lena grew visibly agitated once again and Stanley abandoned his desire to know more. When she remained silent, Stanley retreated downstairs, hoping that her spirits would brighten during his absence. An idea had entered his mind, and as he reached the back door below the attic he had already set the Time Key to a time during the summer.

Many climbers and families of vines grew in the Becker garden and bloomed beautifully in late summers. He knew he would find some behind the house, and his risk of getting caught during the night was low. Stanley approached the back wall of the house and pulled a significantly long vine from the roots. He placed it in a dirt-filled pot that Mrs. Miller had left outside. After watering it, Stanley readied to go home.

He wasn't sure that he could take the pot and plant with him to the future. It was true that he brought his clothes with him through the trips, but at times he found that he was missing a shoe, a coat, or even his socks, which he would find had been left in the present. It was that incertitude that caused him to pause. He would never know whether transporting items back and forth through time was possible if he didn't try. Stanley pressed the pot and vines to him securely before returning home.

∽

There was only silence as Stanley crept to the attic. Lena was in her birdhouse. He placed the pot on the table next to it before he retired to his own room for the night.

If she had been watching, she didn't think it necessary to say a word.

X

The fast-approaching Christmas season had Mrs. Miller in a sour mood. There were many preparations pending in her list of things to complete, decorations to put up, gifts to make, and dinners to prepare. Time seemed to be in a hurry, and the frustrated housekeeper could not seem to find enough of it to finish her daily tasks. On Thursday, December 9—Market Day—she forced Stanley to come along and give her a hand with shopping. No matter what excuse he gave her, there was nothing more persuasive than her resolute authority over him as house-keeper, and Stanley found himself in the carriage facing Mrs. Miller, drowsy and vexed.

"Don't give me that look," Mrs. Miller said. "This'll do ye well, Mr. Becker. A change o' scenery will help."

"I'm all right, Mrs. Miller. There's no need to be concerned about me. I don't know where you get these notions."

She clicked her tongue in disapproval and grumbled something that Stanley could not hear.

Kingston was packed with life and excitement centered on the market square, where it was a wonder how so many souls could fit into one place. It was filled to the rim of a beer jug, as it seemed to Stanley, and the overflow of people was in danger of spilling over. It appeared that all of Surrey had a familiar goal in mind that morning. As the horses pulled the carriage through the busy streets, Stanley saw merchants and vendors pulling wagons of fruits and vegetables, rolls of bread, hanging the various parts of distinct pigs, cows, and fish for all to see; boys in their best rags called out to shine your shoes, women showed off their weaved baskets, and bearded men gave toothless grins with the invitation to take a look at their collection of rare items. The place was a colorful zoo that aroused deprived impulses as consumers acted on their most primal instincts of hunting and gathering goods. The sour scent of body odor repulsed Stanley. At a distance, he watched two women at each other's throats over a plucked hen.

Mr. Miller stopped the horses to allow for Stanley and Mrs. Miller to step into the hectic environment before them. With flushed cheeks and determination, Mrs. Miller marched through the crowd, dragging the very displeased Stanley behind her.

"You've got yer list?"

"Yes, Mrs. Miller," Stanley said, eyeing another group of women in worn-out dresses arguing loudly over the outrageous price of cocoa beans. "This is a woman's domain."

"Nonsense! Now get after 'em. And mind the time!"

While Mrs. Miller searched for ingredients for the Christmas feast, and Mr. Miller hunted down a turkey, Stanley was in charge of finding the fruits and vegetables that accompanied the dinner. He spotted a sack of apples in no time, made no argument about the price, and continued on his way. It didn't seem that it would take much effort when he met the eyes of a man that stuck out from the crowd. Stanley paused when he recognized the bald-headed man. The man seemed to remember him as well, and he grimaced. It was the man with the wooden hand that Stanley had seen in the Romani camp. Something about the man's intense stare compelled Stanley to turn the opposite direction and blend into the crowd.

Stanley felt a chilling sensation of being pursued. In his panic he bumped into a woman with a half dozen children clinging to her dress. She let out a surprised cry but accepted Stanley's stuttered apologies. Behind her, Stanley saw a dark-skinned man, face shadowed by a bowler hat, eyes sinister beneath. Stanley hurried from there, carrying the sack of apples over his shoulder, and took off in a run the moment the crowd dispersed. He didn't know where he would run to, or when he would stop, but Stanley had recognized the shadowed man's presence, and he knew they were after him. The Dream Lurkers were following him.

While the main focus of the day was centered on Market Day, and even more people were gathering and queuing up to the many merchants with their wagons and signs, Stanley Becker was running against the flow of people as quickly as his legs could carry him. He had not been able to find Mr. Miller or the carriage, but he knew he had to lose the shadow men behind him. Whichever way he turned, he saw them. They stood by posts, behind vendors, inside shops, looking out from windows, all with their shadowed faces and yellow eyes, watching Stanley with both amusement and malice.

He had no destination in mind. Stanley's mind was scattered. The chilling sensation that the shadow men, or Lurkers, brought, the feeling that had overcome him the first two times they had appeared, was overwhelming. It chased Stanley as he ran through the streets that misty morning, around corners, through dark alleys, and gave no hint of letting up. Soon enough, Stanley had no idea where he was. The slums were a maze of worn-down houses with dirty-faced inhabitants. If they were shadow men or not, Stanley didn't linger in one place long enough to ask or be approached.

At least a half hour had passed before Stanley realized that he was fleeing from nothing. There were no shadows behind him, and the few passersby in the streets gave him mere glances. He felt foolish. He had been imagining things. Yes, that was it—nothing more than paranoia.

The cobblestone streets, muddied by moisture and caked in black soot, appeared abandoned as Stanley wandered through them in search of anything familiar. Few people noticed Stanley, perhaps seeing his immaculate clothing, but no one stopped him or caught his attention, confirming that he wasn't being followed. What was there to worry about? Hadn't Louis said that the shadows were afraid of him? They couldn't touch him. At the end of the street, and to Stanley's relief, he spotted the welcoming sign of a tavern.

Loud, excited voices greeted Stanley through the doors, and when the few drunken souls in the pub looked up from their glasses, Stanley was aware of their critical glares. These were miserable wretches, drowning their sorrows because the world wasn't as forgiving as their mothers had promised. It had been years since Stanley had felt such unreasonable shame, not since he had moved his family to Woking, away from the thick of the city and most of its complications with classes. Coming from a wealthy family, Stanley had never quite found a neutral place between his high-class background and the society he had chosen to settle in. Woking was a calm suburban town where he had found some peace from his past, but here, in the slums of Kingston, it reemerged.

"What can I get you, mister?" the bartender asked, examining Stanley curiously.

Stanley ordered a pint of beer.

"Come from Market Day, did you?"

"What gave it away?" Stanley glanced over his shoulder. At least the drinkers in the pub had lost interest in him.

"Seems that everyone's gone there this morning. Took half my customers."

"Dandy place you've got here."

"Thank you much, mister," the bartender replied, placing the glass before Stanley. "I suppose we'll know for certain how dandy it is forty years from now, won't we?"

Stanley chuckled, easing out of the conversation. "I'm certain it'll still be standing."

He smiled as he gave the idea more thought. He took a seat in a back corner that overlooked the far window. Outside it, looking through the space between two brick buildings, Stanley could see a magnificent cathedral. What would this great city be like in forty or fifty years? How would it change? Stanley brought out the Time Key and fingered the cold metal.

It was possible that Stanley could visit the future as easily as he could visit the past, although he had never tried to. The thought roused childlike excitement. He found no reason why he could not travel forward. He had the great fortune to not be bound by the natural laws of the universe; he wasn't limited by time. He could travel through it without aging, without the limitations that most men had. Why should he not travel to the future, to see what the next generations would build, the advances that would be reached? Stanley could see no impossibility in what the future could achieve, and he had the key to see all its wonders.

Clearly, Stanley had forgotten why he had even taken refuge in the tavern. The amazing possibilities that held his attention dulled a common sense of warning that perhaps he had really been pursued. For now he sat in his corner, quivering with anticipation. Stanley fumbled eagerly with the little knobs of the Time Key, feeling the small clicks of the long hand count each year mark as he set it. *Forty years.* Stanley added three more ticks. That would mean that the Time Key would send him to the year 1940. He left the other two hands pointing north, knowing the month and days would be the same in the future as he left them in the past.

Stanley waited until the bartender left and the other consumers seemed keen on their own issues before returning his attention to the Time Key. He braced himself for whatever would await him forty-three years from now, and pressed the crown.

∽

The moment Stanley's body materialized, he coughed and bent over to free his lungs of the dust and smoke that choked him. His eyes watered when he opened them, but it was difficult to see through the veil of dust. Breathing through his scarf, Stanley recovered and was able to make sense of the scene before him.

Dust. There was nothing but dust and rubble. His steps crunched when he shifted his position. The tavern, which Stanley had come across forty years earlier, was hardly standing now. Strewn about in rocky piles were the components of what had been a ceiling and standing walls, but now lay destroyed. Boulders and pieces of wood were covered in blankets of dust that had not entirely settled. The table and chair that Stanley had used only seconds before were nowhere to be found, and the window that he had been looking through lay shattered on the cold floor. Outside, Stanley could see that the buildings were in the same condition. Behind them he saw the cathedral, now fractured and in flames.

As he took in his surroundings, Stanley became aware of the ground trembling and shaking beneath his feet. To say that he was afraid would be an understatement, but for the moment Stanley's thoughts were so muddled that even I can't decipher them. His palms began to sweat and his body trembled with the same vibrations coming from the ground. He thought he smelled blood. He was able to stumble to the glass-less window to see what was happening outside, but he saw the mirror image of the destruction in the tavern. The buildings were mere rubble, diminished to rocks and powder. The magnificent cathedral in the background was silhouetted by the red sky behind it, as though it too was hurt and bleeding.

What Stanley heard next made his stomach drop. He covered his ears. An alarm sounded, loud and penetrating, the only living thing in the landscape. Stanley forced himself to look up when another, stronger noise followed the alarm. It seemed to originate from within him;

a sound that began deep in his rushing veins and shook violently. The air itself pulsated, and at last Stanley saw what was making that horrific sound.

They seemed like birds in the sky at first, but Stanley knew they couldn't be. The black shapes with wings could not be the great hot-air balloons he knew could take a man high into the clouds. This was something else entirely, more complex, more advanced, something that could make a man tremble inside and cause the wreckage around him.

This was the future. Stanley fell to his knees in terror.

All this could only have happened in a short time. As the seconds began to catch up to Stanley, he realized that he needed to leave this destroyed future. Trembling fingers set the Time Key to the neutral settings. The flying machines roared and flew above him, trailing fire behind. Stanley cringed as he managed to set the contraption. He pressed the crown just before the fire touched him with hot fingers.

The blinding light swallowed the rubble and ghosts of London. Stanley, at last, could breathe.

⤬

"Mr. Becker! Mr. Becker, can you hear me?"

Stanley felt nauseated. He sensed someone shaking his shoulders. Unable to see through the blurriness, he was afraid that he was still in that bloodcurdling future that had destroyed the world he knew. Maybe it had all been a dream.

A hand clutched his arm and shook him again.

"Mr. Becker! Mr. Becker!"

"W-where am I?"

His tongue was heavy from the dusty air he had swallowed.

"You're back, Mr. Becker."

Stanley recognized the voice and blinked his eyes to clear them. He was surrounded by curious faces, but he caught sight of the young woman speaking to him.

"Nuri?"

The girl didn't smile. She nodded to a boy standing next to her, who reached down and hoisted Stanley to his feet. Dizzy and overcome by another wave of nausea, Stanley leaned on the boy's shoulder and followed Nuri. She pushed away the pub's customers that had crowded around them.

"Move along, then! Nothing to see here!"

85

The boy helped Stanley through the doors but abandoned his side when the man retched out what little he had in his stomach unto the cobblestone street. Wrinkling his nose, the boy was unable to hide his disgust. Nuri patted Stanley's dust-covered back and gave him a handkerchief, pulling his singed sleeve to follow her.

Stanley was able to find his voice as the three crossed the street.

"Where are we going?"

Nuri gave him a sideways glance. Her eyes were a dark gold, determined.

"Away from here."

Waiting on the other side of the street was a hansom cab. The driver jumped down from his perch and held the door open for the boy and Nuri. Stanley hesitated, unsure whether to get in with them or make a run for it. The girl shot him an irritated look and Stanley climbed in. Inside the cab it was cramped and musty, but Nuri sat on the boy's lap to make room for Stanley. She called up to the driver to take them a block south of the marketplace. The boy whispered something in her ear.

"I know that, Pierre! Let me think!"

The boy cast Stanley a regretful look, who was rubbing his temples.

"When did you go, Mr. Becker?" Nuri asked.

Stanley mumbled dryly, "1940."

She nodded, apparently aware of what Stanley had seen.

"The 1940s. Da told me about them."

Stanley was cross. No one had thought to warn him about the future.

"What was it? Does the world end?"

Nuri shook her head.

"War."

Pierre glanced at the window to his right. "Nuri," he said. "There's no time. We have to get back."

"Hurry, Henri!" she called up to the driver, who whipped the horse to a trot. She turned to Stanley. "You have to leave, Mr. Becker. They're after you."

"Who?"

"He's been following you all morning."

"Who is after me?"

"Mà de Fusta! The bald man with the wooden hand. He wants

something from you, but I don't know what! You must hide from him. Don't come back here."

It took Stanley a moment to register what the girl was saying. He remembered the man from the camp, the same man he had seen in the marketplace.

"I knew it wasn't a coincidence," Stanley mumbled. "But what does he want from me?"

"I don't know, Mr. Becker. I'll find out. But you must stay away from him. He is not a good man."

"But what have I done to him?"

Nuri's eyes were somber. "The moment you decided to come into our camp looking for my father was the moment you exposed yourself to something bigger that didn't involve you. For some reason, my father thought it necessary for you to find us, but now you can't escape this. None of us can."

Stanley couldn't shake the feeling that he had been included in something beyond his understanding, and the vulnerability that over-powered him made Stanley remember the little girl in his attic.

"Does this . . . have to do with Lena?"

Both Nuri and Pierre gave Stanley puzzled looks. They didn't know about the girl.

"Who is . . . ?" Nuri began, but shook her head. "I don't know what my father may have told you, but perhaps it's that information that Mà de Fusta is after."

"That's the problem, he didn't say—"

The cab came to a stop and Stanley saw the mass of people still growing in the marketplace, drowning out his voice inside the coach. Henri opened Stanley's door and, before he could protest, Nuri pushed him out of the cab.

"Don't come looking for us, Mr. Becker."

Stanley staggered to the window. "But what—I have questions!"

"We all do. I'll find you when I know more."

With that, the hansom cab left Stanley stranded in the mass of people.

Would Mà de Fusta, the wooden-handed man, find him here? Was he still being followed by the shadows? Anyone in this crowd, glanc-ing at him, smelling his dusty clothes and turning up their noses at his ragged appearance, could be those bloody Lurkers watching his every move, waiting for the right moment to accost or harass him. Snaking his way through any opening in the crowd, Stanley felt every eye stab his back. He searched for any sign of the Millers.

He could still smell the smoke rising from his clothes, and the terror of the future made him tremble. His mind was muddled and bewildered. He didn't know where he was going. The people that noticed him moved aside to avoid touching him.

Someone grabbed his arm.

"Mr. Becker, are you all right?"

Stanley whipped back to see Mr. Miller.

"Tom!"

"Sir," Mr. Miller said, steadying him. "You're not well, sir."

Stanley wanted to laugh and cry all at once. He allowed Mr. Miller to lead him back to the carriage, where Mrs. Miller waited. She cried out her relief in seeing him. Stanley sat across from her and rested his head. He felt feverish. Stanley closed his eyes before he could answer any of Mrs. Miller's questions. He vaguely remembered apologizing to her for forgetting the sack of apples in a pub in the slums.

XI

Lena regarded Stanley curiously as she took a bite of the powdery biscuit he had brought her only minutes ago. Stanley leaned on the armrest of the chair, and his hand held a glass filled with a yellowish liquid that smelled bitter to Lena. Ever since the man had returned from his trip he was quiet and thoughtful, more so than usual. His back faced Lena, long and dark against the crackling fire that he watched so fixedly.

I should venture to explain, in regards to Lena's perspective, that to an extremely small girl the sights, sounds, and smells that we would perceive as ordinary would seem significantly magnified to her. What to us would simply be a man sitting in front of a fire appeared to her intensified and exaggerated. The fire was a yawning pit on the wall, like a burning hell, while the man's silhouetted figure stretched and loomed before her, black and menacing. The shadows cast by the fire danced around her; their pagan movements mocked and taunted her.

The girl, understandably, was uneasy at the moment, but hunger kept her occupied. She studied the container into which Stanley had poured water and took a sip. From the corner of her eye she saw Stanley shift from his unmoving pose. She was unsure, but her voice stirred the man from his thoughts.

"What is this used for?" she asked, holding up the container for him to see. Stanley was visibly troubled when he looked over his shoulder.

"It's called a thimble," he said, returning to his drink. "So you don't prick your finger with a needle."

Nodding, Lena set it down next to her and stretched her arms sleepily. She pouted her lip when she looked down at the rags she had tried to mend yet again without much success. From a splinter she had made a needle, and Lena had thought to join the scraps into an entirely new garment. Her mother had made the dress for her, but now it was a pile of ripped scraps. At least what Stanley had brought her kept her warm enough. The shirt was too large and the fabric too rough, but it would have to do for now. The room with all the houses was always cold, and even more so when the fire on the wall went out, or when she sensed the shadows outside . . .

Taking another bite of the biscuit, Lena looked behind her at the mountains of stacked houses. Some were unfinished, others were broken, but all had been left alone, dusty and plain. Yawning as she rose, Lena limped toward the house she had claimed. Lena liked the small houses. They felt welcoming, and she liked to think that who-ever had built them had made them just for her.

Her fingers ran over the rough and grainy wall of her house, and she stepped back to inspect her work. The white paint looked washed out. She would need to apply another coat. She had made the paint the way her mother had shown her once, but the wood had sucked up the color thirstily. Picking up the brush at her feet, she leaned it against the wall. She supposed she was finished for the night, even though the work kept her hands and mind occupied, which kept the fire tame.

Sleep was calling the girl, who yawned and stretched again, wincing as the cut in her side stung from the movement. It didn't bleed anymore, but it still hurt very badly.

While she tossed aside pieces of wood she had no use for, she heard a creak come from the other side of the room. Startled, Lena peered from behind her house and saw Stanley looking up at the ceiling with an awed expression.

Uncertainly, Lena stepped out from the shadow of the houses and waited as Stanley admired the long vines that were tangled around the posts and climbed high up the walls.

"Thank you," she said, "for the plants."

"I had hoped they would bring you some comfort," Stanley replied as his lips formed a smile. "Did you do that?"

Lena nodded. "I have been working on something else, but . . ." She paused to look over her shoulder. "But I hope it's *a'right*."

Stanley's footsteps thudded below her as he approached, and Lena waited, apprehensive, as he looked over her work.

"You're painting the birdhouse?"

Lena nodded again. "It's a'right . . . ?"

"It's wonderful! And I see you fixed it, too."

Beaming, Lena hurried to open the house's door.

"It was broken, so I fixed the hinge—that's what you call it?"

Stanley's eyes gleamed. "Looks brilliant."

Next, Lena pointed to the vines in the ceiling. "See the flowers in the plants? That's how I made the paint. But I don't have enough."

An odd look slowly glazed over the man's expression.

"I can make more," she added quickly. "But I need more flowers."

"I can bring more."

Lena felt her cheeks burn. She rubbed her arm as she allowed herself a smile.

"How did you get up there?" Stanley wondered.

Lena shrugged. "I climbed."

"But—you are so—how?"

Lena was taken aback by the man's confusion. Hesitantly, she replied, "I'm a *vaelie*."

The perplexed look he gave her confirmed what Lena had suspected about Stanley, her situation, and the strange world that she was stranded in. But she also saw intrigue in those eyes: safe, innocent curiosity. When the man brought his chair and sat down, fixing his unwavering attention on her, Lena's cheeks blushed again.

"Is that what your people are called?" he asked slowly. "Vaelies?"

Lena remained standing and gazed distantly at her bare feet. She nodded.

"Can you tell me about them?"

"You've never heard of vaelies before?"

"Never."

The blood drained from Lena's face, and she could only shake her head in a most injured way. There were no others, none like her, in this terribly cold, gray world. Lena suddenly felt very, very small.

"It's all right, love," Stanley said soothingly. His voice came from far above her, and still Lena had her eyes glued to her feet. "You must be tired. Get some rest."

At his every step, the ground quaked, each thud going farther away.

Lena felt warmth leaving after them. In a sudden panic, she looked toward the window beyond the stacked houses.

"Stanley?"

The steps paused.

"What's wrong?"

Lena's shoulders tensed as she glanced Stanley's way when he returned.

"It's lonely here . . . ," she said. "And I think . . . I think I hear the shadows, sometimes."

Stanley followed her gaze. "The shadows?"

Lena trembled involuntarily.

"I can feel them close."

The shadows had come back. She could feel their coldness reach for her with frozen, hungry fingers, while the burning fire within scorched her in an attempt to escape.

She was so terribly alone.

"You're safe here, Lena," Stanley said. "I promise."

At last, Lena looked up and met Stanley's concerned eyes, a warm smile playing on his lips. Lena, for a moment, forgot the shadows waiting in the night.

Slowly, with a gentleness that was uncharacteristic of the monsters she had always been taught to fear, Stanley dropped to her eye level and said, "Let me tell you a story . . . Have you ever heard of the Bright-eyes?"

⟿

Lena was asleep in her birdhouse. Stanley had promised to stay and watch for shadows. It was a surprise that the story he had told her had helped ease her fear, but then again it had always worked with Maisie, at least to get her to sleep. The obvious connection was not lost on Stanley, but the thought of his daughter still choked him. His heart pounded. It had been hurt and crudely mended, and now it wanted free.

"Papa, I had the dream again—there were shadows, and they came after me."

Maisie's little hand squeezed his tightly.

"That's all it was, love. A dream."

"You won't leave me, Papa?"

"I won't, love."

"Promise?"

The haziness that years of absence had brought was replaced by another voice. Lena's was soft in his head. It would not leave his mind.

"My Maisie," Stanley muttered, watching the dying flames with longing.

How could he chase away the beasts he called Lurkers, the same ones that had followed him in Kingston? How could he promise to keep them away?

As hard as he tried, he could not collect his scattered thoughts. They swam around, knocking against the walls of his mind, pulsating, wanting to be heard. What he heard loudest was the roar of foreign machines cutting through the air, soaring high above his head, dropping fire behind them. Stanley cringed as he remembered the destruction. At least for the future, he was willing to accept it would come in its natural way, and Stanley would wait like everyone else for it to come.

XII

As one might expect from Stanley's experience of December 9 in a Kingston tavern, the man was more cautious in regards to his time traveling adventures, limiting himself to quick trips and only to the past. He was comforted by the thought that at least the past was not unknown to him.

The morning of December 10 found the Becker household with the messenger boy, Tim, at the door with a letter from Stanley's parents. Mrs. Miller tried her best not to mention the letter, but her employer soon found it.

"'Have ye seen the paper, Mr. Becker?" Mrs. Miller said, looking up from the newspaper, hoping to distract him. "They found two bodies by the Thames. That's two more since last week."

"Hmm," Stanley mumbled, slicing open the envelope.

"There's been talk about the murders sounding like those from '88," Mrs. Miller continued, eyeing him nervously. "D'ye remember, Mr. Becker?"

"How could I forget?"

"They say it's that Whitechapel murderer, come back to finish what he started."

"That's barbaric, Norah," Stanley said, unfolding the letter in his hand. "And highly unlikely . . ."

"Well, whoever this killer is—"

"Coming!" he suddenly cried. *"Here?"*

"Now, now, Mr. Becker, there's no need—"

"Of course there's a need, Norah! My bloody parents are coming for Christmas dinner."

"I've enough to prepare, Mr. Becker."

"That's hardly the problem. It's the fact that they come and go as they bloody well please—knowing how *aggravating* their visits are. At least I have the decency of telling them in person. But no, people of high class must sugarcoat everything . . . Why, if it was up to me, I'd—"

I suppose I must shed some light on Stanley's hazy background. The ongoing feud between father and son had deteriorated the delicate relationship Stanley had had with his father for the majority of his life. Frank Becker remained quite displeased with his son, who had always been determined to refuse his rightful position as heir of the family's estates, simply because they could not seem to get along. This tiresome exchange was not uncommon, but it drove the Beckers' only son out.

In 1880, at the age of nineteen, Stanley moved out to begin his own life in London and pursue his writing career. For many years, Frank and Edna Becker did not speak to their only child and had not even attended his wedding. After the accident, however, they faithfully came to visit Stanley once a year to pay their respects and to offer financial help. Stanley always shredded the check they left in an envelope. He hated to see their pity. In his mind, it was all for appearances. The Beckers were a charitable sort with good standing to their name, and they wanted all of England to know that they had not abandoned their black sheep of a son.

Whether this was true in essence, or a result of Stanley's resentment against his father, it didn't change the fact that they would arrive at Stanley's doorsteps the night before Christmas. There was nothing anyone could do about it. To console himself, or to at least try to forget the fast-approaching doom, Stanley would spend long hours in the attic. Mrs. Miller had very strict instructions not to disturb him, unless Dr. Gilmore came to visit.

The doctor usually came once a day when his schedule permitted. His visits, as of late, were quick. He would come later than usual, eyes bloodshot and puffy as though he had not slept all night. When Stanley asked about it, Gilmore only shrugged.

"Mark has been ill," he said. "There's a bug going around. Better to keep indoors until it passes."

Gilmore inspected Lena's cut, which had healed down to a healthy scar. She looked up in confusion.

"Bug?"

"People are getting sick," Stanley explained. "How is he?"

Gilmore shrugged again. "Oh, it's nothing serious. It's the season, I think."

Stanley felt guilty. It had been at least a month since he had seen his nephew and nieces. The least he could do was to pay them a visit.

"I'd like to go outside," Lena piped in, hopeful, but frowned when both men shook their heads.

"Not in those rags, you won't," Stanley said.

Gilmore agreed and Lena folded her arms, insulted.

Stanley had tried to make the girl some clothes, but had a tough time using a needle and thread to join the scraps he had found in Mrs. Miller's stash. Lena always accepted the crude garments, politely. He knew she found his attempts amusing. He had thought to ask Mrs. Miller to make a dress fit for a doll, but had decided against it. It would only confirm to the housekeeper that her boss had lost his mind. It wasn't enough that he spent all day confined to the attic, but she would find him missing for hours at a time. Whenever she asked about it, Stanley would only shrug and assure her that he had been strolling around the neighborhood. Of course this wasn't necessarily true, but Mrs. Miller would not hear the truth for several more weeks.

To avoid being seen vanishing into thin air when he used the Time Key, Stanley had taken his trips during the late hours of the night for safety. He had never tried to make contact with anyone of the past (other than with Lena the first time he had traveled), and wasn't completely certain as to what extent he could interact with them, although the incident with the future and his singed sleeves proved that he was not untouchable by the elements. Perhaps he was not a mere observer of time, but could interact with everything and everyone. It was a theory he had yet to test.

Sheer curiosity, and a promise to Lena, sent Stanley to that spring morning of 1896 to gather flowers from the garden with the rising sun. It had been nearly a week since Lena had been introduced into Stanley's life, and of the few things he knew about her, he could guess the flowers and colors that she preferred. He picked some summer snowflakes, along with some primroses and several early blooming poppies. For the colors she was after, Stanley picked a handful of blackberries. Lena liked the intense pigment they created.

Stanley cut a handful of forget-me-nots and smiled. These reminded him of Lena. Their simple, small existence was tender and hidden, tiny and beautiful. The blue pedals would go well with her skin—

"Mr. Becker?"

Stanley jumped to his feet. He concealed his pickings behind him and smiled innocently at the housekeeper, who frowned.

"I thought I'd seen ye having a lie-down jest moments ago. When d'ye come out here?"

Stanley tried to remain calm. He wasn't a mere observer as he had previously suspected, and he had been right to avoid being seen. He was physically in the past and could be seen by others.

"Thought I could use some fresh air, Mrs. Miller."

The housekeeper was unconvinced. "Ye all right, sir? It's scorching out, and look what ye've got on!"

"Ah, yes." Stanley looked down at his overcoat. "It was a bit cold . . . inside."

The housekeeper gave a nod, leaving Stanley to his oddities, and returned to the stables where Mr. Miller was tending to the horses. Stanley blew out the air in his cheeks and hurried to the back wall of the house, cursing himself for being so careless.

"Hush up, Brutus!" he snapped when he saw the cat staring at him.

He returned home with a thrill in his chest. He was more than an observer of time. He could interact with the people of the past and now had proof of his ability to impact past events. He could go back and change them. There was nothing that would keep him from stopping the accident.

✦

The night of December 11, Stanley found himself in the library, planning what would be the most logical way to go about traveling back to the accident. He wanted to avoid any confrontations with anyone inside the house. It would probably be best to remain outside to wait for the carriage that would take Jane and Maisie, bribe the driver, and leave before anyone noticed. It was simple enough—

A loud crash came from upstairs. Stanley rose and ran to the attic. What could that have been? The Millers had left to make last-minute purchases, and there was no one else in the house. Stanley was alone.

The Bird Room was filled with thick smoke and the fire roared in the hearth, jumping and licking the air. On the floor were the remnants of a broken birdhouse, shattered by its fall.

"Lena!"

Stanley couldn't see the girl, and the smoke pricking his eyes did not help. From beneath the tables, Brutus dashed past Stanley, hissing irritably.

Stanley's stomach dropped.

"Lena, it's all right! Don't be frightened!"

Stanley muttered curses as he scrambled to find her, dreading what might have happened.

"Stanley!"

Her voice was filled with terror. He spotted her. Lena clung to one of the vines that hung from the ceiling.

"Lena, are you hurt?"

She shook her head and Stanley saw that she was sobbing. This time she made no effort to hide it. Stanley reached up to her, but she was frozen with fear.

"Come here, love," Stanley whispered. "It's all right."

Her nimble body weighed nothing when she dropped onto his open palm. She curled up to brace her quivering legs, burrowing her face in her arms to muffle reluctant cries. Stanley whispered softly to calm her. The fire behind him ceased its savage dance.

He was sorry for not being there. It wouldn't happen again.

He was sorry.

Lena's sobs cut him deeply.

⌘

"Why, hello, Mr. Becker. I've only jest—"

"Get that beast out of the house!" Stanley shouted.

He stormed into the kitchen where Mrs. Miller was removing her coat and hat, settling into the warm indoors.

"I will wring his neck!"

Mrs. Miller regarded Stanley calmly, studying the man seething in her kitchen, and sighed resignedly, accepting that he was in a foul mood.

"What's he done to ye now?" she asked, hands on hips. "I've only jest found the poor creature last night."

Stanley was fuming, but he bit his tongue. "Nothing, I—I don't want to see that cat."

Mrs. Miller cast him an annoyed look and replied sardonically, "Yes, Mr. Becker." Spotting the cat on the kitchen counter, she picked him up lovingly. "Come, come, Brutus. Where've ye been, ye naughty cat?"

Stanley stood in the kitchen and attempted to regain some sort of composure before returning to the attic where he had left Lena, sobbing in her birdhouse. His thoughts were agitated and muddled by anger. He felt sick to his stomach about what could have happened in the attic.

But beneath all those layers of emotion, he felt impatient. Everything he had configured was ready to be played out and there was nothing to stop him. In his creaking chair, he glanced to where Lena slept. He did not want to leave her, not like this. He didn't know whether he would be back before she awoke or before another incident were to occur in his absence. There was no telling what would happen, but he knew that if he didn't act, he would have to wait for the next day. No, it would be best to do it now.

He felt ready; the Time Key was set. He had nothing standing in his way. It was five thirty, just before Jane and Maisie left the house six years ago. He would appear in the attic, exit through the back door, and hop in the carriage before anyone would know. Stanley walked to the window where he stroked the Time Key in a solemn manner, promised the silence that he would return shortly, and his thumb depressed the crown.

XIII

The night that Stanley saved Louis Vargas's life marked the beginning of a series of chained events that would ultimately lead to this specific moment, a moment for which Stanley had been training since the first time he traveled to the past. He had at last reached it. The sickness was the same, regrettably, but it was expected. As his sight returned, Stanley's knees buckled beneath him, overcome with vertigo. He braced himself until it subsided before opening his eyes to see the Bird Room in a time where it was used daily for its intended purposes. There was a warm fire in the hearth, and lit candles alongside the windows gave a feel of serenity.

Stanley looked around once and sighed in relief. He did not notice the figure crouching on the floor, staring directly at him, wide-eyed. She gasped. Stanley froze when he saw her.

The girl's blue eyes were fixed on Stanley, and her reddish-blonde locks veiled her face apprehensively. Stanley could not find the words to describe what he felt at the moment he saw his daughter, alive, and just as he remembered her. It was happiness, certainly, overwhelming and suffocating. He tried to calm his breathing, aware that his sudden presence was not only frightful, but unbelievable. Wasn't her papa downstairs, conversing with her mama?

But Maisie had a sharp mind, and she understood that the man who had appeared out of thin air looked like her papa, and there was no doubt that he was. Rising to her feet, she said one simple word that caused Stanley's chest to ache.

"Papa?"

Stanley could not find his voice, but apparently his eyes could produce tears. He wiped them when Maisie approached him cautiously.

"You look like Papa," she said, tilting her head to the side, "but *old*."

Stanley couldn't hold in a chuckle of surprise. The years of hard drinking may have had a toll on him.

"M-Maisie?"

The girl smiled. "Where did you come from?"

At first Stanley was not sure what to say to his daughter that would not sound insane, but she had already seen him materialize from nowhere.

"I-I'm not from this time, Maisie."

Maisie tilted her head to the other side. "Are you from the future?"

Stanley's eyebrows rose. "Yes."

"I thought so."

A few seconds passed while father and daughter regarded one another. Maisie took one step forward. Her extended fingers touched Stanley's cold, pale cheek. He closed his eyes, squeezing out a stray tear.

"How did you know?" he asked her.

"You are my papa."

Stanley forced himself to remember why he was there and what he had to do. Things would be more complicated than he had expected now that he had made contact with Maisie. He had to get outside to stop the carriage.

"Maisie," he began, fighting the urge to hug and kiss her. "Sweetheart, listen. No one can know about this."

She watched him attentively and nodded. "All right."

Stanley paused. This could be so simple.

"Listen, love. You can't—you *cannot* go to the opera tonight."

"Why not?"

"It's complicated. You must promise me that you'll stay home, Maisie."

"I suppose you would know, since you come from the future."

"Yes, love. Will you promise?"

Maisie bit her lip. "Mama will be disappointed. What shall I tell her?"

Stanley's throat tightened.

"Tell Mama that you don't feel well."

Maisie coughed. "All right."

Stanley smiled. "I must go, Maisie."

Just then, Jane's voice called from downstairs. Stanley's stomach flipped.

"Maisie! Come down, darling."

Oh, how he longed to pick Maisie up, place her on his shoulders, and run down to meet Jane. In their presence, he remembered how badly he missed them, how empty his life was without them.

Maisie turned back to Stanley.

"Go on, love."

Maisie paused, leaned forward, and planted a kiss on Stanley's forehead before she skipped out of the room. Stanley leaned back against the wall, closed his eyes, and felt the spot on his forehead burn. He wished he could stay, but knew it wasn't possible. It was time to go home. Whatever awaited him there would be much sweeter than this past that melted his heart. He would have them back, and all would be right.

❧

Back home the sun rose, renewing Stanley's energy. The Bird Room was still. It was unchanged. While the sickness subsided, Stanley listened to the silence. He didn't wish to disturb Lena. Doubt stirred in his mind. Was she even here? The painted birdhouses proved that she must be.

Stanley wasted no time. He ran downstairs. The doors seemed to open for him of their own accord, and the stairs allowed him to glide. It was effortless. He was in a dream.

Plates clattered in the kitchen, betraying Mrs. Miller's early presence to begin the day. She gasped when Stanley entered the kitchen.

"They weren't in their rooms," Stanley blurted, mostly to himself.

"Mr. Becker, you startled me!"

"Could they have gone out for a stroll? H-have you seen them, Mrs. Miller? I must have missed them."

"What are you—Mr. Becker—"

"Jane and Maisie! Did you see them leave? Where are they?"

Poor Mrs. Miller clutched at her apron and tried to remain calm. "Have ye got a fever, Mr. Becker? You're quite delirious."

"I am not! Will you tell me?"

"Come sit down, Mr. Becker," she said, grabbing Stanley by the arm, and she led him to the dining room. "Please sit down, now."

There was doubt, again, that emerged from the anger.

"Norah," he pleaded. "Norah, please tell me they've gone for a stroll . . ."

The housekeeper sat next to him but didn't let his arm free. Stanley's eyes begged.

"Every day I wish I could say it, Mr. Becker. I do. It wouldn't do any good. Maisie and Jane—it's been six years . . ."

The words struck Stanley like ice water. But he could not think, could not feel.

"Mr. Becker, tell me you've not forgotten."

"No, no. I haven't . . ."

"Ye can't be blaming yourself for what happened to them, after all this time. We all knew it. Mrs. Becker, well, she had a harder time, as you know."

Stanley looked at her. "Jane? She had a hard time—what are you going on about?"

Mrs. Miller's eyes grew. "Mr. Becker, please!"

"What happened to Jane?"

There were tears in her eyes and she could not stop them. "Mr. Becker—"

"Please, Norah!"

She swallowed. "A-after Maisie got sick, she wasn't the same. And when Maisie—heavens rest her—when she passed, the missus could not take the sorrow. Please, Mr. Becker."

"What happened?"

She spoke aggravatingly slow. "She-she widnae eat, widnae sleep . . . she'd stare out in wee Maisie's room . . . and then one day— she just did nae have the strength . . . she was not 'erself when it hap- pened—when she went to the bridge . . ."

Stanley was shaking. He had stopped listening.

He rose. He walked.

There weren't tears. Mrs. Miller wailed behind him.

A door. His bed. Dark.

He wished the pillow would smother him, take him away from this. Mrs. Miller's voice rang in his head.

Dark. Silence.

Stanley stared at the ceiling. He touched the empty place next to him. There was no Jane. There never was, never would be. The only thing he had been able to change was their deaths. He, with that cursed Time Key, had changed their fates for the worst.

If there was a next life, would Jane ever forgive him?

In the silence, Stanley closed his eyes and allowed the tears to come.

XIV

Now, I do realize that leaving Stanley in such a delicate predicament is quite apathetic of me, but more pressing matters force our attention elsewhere. I assure you that Stanley will undoubtedly remain secluded in his room for the time being—days to be more precise—and so we now find ourselves in a desolate street, soot-caked and mixed with black slush. There is an abandoned house squeezed in between identical others, its windows are cracked, and the doors bolted shut. Its appearance may stir unexplainable fear in stray passersby, but the surrounding aura of the building itself causes one to choke; so palpable is the terror that it keeps people away, which is certainly how its residents want it. This house that I am referring to is not vacant, but any watchful eye can see that during the late hours of night a handful of men with shadowed faces come and go inside the house with ease.

The district near the Thames has been naturally an uneventful part of the city, and by mere coincidence, it is not far from the same bridge where Stanley attempted to take his life. If you were to cross that dark alley and see the house with cracked windows and bolted doors, you would most likely take off in a run. But take my hand, trust me, as we enter through the door as observers, shielded from what beasts reside inside.

The house is quiet and dark. In what would have once been a cozy room, we see five men pacing impatiently. They don't converse, it is not in their nature, but they seem to be waiting. Up the stairs that creak at each step, we see along the walls that there are still frames hanging on the flowered wallpaper, dusty, with yellowing photographs of a forgotten family. At the top we see three rooms, the doors of which are worn and splintered. Voices come from the left, agitated and rising after each interval. For the moment we ignore that door and draw our attention to the middle door, straight ahead.

If we could scatter our molecules and step through that door with the ease of a specter, we would stand on the other side and soak in our surroundings. The far window of the small room has been sealed shut by boards nailed to the walls; specks of light stream in through the cracks. There is no bed, no table, no embellishments. A single ragged blanket lies on the floor, and at that moment we see a figure reach down to pick it up. The huddled figure wraps the blanket around him and leans back against the wall. A stream of light lands on his face, caressing his cheek, and reveals cuts and swelling around the left eye. His hair is long and soiled. If we imagine a different situation we might see that the man's countenance could be friendly and even pleasant, causing one to wonder about the reason for his current state.

Now that we have thoroughly inspected the scene before us we allow ourselves to take on the perspective of our wounded captive, and I thank the reader for trusting me to deliver them safely through our short journey.

The prisoner gave a sigh and touched his eye, wincing. He wished he could see himself in a mirror. He chuckled quietly. He knew that this current dilemma could only fall on his account. He should have been more careful, should have covered his tracks better. It had probably not helped that before his capture he had carried around a vaelie radiating with energy that the shadow-shifters could easily detect. It didn't matter. He was here now and there was no getting out of it.

From the other room he could hear the low rumble of arguing voices, but he could understand nothing. Most likely they were trying to decide how to get rid of him in the most inconspicuous way. It would be about time. The man had lost any sense of it, but from the little bit of light that came from the outside he could guess that he had been there for a least a week, maybe more. What did it matter? He was to die, anyway.

There were heavy footsteps outside. The doorknob rattled before the door opened. The prisoner looked up to see the dark-skinned man who had been assigned to watch him, standing like a statue with his enormous presence. He did not have to speak for the prisoner to know what he wanted.

"He wants to see me, doesn't he?" the prisoner asked, and the guard gave a nod. "Finally."

The guard watched the haggard figure struggle to stand and followed close behind, keeping his watchful eye on the prisoner's movements. The wounded man wouldn't try anything, knowing firsthand the strength that this guard could muster. Down the hallway the door was open, and inside was a bald-headed man pacing back and forth, holding his hand protectively. It was made of wood.

"Come in," the bald man said, showing his golden teeth. "Take a seat, my friend."

The prisoner obeyed, more thrilled by the prospect of sitting in a chair than by the invitation. He gave the room one look before clicking his tongue, although it made his lower lip bleed.

"Would have thought that the Great Mà de Fusta would choose a lair with less cobwebs."

The bald man smiled. "I see they couldn't beat the humor out of you, Louis. No matter. You know why you're here."

"I suppose you'll ask me where the Time Key is," Louis began, leaning back in the chair. "You should be asking your shape-shifting friends if they saw it while they were pummeling me to a pulp in some dark alley."

Mà de Fusta shot the guard a vindictive look before replying, "Curious you should mention it. They say someone else was there that night. He came to help you."

Louis nodded. "Aye. Don't mean I knew him."

The guard behind him gave a low growl.

"They say," Mà de Fusta continued, "that he's got a strange energy about him. It frightens them, the useless lot."

"Is that why they left so quickly?"

Mà de Fusta's smile vanished. "Don't play me for a half-wit, Louis. You know who he is. Tell me what's so special about him. The shadow-shifters don't seem to know. Perhaps you can enlighten us."

"I'm afraid you know as much as I do," Louis said, shrugging.

Mà de Fusta's fist came down on the desk, hard, but his calm expression belied his rage. "I'm growing tired of this. You know where the Time Key is."

"As I said before, it must have gotten lost in the commotion. And what of your friends? Don't they tell you how they found me?"

"There's much that they don't say," Mà de Fusta replied with a shrug. "But I'm the only one that can help them, now that their shifting has become . . . limited."

"Is that right?" Louis wondered, turning to see the guard's expression. He lacked any.

"Enough small talk. I remember you said something back in Andalusia. You asked for the Time Key in exchange for something else. Do you remember what you promised me, Louis?"

For once, Louis had no rebuttal.

"The fact that you came back to London tells me that you did find what you were after. Am I wrong, Louis? What wounds me the most is that you were willing to forget your promise. You thought that if you went behind my back, I wouldn't notice. That I wouldn't come looking for what was promised me. Isn't that right?"

Louis stared ahead, avoiding Mà de Fusta's gaze as he paced around him.

"You know where it is," Mà de Fusta whispered in his ear. "Perhaps you left it with that man. Where are the Divine Tears?"

Louis clenched his fists.

"Where did you find the Fountain? I must admit that I had my doubts, but you proved me wrong, Louis. One thing I never understood—why do you need the Fountain? I don't see you as the greedy sort, but of course you are a man of surprises."

"Same as you, Johan. I find the chase exhilarating."

Mà de Fusta paused a moment before he turned to face Louis and bared his teeth in a most disagreeable grin.

"Could it be for your Saira?"

Louis didn't breathe.

"Am I warm?" Mà de Fusta asked, drawling the words for effect. "I know where she is. The shadows know her, and you of all people know what they can do."

"What are you implying?"

"Use your imagination."

The bald man's smile caused all sorts of emotions to boil in Louis's chest. He bolted to his feet, but a pair of strong hands gripped his shoulders, forcing him to remain seated. Leaning back against the desk, Mà de Fusta chuckled.

"I will not ask you again. Where is the Time Key?"

"The water is not in that bloody thing!" he spat. "I removed it, but it was lost."

"I don't believe you."

At Mà de Fusta's gesture, the guard stood Louis up and dragged him back into the hallway.

"Don't you dare harm her," Louis said through gritted teeth, struggling against the guard's iron hold. "This is between you and me, Johan. Leave my daughter out of it."

Mà de Fusta's silhouette at the door appeared mocking. Louis was thrown down to the cold floor and didn't have the energy to stand back up.

"I do find some interest in Nuri's . . . peculiarities," Mà de Fusta continued, "but don't doubt she isn't the only one involved in this whole mess."

Louis's eyes widened, and Mà de Fusta bent down to meet his eyes.

"You know well who I'm referring to. Yes, Louis. I remember Dione. You made this about her the moment you came to me. You wanted to travel and I allowed you to find her for only a simple payment. And still you chose to deceive me. Now you know it's not only Nuri who I want. This has *always* been about Dione."

"Please, you can do anything to me—"

The door slammed in his face. Louis stared at it in disbelief, terribly sick to know that Mà de Fusta had gotten to the truth. He had to find a way out of there.

⤜⤛

You may recall my mentioning that any watchful observer would notice the men coming in and out of the abandoned house. Well, as the dark-skinned man came out through the front door, he appeared to feel a presence and paused. Across the street in a wet, dark alley, a slight figure ducked behind a stack of empty crates as she watched through the rising fog.

Nuri's exposed skin chilled under the weather's cold fingers, but she kept her eyes fixed on the dark man standing in front of the house. This was the man she had followed. She had waited the entire time he had been inside, and felt doubtful of what to do next. She had her suspicions about that house and about the man, whom she had seen conversing with Mà de Fusta in the market three days ago. This must be the place where the bald man stayed.

The dark-skinned man continued walking, and Nuri was about to pursue when Pierre touched her shoulder.

"I told you to wait in the cab," she snapped.

The boy, not much younger than the girl, shook his head. "Henri says he'll leave us if you don't come back now."

"Go. I'll find a way home."

"Nuri, this is pointless. We'll try again tomorrow."

"You don't understand, Pierre. I know this is Mà de Fusta's hideout. I can't leave—"

"Tomorrow," he said again, begging with his eyes.

Nuri sighed. "All right, tomorrow."

Pierre led her back to the cab, but the girl continued to look over her shoulder. She did not like the eeriness that the place gave off, but she suspected she was close. She had to find out what Mà de Fusta was doing in England, and what he wanted from Mr. Becker. But most crucial of all was to find the whereabouts of her father. She knew that Mà de Fusta was involved somehow.

As they drove off, Nuri saw the unmoving figure of the dark-skinned man watching the cab leave from the shadow of a dark alley.

XV

Dr. Gilmore could not believe it. Hearing it from Mrs. Miller, he knew she was not one to joke about such things (about anything, in fact), and he suspected that he knew the reason for Stanley's behavior. The man had locked himself in his room for two days and, according to his housekeeper, drank all day and night, tossing the empty bottles out the window.

The plan must have failed. Gilmore had often wondered how Stanley believed he could stop an illness from infecting his daughter, but he had not had the heart to tell him so. Despite all that Gilmore begged, Stanley would not see him, much less anyone else. For two days Gilmore came to tend to Lena three times a day, ask about Stanley, and leave unwillingly. When Lena wondered why Stanley hadn't come to see her, Gilmore explained as well as he could with the little information he had.

Finally on the third day, December 14, Gilmore could not take it any longer. He stormed into Stanley's room where he found the man sitting with a half empty bottle of brandy, facing the window with an unfocused look in his eyes. He gave no acknowledgement that Gilmore was even in the room, and continued to mumble incomprehensible words. With a sigh, Gilmore approached him.

"Stanley, this must stop."

Stanley's lips turned up at one corner, mockingly. "Nothing's happened, Russell."

"Precisely! You're allowing this sorrow to drown out your life again. I had thought this was over."

"Not when it all started up again."

He took a long swig but frowned when it did little to take away the hangover.

Gilmore continued, "This is not the same. This time you have someone who depends on you."

"Who?" Stanley wondered, setting the bottle on the nightstand. "Everyone I love is long dead—"

"Lena."

Stanley held his breath, feeling quite sick.

Gilmore knew he had caught his attention and said, "She needs you, Stanley. You've forgotten her."

"I've forgotten . . ."

"It's all right. She's in the attic."

The man bolted to his feet and staggered past Gilmore, who sighed. His job was done. Things would be all right now. Casting one saddened look at the empty room, Gilmore took leave of the unfortunate Becker home.

In the attic, Stanley swung open the door to the Bird Room and stood back uncertainly.

"Lena?"

From the birdhouse, the girl poked her head out, startled. Stanley approached slowly, aware of his sickly appearance and embarrassed of what she would think of him.

"Lena, I—uh—are you all right?"

Lena regarded him for a moment but did not seem disapproving. She nodded.

Stanley sat in the chair facing her. "Lena . . . I can't begin to tell you how sorry—"

Her hand rose in a silencing manner.

"It's a'right. The healer man told me."

Stanley could not help it when the tears began to sting his eyes, and he held onto the table for support. Lena approached Stanley's hunched-over figure and touched his hand gently. He sighed and smiled weakly.

⁂

"She would have been about your age."

Lena sat dangling her feet at the edge of the table, eyes wide and attentive, while Stanley spoke.

"That is, if life had been kinder to her."

"What was she called?"

"Her name was Maisie."

She repeated the name in a hushed voice. "Beautiful . . ."

Stanley nodded, unsettled by the memories he was retelling, but it helped to talk to Lena again.

"And she was too. She inherited her mother's looks, thankfully. And she had her spirit."

"What happened to her?"

Stanley was unsure of how to begin. "Do you remember the Time Key?"

Lena nodded.

"Six years ago, my Jane and Maisie were in a terrible accident. They didn't survive." He paused, seeing Lena's eyes grow wide. "I used the Time Key to return to that night and stop the accident from ever happening, but somehow it failed. I think that it created two realities. My reality is still the same, but I can see fragments of other memories. Somehow, by changing the past, I succeeded in avoiding the accident, but I caused their . . . deaths to come differently."

Lena nodded again, doubtful.

"The new reality that I created—well, my Maisie died of an illness, and her mother lost her will to live. I can still remember the accident, but I can also see Maisie sick in her bed. I can see Jane with hollow eyes . . . How can that be possible?"

Lena shrugged her shoulder.

Stanley concluded, "Apparently time travel has more complications than I had imagined."

After a long moment of silence, Lena looked up at Stanley, who was staring at the floor in defeat. "What will you do now?" she wondered.

"I can follow my original plan and avoid speaking to Maisie at all. It might work."

"You will go back?"

Stanley nodded. "I will prevent the carriage from coming. Perhaps that will be what saves them."

Lena wasn't so sure. "Will you go back to the old reality or the new one?"

"I suppose that when I get there I'll find out."

Stanley had not thought about going back very thoroughly, but he was tired of sitting in his room, wallowing in misery. He was unconvinced that there wasn't anything he could do to change Jane and

Maisie's fates, but the uncertainty made him nervous. What would he find when he traveled back?

"Can I come with you?"

Lena's question took Stanley by surprise, and was about to decline when he saw her imploring look. Could he take her along? True, he had brought things from the past to the present, but at times some items disappeared through the journey. Perhaps with Lena it would be different.

"If you wish," he consented. "Are you not afraid?"

The girl leapt to her feet. "I'm not afraid of anything!"

"Then you must promise to remain with me at all times. We wouldn't want for Brutus to find you again."

The thought made her uneasy, but she didn't reconsider. "When will you go?"

There were still things he needed to finish that morning, work he had been neglecting while secluded in his room.

"Tonight at *five*. It should give us enough time."

Stanley sat back in the chair, running his fingers along his jaw as his thoughts began to race. It was thrilling to think that he would travel once again, but the sorrow still lingered and it was difficult to cast away. To see them, to feel their presence, to have Maisie in his reach, and to have them die again was excruciating. Going back had erased the six years of emptiness, of pain, but to lose them a second time—Stanley could not bear the thought that it had been his fault.

The day dragged on. Much to Mrs. Miller's relief, Stanley finished his work, changed into clean clothes, shaved the ragged stubble on his face, and seemed to regain some appetite. When she wasn't looking, he grabbed a handful of scraps where Mrs. Miller tossed ripped up garments and fabrics for sewing and took them to Lena, who desperately wanted to make herself extra warm clothes.

That afternoon, just as the sun sank below the horizon, Stanley announced that he was going for a stroll. Mrs. Miller, aware of his delicate state, certainly tried to stop him by voicing her fear of that vicious criminal roaming the streets of London paying Woking a visit. Despite her protests, Stanley left the house before the light of day vanished entirely. Shrugged in his coat, he walked as smoothly as he could.

The small bulge in his coat pocket shifted to a more comfortable position. Stanley was apprehensive about Lena riding in there, but there had been no arguing with the little, short-tempered girl. Crossing

114

through the gardens, Stanley was careful to remain concealed from any watchful eye, and when he reached a tree, he crouched behind the bare bushes.

"Are you sure you want to do this, Lena?" he asked quietly.

Her irritated voice was muffled. "Yes!"

"It will be quite unsettling," he warned. "But the side effects should pass quickly."

"A'right."

Stanley double-checked the settings in the Time Key before he pushed the crown.

"Hang on, Lena."

∞

After the blindness, Stanley realized he was quite cold.

"Lena?" he whispered, looking around him wildly. His overcoat, lounge coat, and shoes were missing. "Lena, are you here?"

When he received no answer, he suspected that along with his clothes, she had been left behind in the present. If this was the case, then there was nothing he could do. He rose and made his way through the garden toward the back of the house. He could easily see through the lit window in the Bird Room. If he had traveled back to the original reality then his plan could work, but if this was the alternate past then he would see his past self materialize inside the Bird Room.

It didn't take long for Stanley's hopes to be crushed. Above him, in the warmth of the Bird Room, a figure suddenly appeared out of thin air and stumbled to his knees. He would see Maisie and give her instructions to remain at home that night. Stanley knew what would happen, and that knowledge crushed him. There was nothing he could do. Past Stanley had set the alternate course and nothing could change it.

The freezing weather didn't seem to affect Stanley as his downcast figure walked through the gates of his house and down the street with no destination in mind. Maybe if he walked far enough, long after losing any feeling in his feet, he would receive a sort of answer. Or maybe he would be fortunate enough to get run over by an uncontrolled carriage. It didn't matter to Stanley, who looked up pleadingly as if to find a solution in the bright stars above his misty breath. Whatever sort of being lived up there, manipulating his actions like a puppet, was no doubt enjoying Stanley's misery.

The night was a peaceful one. Stanley walked on, alone. No one

115

would be outside in that cold night. As his frozen feet trudged on, Stanley tried to keep his mind blank to minimize the ache in his chest.

After ten minutes of walking he heard the sharp *clip-clop* of horses echoing behind him. Stanley looked back as the coachman of a cab pulled up next to him on the street, gave him a queer look, and stopped the snorting horses. Pausing, Stanley tried to take a peek at whoever was riding inside. The curtains parted and Stanley staggered back in shock.

"Ought to be cold without shoes," the man in the carriage said. "I'll give you a lift."

The man inside the carriage was Stanley.

XVI

Whether it was disbelief or distrust, Stanley could not find the will to take his eyes off the man sitting across from him, who was looking out the carriage window vigilantly, as if expecting a surprise attack from outside. It was as though Stanley was facing a mirror, and his reflection had a mind of its own, could talk back, and kept giving him annoyed glances. Stanley supposed that he would be annoyed too. It had taken him a long while to accept that the man riding inside the carriage was indeed himself. He was confused about his sudden appearance and the fact that the man seemed no more surprised to see him, as though it were a common affair. This led Stanley to conclude that the man in the carriage could be none other than a future version of himself. Stanley had often feared being caught by his past, but had never imagined he would be visited by the future.

When Future Stanley deemed it safe to acknowledge him, he closed the curtains, picked up a full bottle of brandy, and nodded to himself.

"Rather shocking, isn't it?" Future Stanley began, giving him a knowing smile. "I assure you, it isn't any easier for me."

Stanley was able to find his voice, though it sounded hoarse and breathless in comparison. "When—why? *How?*"

"I know you have questions, and I'll do my best to answer some of them. But first"—he held up the bottle—"care for some brandy?"

For once, Stanley declined.

"Probably a good choice," Future Stanley said, taking a drink straight from the bottle. "As you might suspect, I came from your future. I knew you'd be here, obviously. And I know what you are feeling."

117

Stanley swallowed, sensing the foreshadowing of some approaching doom that he was unprepared to hear about. He couldn't shake the strangeness of the situation. How many times in life could one speak to one's self?

"Let me tell you something about the past," Future Stanley continued. "You've probably already figured it out."

"Can't be changed."

"In theory, it can." He paused for effect. "But, of course, there are powers beyond us that control the flow of the world. You could call it *fate*."

"I changed their fate," Stanley murmured, "didn't I?"

Future Stanley's eyes drilled deeply into his, studying every emotion that came across Stanley's face, perhaps measuring how ready he was to know the truth.

"That is what I want to explain to you," he said slowly. "We can't blame ourselves for what happened to Jane and Maisie. The accident that should have happened tonight only made their deaths come sooner. Perhaps Maisie had already caught the influenza from who-knows-where. I don't know. What you did only revealed their true fates."

Stanley shook his head dizzily. "But is there no way to change it?"

"This was the role they were meant to play," Future Stanley replied simply.

"It isn't fair to them."

Future Stanley paused, furrowing his brow, and Stanley wondered if that was really what he looked like when he felt impatient.

"Think a little deeper. If they had not died, we would have never gone to that bridge six years later. As a result we would have never met Louis and his family. More importantly, we would have never been there for Lena. Who knows what Louis would have done with her?"

This thought stirred something in Stanley's chest, causing the blood in his veins to rush and boil. When he looked up he saw Future Stanley's expression mirrored his own feelings.

"What about our past, the Stanley from this reality?" Stanley wondered. "He won't go to the bridge. Why would he?"

"Perhaps he does, perhaps he doesn't. But you and I have this role to play, and so does he."

Stanley nodded. The fragmented memories he had of another reality showed his dear wife with hollow and faded eyes. They showed glimpses of the darkened bridge, of a figure standing at the edge. Stanley could hear his own voice pleading. In the memory, Jane had jumped. Stanley shook his head to cast it away. He knew why Past Stanley from this new reality would go to Kingston Bridge six years later.

"Wait just a moment. If you are my future, wouldn't that make me your past—the past that you changed?"

At this, Future Stanley smiled. "I thought you might ask that," he said, taking a second swig from the bottle, but didn't seem to enjoy it. "I tried to change this night many more times than you, but I never was able to save them. Ultimately I went back to the first night that I tried, before I spoke to Maisie, and stopped my past self. I was able to stop all of it from happening; therefore it created your reality, the same as mine. It allowed you to experience everything that I have already done."

"That's quite confusing."

"And because you have not done that, and probably won't, the Stanley of this reality is changed. But the universe has a way of fixing things to get on the right track." He shrugged, as if there was no need to be concerned.

"Then," Stanley began. "Then none of it has a purpose. We are only puppets, aren't we? We can't even control what we do."

Future Stanley looked up at the ceiling of the carriage, sighing. "That is something I've been trying to have answered. But know this: everything you and I have done was our own choice and no one else's. If we were to do it again, we would make the choices that seem best at the moment. The same choices. Would you not?"

There were several instances that Stanley could think of that he would rather change, to choose a different path, but as he thought deeper, he could not disagree with Future Stanley. All the choices he had made carried him through this adventure, pushing him further into the unknown. Would he rather not know about it all? His thoughts returned to Lena. He would not have been there to care for her, to be influenced by her innocence. In a way, Lena was allowing him to be a father once again, and the more Stanley realized this, the more urgent the need to return to his present became. One look from Future Stanley told him that he knew exactly what he was thinking, and he was glad that Stanley finally understood.

Future Stanley poked his head out the window and called out to the driver.

"Where are we going?" Stanley asked.

"Home," he said. "You need to get back to Lena."

Stanley nodded, feeling his chest grow heavy with worry.

"If you choose to travel with her again, you must be more careful. Anything that isn't touching you directly might get left behind." Future Stanley motioned to his shoeless feet.

"I suppose you would know."

"Yes, I'm your future," Future Stanley replied, "but that doesn't give me the right to take away your own choices."

Stanley could not help feel bitter. "That's mighty kind of you."

"And to return me the favor, promise me you'll do what I just did in your future, for the sake of our past self. No one came for me, you know. Does it help to know that you could do nothing more?"

Stanley shook his head.

"It was worth a try."

The horses slowed to a stop and Stanley saw that they were back home, where the lights glowed brightly inside and figures moved to and fro. He stepped out, breathing with relief.

From the carriage, Future Stanley parted the curtains. "Stanley," he said with hard eyes, "that girl has grown to mean so much to me. Make sure you care for her, like you would Maisie."

Stanley nodded. "Do you know where she came from?"

Future Stanley shook his head. "You'll find out soon enough."

After a nod, Future Stanley instructed the driver to get a move on, who looked back at Stanley and shook his head in disbelief. Now that his future self was gone, Stanley began to feel overwhelmed, but he knew he could not think too much on it without going insane. He trotted back to the house, opened the gates quietly, and took refuge behind the bushes to witness the scene inside the house one last time. Through the window he could see the library and a hunched-over figure scribbling away furiously on his desk. Would this Stanley finish the story about the aspen folk? At the opposing side of the house he could see into the dining room where Jane and Maisie's silhouettes were sitting and telling stories. The Millers came out of the house through the front door and headed off to their own little house for the night. It was peaceful, and for now it mingled in the Becker home.

Not wanting to disturb them, Stanley returned to the present.

There was a bundle on the dry grass hidden by bushes under a tree, and when Stanley touched his warm overcoat he knew that not much time had passed since he had left. Carefully, he lifted the coat.

"Lena," he whispered. "Are you hurt?"

He found the bulge in the pocket and a very startled head poked out from inside. Stanley felt relief. In the dim light he could barely pick out her small features.

"Are we in the past?" she wondered.

Stanley couldn't help smile as he shook his head. "I'll explain once we're inside."

Mrs. Miller appeared surprised that it had been quite a short stroll, but was relieved to see Stanley unharmed. Without question, she accepted his excuse that it was too cold for walking. In the Bird Room Stanley seemed to breathe unrestricted for the first time since stepping into that carriage. From his pocket, Lena climbed out with the greatest of ease and leapt onto the table, all in quick, graceful movements. Stanley regarded her with awe.

"That's a trick I've never seen before."

Her impatience was clear on her face. "What happened, then?"

Stanley shed his coat and knelt down to feed the fire in the hearth.

"I traveled back without you," he explained. "My coats and shoes were left behind."

Lena appeared disappointed. "What did you do?"

"I went back to the new reality. There was nothing I could do."

"Oh."

Stanley paused, remembering.

"I . . . I ran into myself."

Lena's confusion was understandable, and Stanley explained as well as he could the events of that night in the past, but when he vocalized them, they seemed like a dream. Perhaps by using the Time Key he had opened up many other possible choices, different paths, many other Stanleys capable of making choices of their own. Perhaps he and Future Stanley came from the reality of the accident, while other Stanleys came from this one by the mere fact that Stanley chose not to stop himself from speaking to Maisie. What did it all mean, exactly? There were infinite possibilities, and the thought caused Stanley's skin to crawl. He could not view time the same way he had previously. One thing he did know—the past that he wanted to change was out of his reach, but he was convinced that the future was the only time he could change himself.

Oddly enough, he felt resentful toward Future Stanley, who knew everything that lay ahead of him and yet chose to keep it to himself. That Future Stanley whose experiences were ahead of Stanley's, who knew so much more, had not felt enough pity to lend Stanley a hand. But he had come back to speak to him, to help him sort through his emotions and thoughts, to direct him in the right direction, to save him the trouble of trying to change the past countless more times. He had a least saved him from further misery. Perhaps Future Stanley wasn't all that different from him.

In the crackling light, Lena's skin glowed mystically, and her eyes seemed to sparkle as she watched the fire dance. She fingered the beads in her hair mindlessly and closed her eyes. Stanley watched the fire and felt the remaining mystery of his retold experiences linger between them. No one knew what to say. How could such incredible things be possible?

Suddenly, Lena's head perked up and her gaze turned to the window behind her. She rose to a crouching position, as though ready to run.

"What's wrong?" Stanley whispered.

"I can hear them. They're watching."

Stanley stood to peer out the window. Below them, shielded by the shadows, was a handful of figures. Stanley felt his throat tighten. One of the figures took a step forward under the light that the window cast into the garden and looked up with an intense expression that Stanley could faintly see. After a few seconds the figures backtracked and vanished into the night. Stanley noticed that his breathing had become agitated. He looked over his shoulder. Lena hugged her legs to her chest. The fire crackled loudly, threatening.

Stanley hurried to her side. "It's all right. You're safe."

The girl trembled visibly and covered her face with her hands. Stanley placed his hand against her back comfortingly, hoping to relieve her fear.

"Lena, as long as you're with me, they can't come."

Her eyes peered from between her fingers.

"They're afraid of me, Lena. They won't come near me."

"They won't?"

Stanley shook his head.

The fire behind them subsided slowly.

"Why not?"

Stanley gave her a smile and wondered how subtle his explanation should be.

"They have never confronted me. Louis said they were afraid of me."

"Louis?"

"You must remember him. He's the man that left you here."

After a moment, her eyes grew wide. "That man!"

"Yes, Louis—"

"He put me in a bottle! It's his fault I'm even here!"

Stanley frowned. "What do you mean?"

Lena continued as though he had not spoken. "I didn't know him, but he found me after we crossed. I was afraid of him, and that caused a fire. He put me in a glass bottle and kept me hidden for I don't know how long. I only remember being very hungry and frightened. Then you appeared. And you dropped me!"

Stanley pondered over her words. "What do you mean crossed?"

Lena became silent, her eyes downcast as she remembered something that Stanley could only guess at.

"Where did you come from, Lena?"

Before the tears could even come, the girl rubbed her eyes furiously. Stanley placed his hand against her back once again, and the girl looked up longingly. She rested her head on his fingers and closed her eyes.

"It's all right," Stanley said. "I'm here."

⚭

Lena was asleep. She had curled up in his hand, exhausted and oddly comforted by him. She had asked to hear a story, and Stanley had only begun to weave a tale when he heard her soft snoring. He had placed her on a bundle of handkerchiefs and covered her warmly.

Now, he could only finger the Time Key anxiously. His finger traced the intricate design of a rose before he opened it. Future Stanley's words of caution returned to him, but brushing them aside, he set the hands. Each *tick* resonated in the walls of the Bird Room, each stirring a deeper desire inside him, hurling his emotions on a confused race against time. They spun about within him, like the particles of his being soon would, and he smiled the moment he knew he was ready to see the face of happiness.

Silently, he walked out of the room, and turned to face the closed door to the Bird Room. He knew Lena wouldn't miss him while she slept. Placing his thumb on the crown of the Time Key, Stanley tried to ignore the hint of guilt that clung to him.

He deserved this. Stanley took a deep breath and pressed the crown.

❧

His hand shook as he turned the doorknob. Candlelight welcomed him. The vision of a faded memory met him, now crisp and clear in front of him.

From behind her work, Jane looked up.

Part Two

XVII

The cold mist soaked Stanley as he ran through its smoky veil, gasping for breath and looking over his shoulder in that paranoid sensation that someone is about to tackle you from behind. But there was reason for Stanley's fear, as four figures chased him, and the cold panic that preceded them was unsettling. Stanley's feet stumbled. Ahead he saw lights moving at incredible speeds. Without question, he headed for them.

He felt the pavement beneath him and realized too late that the lights were moving toward him. They blinded him. Holding on to his collar, Lena suddenly cried out, when Stanley saw one of the men lunge at him just as a loud honking sound—

I apologize. I seem to be getting ahead of myself. For Stanley's sake, I'll backtrack to a more logical scene to continue our tale, as he would have intended. Although it is cruel of me, I am obligated to present the events leading up to Stanley's current predicament in the natural order that our hero lived them. We now travel through time and space to the busy streets of London, where we hear women calling, horses trotting, men on the docks at a distance, and children laughing without a care in the world, the streets on which Stanley walked. He passed vendors, shoeshiners, and boys running by, but he knew better than to allow them easy access to his wallet. The date was December 24, 1897. Stanley Becker wandered the streets where he had spent the early years of his childhood before his family relocated to the country.

Past beggars and desperate vendors came more calm and majestic neighborhoods, sharing one city and yet so distinct to the grime and chaos surrounding them. He felt as if from Hell the Creator had granted him safe passage into Heaven. The red-bricked houses blended together, all identical and well maintained, bringing the memories back. Stanley kept loose fists inside his coat as he strolled through the familiar scenery. He had been toying with an idea for quite some time, and as he stood facing his childhood home, his stomach fluttered wildly.

Under a tree he crouched low and set the Time Key. He felt a rush of excitement throughout his body. His fingertips tingled. Unable to conceal a boyish grin, he traveled to the summer of 1868.

The air felt creamy seeping down his lungs; it brought warmth and longing for the simple life of the past. Strewn about the front yard were boxes and suitcases, old furniture and decorations that had once embellished the old Becker home. Burly men lifted and loaded them onto a wagon as servants scurried about finishing last minute packing. Stanley watched from the security of the trees, attempting to remember the events of the day twenty-nine years ago, and hadn't noticed the little boy watching a few feet away.

"Where'd you come from, mister?"

Stanley jumped in surprise and turned to see a dark-haired boy with expectant blue eyes, studying him from under furrowed brows. His foot tapped the grass impatiently when Stanley didn't answer right away.

To appear nonthreatening, Stanley crouched. "I've been standing here all along."

"No, you haven't! I saw you appear out of nowhere!"

Seeing the boy's obstinate scowl, Stanley knew it was pointless to argue. He leaned forward playfully.

"Do you want to know a secret?"

The boy nodded.

Stanley paused.

"I'm from the future."

"No, you're not," the boy said, wrinkling his nose. Apparently he would not be as easily convinced as Maisie. "That's impossible."

Shrugging, Stanley replied, "Believe what you want."

The seven-year-old took a step closer. "If you came from the future, wouldn't you need a time machine?"

Stanley chuckled in amusement. The little writer had come up with the idea of a time machine even before H. G. Wells himself. From his pocket, he slipped out the Time Key to show the boy, wondering briefly if by doing so it would cause problems in the future.

"I can use this to travel to whatever time I'd like."

The boy considered it. "I wish I could go to the future, then I wouldn't have to leave."

"And why would you wish that?"

"I dunno . . . Father says we're going to the country."

"Are you afraid you won't make friends?"

"I know I won't have any. There are only servants there."

Stanley tried to sound reassuring. "You'll have Mrs. Miller."

"How do you know her?"

Caught off guard, he stuttered. "I don't know her. It was only—I know of her—"

The boy continued, frowning suspiciously. "She's only my nanny. It's her job to be my friend."

As he spoke, Stanley noticed a young woman calling from the house. She wore a familiar scowl of disapproval and spoke with a thick Scottish accent, which would somewhat mellow out over the years. The twenty-some-year-old nanny could see only the boy, fortunately.

"I must go," Stanley told the boy. "What's your name?"

The boy rubbed his nose. "Stanley Frank Becker."

It was a dreadful name, but Stanley smiled as he watched his seven-year-old self run off. Mrs. Miller received him in a warm embrace, pointing toward Stanley's hiding place, and he knew his fun was over. With the Time Key, Stanley left the past.

In 1897, there was a widespread conversation, although hushed and fearful, about the numerous mystery murders and counting. The horrible idea of an uncaught killer seemed to excite the residents of London, as it wasn't the first time that a notorious individual had made headlines for unsavory crimes. Despite local officials' assurance that these crimes were clearly lacking in evidence to be related to those of 1888, Londoners' love for the theatrical made it a certainty that Jack the Ripper had returned to finish what he had started a decade ago.

Oblivious to the city's terror, Stanley didn't feel unsafe, even though he distinctly remembered Nuri's warning. It had been at least two weeks since he had last seen her.

Down a familiar street, Stanley picked up the sweet aroma of freshly baked goods. In front of the coffee house, Stanley stood with hands stuffed inside pockets, chest heavy and heart racing, ready to travel once again. This trip was no mere enjoyment. It was a nostalgic gesture, more than anything, to find closure and move on. He was to travel to his past one last time.

June 8, 1881. Stanley observed in silence from inside the coffee house, his cup untouched, his fingers folding and unfolding a small note on the table. It wasn't long before Stanley saw his twenty-year-old replica, walking briskly as his eyes scanned the contents of a magazine where his most recently published work had been viciously criticized. With furrowed brows, the young man didn't look up in time to notice a young woman with a loaf of bread under her arm, and before Past Stanley could stop, he rammed into her. The young woman gave a scream and fell onto her back. Stuttering clumsy apologies, Past Stanley helped her up, but the moment she laughed, he appeared dumbstruck. Inside the coffee house, Stanley smiled.

He remembered the incident vividly, and it was quite heart-wrenching to witness it from an observer's view. He would invite the young woman for some coffee, apologizing profusely for his gracelessness. Inside, he would sit facing her, awkward and nervous. He would learn that her name was Jane, that she was a passionate painter, and that her laugh sounded as though it came from an angel.

"I've just returned from Paris," her melodious voice flowed like spring water through the coffee house. "Their ideas are absolutely revolutionary. Have you ever seen Monet's impressions?"

Stanley couldn't hear what his younger self replied, but it didn't matter. Jane's voice had taken his hand and was leading him into another time, one he could only see in his mind's eye.

XVIII

On the night of December 14, 1897, Stanley had ignored Future Stanley's warning and traveled to 1884 in search of the happiness he believed he deserved.

It had been six long years, and when Stanley saw Jane at last, he was taken aback by the apprehension in her teary eyes. His immediate response was to take her in his arms and kiss the tears from her cheeks, but it would have been a mistake. Her fear came from seeing him, the unkempt and decrepit version of the husband she knew. Stanley was visibly older, and understandably, it caused her to feel afraid.

Keeping one foot outside the Bird Room, Stanley raised his hands, but did not approach her.

"Who are you?" she demanded, although her trembling fists betrayed her challenging stance and authoritative voice.

It was difficult to resist his natural impulse, but Stanley understood that Jane did not know about the accident, or even about Maisie's illness. She had no idea that in the future, because of their deaths, Stanley would travel back in time to see them, and even attempt to save them. Stanley accepted that he was a stranger.

He simply said, "It's me, Janey."

Jane's eyes were dubious, but she tilted her head to the side as curiosity set in, and at least for the time being, she cast away the lingering fear between them.

"How can that be possible?" she asked. "You couldn't be my Stanley."

"It is me, Janey. You know me."

Jane took a step forward. "But you can't be my husband."

She nearly cringed at the word, as though it gave her a bitter taste. It had not been by mere chance that Stanley had traveled to this particular time, this exact night. He remembered the arguments, the hurtful words, and knew the reason for her sadness. Stanley entered the room and offered his hand. After a moment, she accepted it. Her touch made the pounding in his chest quicken, causing ripples of excitement and desires to pulsate through his body.

Jane must have sensed that Stanley was in dire need of affection, or at least a simple act of sympathy, when she placed her hand on his cheek.

"Where did you come from, Stanley?"

With closed eyes, Stanley found he could control his emotions enough to speak.

"Somewhere far away."

"Tell me."

"You wouldn't believe me."

When Stanley finally opened his eyes, he saw her smile.

"I'm in need of a good story," she said.

Stanley remembered that on this particular night he had stormed out of the house, mounted his horse to calm his anger and clear his thoughts, and left Jane weeping in the Bird Room. Although the thought made him nervous, Stanley supposed it wouldn't be too risky to stay a little longer, if it meant that he could comfort Jane.

Jane knew what he was thinking.

"You've gone for a ride . . . the other you, that is." At this, she laughed hoarsely. "I must be dreaming."

Stanley waited. Jane was shaking her head.

"Jane, I-I'm sorry, I shouldn't have come—"

"No, no!" she cried, grabbing his sleeves. "I'm all right. Please, stay."

Stanley hesitated but followed Jane's lead when she sat down.

"Don't concern yourself over me," she assured him. "Please, tell me about you."

Stanley couldn't tear away his eyes, even though Jane was as visibly unsettled as he should have expected. When he still didn't answer, she giggled quietly.

"I do wish to hear a good story."

Stanley began in a hushed tone. "You're right, Jane. I'm not the Stanley you know. I'm a different version of him. An *older* version."

Her smile started to fade.

"I know how this must sound, but listen to me, Janey." Stanley's fist opened, and on his palm rested the Time Key, winking in the candle-light. Jane appeared interested, and Stanley continued, "This contraption allows me to travel through time. I am a time traveler. Do you believe me?"

"Time traveler," she echoed. "That's not possible."

Stanley took her hand gently and smiled sympathetically.

"If you truly are a time traveler," she said, "then when do you come from? You certainly *look* older."

"I come from the year 1897," he replied with a chuckle.

Jane's unease appeared to vanish. With a twinkle in her eye she exclaimed, "Why, Mr. Becker! You're an *old man!*"

Stanley laughed out loud, surprised and delighted by her teasing.

"I'm only thirty-six!"

Jane squeezed his hand.

"So, you're my future, and I am your past."

Stanley nodded.

"Incredible . . . but how does it work?"

With the Time Key in hand, Stanley showed his wife all he had learned about traveling through time with the contraption and found that it all felt much like a dream. The nagging in the pit of his stomach reminded him of his body's dislocation in time, and Stanley knew the night couldn't last forever. Soon, Past Stanley would return, and he couldn't let himself be seen. When he announced that it was time for him to return home, Stanley saw a faint flash of disappointment visible on Jane's expression.

Jane stood up with him and gave him a hesitant kiss.

With a lump in his throat, Stanley stepped out the door. Jane watched nervously, and when Stanley pressed the crown, she gasped. Stanley's body vanished before her disbelieving eyes. Crying out, Stanley stared at the splintered wood, touched the icy doorknob, and fell to his knees. His cheek still burned where Jane had kissed him.

In the quiet, Stanley sobbed.

∞

It was an addiction. He had tried it once and couldn't stop. He found any excuse to return, even though he knew the heartache was tearing him from within. The little peace he felt in the past would only melt away in the present, and Stanley felt as though he were dying. He *needed* Jane.

The night after he had visited Jane the first time, Stanley prepared to return. He stood outside the door to the Bird Room on December 15, trembling with anticipation, and set the hands of the Time Key.

"Stanley?"

He looked up to see Lena emerge from her birdhouse. He had probably roused her with his footsteps.

"Yes, love?"

The girl seemed uncertain. "Are you leaving?"

"I won't be long," he promised, closing the door. He caught a glimpse of sadness in her pleading eyes. Stanley paused when the door shut.

She will be all right, he told himself as he pressed the crown.

The attic drowned in the bright light. His body dispersed during the jump, and once the light subsided he could make out Jane's figure behind a large canvas, lashing out her rage with aggressive brushstrokes. The door to the Bird Room was open, and Stanley stepped in cautiously, leaving guilt and shame behind as he entered.

"I didn't mean to wake you," Jane said without looking up. "I couldn't sleep."

"You didn't," he replied.

Startled, Jane looked up and her eyes widened in surprise. It had been at least a few weeks since Jane had first seen him, and Stanley could see that his sudden appearance stirred similar emotions from that night.

"I thought you had been a dream," she said, putting down her brush.

Stanley's cheeks flushed red. "I couldn't help myself. I had to come back."

Wiping her hands on her apron, Jane watched him sit down dizzily.

"Time travel can be quite exhausting," he said.

She took a seat next to him, unable to tear her eyes off the apparition that was her husband from the far-off future. Stanley wondered what she was thinking.

"I can't imagine," she replied, uncertain.

Stanley smiled warmly.

"It is true, then. You're from the future."

He nodded.

Jane gave him a lighthearted smile. "All right, Future Stanley, what is it like there?"

"In the future?" he asked, taken by surprise.

"Well, yes." She sat down next to him, crossing her legs in the trousers she liked to wear to paint, and seemed eager to hear his answer. "How have things changed?"

"I suppose everything is still quite similar."

"Well . . . what do women wear in 1897?"

Stanley tapped his lower lip thoughtfully. "Oh, fashion hasn't changed all that much, only they wear mutton legs as sleeves. And the dresses still make them look like skinny whales."

Jane let out the sweet laughter that Stanley missed so much.

"I had actually hoped we could get rid of it all—the skirts, the corsets, the whole lot," she replied. "And things at home? Tom and Norah?"

"Still the same, I should think," Stanley answered. He could not make himself look away from the lovely image of his wife before him. "Mrs. Miller's quite stressed. It's Christmas in a few days and my parents are coming for dinner."

"Oh, that's unfortunate."

"It will be quite unpleasant," he agreed.

Jane's eyes were warm. "What about us? I take it I haven't snatched up all your money and stolen away on your horse one night, Mr. Becker."

Stanley chuckled at the familiar joke, but broke his gaze, unable to suppress his emotions. Jane was still curious.

"I suppose I shouldn't ask to know about the future. It could cause a split in the universe, or some rubbish."

Stanley nodded and noticed her fingers fumbling on her lap. He knew what she really wanted to know about the future.

"Stanley," she began, licking her lips. "I won't ask anything else, but can you tell me one thing?"

He forced himself to look up and give her a knowing smile. "What do you want to know?"

"Do we have children?"

They were silent for a long minute, and then Stanley reached down to hold her hand. He knew the pain, or at least could understand it now that it had all passed. His younger self didn't know the emptiness that Jane felt inside her, the longing for that warm seed to grow within her, the nurture she wished to give; a gap had formed between them because of Stanley's inability to understand. In time it would be mended, but Stanley wanted to give Jane the little bit of hope she so desperately craved.

"We have a beautiful girl," he said at last.

Jane's eyes twinkled. "Maisie."

Stanley's brows lifted. "How did you know?"

"I have dreams of her."

"You never told me."

Jane shrugged. "You never asked."

Stanley struggled to control his emotions, the yearning that he felt, and so it was time to return home. He rose, but was uncertain how to say good-bye.

"I understand," Jane said, standing next to him. They still held hands. "I won't ask about the future. I promise."

She patted his cheek, and Stanley closed his eyes.

"Will you come back?" she wondered.

"If you would have me."

"I would."

∽∞∾

It was uncertain what sort of influence his visits would have on the past, but he knew that it was impacting his present. He could feel himself growing distant, irritable, and simply unstable. It was worse than the poison he had drank for six years, as he was aware of the disappointed looks that Mrs. Miller often shot him. Gilmore could sense his rapid regression as well. From Stanley's visits to his nieces and nephew, the doctor could read the troubled expression on his brow. Gilmore never asked, and Stanley never explained.

With Lena, he felt shame.

On December 19, he spent the day in the Bird Room working while Lena occupied herself with making paint. For the moment she had paused to munch on a piece of cheese atop her birdhouse. Fresh paint on the outside walls were a soft hue of teal, a new mixture she had made.

"Do you ever see them?"

Stanley looked up from his work, confused by her question, and dipped his pen in ink once again.

"What do you mean, love?"

Lena took another bite and chewed thoughtfully before swallowing.

"I mean, when you travel—do you ever go see *them*?"

She fingered her beaded hair nervously, and Stanley finally realized who she was referring to. Lena never used their names. Perhaps she feared he would be sad in hearing them.

"I visit them, sometimes."

Lena bit her lip uncertainly.

"It would be painful," she said. "Wouldn't it?"

Stanley nodded, studying the black splotches where he had let ink drop.

"It is."

"Do they know you are from the future?" Lena wondered.

Stanley set down the pen. "Jane knows, and I told Maisie only once. It's quite unbelievable to say the least."

Lena took one last bite of cheese and climbed down. Stanley abandoned his work and leaned back in his chair, sighing in exhaustion. It would probably be a good idea to take a break that night and catch up on some much needed sleep.

"It is strange," Lena continued, peering down Stanley's inkwell in fascination. She touched the rim and studied the black substance on her fingertips. "It's almost as if they are alive, but you can only see them with your Time Key."

Stanley nodded slowly. "I suppose that's one way to see it."

Lena dipped her hand inside the inkwell and marveled as her fingers returned pitch black. Stanley chuckled when she hurried back to her birdhouse, smearing ink on her other palm, and pressed both hands on the wooden walls of her home. Her tiny prints stood out clearly. Lena giggled and repeated the process.

Stanley stared at his hands and felt the always-present emptiness in his stomach churn.

❧

The quick visits to the past continued for the next week or so, filling Stanley with the joy he had wanted for so long, quenching the thirst that had been left unsatisfied for six years. However, in returning to the past one night, he found that his visits had had a terrible impact, not only on him, but on Jane as well. He heard her sobs before he saw her, and the moment he revealed himself she hurled the rage his way.

"So you're back," she said between gritted teeth.

Stanley hesitated at the door.

"Janey, what—"

"Don't call me that," she snapped. "You have your own Jane. What do you want me for?"

Stanley stood frozen, as though he had been splashed with icy water. Jane's fists shook at her sides.

"Why?" she asked. "Why do you come here? Why aren't you home? Why aren't you with Maisie? With *me*?"

Stanley couldn't speak.

Jane no longer held back her tears. "What happens in the future?"

Hanging his head, Stanley fumbled with the Time Key.

"I'm sorry," he mumbled. "I'm so sorry."

Jane had her face buried in her hands when Stanley traveled, and her sobs echoed in his ears.

❧

Stanley leaned back against the wall, gasping and trembling. There was nothing he could have said that wouldn't have given away his reason for coming back. He had been so stupid, so careless for seeing her, only to appease his own suffering. Stanley had hurt Jane.

Calming his pounding heart, Stanley took a deep breath and climbed down the attic stairs. The hush of the house gave off a sort of peace as Stanley walked to his room. At the open door, Stanley watched the darkness. There were two figures lying on the bed. His body cuddled against Jane's, embracing her. At the foot of their bed was an unmoving bundle in a bassinet, a tiny infant spending her first hours of life in peaceful sleep. Listening to their quiet breathing, Stanley sighed and opened the Time Key.

Several months forward, Stanley entered Maisie's room where he saw her grasping the bars of her crib, eyes wide, and suckling her thumb. His chest felt heavy, but the infant stirred tender warmth in him.

"Hello, love," he whispered.

Maisie, only six months old, raised her pudgy hands toward him. Stanley reached down and took her in his arms. It was difficult enough to handle his many mixed emotions, but for once, Stanley allowed himself to let this moment be what it would be. With the memory of Jane's agony, Stanley let the tears soak his cheeks. Lena had been right. To hold Maisie's warm little body against him, to look into her living eyes once again, meant that Stanley's past, although it had already passed in his perspective, was still happening now. It meant that although he would have to return home, Maisie and Jane were still alive here. It would have to be enough.

Once she had fallen asleep, Stanley placed her in the crib and traveled.

∞

Four years forward, Stanley saw that a bed had replaced the crib, and there was a girl instead of a baby, whose head peered from beneath the covers to see her papa at the foot of her bed.

"Papa?"

Stanley jumped at the sound of her voice. He had thought she was asleep.

"Yes, love?"

"I can't sleep."

Stanley sat down next to her when she made room for him. It wasn't his first time visiting Maisie in her bed, but his chest pounded loudly as he convinced himself this would have to be the last.

"Was it a dream?"

"Yes. There were shadows, Papa."

Believing him to be her papa of this present, not the future, Maisie climbed onto his lap as though it would protect her from the nightmares. Her warm little hands grabbed his arms and draped them over her. Stanley held her securely, in fear that she would vanish at any moment. He kissed the top of her head.

"They can't hurt you, love."

"Can you tell me a story?"

Stanley thought for a few seconds.

"The Bright-eyes?"

"You've already told me that one."

"Right . . . hmm . . ." He smiled after a moment. "You've never heard of vaelies, have you?"

Maisie turned her head to look at him with interest. "No. What are they?"

"They are people that live in the trees."

"How can they live in trees?"

"Well, they are quite small, you see."

Crossing her arms, Maisie scoffed. "Have you ever seen them?"

Stanley chuckled. "I know one. Her name is Lena."

"I don't believe you, Papa!"

"It's true," he replied. "She lives in the Bird Room."

"I've never seen her."

Stanley lowered his voice. "If you listen you might hear her. She likes the quiet, you know . . . and milk with honey."

"Milk with honey?"

"Oh, she loves it. She can't resist it."

Maisie pondered his words, as though committing the information to memory.

"Does she have a family?"

Stanley sighed. It had been weeks since the girl had come into his life and still he knew very little about her. "I suppose she does, but she won't tell me about them."

"Maybe she ran away."

"What makes you say that?"

Maisie shrugged. "I dunno."

Maisie's eyes were heavy and she struggled to keep them open. Her small fingers entwined with his, laced tightly together. Stanley pulled the covers over them both and rested his cheek on her head, breathing in the peace that this moment offered. He knew this could not continue. The past needed to return to its natural flow, and Stanley could not intervene any longer. In his silent way, Stanley said good-bye to his daughter for the last time.

⌘

Lena never mentioned that she felt alone, neglected, but Stanley could see it in her eyes whenever he readied himself to travel to the past. Lena was aware of his trips to the past, and what they meant, but Stanley couldn't bring himself to explain his agony. He supposed she knew. On December 23, however, she watched him disappear, his body glimmering in the light of the setting sun, with a promise that he would return soon.

Stanley traveled again, to say good-bye to his wife.

Jane was looking out the window when he appeared.

"Jane?"

She didn't turn. "You're back."

Stanley was unsure whether she was still angry with him, but he continued, "I can't come anymore, Janey."

Jane turned to reveal the tears on her cheeks. "I know. This isn't natural."

They approached one another, and Jane embraced Stanley, who melted in her arms.

"I only have one husband, you know. I couldn't stand *two* Stanleys."

Stanley's surprised laughter sputtered out. "I love you very much, Janey," he said. "Have patience with him—*your* Stanley. He loves you, but he is only a boy. He has quite a bit to grow into."

Jane held his hand and planted a soft kiss on his lips. "This is quite strange," she whispered. "But it looks like you need it."

"Thank you."

"Go home, Stanley. Take care of your family."

"I will."

⚬

It was a dark night in what he assumed was still December 23, 1897, by the fire in the Bird Room that was slowly dying. Wearily, Stanley knelt down to feed it when something caught his eye.

Lena watched the outside world from the roof of a tall birdhouse, shoulders tense and eyes narrowed.

"Lena?"

The girl didn't glance his way.

"There's someone outside," she said, pointing her finger. Stanley approached her. "In the trees."

Stanley squinted. "Is it one of the shadows?"

Lena shook her head. "I don't feel them. They are cold. It isn't cold now."

Stanley tried to see through the dark night, and at last he saw the figure.

"Who is it?" Lena asked.

Frowning, Stanley replied, "I don't know."

The figure stood at the fringe between moonlight and shadow, and looked up from under a hood. Feeling a sudden surge of anger, Stanley marched to the door and grabbed his coat.

"Where are you going?" Lena cried, frightened.

"I'm going to see who that is," he said, stuffing his arms through the coat sleeves. "I'll be back soon."

"Let me come," she said, standing up.

Stanley hesitated. "I can't have you in harm's way, Lena. Stay here."

Lena wrinkled her nose defiantly, but she turned back to look out the window. Stanley raced downstairs to the back door. With his heart in his throat he stepped into the night.

Stanley shivered inside his coat, scowling through the veil of blackness. Behind the trees, he could faintly see the shape of a figure, accentuated by the moonlight that betrayed its presence. He took a step forward, attempting to appear menacing.

"Who are you?" he called. His voice sounded frail in the thick silence. "What do you want?"

The figure behind the trees remained motionless, but seemed to regard Stanley with the same intensity. In turn, Stanley was growing impatient. He wished he would have thought to bring his worthless pistol when he approached the figure with renewed determination.

"Are you one of them?" he demanded, crushing through the undergrowth. "Are you one of the shadows?"

The moonlit outline of the figure possessed delicate curves that gave hints of belonging to a woman. Stanley frowned. He recognized the velvet cloak.

"How . . . is that . . . ?" he stammered. "That belonged to my wife!"

It could not be Jane's.

He was only a few yards away when the figure held up her hands and stepped in the clear.

"I'm sorry," the woman said, gesturing for Stanley to keep his distance. "I—I only wanted . . ."

"Who are you? What are you doing here?"

"I only wanted to . . . I needed to see you . . ."

Stanley took another step and the woman turned to flee.

"Who are you?" Stanley pleaded, running to the place where the woman had been, but he could not see where she had gone. The gardens were silent and the woman was nowhere to be found.

He paced desperately, and finding no answers in the silence, returned to the house unwillingly.

It could not have been . . .

It wasn't possible.

Stanley shook his head to clear it. It hadn't been Jane. It hadn't been her voice.

Stumbling back inside the Bird Room, Stanley met Lena's concerned look from the birdhouse, and was reminded of the oddities taking place all around him. The shadows, the vaelie, a mysterious woman, and the disappearance of a man who had left him a contraption that allowed him to travel through time. He had ignored his unsettled thoughts regarding an unseen world that, only weeks ago, had begun to make itself known. And now, having said good-bye to the past he had desperately longed for, he was awake to see the possible terrors in his present.

"Who was that?" Lena asked in a small voice.

Finding his own voice, Stanley collapsed on his chair.

"I don't know."

Lena climbed down from her birdhouse. "It wasn't a shadow," she repeated.

"I don't think so."

Uncertainly, Lena waited while Stanley's mind raced.

"Where did they come from?" he mumbled. "Who was that woman? Why in blazes was she watching us?"

"It was a woman?"

Stanley didn't seem to hear her.

"Lena," he said abruptly. "None of it makes any sense. The shadows, the woman . . . Where do they come from . . . ? Where did *you* come from? You must know how you came here."

Startled, Lena clutched her shirt. "I told you!"

"You told me about Louis, but how did he cross? If he brought you here, there must be a way to take you home."

"I don't know!" she cried.

Stanley sighed. "I don't understand any of this."

Stanley passed a hand over his eyes in exhaustion and frustration, desperately wishing he had answers. Frankly, he was tired, and the past he had returned from was still vivid in his mind.

"If I knew how," Lena said suddenly, "I would already be gone!"

Stanley looked up in surprise. At the edge of the table, Lena shot him a furious glare, her little fists shaking at her sides. In anger, the girl bared her teeth.

"Do you think I stay here because I want to?"

The crackling fire burned Stanley's back as the flames in the fireplace grew and devoured the wood he had thrown in. Stanley had never seen her quite so enraged.

"Lena," he said slowly. "Calm yourself. I didn't mean any . . ."

With narrowed eyes, she cried, "I want to go home!"

Turning violently, the girl stomped her feet and disappeared inside her house. Stanley rose uncertainly, walked toward the table, and peered inside the birdhouse.

"Lena, I didn't—"

From the entrance, her drinking thimble went flying out, bounced on the table, and dropped at Stanley's feet.

"Go away!"

Stanley cursed himself.

He had hurt her. He hadn't meant to, certainly, but he had. During his pathetic travels to the past, he had left the girl all alone—a *child*. Sighing, Stanley retrieved the thimble and set it back on the table.

"I'm sorry, love," he said simply. "I hadn't meant to upset you."

Lena didn't answer, and Stanley hung his head in shame. After one last look through the window, and seeing nothing unusual, Stanley returned to his place in front of the fire and leaned back in the chair.

"I'll watch for shadows," he promised.

Lena said nothing. It wasn't long before Stanley felt the embrace of sleep while he stared at the dancing flames, chin propped on his chest, as his mind struggled to forget the past. In his drowsiness, he tried to comprehend the nature of shadows and of a fiery little vaelie living in his attic.

XIX

The sounds of clattering spoons against cups, the rumble of blurred conversations, and the rush of his own heartbeat pounding in his ears finally awoke Stanley from the memories and into his current present: the day he had met his wife in 1881, the moment in which he was a mere observer, where he remained hidden to whisper the last good-byes necessary to carry on with his life. At the other end of the coffee house, Past Stanley had been successful in making Jane laugh once again.

A smile formed on Stanley's lips as he studied the note in his hand. That morning he had risen to the sounds of a gentle brush splattering paint on a wooden surface. Seeing him awake, Lena had dashed to a newly discovered birdhouse, calling Stanley's attention, and had retrieved a neatly folded note. She had handed him the small paper, curious to know what its contents read. Stanley had been surprised by her eagerness, an innocent gesture that had no trace of the hurt from the night before. Presently, as he read the cursive writing for the third time that day, Stanley chuckled at the red smudges Lena's fingers had left around the edges of the note.

∞

My Darling,

You were right. She was born last night, and she is lovely. Whatever happened in your past, leave it. Love and live. Embrace what you have, because time forgives nothing and cannot be controlled, not even with a time machine.

With love,

Janey.

It was time for Stanley to leave. The past had no place for him anymore. Shrugging in his coat, he tilted his hat forward to walk by the couple unnoticed. Not that it mattered. Past Stanley and Jane gazed intently into each other's eyes, love-struck.

Outside it was quite warm, and people around Stanley gave him queer looks, although they were not as stunned as the people of 1897, who could have sworn that they had just seen a man appear out of thin air. But Stanley didn't stop to explain, finding that two hours had passed since he had left, and hurried to the street where Mr. Miller so faithfully awaited him.

Mr. Miller didn't say a word as Stanley climbed in, shivering from the cold, and looking over his shoulder as though he were being pursued. Before coming to London that day, Mrs. Miller had yet again warned them of that mystery murderer, and from Mr. Miller's scowl, Stanley knew the coachman was thinking of it now.

In his habitual manner, Mr. Miller asked, "Where to, Mr. Becker?"

"Canbury Gardens."

"In Kingston?"

"Yes."

Stanley had seen one of the shadow men—or at least had thought he had seen one—leaning his back against the wall of an alley, watching intently as Mr. Miller urged the horses forward. Stanley had seen this man before; it was difficult to forget his dark skin and yellow eyes, and even less the coldness that surrounded him. It had been a long time since he had seen the shadows.

At the gardens, Stanley was disappointed to find the clearing free from any visible Roma. Feeling once again at a dead end, he sighed. He had not received word from Nuri since Market Day, and Stanley had hoped she would have answers. The shadow men had not bothered him since the night he had returned from speaking with Future Stanley (other than the occasional observer), they hadn't a clue as to finding a way home for Lena, and Stanley still had questions that only Louis could answer. Now that his time traveling to the past had reached an end, Stanley's entire focus was on the vaelie, whose origins remained unknown. Finding a way to take her home was his top priority, and who other than the Roma would know about the place she belonged to, and how to get there?

From the corner of his eye, Stanley saw the dark-skinned man once again, watching him from under a tall oak with the same intensity. Stanley approached him, and the shadow man walked away.

"They're not ones for talking."

Stanley looked back to find a bald-headed man studying him from the clearing, his left arm hung limply by his side. Inside the sleeve, Stanley knew the hand was made of wood.

"Who are you?" Stanley demanded, feeling a lump in his throat.

"They call me Mà de Fusta," the bald man answered, and his lips parted to show an arrangement of golden teeth. "And by 'they' I mean the Roma. And you might be?"

"Where are they?"

Mà de Fusta chuckled. "I've been looking for them, as well."

The man's voice sent an unexpected chill up Stanley's spine, embracing him with a blanket of ice.

"But enough with the formalities," Mà de Fusta said. "I know you spoke with Louis before his disappearance."

Stanley did not reply.

"I know he gave you the Time Key."

Swallowing, Stanley tightened his hold around the contraption in his pocket.

Mà de Fusta continued, "It's very crucial that I have it back."

"I don't know what you are talking about, sir."

The man's eyes were hard, measuring Stanley's ungainly figure as though he were an irritating insect he wished to squash. "I suppose I should warn you," he said slowly. "I'm a man of little patience, but since we've only just met, I will let you off with some words of advice."

Stanley saw the shadowed figures emerge from behind trees, scrutinizing him with their yellow eyes.

"Find the Time Key, hand it over willingly, and we'll leave you alone. Fail to do so and they will take it by force. Fret not—they know where to find you. Do we understand each other?"

Stanley tried to appear unmoved.

"I'll be a gentleman," Mà de Fusta said, "and give you until Christmas to decide, eh?"

By Mà de Fusta's sign, the shadow men dissolved back into the shadows of the trees. Mà de Fusta walked away. As though he had at last emerged from underwater, Stanley gasped for air the moment he realized he had been left alone.

❧

Mrs. Miller had grown used to Stanley's frequent trips to the Bird Room, where he spent most of his day secluded doing heavens-knew-what. She had been faithfully obedient to his instructions to stay away. But on that day curiosity surfaced, and as she climbed up to the attic, she couldn't shake the tension that her employer would catch her nosing around. The door creaked softly when she opened it, and the sight that welcomed her inside the Bird Room caused her to gasp.

Arranged in a web, twisting this way and that, were gorgeously thick and luscious vines growing up the walls and around the posts of the vaulted ceiling, raining down above the housekeeper's head like a rainforest. All about the cabinets and tables were planted pots of colorful flowers and ferns, giving off fresh scents of spring in the dead of winter. Mrs. Miller pressed her hand to her chest, awed by the beauty. She inspected the various birdhouses that hung down from the ceiling, little floating homes fit for the birds. So this was what Mr. Becker had been working on for so long. It made the housekeeper smile. And to think she had long been questioning his sanity.

When she heard the front door open downstairs, the housekeeper forced herself to leave the Bird Room, unwilling to keep it a secret. At the kitchen, she passed Stanley, who rushed upstairs in a panic.

"Sorry, Mrs. Miller," he stuttered apologetically. "I'm in a bit of a hurry."

"Mr. Becker, dinner's in an hour. Ye really must get ready."

"I know, Mrs. Miller. I won't be long."

It startled Lena when the door opened once again and shut loudly, but when she saw it was Stanley, she poked out of her birdhouse hanging from the ceiling. She preferred to sleep there, comforted by the altitude, and snuggled as though by a cloud floating in the air.

"Lena, are you here?"

Stanley scanned the room with a sick look on his pale face.

He saw the girl climbing down a vine to the window, and in relief, he blew out the air in his cheeks as he sat on the chair to face her. She raised one eyebrow and watched him curiously, with still no hint of the anger Stanley had seen the night before. He supposed that if the girl didn't acknowledge it, neither should he.

"Where else would I be?"

"I thought that perhaps—no, it's nothing."

Her hand waved at him to follow her. Lena led him to a pair of bird-houses that she had recently finished. Stanley nodded, knowing what to do with them.

"Where do you want them?" he asked, picking one up and standing on a stool to reach the posts.

It was incredible to witness the girl climb up the vines with such agility and ease, giving high leaps to reach the top in a matter of sec-onds. Stanley struggled to spot her running through the lush greenery above him, until she called down to the place she had chosen to hang the birdhouse.

"You've made good progress," Stanley said, fastening the wire that was attached to the birdhouse onto the post. "Looks wonderful."

Lena never knew how to accept a compliment, but he saw her face blush behind the large leaves of the vines. After the two newest bird-houses had been hung up, Stanley stood back to admire her work, grin-ning widely at the transformation that the Bird Room had undergone.

"Beautiful."

Stanley turned to see Lena hanging from a vine to look out the window as the sun descended into the horizon. Her eyes pleaded and her body radiated with yearning in her silent way. Feeling guilty, Stanley sat down behind her and sighed. Lena loved to go outside; it was her natural instinct, but Stanley only allowed for her to go very few times a day in fear that the shadow men would find her. He didn't know what they would do to her.

"Sun will go down soon," he told her, but the girl only nodded. "You'd best put on some warm clothes. It might snow."

Lena looked back with dubious eyes.

"I can come?"

Stanley smiled. "Only if you're up to it."

Her squeal of excitement made Stanley chuckle.

Out in the cold weather, Lena burrowed herself against Stanley's neck. Stanley had found that if he loosened his collar enough, the girl was able to ride comfortably next to his neck. There, she was protected from the biting cold, even though she preferred to be up in the trees.

Stanley remembered the first time he had seen Lena climb up a tree and disappear into the leafless branches. Her soundless movements had created ripples of mystic thrill. Once in a while he would hear her soft laughter echo through the dead of winter, bringing warmth with her voice. He had never been entirely certain where and how he had collected the idea to write about people like her living in trees, but seeing Lena running and leaping from branch to branch, gliding through the air without the slightest effort, he knew it was something he would never fully understand. Like the place she had come from, Lena's innate behavior and attraction to the trees, the natural abilities she possessed, could never be explained to Stanley, as he could not grasp what they meant or what miraculous world could create such mysterious creatures as she. The more he thought about it, the less he was convinced that she could have somehow come from his imagination.

A trail behind the house led them into the woods, allowing them the unconcerned privacy Stanley preferred. At least, he felt safe enough. Against his neck, Lena shivered slightly.

"There was a woman today—she came to the Bird Room. Who is she?" Lena wondered.

Startled by her question, Stanley stuttered, "You saw . . . Mrs. Miller?"

"She came to the Bird Room. She liked my plants. And the birdhouses."

"You've not shown yourself to her, I hope."

"I think that I'll scare her."

Stanley agreed. "You're quite frightful."

The girl giggled and cried, "I am not!"

To the west they heard the trickling river that ran through the little forest, and when Lena asked if it was *a'right* to climb, Stanley consented. Reaching up as high as he could, he raised Lena to the nearest tree. She leapt off skillfully and vanished into the bare branches. Stanley watched until his inept vision lost sight of her.

"Don't be long," he said, although unsure whether she could hear him.

Stanley walked through the underbrush, following a hidden trail that crunched under his shoes. It would eventually take him to the river. He brought out the contraption that was responsible for the current dilemma that his mind mused over, as he tried to solve the puzzle that Mà de Fusta's ultimatum laid out. Stanley opened the rose-like insignia that served as a cover and window, and he examined the long hand that

150

usually spun in an idle counterclockwise manner. It pointed toward the river, unmoving, with its little attached hand spinning wildly. Stanley had yet to discover what type of energy the Time Key was attracted to or what that information entailed.

From the corner of his eye, Stanley noticed a figure, shadowed by its own dark aura. Stanley was ready. He turned, faced the dark-skinned man, and approached him. This time the man didn't flee; instead, he crossed his arms as Stanley came closer.

"Who are you?" Stanley shouted. "Why are you following me?"

The man watched him with a calm expression that made Stanley anxious but did not answer. Stanley maintained his aggressive confrontation.

"What do you want?"

The man's nostrils flared, and at last he spoke. "We've been watching you for some time. We know you have the Time Key."

Stanley scoffed. "In case you weren't informed, your boss has already made that clear."

The dark-skinned man shook his head, appearing slightly amused. "Not boss. We do his bidding as an agreement. None of us is loyal to him."

Briefly, Stanley wondered why this man, this Lurker, always appeared to be alone.

"He doesn't know you're here," Stanley asked, "does he?"

The dark-skinned man, large and robust, clenched his thick hands. "He believes you possess an item of great value," the man began. His voice was deep and rough, as if he rarely used it. "A very powerful item, but in fact it has been lost. The wooden-hand man has been so blinded by his desperation to possess such power that he doesn't see it's not in the contraption."

Stanley's hand gripped the Time Key in his pocket. "Why are you telling me this?"

The man's yellow eyes regarded Stanley pensively as he continued, "He'll come for it whether you give it up willingly or not, but he will come. And yours is not the only life you treasure."

Stanley's mind raced, feeling his throat tighten.

"Is that a threat?" he challenged in a hoarse voice.

"It's a warning. You'd do well to be prepared. Once he knows you don't have what he wants, you'll be of no use to him." The man looked

151

toward the trees, brow furrowed in thought. "And there are other things that may interest him."

Stanley heard a crackling noise, like a small explosion, and caught a whiff of smoke.

The man turned away to leave.

"Tread lightly. Things are about to become . . . difficult."

The foreboding was not lost on Stanley, whose weak knees threatened to buckle beneath him as he watched the man disappear behind the rising fog. At last he understood the gravity of the danger to which Louis had exposed him and those around him. What awoke Stanley from the trance was the open flame devouring the branch above him, which he instantly reached for and knocked down, stomping on it before the fire grew.

"Is he gone?" Lena called down from somewhere above him. Her voice was shaky and clearly distressed.

"Yes, Lena. He's gone," Stanley answered, putting out the last of the fire. "Did you do that?"

"What did he want?"

Lena's voice was close, allowing Stanley to easily spot her on the tree. She accepted his outstretched hand. Stanley jumped when he felt her cold body against his neck.

"To warn me," he replied. "We'd best go home."

He walked briskly, as though sensing a pursuer, but he saw no one behind him. The shadow man had come alone. Only when they were at a distance from the little forest did Stanley feel secure.

"You caused that fire, didn't you?" he asked in an attempt to distract his own thoughts.

"I'm sorry. I was frightened."

"Does it happen often?"

After a pause, and much to Stanley's surprise, the girl answered, "Sometimes when I'm angry or scared. I can't control it when the fire starts."

"You don't know how it happens?"

"No. I suppose it's a curse."

Stanley felt uneasy about Lena's explanation. It confirmed the fact that he knew very little about the girl and the world that she came from, and considering his fortune to have gotten an answer without angering her, Stanley thought it best to avoid questioning her further.

"He came to warn me about something," Stanley said, addressing Lena's question about the shadow man. "He wasn't there to hurt us."

"Warn you about what?"

"About someone," he replied slowly, "who wants possession of the Time Key, or rather what was inside it."

After a pause, Lena said, "You can't trust them, you know. They're shadow-shifters. They kill humans."

"Shadow-shifters, eh?"

"They're shadows—beasts that behave like shadows and prey on a being's soul. When they kill a human they can take on his shape. That's how they can hide among you. But they don't fool vaelies."

Instinctively, Stanley quickened his pace.

"But you said they can't hurt you," she continued. "So there's nothing to worry about."

Stanley realized he needed to maintain his confidence in the idea that he was untouchable, at least for Lena's sake, although he feared he was mistaken.

"Nothing to worry about."

In reaching the house, Stanley saw that a familiar carriage had pulled up to the gates. He cursed. The carriage belonged to his parents. As quickly as he was able, he stole inside the house through the back door, left Lena in the Bird Room, and changed into the best suit he owned. One thing that his parents strictly demanded, among many, was a good impression. Accepting the limited time to make himself more presentable, Stanley took a deep breath, nodded to his reflection in the mirror, and walked out. Mrs. Miller awaited him in the kitchen.

"They're cross ye didn't receive 'em," she whispered, grabbing his arm. "Where in blazes were ye?"

"I went for a stroll," he defended. "I thought they weren't coming until tomorrow!"

"I told ye this mornin'!" she snapped. "D'ye never listen—doesn't matter. Go in there and try not t'make a fool o' yerself."

As previously mentioned, Stanley's dismissive opinion of his parents was partly due to an ongoing feud between him and his father, and as he walked into the library, familiar resentments surfaced. He paid little heed to his emotions, as was courteous, and extended his hands in feigned delight to see his parents.

"Pardon my tardiness," he said. "Couldn't find the right suit to wear."

His mother, majestically elegant as always, rose from the armchair (which her critical eye had been studying moments before) and embraced Stanley. Behind her, his father turned to face him, although his attention remained on the stack of manuscripts he had been fumbling through with disdain. Frank Becker gave his predictable business grin. Both seemed older than when Stanley had last seen them, but their grand influence remained intact, always prepared to reveal that they were wealthy beyond belief.

"It appears you never did," Frank muttered loud enough for his son to hear, in regards to Stanley's statement.

Edna's embrace left fragments of warmth. "Oh, my Stanley!"

"Hello, Mother," Stanley said with his best smile. "I hope the trip wasn't too troublesome."

"Indeed it was," she replied, touching her forehead with the back of her hand in a demonstration of regret. "Dreadful weather we're having. It makes it nearly impossible to step outside without getting a layer of mud on your shoes."

"I regret to hear that, Mother," Stanley replied with sympathy. Frank had reached them and now offered his hand to Stanley, who shook it grudgingly. It was a sort of tradition, a ceremony in which they measured each other's strengths. Frank would always win.

"Father," Stanley said, nodding. "I take it you're well."

"Could be better." Frank's eyes remained intently fixed on his son.

"Stanley," Edna said, interrupting the exchange. "I'd like to freshen up before dinner."

Stanley nodded and called for Mrs. Miller, who brought a tray of tea, which regrettably no one would touch. The housekeeper led Edna out of the room, leaving Stanley alone with his father, whose attention returned to the desk by the window.

"I see you've started writing your stories again." Frank fingered through the stack. "Have you had any printed?"

Conversations with Frank always began with two things: politics and money. At the moment Stanley suspected this conversation was inclined to the latter.

"Not yet," he replied. "I still write for the magazine."

"Of course. Pity you won't come to the estate. I could use someone with your talents."

Stanley was unsure of what he meant. It was a habit to search for hidden messages in everything that came out of his father's mouth. Fortunately, Mrs. Miller called them to the table, where a fancy dinner had been laid out. Mr. Miller pulled the chair out for Frank, while Mrs. Miller shot Stanley a warning look to behave. At the entrance to the dining room, Edna eyed the lack of embellishments on the walls.

"Stanley, dear," Edna said. "You really should consider changing the wallpaper. A much brighter design should liven up the house."

Stanley took a seat across from his father, who was polishing the impeccable silverware with the tablecloth.

"I'm afraid I know very little about interior design, Mother."

Edna sat down by Frank. "We just changed the walls in one of our rooms. Didn't we, Frank?"

"Yes, and now it's covered in sunflowers," Frank said. "Gives me a headache."

Edna ignored her husband. "It really does wonders for the feel of the room. Also, dear, your furniture is grossly outdated. I'll have a word with Norah."

The Beckers were far from the religious sort, so when everyone at the table was ready, Mr. Miller prepared to slice through the roasted turkey. Mrs. Miller poured red wine into their glasses, beginning with Frank, and the dinner took off. To Stanley's relief, it was not quite as unpleasant as he had expected, but he kept his guard up just in case.

"You probably haven't heard, Stanley," Edna said between small bites, dabbing her lips with her napkin. "Our two Arabians are foaling in the spring."

Stanley was slightly interested. "Are they now?"

"You really should come by, dear. We know how much you enjoy riding."

Frank cleared his throat. "Your Clydesdales are well, I assume? I'd like to see them in action."

"Mr. Miller can take you around the village. Won't you, Mr. Miller?"

"It would be my pleasure," the coachman said as he cleared empty plates.

Mrs. Miller brought out cakes for dessert.

"What about you, dear?" Edna asked, determined to convey how much they cared for their son's well-being. "You've been well?"

"Couldn't be better."

"We just had to come for a few days, Stanley, since you won't come to see us."

"I'm sorry, Mother. I have been busy."

"Three long days," Frank added, looking around through his eyelashes with disdain.

Stanley couldn't help the sneer that crawled up his face. "Now if that's quite the sacrifice for you, Father, you're welcome to stay at a hotel in London's finest. Such a humble home as mine is probably well below a respectable businessman such as yourself."

Edna shook her head. "Stanley, dear—"

"It's all right, Edna," Frank interrupted, clearly unmoved that such a pleasant evening had taken a bitter turn. "We shouldn't lie to our only son. It makes for the spoiled ingrate that he's turned into."

"We were planning to go to London, anyway, Stanley," Edna explained. "You understand, don't you?"

"Of course, Mother. It's quite a relief, really."

Frank grimaced. "We're to see my old friend Charles Neeld, from the club. You remember him, surely."

"I make sure to update my list of all your friends, Father."

Behind Stanley, Mrs. Miller thumped him with a tray in the back of the head when the guests looked away.

"He's recently started a new business that travels to Africa for a few months at a time. He mentioned he was in need of someone to oversee a handful of crewmembers—"

"I have a job, Father."

"But think of it, Stanley," Edna piped in. "It would be so exciting to travel."

Stanley took a sip of wine, rubbing the back of his head. "I'm quite content here."

"Yet you've done nothing with your life!" Frank cried. "Look at you—you're still in the same position you were six years ago."

Stanley held his tongue and avoided looking at his father.

Edna placed a hand on Frank's. "We only worry, dear. That's all."

"Thank you, Mother. But I'm quite all right."

"You know, Stanley," Edna said slowly. "What happened to Jane and Maisie, it couldn't have been stopped. We can never change it."

Stanley nodded. This wasn't the first time she had given that speech. Stanley knew that she was referring to Maisie's illness and Jane's suicide, but it served as a logical excuse for both realities.

"I know that now, Mother."

≈

Evidently dinner had not been as torturous as Stanley had expected, but he was relieved to say good-bye to his parents. Mrs. Miller would not let him lift a finger to help clean and sent him away. At least Stanley deemed the night a success by the mere fact that he had not opened the bottle of brandy that he had been so tempted to drink during the long conversations. He took leave of the exhaustive evening and went to visit Lena with a salad. He didn't dare offer her turkey, remembering how she seemed to detest any meat. In the Bird Room, he found her hanging upside down beneath a birdhouse to inspect the bottom part of it. Her delight to see him always made Stanley forget his troubles.

While she ate, Stanley concocted a plan to find what had happened to the little vial inside the Time Key that Louis had removed, and cursed himself for not thinking of it earlier. If he could find the vial, or at least see where it had been lost, he could hand it over to Mà de Fusta without all the fuss, and he and the Lurkers would leave Stanley alone at last. It was as simple as traveling a few weeks into the past and playing the observer. Stanley was both experienced and skilled in that field.

Lena saw the sudden concern in Stanley's face.

"Are you worried?" Lena asked with a mouthful of spinach.

Stanley looked up from the Time Key and shook his head, but something told him it wouldn't do any good to hide his plan from Lena. He didn't like to hide things from her.

"I think I'm going to travel one last time."

Lena swallowed.

"I'm going to find out what happened to Louis the night he left you here."

"You'll try to talk to him?"

Stanley shook his head. "He took a vial that was hidden inside the Time Key. I'm going to follow him to see where he took it before his disappearance."

"Can I come with you?"

"If you'd like. Couldn't be too dangerous, I suppose."

The girl jumped to her feet. "When do we leave?"

157

"Now. It should take us back just a few minutes before I walk into the house."

For a moment, she seemed concerned.

"Will it hurt?"

"It's a bit nauseating, but it passes quickly."

"How do you know it will take you when you want to?"

Stanley demonstrated how to change the hands. "I move the years hand counterclockwise to go back, but just a bit. The date was December fourth—a Saturday. We turn the seasons to the end of autumn, a bit past the last marker to indicate the month of December. And the days hand to the middle marker for Saturday. The hour will remain the same as it is now. Are you ready?"

Lena slipped on the shoes she had made and stepped onto Stanley's open palm, nodding fervently and clearly thrilled. Stanley raised her up to his eyes, solemn.

"Promise to stay with me at all times?"

Lena nodded impatiently.

"Promise?"

"Yes, yes, promise! Let's go!"

Stanley chuckled and the girl squealed with delight as she took her place burrowed in Stanley's collar. They were all set, and trembling with anticipation, Stanley readied to activate the Time Key.

"Hold on to me tightly, Lena," he instructed. "Don't let go."

And they traveled.

∽

Stanley's head spun, but he was used to it enough to keep steady on his feet. The Bird Room was bare and musty, unused. Against his neck, Lena's hold was limp. Stanley reached up to her.

"Are you all right?"

"No," she mumbled. "I feel sick."

"It'll pass. Do you want to continue?"

Lena consented with a sigh. The moment he stepped out, Stanley heard the door open downstairs and shut again. Finding that his shoes were missing was a relief as he walked silently through the dark corridors of the house. He stopped in the kitchen when he heard voices.

They waited several minutes in the dark kitchen.

"Stanley?"

"Yes, Lena?"

The girl shivered. "I can sense a vaelie close by."

Stanley pursed his lips as he remembered.

"That's you," he replied. "In the other room."

From the library, Stanley heard his own voice rise in irritation. The moment was approaching. He listened intently.

"Thanks for your time," Louis's muffled voice said. "And for the scotch. I had a glass or two."

It was time. Louis would exit the house at any moment, and Stanley would be watching. As silently as he was able, Stanley backtracked and headed for the back door. Lena hung on as best as she could despite the dizziness. Outside it was quite cold, and the moon cast its bright light on the house through the clouds gathering in preparation for the coming snowfall. Of course, this wasn't the first time that Stanley had been forced to walk out into the winter cold without shoes, but tonight he didn't waste any time in regretting it.

He took cover behind the adjacent wall of the house to see Louis step out and close the door behind him. At the gates, Louis hesitated. Did he doubt whether he had done the right thing to leave Lena? Was he aware of the consequences following Stanley's involvement? Ire stirred within Stanley as he watched the man saunter off without the slightest concern, wondering how he could seem so guiltless after leaving a creature as vulnerable as Lena at the mercy of a drunken man, without giving any sort of explanation.

Stanley felt Lena shiver weakly again and forced himself to return to the present moment. Louis had turned to close the gate, but before Stanley could sneak closer, he saw the shadows slithering like snakes from dark corners in the street.

They were the same Lurkers Stanley was familiar with, the ones that had come to that dark alley the night this had all begun. But these were not men. Frozen in his hiding place, Stanley watched as the shadows reached Louis and overtook him from behind, pummeling the man to the ground. The beast-like forms that attacked him had undetermined shapes, constantly molding and shifting, were the size of horses, and had yellow eyes as the only thing betraying their animated existence. Their morphing bodies were black as the night surrounding them. When Louis's body lay unconscious on the wet street, the shadows suddenly hovered over him, dissolved into the darkness, and, along with Louis, they vanished as quickly as they had appeared.

Stanley waited. In the silence, Lena gave a soft whimper. It couldn't be—Louis, along with the vial, was gone. The bloody Lurkers had been behind it all along.

Despite Lena's protests, Stanley rose and ran to the place that Louis's unconscious body had been only seconds ago. He must find the vial. Perhaps it had fallen in the street as Louis was being clobbered senseless. Stanley could see nothing in the dimly lit street. He cursed. Lena was near tears.

"Stanley, I don't like this place," she begged. "Let's go, please. The shadows could come back."

Stanley, on all fours, hung his head. This could not be another dead end. Lena was pulling the hair on the back of his neck desperately.

There was no vial.

"Please, take me back to the Bird Room!"

Stanley smelled smoke.

"All right, Lena. You're right. I'm sorry."

Without another word, Stanley left, and Lena trembled in his collar. They headed back to the house in defeat. There was nothing more they could do, and now Stanley faced the difficult reality of what would come when he traveled to the future. Mà de Fusta and his loyal minions would come for the vial that Stanley did not have, and he could only imagine what sort of terror they were capable of inflicting.

As they passed the library on their way to the back of the house, Stanley hesitated when he heard movement through the open window ahead. Past Stanley had just picked up the bottle. Soon it would come rolling out through the window and shatter on the stones where he now stood, injuring Lena inside. Stanley couldn't will his feet to take another step.

"What are you doing?" Lena whispered.

"You're about to come crashing down. You'll almost die. I can't allow that to happen again."

Lena hesitated, probably trying to grasp the reality that she was in the past and all that had happened to her was actually the present moment for an identical version of her.

To Stanley's surprise, she replied, "You can't stop it from happening."

"I can catch the bottle. Nothing will be different."

"*Everything* will be different."

Stanley's mind raced. Lena was right. If the bottle didn't shatter, wounding the girl, would Stanley even help her? Would he dismiss the entire event as part of his imagination? Lena would be left abandoned and alone. She would die in that bottle.

Without another word, Stanley went back inside. He heard the bottle shatter on the stones when it fell. Some fragments hacked at Stanley's heart. Lena sobbed quietly. They traveled home in silence.

XX

Allow me to leave the Becker home for a moment and draw your attention to an event that occurred only hours prior to Stanley and Lena reappearing inside the Bird Room as they arrive safely from their adventure. In the early hours before dawn, the environment in Kingston was peaceful, and the society at the shores of the river Thames seemed unbothered before the start of the new day. At least for now, there had been no new murders to terrorize the streets. But such thoughts did not seem to alarm a certain girl who waited in the cold silence, watching the abandoned house. She had risen to a black morning to watch the house, but she did not intend to remain an observer for long. She had come every day for the past week and knew that the moment the residents of the house left, there would only be one man to worry about: Mà de Fusta. But the bald man didn't concern her. She was a stealthy thief, and breaking into the house without his knowledge would be quick and effortless.

Five men emerged from the house, and Nuri waited. After five minutes, the last man walked through the door and headed a different direction from the rest. With a grin that she couldn't contain, Nuri made her way to the house. Her soft-padded leather boots made no sound as she ran. In reaching the front door she found that it was locked. From her hair she removed two pins to pick the lock. It wasn't difficult, and once inside, the girl stood in the dust-filled air of the abandoned house. It was musty, and Nuri could not stop her nose from wrinkling.

Up the stairs she was careful to step lightly, and she froze when a board creaked. No disturbance in the house followed, and she continued. There were three doors at the top of the stairs. Nuri hesitated. She heard a voice coming from the room to the far left. She opened the room at the opposite end of the hallway and, seeing it was empty, hid inside to wait.

She recognized Mà de Fusta's voice. Her hand reached under her skirts where, latched to a belt around her leg, she kept a hidden knife. Breathing slowly, heart thudding in her ears, Nuri peered and saw Mà de Fusta emerge from the room. At the stairs, he turned away from her. Nuri stepped out, knife gripped so tightly in her fist that her knuckles turned white. She had one goal in mind. Surely with the threat of a sharp knife to his throat, the bald man would talk.

A hand shot out from behind Nuri. It clutched her face while another arm wrapped around her waist. Before Nuri could react, her oppressor pulled her back inside the room. A scream gathered in her throat, and a voice hissed in her ear.

"Don't make a sound."

Nuri couldn't say what caused her to submit. She waited in silence as the man closed the door soundlessly. Mà de Fusta's steps resonated down the stairs.

"I've been watching you for some time," a deep-throated voice said, blowing cold air down her neck. He still held her tightly. "Mà de Fusta would have slit your throat if he'd seen you."

Nuri wrestled her face free. "Not if I had slit his first," she snapped. "Let me go!"

"What did you think would happen?" the voice wondered, with a hint of amusement in it. "We're shadows. We see all."

"Where is my father?"

From Nuri's right came a thump on the wall and a muffled voice called, "Who is that?"

Nuri gasped. "Da! You're here!"

The voice on the other side of the wall cracked. "Saira?"

Downstairs, the front door opened and slammed shut. The man holding Nuri suddenly picked her up in his big arms, despite her struggles. She felt a biting cold embrace her. To her horror, the man that held her became a silhouette, the featureless shadow of a man. She tried to scream but had no voice. She saw the shadows crawl up and overtake them, swallowing them in frozen blackness. Suddenly there was no depth, nothing tangible, nothing she could see, as though she were part of a nightmare.

After what seemed like hours, she felt the cool fingers of the early morning chill stroke her face. The big arms carefully set her limp body on the wet ground. She leaned back against a wall and blinked several times before she recognized the alley. She was back in the place from where she usually observed the abandoned house.

The dark-skinned man looked down at her without expression. A faraway streetlight faintly reflected off the hard features of his face.

"Don't come back here. Not alone."

Nuri braced herself in the dizziness. "Let my father go."

"The wooden-hand man wants the Time Key for what it carries," he continued. "He'll do anything to get it."

Nuri gritted her teeth, knowing what the shadow man was referring to.

"Why are you telling me this?"

For a moment the shadow man's yellow eyes softened. "We came to him because we believed he could help. We made an agreement, but he wouldn't hold his end of the bargain. We are growing weak. We must find a way to return."

"You're from there—the other world. Aren't you?"

"All we want is to go back."

Nuri sat up. "What can I do to free my father?"

"Your father will be executed tomorrow, whether the wooden-hand man finds the Time Key or not. But he will not find it. You'd do well to warn the man who has possession of it."

After a moment, Nuri was able to stand up. Her eyes never wavered from the shadow man, who had little interest in what she would do or say next.

"How can I trust you?"

The man regarded her blankly. "You can't."

When the big man handed her the knife, Nuri snatched it up to hide back inside her skirts. It seemed that nothing more would be said. The girl turned around and ran to the place where the hansom cab awaited her. Seeing Nuri, Henri climbed on his perch to await her instructions.

"To Woking," she said, looking over her shoulder. No one had followed her.

"To the camp?"

Nuri shook her head. "Mr. Becker's house."

The cab left the dark streets as sunlight peered over the horizon and began to sprinkle its warmth over them. Nuri didn't see any pursuers or shadows. She leaned back in her seat and sighed. She felt both drained of all energy and invigorated by adrenaline, but guilt poisoned her thoughts. She was leaving her father behind.

XXI

They had been back for no longer than a few minutes when Stanley saw the sun peek through the clouds on the horizon, stretching warm arms of light across the yawning sky, and although it implied a peaceful dawn, the travelers felt nothing less than agony as their thoughts recollected the events of the past. Lena wasted no time to retreat to her birdhouse, casting Stanley only a wounded look before she disappeared inside. Stanley watched the sky through the window, unable to sort out his cluttered thoughts. Today was probably Christmas, the day that Mà de Fusta and the shadow men would pay him a visit, and Stanley didn't have what they would kill to possess.

It wouldn't do any good to sit and sulk, knowing now that his life and those around him were in jeopardy. He would have to send the Millers off for a few days while the danger passed. At least they would remain safe away from him. Lena was a different matter. Knowing the girl, she would not want to go off on her own even if she could. There was nowhere for her to go. They had yet to find a way to send her home, and there was no guarantee that she would be safe. The only solution that Stanley saw was to take her to Gilmore's house, and that would mean putting him and his family at risk if the shadow man were to tell Mà de Fusta about her existence. Perhaps Gilmore could be persuaded to leave Woking with her, possibly to his parents' residence in London, away from the danger, but it would not be easy. As Jane's brother, they shared a common stubbornness. He would not do Stanley's bidding without an explanation.

A knock came at the door and Stanley turned to see Mrs. Miller enter cautiously.

"Mr. Becker," she said uncertainly. "There's someone at the door for ye."

And so this was how it began. Stanley tried to appear composed, regretting that he had not been given any more time. In a hoarse voice, he asked, "Who?"

"A girl."

Her answer took him by surprise, but he followed her downstairs.

"She widnae say 'er name," Mrs. Miller explained. "She's waiting in the library."

Stanley straightened out his collar as best as he could. He walked through the hallway in apprehension, shoeless and silent. At the library, Stanley saw his visitor and felt a rush of both relief and confusion. Nuri, wild-haired and unsettled, stood in his library. The image of her exotic presence stood out among the mundanely ordinary items of Stanley's library. When she saw him, there was panic in her expression.

"Mr. Becker!"

❦

Her slender fingers gripped her spoon tightly as she stirred the milk and tea together with such aggression that Stanley was afraid the cup would shatter. Her arms trembled from either cold or fear, Stanley could not be sure. She gratefully accepted the thick blanket from Mrs. Miller, who couldn't help stare at her with both fascination and distress. When Stanley nodded for her to offer them some privacy, the housekeeper obeyed hesitantly. Nuri brought up the teacup, cuddled it in her hands, and sipped the warm drink with closed eyes. Stanley cleared his throat uncertainly.

Nuri set the cup down to look at him with coal-black eyes, fearful and clearly upset.

"I apologize," she said, "for coming here."

Stanley left his cup untouched. "Is everything all right? You're not hurt?"

The girl shook her head, and still her familiar smile refused to make an appearance.

"How did you know where to find me?"

"Word gets around," she replied.

Stanley wouldn't take his eyes off her, who in turn was fixedly watching the tea in her cup as though it held answers that she struggled to decipher. After a long pause, she finally sighed in resignation.

"I found my father."

Stanley sat up in his armchair, fists clenched. "Where is he?"

"Mà de Fusta."

Wide-eyed, Stanley could not find the words to ask. "Is he . . . ?"

"He's alive, at least for now. I heard him. But the shadow man took me away before I could get to him."

"Did they hurt you?"

"No. This one, he seemed . . . safe."

Stanley paused. "What did he look like?"

Nuri frowned pensively. "Dark skin . . . He was quite tall, and very large. Do you know him?"

Stanley tapped his lip. "He came to warn me last night. I don't suppose we can trust him."

"I can't say I do, but I don't understand why he would warn us both. He said all they want is to go back. He said that they are weak."

The girl took a long sip of tea, warming her shivering body, and Stanley asked, "Go back?"

"To their world."

Her answer made Stanley's skin crawl. From his waistcoat he brought out the Time Key. "They want what was in here. But your father took it, remember?"

Nuri nodded. "He wants the water from the Fountain. The Divine Tears."

Stanley wanted to ask about this strange new information, but chose to stay on the subject that was most crucial. "The shadow man said Mà de Fusta would come for it, whether I have it or not."

"He'll find you. Wherever you are."

Stanley stared at the contraption in his palm. "I went back. I saw the Lurkers, the shadow men, vanish with him. I searched everywhere, but I didn't find the vial. What more can I do? Mà de Fusta, he . . . he threatened me. We *must* find it—"

"No!" Nuri snapped. "That water is more powerful than anything you can imagine. If he gets ahold of it—it could be disastrous!"

"What could it possibly do?"

Nuri looked at her cup again. "It's an old story that my father would tell me as a child."

Her eyes turned a misty green as she retold the fairytale from her childhood.

"There was a Fountain where the gods wept for every injustice in the world, for every sad girl, every lost boy. The gods looked down at the worlds they had created, saw all the terrible things that man did, and their tears were so many that it created waterfalls to pour down from the Heavens into the mortal world, connecting both Heaven and Earth. Because the water from the Fountain was filled with the gods' tears, it was influenced by their divinity. It was said that the water possessed supernatural properties."

Nuri paused, chuckling quietly at the thought. Stanley wanted to brush aside the mystic influence that had taken control of the conversation.

"The gods feared that a mortal would use the power from the Fountain, so they called a guardian, a protector, to watch over it. No mortal could ever find such a place."

"But Louis—he found it."

Nuri nodded, uneasy. "They were only stories. I never believed them, until I saw him cross over with my own eyes."

Stanley sighed, feeling the heaviness of mystery and the unknown utterly exhausting. He couldn't say that he believed Nuri's story. It wouldn't matter. He still did not know what to do about Mà de Fusta or his ultimatum, and knowing that Louis still played a crucial role in all this only magnified his distress.

"What's next, then?"

After a pause, Nuri looked him directly in the eyes. "Come to our camp. Mà de Fusta will find you there, but we can protect you. At least you will be away from those you care about. No one else will get hurt."

The idea had logic to it, and Stanley saw no other direction to take. He consented. He didn't know where the impulse came from, but he hardly realized what he was saying as the words slipped out.

"Nuri," he said. "The Time Key was not the only thing your father left me."

Her eyes grew with interest.

∞

Grief lingered in the quiet Bird Room. It made Stanley's chest heavy when he opened the door, and yet a familiar thrill surged within him as he remembered the first time he had spoken with the little vaelie. The sensation seemed to infect Nuri in the same way when they both entered. She marveled at the green canopy of vines above them, and smiled at the

169

birdhouses hanging in the air. When Nuri turned to cast him an expectant look Stanley walked to Lena's birdhouse by the window.

"Lena," he said softly. "I've brought someone to meet you."

Understandably, Nuri scowled at Stanley, as though wondering if he was insane. From inside the birdhouse, Lena emerged slowly, wide-eyed, and peered out from the opening. Nuri froze and made a choking noise.

"Before his disappearance," Stanley explained, as Nuri took a seat in a daze, "Louis left her to me. I don't know the reason, but might you have an idea of how to get her home?"

Lena studied the Romani girl pensively, and in return, Nuri could not tear her eyes from the vaelie. Finding her voice at last seemed to help drain the shock.

"Da told me stories about them. I thought that's all they were."

Stanley's hopes sank, but he had expected as much.

"I wouldn't know how to get her home," Nuri continued. "But I'm certain my father does . . ."

In her usual silence, Lena retreated once again into the birdhouse without giving Stanley more than a mere glance that reminded him of the past he had not changed. Nuri took a deep breath and rose quickly, shaking off the obvious unease that Lena's existence gave her. She headed for the door and Stanley followed. It seemed that their conversation was over, and Nuri was eager to leave. At the front door, Stanley stopped her.

"Come to the camp," she repeated. "We can help you there."

"And Lena?"

She shook her head. "Leave her here. This is the safest place for her. If Mà de Fusta were to hear about her—well, he's a greedy merchant."

It was agreed that he would meet her at their camp, which she revealed was only about two miles north of his house, near a stream broken off from the river Thames. Nuri left him with the hope that all would be made right, explaining that Mà de Fusta was only after one thing, and by pretending to have it in his possession, Stanley would demand to have Louis set free in exchange. Nuri seemed less concerned about the shadow men than Stanley was, and claimed that their disloyalty to Mà de Fusta gave them an advantage. As he watched the girl drive off in the cab, Stanley hoped it would be as simple as she promised.

XXII

For the past two weeks, Stanley had visited Gilmore's sickly son each day, disturbed by the fact that Mark's condition seemed to worsen at each visit but relieved that the boy still had the energy to appear excited when he walked through the door. Stanley would bring a collection of the boy's favorite books and some toys to distract him from the obvious discomfort. The boy's pale skin looked gray, and the constant coughing shook his frail body. Images of Maisie ill in her bed flashed in Stanley's mind, and he could not help but fear for the boy.

"I brought you a new toy," Stanley told his nephew, whose eyelids looked too heavy to lift. He showed him the round object with a string tied to the center pole wedged between the two halves.

"What is it?" Mark wondered, taking it in his hands very gently. Pressed tightly to his chest, the boy held the old stuffed bear that Stanley had brought him a week before.

"They call it *the Prince of Wales toy*," Stanley said, fitting the string to his finger in a loop to keep it in place. He rolled the string and let go. The toy dropped down, bounced when it reached the end of the string, and loyally returned to Stanley's waiting hand. "I hear that in America they adopted the name *bandalore*. But my favorite is the *yo-yo*."

The demonstration captivated the seven-year-old, who couldn't wait to try it himself. With his two sisters, Minnie and Mabel, watching in hushed excitement, Mark copied Stanley's movements with the toy, but could not get it to come back up. Stanley kissed the boy's sweat-dipped forehead and promised that he would soon master the toy.

Gilmore's wife, Mary, watched weakly from the door. Stanley smiled at her encouragingly.

It pained Stanley to see the young boy so frail, and Gilmore's despondency only added to the anguish. The doctor sat outside smoking his pipe and rubbing his hands to warm them when Stanley stepped out. Gilmore hardly looked up when his brother-in-law took a seat next to him.

"He seemed quite taken with the toy."

Gilmore sighed. "Your visits always help."

Stanley was at a loss for words. For six years Gilmore had been the one to give him advice, to listen to his endless complaining, to be his faithful friend. Now roles had been reversed, and Stanley was unsure how to ease the pain of the inevitable.

"How is Lena?" Gilmore asked. He hadn't seen the girl in over a week.

"She's transformed the Bird Room entirely," Stanley said. "She's brilliant."

"I'd like to see her soon," Gilmore replied. "I have this idea in my head that if she's real, a living, breathing being, then anything could be possible. Anything at all. Perhaps where she came from you could find a cure for any illness."

The statement choked Stanley. He knew his brother-in-law's agony.

"I would think Lena might like to meet Mark."

Gilmore agreed.

The mention of Lena reminded Stanley of Mà de Fusta and his coming visit to the Roma's camp, stirring feelings of anxiety, but overall Stanley found a little bit of comfort in the idea that all would be over that night.

"Is something the matter?" Gilmore asked, eyeing Stanley as he blew out a puff of smoke.

"I may be in a bit of trouble, Russell," Stanley replied with a sigh. "Trouble I'm uncertain of how to get out."

"What do you mean?"

It was time to tell Gilmore everything. As though he had memorized a script, Stanley related all he knew, all that had happened from the night that he had saved Louis from shadows, to the morning he had had tea with a Gypsy. He found it strange to tell. It was as though he were a narrator in someone else's incredible life, the mere witness of a protagonist who knew very little about the events that had shaped it and, if his intuition was correct, the arriving end of it. Stanley couldn't say what caused him to suspect this approaching doom, but he was surprised to realize that he fully accepted whatever was to happen that Christmas night. Knowing that his family and Lena would be well away from danger gave him a little bit of peace.

"If anything happens to me, be sure to care for Lena."

Gilmore nodded. His eyes were wide and overwhelmed. "How will I know?"

"If you don't receive word from me, find the Roma. Nuri will find a way to get Lena home."

"Stanley, I really must insist that I come with you."

Stanley shook his head. "You have your family. I'll be all right. It's only precautionary."

Gilmore smoked his pipe fervently, digesting the load of information. Stanley offered his hand and Gilmore shook it.

"You've always been a good friend, Russell. Thank you."

"Only because you married my sister."

They both laughed, perhaps too long and too hard, but it sounded comforting in their ears.

∞

"Why do you need to leave?"

Lena watched Stanley pace the length of the Bird Room from a birdhouse next to the window, where she had been staring longingly at the sky outside as dark clouds swallowed the sun. Her nose had wrinkled obstinately the moment Stanley announced his departure.

Stanley struggled to put into words a simple explanation that would both omit his suspicions of the danger that awaited him at the Romani camp and satisfy Lena's curiosity about where he was going that she wasn't allowed to come, all the while trying to keep his emotions under control so that she wouldn't see the concern in his eyes.

"It will just be tonight, Lena."

"Where are you going?"

"It's not far."

"Then why can't I come?"

At last he stopped pacing and faced the birdhouse, where she dangled her feet and leaned her head against the circular entrance. Stanley didn't want to leave. Her companionship over the last month had grown within him like the thick vines that embellished the Bird Room, two beings intertwined and unwilling to separate. Not having her close was nearly unthinkable.

"I'm sorry, Lena," he said slowly, wincing at her look of disappointment. He had been the cause of many of those looks. "I won't be long, but Russell will come by to see you."

"The healer man?"

"Yes."

Lena consented and seemed satisfied with his promise. It never ceased to amaze Stanley how willingly Lena always appeared to trust him, even if he failed to keep a promise. The girl stretched out her hand, as she always did to say good-bye.

Stanley failed to swallow the lump in his throat. He was useless at good-byes. Regardless of whether his intuition was accurate or mistaken, the idea that he wouldn't be around to see Lena again, that the friendship they had shared would be broken, deeply troubled him. If he were never to return to her, would she be safe? Stanley fully trusted that Gilmore would keep his promise, but would she ever find her way home? He deeply regretted being unable to help her find her family. Remembering all the past events they had shared together, it was not lost on Stanley that without the girl his life would have continued on that same numbness that had consumed him. Without her, he could not have been privileged to experience the responsibility and affection of a father once again.

Stanley accepted the gesture with his finger, touched her minute hand, and felt a rush of energy flow through him.

Her smile warmed him.

❧

It would be absurd to relate every minute of Stanley's day as he waited for any indication that it was time to set out, but at long last the time came. As we have learned from Stanley's experiences, the man was a planner, and it was highly uncharacteristic of him to function on mere impulse, as he feared taking risks unless he was unlikely to get hurt. But as a time traveler he had learned that without risks nothing else would set things in motion.

When he told Mrs. Miller that he was to leave that afternoon, her hands went to her hips, her mouth made a grimace, and her voice became very shrill.

"Where're ye off to now?"

Stanley stood outside the carriage while Mr. Miller prepared the horses.

"To meet some old acquaintances. I'll be home tonight for dinner."

The housekeeper sighed. "I can see there's nothing I can say t'make ye stay. Do be careful, Mr. Becker."

Stanley smiled. "You've always looked after me, Norah."

"Since ye were a wee scunner—"

To the housekeeper's surprise, Stanley leaned forward and wrapped his arms around her in a gesture of warmth that he had not shown in a very long time, and to Mrs. Miller, it brought back the sweet memories she cherished of a little wild boy. Stanley whispered "thank you" in her ear.

They left Mrs. Miller at the gates, wiping sudden tears in embarrassment, and Stanley instructed Mr. Miller where to take them. The horses followed the road northwest, every minute getting deeper into a dense undeveloped region, leaving behind the civilization that Stanley was comfortable seeing. For two miles they rode, and Stanley feared that he had gotten them lost, but soon he saw the tall grass and the road that came to an end, just as Nuri had instructed. He had Mr. Miller stop the horses before he stepped out into the cold.

"That will be all, Mr. Miller."

The coachman jumped down from his perch as Stanley trudged away through the grass that led to a trickling stream not far off from where they had stopped. He cast the horses a glance and followed Stanley.

"Go home, Mr. Miller," Stanley said when he heard the coachman running after him.

"Wherever it is you're going, I'm coming along. I promised Mrs. Miller that I'd look after you."

Stanley cast Mr. Miller a glance, surprised by the man's sudden impulse to disobey an order, but when he saw that the coachman would not be easily dissuaded, Stanley assented with a grunt.

"Are you certain, Mr. Miller?"

The coachman nodded willfully. Both men continued.

"Can't say I didn't warn you."

Giving the horses one last look of concern, Mr. Miller trudged on behind his employer's quick pace at a nervous two-stride distance. The wide fields ahead were covered in the same tall, yellow grass; across the river, Stanley was able to make out the angled tops of various tents. Soaked to the knees in river water, the men approached the camp that rested alongside a line of trees at the edge of the thick woods surrounding them. Behind Stanley, Mr. Miller grew agitated.

"Stay with me, Tom. We'll be all right."

"That's a Gypsy camp," the coachman muttered.

"I know that."

"What sorts of business have you with Gypsies?"

"It's quite a long story, and we don't have the time . . ."

A group of young men, whom Stanley immediately recognized, were chatting and playing cards on a crudely made table under a bare tree. As soon as they saw the two men approach, they rose in unison. Mr. Miller remained close to Stanley, prepared to fight at the first indication that their lives were under threat. Stanley nodded to a young man from the group.

Pierre gave him a sideways glance and motioned for them to follow. "You came just in time."

The boys parted to let them pass, talking excitedly in a foreign language. A few of them gave the men friendly pats on the back.

"Don't let them near your wallet," Stanley whispered to Mr. Miller, whose scarf was being examined by two of the boys. Turning back to Pierre, Stanley added, "Nuri is expecting me."

The boy nodded. In entering the camp, Stanley felt as though he had stepped into an exotic land, where he was the foreigner among a mass of beautiful, extravagant natives. At least there was no contempt that Stanley could read, and the slaps on the back that they received he took as a welcoming sign. From the Roma, at any rate, there would be no trouble he should fear.

It appeared that the camp was in preparation for a Christmas feast, and among the mass chaos chickens clucked, dogs barked, and donkeys snorted alongside the various voices of calling women to crying children and laughing men. Whichever way they looked there were big fires roasting various deceased animals. Strong scents filled Stanley's nose, some mouthwatering and others rather displeasing. Women were busy preparing delicious platters of colorful foreign foods, and men tended to horses and mules; boys fought each other with sticks, and babies sat on the hips of girls not much bigger than themselves. At each turn Stanley and Mr. Miller received pleasant looks of curiosity.

"Do they know us?" Stanley asked Pierre, managing to free himself from a pair of elderly women who asked him questions in a foreign tongue. He didn't recall having received as much attention in Canbury Gardens.

The boy nodded. "Nuri told everyone about Louis and that he had contacted you for some reason. They remember you. They think you know how to get him back to us."

Stanley swallowed with difficulty. As they passed the last of the dwellings, Stanley saw a familiar tent isolated from the rest, and his chest tightened when he saw Naomi outside it dusting a rug. Her look of surprise implied that she had not been expecting them.

"Mr. Becker!" she exclaimed with raised eyebrows. "What brings you here?"

Pierre was about to explain when the tent flap opened and Nuri's head poked out, wearing a grin full of mischief. She waved her hand theatrically.

"Come in! Come in!"

Naomi sighed. "Of course."

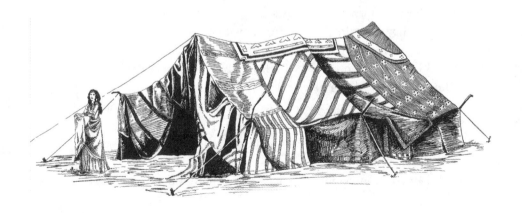

XXIII

Mr. Miller's busy hands clasped together, fingers latched nervously in between each other as a sort of mechanism, while he blew air on them as though to warm them. Sitting on feathered cushions that lay scattered on the floor of their hosts' tent, Stanley waited patiently while Nuri and her mother argued in a foreign language. Stanley thought he heard a trace of Spanish, but he couldn't be sure. When Mr. Miller shifted uneasily, Stanley glanced at him.

"Your hat, Tom?"

The coachman reached for the hat that should have been on his head, found it missing, and blushed.

"The boys took it," he said. "Along with my scarf."

"I don't think you'll find them again."

"I don't mean to pry, Mr. Becker," Mr. Miller whispered urgently. "But what are we doing here?"

Before Stanley could answer, Naomi's voice rose as she grew agitated. "*Achanta la muí!*"

For a moment, Nuri's eyes widened in surprise, but their hardness returned instantly in a flash of red.

Naomi continued in English, either in confusion, or for the guests' sake.

"I knew you were up to no good," she spat. "Going on all those trips with Pierre. And now you've dragged Mr. Becker into it!"

Nuri's fists were clenched. "*Mare*, this is important—"

Naomi's hand flew up to demand silence, and Stanley didn't dare say a word. He felt guilty for Naomi's frustration, as he was partly

178

responsible for her daughter's secret trips to stalk Mà de Fusta and his minions.

"I don't understand it, Nuri. Ever since we came here, you have been uncontrollable. You come and go to who-knows-where. I worry you'll catch trouble, or worse. Can't you understand that I'm your mother, that I've enough gray hairs from your father already? You're just like him! And now with his disappearance—"

"I know where Da is!"

Naomi's mouth gradually closed as she studied her daughter. Then, she turned to Stanley for the first time since they had come into the tent.

"Mr. Becker knows too, *Mare*," Nuri said. "Don't you, Mr. Becker?"

All eyes in the tent scrutinized him, and Stanley felt resentful for being involved so insensitively into the argument. He quickly nodded.

"You'd best tell her the whole story," he said to Nuri, whose triumphant gleam gave away the cruel advantage she had over her mother.

Naomi slowly sat down on a cushion, eyes fixed on the ground, to await Nuri's explanation. The girl sat directly across from Stanley and waited a minute or so before she turned back to her mother to retell her story.

"Pierre and I have been following Mà de Fusta ever since he appeared in England. By the river in Kingston, we found an abandoned house where he goes each night. We saw men with him too. The shadows Da told us about. There were six of them."

Naomi whispered, "The murders."

A chill shot up Stanley's spine. The mystery murders, of which Mrs. Miller had repeatedly warned him about, were the Lurkers' doing the entire time. Lena's explanation about the creatures began to make sense. In entering this world as shadows, the beasts would have had need to hide, to blend in. Logically, they would have had to kill a man to take his shape.

Mr. Miller fumbled his thumbs uneasily as he tried to understand the conversation.

Nuri continued, "This morning I went inside the house when the men left."

"You went inside!"

"I know it was stupid, but I found the place where they keep him, *Mare*. I was there. I heard his voice. Mà de Fusta has kept him there this whole time."

"But the shadows—they work for him?"

"As an agreement," Stanley put in. "One of them came to warn me. They do his bidding in exchange for a way back to wherever they came from."

"You spoke to a shadow-shifter?" Naomi asked, eyebrows raised.

"He helped me, *Mare*," Nuri said. "He got me out of that house before Mà de Fusta could find me. He warned me of the same thing. All they want is to return home."

"And Mà de Fusta?"

Stanley's hands became moist as he spoke up. "He's coming to retrieve the Time Key for what it carried. Only, he doesn't know . . ."

"It's been lost," Nuri finished.

Naomi nodded as her face turned pale.

"I used the Time Key to go back to the night that Louis came to retrieve the vial," Stanley explained. "I saw the shadow men take him. I searched everywhere, but I didn't find anything."

"And Da couldn't have it. Otherwise Mà de Fusta would not be after Mr. Becker."

"Mà de Fusta threatened me that he would come, whether I gave up the Time Key willingly or not, but obviously I have no vial. He'll come to the camp, because I'm here."

Naomi's hands shook. "I gather you've already thought of a plan, Nuri. What do you propose we do?"

An impish grin crawled up the girl's face, giving Stanley flutters in his stomach. He had been waiting for this moment.

"Mr. Becker will stay here with us. Mà de Fusta will come, and we'll make a trade."

Naomi stared at her hands as she replied, "A trade? Don't expect to fool him. The man isn't stupid."

"It's only a diversion, *Mare*."

Stanley caught on immediately. "We'll free Louis ourselves . . ."

Nuri grinned. "I've already spoken to Toma. He's sent five men to watch the house. They'll wait until Mà de Fusta and the shadows leave to set Da free. It won't matter that Mr. Becker doesn't have the vial, because while we distract him, Da will be long gone."

Naomi didn't look up from her shaking hands.

"It's so simple, *Mare*," Nuri urged. "Mà de Fusta won't see it coming. We'll have Da home by tonight!"

The plan seemed simple enough, and the thrill that Stanley had caught from Nuri muddled the few doubts he still had. Naomi stared blankly into the distance without saying a word. For the first time, Mr. Miller coughed to make himself known.

"I don't mean to interrupt," he said as all eyes turned to him, "but this shadow man . . . how can you trust him?"

Nuri's eyebrow rose. "I'm sorry—who are you?"

Stanley cleared his throat. "I apologize. This is Tom Miller, my driver."

Mr. Miller continued, "These men, they don't appear to be trust-worthy. How do you know that it's not all a trap of some sort?"

An uneasy silence followed as everyone digested the question and allowed doubt to enter. Stanley knew he was right. They could not trust the Lurkers, the murderers and kidnappers that they were. He had wondered that himself countless times but could see no other alternative. Nuri gave a sigh and answered with the innocence of a tired child who only wanted her father to come home.

"There's nothing more to do," she said. "The shadow man said Da will be executed tomorrow, whether Mà de Fusta gets the Time Key or not."

A stifled cry escaped Naomi, and Stanley instantly went to her aid. He took her hand and whispered, "He'll be all right. I'll do everything I can to get him back to you."

The woman's lips quivered, but no one was able to do anything more when they heard a sudden racket outside and a flurry of hands opened the tent flap. Before Stanley knew it, he was dragged outside into the crowd, ears ringing with the sounds of pots and pans banging, people calling and yelling, whistles and laughter. In the confusion, Stanley saw Mr. Miller being pulled by an old woman who was explaining something he clearly couldn't understand. Amongst the chaos, Stanley felt a small hand grab his sleeve to pull him aside. He looked down to see a big-eyed, dirty-cheeked little girl with black frizz for hair smiling up at him.

"You can come with me," she told him, pulling Stanley's hand. "My name is Ann Marie. That's my brother Pierre."

Stanley looked to where she pointed and saw Pierre follow Nuri in the crowd.

"I'm Stanley."

"*Bonjour.*"

"What's happening?"

"It's Christmas," she said plainly, as though that would explain the chaotic event. She pointed ahead where the noisy crowd was making its way to a large bonfire. "We all go there to eat and dance."

Stanley was not accustomed to such lively celebration, and the hectic environment made him uneasy. Touching elbows with others from the crowd, Stanley followed Ann Marie to the bonfire surrounded by logs used as seats. They found a place to sit and the girl motioned for Stanley to stay.

"I'll bring food," she told him and dashed away.

The people were eager and excited. Above the noise Stanley could hear singing and clapping, feet stomping, and even a guitar playing. Near the fire he saw Nuri in her long dress, pinning up ribbons to her hair in the shape of a flower, while Pierre tuned an old guitar with his ear to the strings. Having escaped his elderly captor, Mr. Miller managed to reach Stanley, who couldn't help smile at the sight of the frightened man.

"W-what was all that about?" the coachman cried.

"It's their Christmas celebration, I suppose."

Mr. Miller looked up at the darkening sky, which the sun had set ablaze in crimson. "I do hope they have turkey."

What Ann Marie brought back to them could not have been turkey, seeing its disagreeable appearance. It was also quite tasteless. Stanley managed to tolerate swallowing the meal, while Mr. Miller picked at it uncertainly. As soon as they were finished, their hosts were not slow to set down another plate on their laps. At least the second time around Stanley tasted ham.

Ann Marie, who couldn't be older than six, sat confidently on Stanley's lap when the event commenced. What had been a tumultuous din of voices slowly began to shape into singing accompanied by all sorts of instruments. The music was foreign but lively and harmonious. In the background, people clapped to a beat only they understood as bodies leapt up to move around the bonfire. Stanley realized that they were dancing, their movements choreographed by rules he did not recognize. It seemed more like a provocative competition than a dance. Women raised their arms high in the air, embracing the night and manipulating their movements with fervor. Men followed behind, faced the women, and moved their legs and feet in a complicated fashion. Drums beat, a *kanun* played, guitars strung their tune, and there was even a violin. Tongues clicked, hands clapped, bodies moved in pagan motions that captured Stanley's fascination.

Suddenly, Pierre took the stage, which was merely a wooden surface that faced the fire. He took a seat on a stool and began to play an intimate tune with quick fingers. Ann Marie bounced with excitement.

"*Flamenco*," she explained. "My cousin Nuri will dance."

"What is flamenco?" Stanley asked, but the young woman who took the stage next caught his attention.

Nuri had on a red dress with ruffles at the ends of the skirt and sleeves. A shawl draped over her shoulders, and her hair was pulled up in a bun adorned by a flower. She gazed intently into the fire and posed for her audience as another voice began to sing. Stanley immediately recognized Toma standing next to Pierre, the big man who had introduced Stanley to Nuri and her mother so long ago. His deep voice echoed as he dictated Nuri's movements. Her arms circled around her and her hands moved in elegant waves, rose up above her head; then her torso twisted dramatically while her legs followed in a flowing movement. The shoes she wore *clip-clopped* to the beat of the guitar, creating intricate rhythms. Like an enchanted snake, the girl slithered elegantly, moving the air around her, and stirred emotions in those whose attention she had captured. Her body was red smoke, intoxicating and invigorating, full of such grace and enchantment that Stanley realized he had been holding his breath.

The dance could not have lasted more than a few minutes, but when Nuri was replaced by other dancers, Stanley regretted to see her leave. Such a dance performed by as graceful a creature as she could not have come from this world. When he turned, he saw that Mr. Miller had been struck by the same vision.

More dances followed, encouraged by drinking and eating, and Mr. Miller was dragged onto the stage by the old woman who could easily be a hundred years old. Ann Marie jumped from Stanley's lap and pulled his sleeve impatiently.

"Dance with me!"

Stanley stuttered, "I'm afraid I don't know how."

But the girl would not be dissuaded. The people around the bonfire laughed when the two *payos* attempted to follow this curious dance, but they were surprisingly encouraging. Stanley blushed as he tried to move his legs and stomp his feet to a rhythm he could not follow, but laughed as he imagined how ridiculous he must look. Ann Marie twirled and bounced around him, squealing with delight.

❧

Soon enough Stanley was able to steal away from the chaotic dancing, and after declining several more offers of food, he managed to find a quiet place where he could overlook the lively celebration. Naomi stood at a distance, eyes downcast, lips pursed, but she smiled when Stanley approached her.

"Are you all right?"

The woman nodded, rubbing her arms. It reminded Stanley of Lena, who always made a similar gesture when uneasy or confused. Stanley missed her.

At last, the woman sighed. "You should not have come here, Mr. Becker."

"Please, call me Stanley."

"Your life is in danger."

"I know that, and I understand, but—"

"No. There's something you must know about our family."

Stanley held his tongue, sensing Naomi's hesitancy to share something she had never told a soul, which was somehow relevant to Stanley's well-being. The woman took a deep breath and stared ahead toward the bonfire where Nuri had once again taken the stage.

"Nuri's not our only daughter. We had another girl before her. She was only two when I last saw her. We called her Dione."

Stanley saw a gleam of sadness.

"From the moment she was born the old women knew she had a demon in her. We lived in Andalusia then, with other *Calé*—Gypsies."

"I had assumed you were Roma."

"Englishmen have never heard of *Calé*, so we refer to ourselves simply as Roma."

Stanley nodded when Naomi paused.

"In Andalusia, we spent months in isolation to restore the *kuntari*—the balance. After we were allowed to rejoin the clan, we noticed nothing out of the ordinary. She was a normal child. This was around the time when Mà de Fusta first came to our settlement and Nuri was born. That day, after Nuri's birth, Dione disappeared, and so did Mà de Fusta."

Stanley held his breath. "D-do you think—"

Naomi shook her head. "If he did, or did not, have something to do with her disappearance, I may never know. We found the man in a ditch three days later. His hand had been . . ." Naomi motioned to her own hand, wiggling her fingers.

"It was cut off?" Stanley asked. "How?"

"He never told anyone, and he claimed to never have seen Dione. I never saw my daughter again. They said it was because of Nuri that Dione went missing. They say that Nuri brings bad luck, because her demon was never cast out properly."

"A demon . . . ," Stanley muttered, uneasy at the word.

Naomi sighed. "Nuri, she . . . she's not right."

"In what way?"

"She sees and . . . hears things . . ." Naomi cast a look toward the stage where her daughter danced. "Very few people notice, but her eyes . . ."

Stanley nodded vigorously. "They change in color, don't they? I had thought I had imagined it."

Naomi regarded Stanley curiously and continued with a nod of her head.

"In any case, we could do nothing to get our daughter back, and there was the matter about Nuri's condition. Even now the old women say her bad luck is not allowed in the camp. We stay with the clan, but in isolation, mostly. Years ago, Louis made an agreement with Mà de Fusta to grant him a way to cross to the other world and find a cure for Nuri."

Stanley understood. "The Time Key in exchange for the water."

Naomi nodded. "That was the agreement, but that was never Louis's intention. We needed the water to cure Nuri. Although, I am afraid that the water is not the only thing Mà de Fusta has taken an interest in."

"You think he wants something with Nuri?"

"I have my suspicions, but I can't be certain. After Dione's disappearance, a woman called Sibyl came to see us. She assured us that she was safe. I don't know where she might be now, but I take comfort that Sibyl would watch after her. She did give us a word of caution: we had to stay away from Mà de Fusta."

"But Louis—"

"Yes, he broke the agreement, but it was done in desperation. The promise of a cure for Nuri's curse was too good to pass up. If you had children of your own, you would understand."

Stanley nodded. He would have done anything, walked to the ends of the earth, if it meant he could have saved his family's lives. One thing, however, he could not understand.

"What could Mà de Fusta want with Nuri?"

Naomi only shook her head. "I'm afraid I don't know. The world is out of balance. Things do not seem to make sense."

Stanley could only agree. Before he could reply, a commotion stirred up the crowd around the bonfire. Everyone faced the river, pointing to a thick darkness. Naomi took Stanley's hand and squeezed it, desperate fear in her eyes.

"You do not have to do this. You can leave and no one will know."

Stanley patted her arm reassuringly.

"I must do this, for you and your family."

Taking a deep breath, Stanley tried to arm himself with the courage he lacked, uncertain about the events that would follow.

XXIV

erry Christmas!" His voice echoed through the black night, sending waves of distrust through the crowd that had gathered by the river shore. "I heard dancing and thought I'd stop by for a visit."

Mà de Fusta was a lone figure on the opposite shore of the river. At the moment, Stanley could not sense the coldness that preceded the Lurkers. It surprised him that the bald man had come alone, without the protection of his shadows, but Stanley wasn't about to question it. As he elbowed his way through the crowd, Mà de Fusta's voice chilled his bones. He reached into his pocket where the cold pistol sat and waited.

Somewhere to his left, Stanley heard Toma's booming voice growl. "You're not welcomed here."

Mà de Fusta's figure shook slightly when he laughed. "I'm not here for you Gypsies. I've some pending business with someone among you. Perhaps you know him?"

Stanley breathed in deeply, puffed out the air, and braced himself. He stepped forward, breaking the silence that had followed Mà de Fusta's question. He gripped the pistol tightly in his coat pocket. He didn't expect for things to go badly, but one could never be sure. Before Stanley could speak, Nuri stumbled out of the crowd and stepped in front of him.

"He's one of us now! Whatever you have to say to him you say to all of us."

Stanley waited. He sensed the crowd behind them holding its breath. Mà de Fusta's piercing eyes drilled into Stanley. This was a delicate situation, and Stanley understood that Nuri was hoping to buy time, but he feared that Mà de Fusta would lose his patience. Stanley cleared his throat and wished his voice wouldn't tremble quite so much.

"They tell me you're a merchant."

Mà de Fusta crossed his arms. "And?"

"Then let's make a trade. I'll give you what you came for only when you deliver Louis Vargas safely back to his family."

In the dim light of the crowd's torches, Stanley could just make out Mà de Fusta's eyes watching him intently, as a cat would watch a mouse. Stanley hoped he had not made a mistake. Next to him, Nuri waited for Mà de Fusta's reaction. The crowd behind them was motionless. The hush dragged on, until at last Mà de Fusta shrugged his shoulders innocently.

"I daresay I don't know what you mean."

"Don't take us for dimwits!" Nuri snapped. "We know you took him hostage. We've been watching you."

At this, a greasy smile formed on Mà de Fusta's lips and Stanley knew that Nuri had gone too far.

"I know you have, my dear."

The night air dramatically dropped in temperature. A sort of fog drifted through the camp and slithered its way to Mà de Fusta. Under the light of the torches, Stanley saw the mist take on shapes behind the bald man and immediately knew the Lurkers had come. Five men materialized before their eyes, faces twisted up in terror, as five shadow men held them tightly with knives pressed to their throats. The only indication that they had been shadows just seconds ago was the black mist still clinging to their bodies like vapor. As the vision before them unfolded, the crowd gave startled screams, shocked to see the turn of events become so deadly.

With a voice full of loathing that hardly concealed his fear, Toma yelled, "Let them go!"

Next to Stanley, Nuri cursed. He grabbed her arm desperately.

"What do we do now?" he asked her, sounding harsher than he would have liked.

Nuri looked up in defeat. She had not expected for this to happen, and the hope of her father's freedom was bleak.

"I don't know."

"I hear they call you Stanley," Mà de Fusta said loudly, still grinning.

Stanley turned to face the bald man and, with gritted teeth, made his way to the river. He brought out the Time Key and held it tightly in his fist as he stepped into the icy water. Mà de Fusta nodded approvingly.

"That's it, now. You seem like the only sensible one from this lot."

The cold water numbed Stanley's skin when it reached his ankles. He held the Time Key for Mà de Fusta to see and nodded to the men.

"Let them go first."

Behind him, Stanley heard murmurs and agitated movements. Toma whispered commands to those around him, and slowly a line of men armed to the teeth emerged from the crowd to stand behind him. Stanley didn't take his eyes off the bald man, who took a step forward.

"The Time Key, if you please."

One of the men cried out in terror when the knife that was pressed to his neck pierced the skin. A few women in the crowd wailed. Stanley couldn't help that his arms shook. He was unable to will his feet to step closer to the man who could so easily take the lives of five innocent men. Somewhat indifferent, Mà de Fusta approached Stanley and snatched the Time Key from his fist, chuckling. Instantly, he felt empty. Stanley had never parted from the contraption since Louis had left it to him, and now it was in the hands of the man who was keeping him hostage. Stanley felt stripped down and helpless.

On his side of the river, Mà de Fusta worked the knobs impatiently. Looking back over his shoulder, Stanley saw the men at the ready for battle. Toma's face distorted in his rage.

"And the men?" Stanley asked.

Mà de Fusta didn't seem to hear him. His thick fingers pried open the little chamber where a vial filled with water had once been. Seeing the chamber was empty, Mà de Fusta's face turned a deep hue of red, as though he were suffocating. His eyes flashed when he looked at Stanley.

"You tried to deceive me."

Stanley opened his mouth to try to appease the situation, when the bald man gave a quick nod and the shadow men's knives struck. The five captives, throats cut, dropped lifeless on the ground. Stanley staggered back. Nuri, along with a dozen other women, screamed in shocked horror. The armed men, at Toma's gesture, charged with their own knives and daggers, pistols raised to fire at the shadow men, who were ready for the attack. Stanley, finding himself in the middle of the battle, did not know what to do. His fingers scrambled to find his own pistol. Mà de Fusta's fist struck his face.

"What have you done with it?" Mà de Fusta demanded, pulling Stanley above the water by the collar. He gripped the Time Key inches from Stanley's bloodied face. "Where are the Divine Tears?"

Stanley could not reach the pistol in his coat.

"I never had the vial!"

Mà de Fusta cursed, threw the Time Key in fury, and pushed Stanley under the water once again. He pressed down firmly on his shoulders. Stanley struggled, unable to free himself. He swallowed a mouthful of icy water. He tried to scratch, punch, grasp at anything that would let him free, but Mà de Fusta had a surprisingly iron hold on him.

While Stanley fought for his life, the battle around them was chaotic and bloody. It lasted no more than several minutes, but the struggle seemed to drag on for most of the night. As you may remember the shadow man telling Nuri about their diminishing strength, it was clear that their weakened state had an effect on the way the shadows behaved. They were limited to their human shape, unable to melt back into the shadows around them as a way of protection. The Roma used this to their advantage. Wounded shadow men refused to retreat while the Roma fought furiously.

In the chaos, Nuri found Mà de Fusta's figure determined to hold down Stanley in the water. Knife in hand, she pressed the blade to his neck.

She cried out as she struck.

Stanley felt the hands release him. He sat up, gasping desperately for air. He whipped his head and saw Mà de Fusta elbow Nuri's face. She fell to the ground. Mà de Fusta wrestled the knife from her hand, touched the bleeding cut on his neck with surprise, and then turned back to the girl. Stanley wasted no time to jump to his feet and tackle the bald man to the ground.

"The water was lost!" he said, landing punches of his own. "What more do you want from me?"

Shots rang out to Stanley's left. He looked up to see a man strike down with his knife, embedding it in a shadow man's chest. The creature fell and vanished in black mist. At Stanley's hesitation, Mà de Fusta hit his belly with a closed fist. Stanley buckled over. The bald man pushed him aside. His hard-soled boot pressed down on Stanley's chest.

"I have no quarrel with you," Mà de Fusta said. "But it does appear you breached our agreement with that little trick. The shadow-shifters know about you, and they know you protect a certain child. It would be most unfortunate if some accident were to befall her, now, wouldn't it?"

Stanley choked. The bald man smiled as he retreated toward the dispersing shadows. One of them grabbed Mà de Fusta in a protective gesture and vanished with him, leaving the field of wounded men. The Roma looked about them in confusion, seeing at least half a dozen men lying motionless, unable to believe that their lives had been taken so savagely.

In a daze, Stanley attempted to get up when someone grabbed his arm to stabilize him. Stanley looked up to see Mr. Miller, a deep gash above his left eye and a cut lower lip that grimaced painfully.

"You all right, Mr. Becker?"

"Tom, we must go home!"

"Right, sir."

To their left, Naomi crouched next to her daughter and held a rag to her bloodied nose. Nuri looked up, eyes filled with regret.

"I'm sorry, Mr. Becker."

Stanley knelt in front of her. "There's no need to apolo—"

Nuri grabbed his arm. "Sibyl will know what to do. Remember—one-hundred fifteen clicks."

Stanley didn't have the heart to tell her that he had lost the Time Key. He nodded and rose.

"Be careful," Naomi said, as he and Mr. Miller fled from the confusion and despair.

The two men ran as quickly as their shaking legs would allow, and Mr. Miller kept a strong grip around Stanley's arm in case he were to stumble. Stanley's determination carried him all the way back to the carriage, where they found two very vexed horses still strapped to the coach, snorting and pawing at the ground. Mr. Miller helped Stanley inside.

"I apologize for involving you, Tom," Stanley said. "This did not turn out the way we had hoped. You were right. It was a trap."

The coachman had nothing to say but placed a metal object inside Stanley's trembling hand. Stanley stared in disbelief at the Time Key.

"How did—"

"Snatched it up from the river. I was lucky to come upon it in the dark."

Mr. Miller closed the door and hopped onto his perch. He urged the horses to a fast run. Stanley held on inside the carriage, and marveled at the Time Key that he had been convinced had been lost. Nuri's voice echoed in his mind as he fumbled with the knobs in the dark. Held up to his ear, Stanley heard the Time Key's tiny clicks as he set it forward, counting each one.

Sibyl will know what to do . . .

Stanley had often wondered who she was and why she seemed to be so important to the Roma. He supposed he would find out soon enough. The only thing that mattered was to get home before the shadows found Lena.

❦

The sight of his house up in deadly flames wrenched at Stanley's heart. It was suddenly difficult to breathe. The back of the house, where the attic was located, was engulfed in crackling fire. A veil of black smoke rose from the house, yawning and stretching into the night sky. Mr. Miller stopped the horses at the gates and jumped down just as Mrs. Miller approached them, coughing convulsively into a handkerchief, and holding tightly onto a very cross Brutus.

"You're all right, Norah?" Mr. Miller asked, embracing her shaking body.

The housekeeper nodded. "I-I couldn't stop th' fire. I tried t' put it out in the attic, a-and I 'eard voices—Mr. Becker, dinnae go inside!"

The hot smoke burned Stanley's eyes the moment he entered the house. He breathed through his scarf as he squinted to make his way through the hallway. In the kitchen were the ruined platters of a dinner they would never eat. Stanley knew his way up the stairs to the attic, around the stored boxes and furniture, and reached the door to the Bird Room. It appeared that the fire had originated from the Bird Room and spread quickly, threatening to consume the entire house. Afraid of burning his hand on the metal doorknob, Stanley kicked at the door with all his might. After several tries, he succeeded to break inside.

It was a miracle he still had his pistol. Stanley held it at the ready. He walked into the room being devoured by flames. Stanley shielded his eyes from jumping sparks and fire reaching out to touch him. Struggling to breathe inside the terrifying inferno, he called Lena's name. Through the smoke he made out a black figure by the opposite window. Stanley pulled the trigger and shot at the vanishing mist.

192

"Lena!"

He didn't know where to look. The fire had disintegrated the vines on the ceiling, and most of the birdhouses had caught fire. Calling out the girl's name, Stanley pulled down the birdhouses he could reach and looked inside each one. A loose board cracked and fell next to him, engulfed in flames. Through the smoke he made out the vaelie's frozen figure peeking out from one of the birdhouses hanging in the air. She pressed her hands to her ears in both fright and pain. Stanley reached up to her.

"Lena, come with me! The shadows are gone!"

The girl managed to drop down onto his hand, and Stanley immediately left the Bird Room. Through the smoke, Stanley made his way downstairs. There, he found the air easier to inhale. Once outside, he staggered to the garden and fell on his knees, coughing and sweating in the cold night. Lena burrowed herself in his collar beneath the scarf, shaking and whimpering.

Stanley, understandably, had not noticed the three figures running up to him from the gates until they were nearly upon him, and was ready to fire the pistol again when he heard Gilmore's voice above the roaring flames behind them.

"Have you gone mad?" Gilmore demanded and grabbed Stanley's arm when he rose. "What were you doing in there?"

Stanley wheezed as he replied, "Lena."

"She was inside? Is she all right?" Gilmore asked, but when the Millers approached he dropped the subject. "What happened? I saw the fire from my house—"

Stanley grabbed Gilmore's collar rather harshly. "Take Tom and Norah with you," he said with urgency. "Don't go home. Tom will explain what happened."

Uneasy, Gilmore nodded. Stanley hoped he understood the gravity of the situation. Stanley stumbled toward the gates, ignoring Mr. and Mrs. Miller's questions. Ahead he saw a crowd gathering, curious neighbors with buckets of water. It would take a while for the firemen to come extinguish the fire, if there was anything left for them to save once they did arrive. Amongst the crowd, Stanley saw four shadowed figures watching him intently. He reached the carriage and jumped on Mr. Miller's perch. As he urged the horses forward, he saw Gilmore leading the Millers to his own carriage. Behind them, a dark-skinned man regarded the scene calmly, nodding to Stanley, who didn't look back once the horses began to run.

He was uncertain where to go, but he sensed the shadows pursuing after the carriage. He steered the horses toward the road to the Romani camp. Stanley whipped them to run faster, and all around them other carriages veered off to avoid a collision. Under the light of streetlamps, Stanley saw the shadows slithering like snakes. People cursed and yelled for him to slow down. Stanley couldn't shake the shadows. In reaching the desolate road, Stanley smelled smoke.

Lena coughed weakly and whimpered. Stanley could feel her body trembling against his neck. The shadow men's cold influence was palpable. A sudden explosion roared to their left, a tree was engulfed in flames, and Stanley heard the shadows shriek. Once again, behind them, the air crackled.

"Lena! Are you doing that?"

The girl poked her head out from the scarf. "I don't know—I can't help it!"

Gritting his teeth, Stanley saw that for the moment the shadow men were behind them. He saw no way out of this. They would continue to pursue, and Stanley had no hope of fighting them off alone.

"Lena!" he cried. "We can't shake them. I'm going to jump!"

"Jump?"

"Hold on to me!"

"A'right!"

Cupping a firm hand over the small bulge beneath his scarf, Stanley took a deep breath, and dropped down. Landing on his feet, he stumbled and fell on his back. The impact knocked the air from his lungs. He rolled for a few yards before he finally stopped. He gasped for breath. After a moment, he sat up and brought out the Time Key.

"Are you all right, Lena?"

"Y-yes."

Stanley saw the shadows take four human shapes, silhouetted by the scorching fire behind them. They approached him. He didn't see the dark-skinned man among them, but he couldn't be sure. With his thumb on the crown, Stanley did not allow himself to remember the dread that the future had brought him in the past. Instead, he thought of the person he had to find in order to save Louis and set things right.

As the black shapes came closer, Stanley tried to calm his breathing. He activated the contraption.

"Hang on, Lena!" he cried, just as the white light blinded their vision.

XXV

I have had the privilege of hearing Stanley retell his experiences in his own words, and while relating the events of the night that he traveled to the far-off future, he had hinted at his surprise to find that he had not materialized into reality as he had expected. Instead, the white light had remained as he drifted off weightlessly. He felt nothing. No pain, at least. There were no sounds, no smells, and no disturbances. Stanley said to me once that being in the presence of the Divine was like being cold in hot water, like sweating in a snowstorm, and although it felt like a dream, Stanley never doubted it was real. Now that I have recounted the events leading up to Stanley's journey to the future, allow me to return to his dream-like vision of the goddess.

He found that he was able to walk through the white mist. It felt soothingly moist against his skin. The air was clear and fresh, sifting down his throat and filling his lungs, and although the endless white mist seemed to go on forever, Stanley knew he was only waiting. For what, he did not know.

After what seemed like hours, there came a rumbling that shook Stanley to the core. He remembered the quaking from the future he had once visited and feared he had returned to it, but after a moment he sensed another presence in the mist.

A loud voice spoke, melodious and harsh, both soft like a whisper and deafening like thunder, but he recognized it belonged to a woman. When he turned, he saw her. From what Stanley could make out, the woman's tall elegance magnified her terrifying, numinous beauty. Her dark skin glistened as though it were made of diamonds. She wore a white robe and an intricate veil over her hair. Under furrowed brows, intense eyes full of rancor regarded Stanley with impatience. She had been speaking for a few seconds before Stanley finally understood her words.

"Restore the balance," her voice rumbled and echoed. "Oma and Asa must remain in separate harmony. Do you understand me, mortal?"

Stanley staggered back, shaking his head, which seemed to infuriate the woman.

"Restore the balance," she repeated before a white light swallowed her image and Stanley was deposited back into reality, where the cold night welcomed him with a strong wave of nausea.

The grass under his head pricked his neck in a most irritating way, but Stanley was busy recollecting the memories of the night. He remembered the fire, the race to escape the shadows, the jump, and the strange out-of-body experience with a woman giving commands that seemed more and more like a dream. Once he felt the sickness pass, Stanley touched the scarf around his neck and whispered to the silence.

"Lena, are you here?"

He didn't feel her against his neck. Stanley sat up and listened to the calm, beginning to panic. He could not believe that she had been left behind when they had traveled. She *must* be here. Calling Lena's name, he searched with squinting eyes in the darkness, hoping she was in the grass.

"I'm here!"

Her little voice came from the bare bushes near him, and Stanley breathed again. He crawled to where he could faintly see her figure perched on the branches.

"You wouldn't wake up, so I hid," she said in a hushed voice.

"Have I been asleep long?"

"Only a minute," she replied, hopping onto his hand. "I was watching the shadow-shifters."

Stanley swallowed. "They're here?"

Lena pointed ahead. "They look confused, but they haven't seen us."

Sure enough, four figures were stumbling around several yards away; some groaned in pain while others knelt to empty the contents of their stomachs. Stanley rose slowly and placed Lena on his shoulder. They had to get away before the shadows found them. Lena held on to his collar weakly. Up ahead, they could see lights moving.

"They see us!" Lena cried.

The four figures had noticed Stanley's retreat and gave chase, although they struggled to keep steady on their feet. Running as fast as his shaking legs would allow, Stanley headed for the moving lights.

The cold mist soaked them, and as he ran, Stanley could feel the shadows' icy breaths reaching for them. He anticipated the beasts to seize him from behind at any moment. Stanley stumbled. Lena cried out. He felt the paved road under him and looked toward the approaching lights. They moved at incredible speeds. Stanley froze in his tracks.

One of the shadow men was only feet away from him when a deafening *honk* preceded screeching tires and a vehicle collided with Stanley's pursuer. To Stanley's horror, the shadow man's body was thrown back like a rag doll, landing motionless on the street. Black mist emanated from him. Stanley ran to the other side of the road before any more vehicles came. The three remaining shadow men watched, still disoriented, but did not pursue.

As Stanley fled the scene, he heard a man climb out of the vehicle, yelling out enraged obscenities at no one in particular. More of the strange machines stopped in the middle of the road. True, Stanley had seen automobiles before, but never any quite like these. The sight of them terrified him.

He ran until his sides burned and it became difficult to breathe.

The cold night was dimly lit by lamps alongside the road. In the distance, Stanley could see the outline of several houses behind a wall of trees. Stanley followed the road toward the bright lights of the city ahead, keeping well away from the traveling vehicles zooming by at blurred speeds.

Lena tapped his neck.

"I don't sense them anymore," she said. "They're not here."

"What sort of place is this?" Stanley muttered, gasping, as he slowed to a walk.

"Stanley, where are we?"

Stanley sighed and answered, "In the future."

He continued on a brisk pace, comforted by the thought that each step took them further away from danger.

"How do you feel?" he asked Lena.

"Sick."

"It will pass, I promise."

"What do we do now?"

"I don't know."

It had been absurd of him to think that once in the future he would have no trouble finding this Sibyl woman, but for the moment he was determined to keep on trudging. Surely, he was bound to find someone he could ask for directions.

"Stanley?"

He snapped back from his thoughts. "Yes, love?"

"I'm sorry about your house."

"It wasn't your fault."

The girl didn't reply.

"Don't blame yourself, love. You were frightened. They . . . they could have taken you . . ." Stanley clenched his fists at the thought.

The streetlamp above his head flickered, revealing a sign with the name of the street, and Stanley was glad to recognize it.

"At least we're still home," he said.

"Why are we here?"

Stanley remembered that Lena knew nothing about the night in the Romani camp.

"We must find a woman named Sibyl," he explained. "The people I went to see back in the past mentioned her several times. They said she has answers to my questions."

"Do you know where to find her?"

"I don't have the slightest idea."

A few minutes passed, and still they saw only dark streets with bright lights that zoomed by. Stanley wondered if he had been right to travel to the future, when he saw a stray pair of lights shine on them as a vehicle slowed down and pulled up next to them. Stanley watched as the automobile stopped, and one of the windows magically rolled down to reveal a young woman. She studied Stanley curiously under furrowed brows.

"Need a lift?"

He took a cautious step back.

The girl leaned forward as she explained, "I was told I'd find you here. She said you'd need help."

Stanley held his breath. "Who?"

The girl's hazel eyes were doubtful. "They call her Sibyl."

⚬✖⚬

His hand gripped the armrest tightly, turning his knuckles white under the pressure. As much as he tried to appear unmoved, Stanley could not deny that he was deeply terrified. Never in his life had Stanley been in a horseless carriage that could travel at such unbelievable speeds, capable of blurring the scenery outside beyond recognition. It was with both fascination and unease that Stanley studied the interior of the vehicle as inconspicuously as possible. He was struck with wonder that this machine could have been invented and designed by man, but of course, anything could be possible 115 years in the future.

Lena had fallen asleep under the concealment of his scarf, and she shifted positions when Stanley leaned back restlessly in his seat. The young woman eyed him curiously as she reached forward to press a button on the dash. Immediately, a startling noise rang all around them. Stanley jumped. Lena stirred. The girl, whose identity still remained a mystery, turned a knob and the noise died down.

"Don't like rock?"

Stanley didn't know what she meant, but she wasn't expecting an answer. In her pause, Stanley studied her. It surprised him that despite the biting cold, this girl had more exposed skin than not, and her clothing was as foreign to Stanley as the vehicle they rode in. The girl, who must have been in her early twenties, had long light-brown hair that cascaded down in waves over bare shoulders. A colorfully knitted blouse draped loosely over her torso to rest on extremely short trousers. Stanley had never seen such provocative clothing exposed so unconcernedly in public. His cheeks blushed red when the girl noticed him staring.

"Where'd you come from, anyway?" she asked him indifferently. He was unsure of how to answer, and at his silence, she shrugged.

Stanley cleared his throat, feeling soothed by the warm interior of the vehicle. He wondered where the heat came from.

"Who is this Sibyl?" he asked. "How did she know I would be here?"

The girl looked ahead as she steered the vehicle around a curve. "She just knows things. I guess that's why they call her Sibyl."

Stanley nodded, though his question was far from answered. "What is the date?"

The look she shot him hinted that she was considering whether he was confused or simply an idiot.

"Christmas."

Stanley pressed on. "What year?"

"The same it's been all year—2012."

So it had worked, but hearing a native of this future confirm it made it all the more astounding. Blowing out the air from his cheeks, Stanley leaned back once again, suddenly weary.

"Were you in an accident or something? You smell like smoke. And . . . looks like your suit is ruined."

Stanley looked down at himself. He hadn't considered that people of the future would have developed a distinct sort of fashion over a hundred years later. It reminded him of Jane's wish that by 1897 women would have discarded dresses altogether, and seeing that this future was close to that expectation, he wondered whether it was considered more fashionable the fewer clothes one wore.

Finding the conversation at an end, the girl pushed the button on the dash once again and the dreadful noise boomed in Stanley's ears. Lena stirred against his neck. If this was music, Stanley could not believe it had strayed so far from the lovely melodies he was used to. Most importantly, he could not figure out where it was coming from.

"Mind if I stop at a gas station?" she said suddenly. "I'm starving! They gave us food in the airplane, but it's like eating crumbs."

At Stanley's confusion, the girl added, "I just flew in from LA."

Stanley nodded as though he understood.

"What's your name, anyway?"

"Stanley Becker."

The girl smiled politely. "I'm Rosie."

"Pleasure."

The reader may take notice of Stanley's ignorance about certain aspects of the future he is visiting, but for a man who was born into the nineteenth century this is understandable. I will do my best to refer to everyday things in the year 2012 as though they were common knowledge to the reader, assuming you are familiar with the culture of the twenty-first century.

In a few minutes, they had reached a filling station where Rosie stepped out to pay inside, leaving Stanley in the car. His mind struggled to take in all the miraculous innovations of the future. He studied the bright lights around him, captivated by this strange new world filled with enlightenment, in all senses of the word. Stanley found it strange to think that he was living in a time after his generation had been deceased for at least sixty years.

Clicking off the belt fastened around him, he whispered softly, "Lena?"

The girl groaned. "Where are we?"

"It's called *gas station*."

"What is it?"

"I'm not certain. I suppose it's where they fill the carriages with fuel."

She poked her head out from inside the scarf, took a deep breath, and climbed down his arm to perch on his hand.

"How do you feel?"

"Better," she replied in high spirits. "And the shadows?"

"I haven't seen them. Not after we left the road."

"Is that girl taking us to Sibyl?"

"So she claims."

At Lena's bidding, Stanley raised her up to the window. She pressed her hands to the cold glass, leaving tiny prints where she touched.

"It's all so bright . . . It looks like day!"

"It's incredible," Stanley added.

Lena paused for a moment and held her belly, letting out another groan.

"Are you hurt?" Stanley asked, inspecting her.

The girl shook her head. "I'm not dizzy anymore, but I feel . . . strange."

Nodding, Stanley smiled apologetically. "It's a side effect from traveling. You'll feel . . . *off* for quite some time. It might even worsen."

"But it doesn't bother you?" Lena asked bitterly.

"I'm used to it, love. I've practiced, but I can still feel it. Your body knows it doesn't belong. You'll slowly get accustomed."

Sighing, Lena rubbed her arm.

From the building that Rosie had entered, Stanley saw the girl emerge carrying a plastic bag, her bare legs chilled in the cold.

"Lena," Stanley whispered. "Time to hide."

"But I want to look!"

"I don't know how she'll react if she sees you."

Mumbling angry complaints that she was tired of riding in pockets, Lena obeyed and dropped inside Stanley's coat pocket just as Rosie reached the car. She fueled the vehicle before climbing back in and offered Stanley chips from the bag she had opened. He declined. Lena moved inside his pocket.

"We'll be there in a half hour," Rosie announced.

Stanley nodded and gripped the armrest tightly once the vehicle began to move. Rosie glanced at him and grinned with amusement.

"Does my driving make you nervous?"

He couldn't help it when he bit his lip. "I've never ridden in one of these."

"Really?" Rosie's eyebrows shot up. "Were you raised in a cave?"

"How fast does it travel?" he asked, looking out the window as the trees and houses blurred once again, melting together with the bright lights all around.

"We're going sixty."

Rosie noticed his confusion.

"Sixty miles an hour."

Stanley shuddered, having a difficult time comprehending how such a thing could be possible. Back home, the few times he'd seen the silly machines chugging through the streets, they had never come close to traveling at such speed. Rosie suddenly laughed and took her eyes off the road to see his reaction.

"Where did you come from, really? It almost looks like you should be wearing a top hat or something."

Stanley didn't answer.

"Why were you walking in the dark on the side of the road?"

"I was lost."

"Being lost is not your only problem." She gave his clothes one last look.

Clearly the girl had no idea he was from the past, and Stanley wasn't about to explain it to her. He kept his answers as simple as possible.

"I came here to look for Sibyl, only I didn't know where to begin. I'm quite fortunate you found me."

Rosie nodded, giving a shrug. "The plane had just landed when she called me, which surprised me because she doesn't use phones. Anyway, she knew exactly where to find you. That's my grandmother. She just seems to know things."

Stanley felt relieved that if Sibyl had known he was coming, then she would probably know how to help him and Lena. Things would work out after all.

"What do you want with Sibyl?"

"I was told she could answer some questions."

"She probably can."

Stanley nodded, and after a long pause, licked his lips uneasily.

"What's a plane?"

Rosie shot him a surprised look. "Seriously?"

Stanley cursed in his mind. He was drawing unwanted attention to himself.

"You know," she replied slowly. "Airplane, public transport . . . You fly from one place to the other."

Flashes of flying machines, leaving fiery trails behind, that had destroyed London ran through Stanley's head as he remembered his visit to 1940. Perhaps, according to Rosie's claim, they had been more than death machines. Man had at last conquered the skies, and Stanley was alive to see it. He wondered what other milestones the future generations had achieved.

Rosie mumbled, slightly annoyed. "Never heard of planes, never ridden in a car . . . Where have you been the last hundred years?"

Stanley didn't answer. It wouldn't do any good to try to explain where he had come from. If the girl didn't know, she would not believe him. He could not afford to jeopardize his only way of finding Sibyl.

They had reached a place where little homes, identical to one another, appeared old and worn, joined together row after long row. The streetlights shimmered and the fog thickened. Stanley saw various houses adorned by brightly colored lights, conveying that in this future the celebration of Christmas continued, festive traditions brought on by his own time and developed by the following generations.

"Where are we?"

"Kingston."

Stanley felt the vehicle slow down until it stopped in front of an old house with chipped paint and broken shutters. Colorful lights blinked and glimmered to outline the house as a show of celebration. Even the leafless tree outside was covered in red and green lights. It was a humble home that looked welcoming.

Rosie shut off the engine and, without a glance, stepped out of the car.

"This is it."

Stanley wasn't all too quick to follow. At the back of the vehicle, Rosie opened the trunk. She unloaded a single suitcase and strapped a guitar over her shoulder. With a wave of her hand, which Stanley took as a command to follow her, the girl walked up to the house just as the front door swung open. A little girl, perhaps eight or nine in age, ran to Rosie.

"Good to see you, too, Daisy," Rosie said, embracing the girl warmly. She took the little girl's hand to lead her inside, where a woman welcomed them. Stanley walked behind them several steps in delay, unable to hide his uneasiness. The woman at the doorway hugged Rosie and cast Stanley a curious look. Oddly enough, there was something about the woman that Stanley recognized. He supposed it was the familiar way that the woman ran her hands tenderly over her rounded belly. Stanley remembered Jane making a similar gesture.

"Whose car is that?" the woman asked Rosie, who answered something unintelligible.

Next to him, Stanley noticed the little girl had reached his side and was pulling his sleeve.

"Are you here to see Gram?" the girl asked. Her round eyes sparkled.

Stanley nodded, feeling out of place as he studied the girl. Her white dress contrasted her dark skin, and wild ruffles of hair fell over her smiling face. The little girl stuck a lollipop in her mouth when she grabbed his hand and pulled him along. Stanley was hesitant to go inside. The pregnant woman held the door open.

Inside, Stanley was comforted by the warmth and taken aback by the sudden sounds and visions in the room. A boy sat on a worn couch, eyes glued to an object in his hands. A long wire attached to it was connected to the boy's ears. Across the room, a box-type object emitted a horrible noise. Lights flashed from it, intense and nauseating. Stanley glanced at the box, but turned away immediately. He didn't feel ready to face any more inventions of the future.

The little girl let go of his hand to sit on the couch, and the pregnant woman led him to another room. From the kitchen, a tall man, dark-skinned like the little girl and boy, stood at the arched walkway and nodded to Stanley. Feeling rather uncomfortable by the strangers, Stanley nodded politely and looked away.

They walked through a narrow hallway decorated by photographs. He took a moment to inspect them closely, surprised to see such clarity and brightness in their colors as he had never imagined outside a canvas painting. They continued past two bedrooms. At the end of the hallway they reached a room where a beaded curtain replaced a door.

The pregnant woman continued to study Stanley as she asked to take his coat.

"That's quite all right, madam. Thank you."

The woman nodded. "Sibyl's been expecting you."

Exhaling deeply, Stanley thanked her again and moved the curtain aside as he stepped through. His steps resounded in the expectant silence.

XXVI

All the events and experiences that Stanley Becker had struggled through had led him to this precise moment; a dimly lit room in the future, a place that seemed as though it were a different country altogether, and the life he had been thrown into suddenly seemed to culminate at each step he took through that dark room. At his feet were scattered sheets of paper, marked books with broken spines, embellished vases and pots acting as pedestals for more and more books. Along the walls hung rugs with stitched designs, woven blankets with curious patterns, clay trinkets stacked on towers of books that nearly touched the ceiling. Statuettes from foreign cultures watched him with fixed, lifeless eyes.

Stanley couldn't restrain himself. His hand stroked the spines of the books nearest him as he recognized several titles and authors. From the classics he found Plato's philosophies and Homer's epic poems. On the next column he was not surprised to find Thoreau, Emerson, and Darwin, and was quite pleased to see Hugo, Doyle, Verne, and even Wells himself. Stanley patted *The Time Machine*, remembering the time in which the book had been written, the time he had left, and wondered whether Mr. Wells could have seen that the improbability of time travel was actually possible. Continuing on, he wondered about the other writers that would leave, and had left, a mark on this world to last the centuries. Names such as Orwell, Fitzgerald, Tolkien, and Rowling meant nothing to Stanley, but he wondered what sort of voice they had left in this century.

In his pocket, Lena stirred. Stanley remembered what he had come here to do. He walked past the columns of books and around oddly placed furniture, in search of the woman they called Sibyl.

"I am a lover of good books, as you can see," a voice said, soft and smooth, like a bubbling brook. "I can't read them now, but I keep collecting."

Stanley at last found a figure in a rocking chair next to a window, staring fixedly ahead. The woman's long hair rained down over her shoulders, splashed with silver strands. Her hand stroked a ginger cat on her lap whose yellow eyes watched Stanley with intent. Stanley remained a few steps back.

"Come, sit with me," the woman said, motioning to a chair that faced her.

As he walked past her, Stanley studied the woman. Her eyes were glazed and staring, and he realized that they saw nothing. Her smile was comforting.

"Thank you," Stanley said, removing his overcoat slowly as he took a seat. Lena peeked out briefly. "You must be Sibyl."

"And you must be Stanley Becker."

Stanley stuttered, "I am."

The woman's smile remained. "You've traveled a long way from home, Stanley. And I see you've brought a friend with you as well."

Taken aback, Stanley hesitated. The old woman's smile was filled with delight.

"How—what do you mean?"

"Like the Time Key you carry, I can sense very powerful energies, Stanley Becker. Despite my lack of sight, I can see certain things even if they're hidden. Although it has been quite a long time since I've sensed the presence of a vaelie."

Lena peered from the pocket again, red faced and timid. It seemed pointless to remain in hiding. Stanley nodded to her that it would be all right to come out. Wary of the cat, the girl climbed out slowly. She sat on his palm and watched the woman attentively.

"How did you know we were coming?"

"I know quite a lot of things. That's why I'm called Sibyl."

Stanley was growing tired of that repeated response. "I was told you could help me, that you could answer my questions."

The woman nodded. "I may be able to, but there are more urgent matters at hand. The gods have shown me the imbalance of the world."

Her fingers tapped her lips pensively, and Stanley shuddered as he remembered the strange vision that had come to him before waking up in the future. Sibyl appeared to be gathering her thoughts, organizing them in her head before revealing anything to Stanley, who feared that whatever she was about to say would disclose information he was not yet ready to hear.

"There is something you must understand before I can answer your questions," the woman began, taking a deep breath. On her lap, the cat's watchful eyes did not blink. "Each day you will visit me, Stanley Becker, and I will explain things in a way that seem most natural to me. I will allow you to ask questions, but I cannot guarantee they will all be answered before your last visit. Do you understand?"

Swallowing, Stanley nodded.

"My eyes are not what they used to be, Stanley."

"Yes—my apologies."

Sibyl closed her eyes as though to ask for inspiration, shaping her lips into a solid line, and began the first story of many:

"At the beginning of the world Oma was created alongside Asa, Brother and Sister, to raise and nurture the many creations of the gods. However, Oma grew jealous of His Sister because the gods favored Asa for Her gentleness, for Her kindness. Oma rejected His Sister and the link between them was severed, cutting off any contact between them and the creations in their dominions. But Oma was never meant to be alone, so the gods sent a messenger, a Keeper of the Peace, to watch over Him and to act as mediator for the gods. She, the Keeper, was allowed to visit Oma and Asa. She was given the task to oversee the gods' creations within them. Despite her efforts, Oma grew increasingly obstinate and would have nothing to do with the gods. Asa was more understanding, yet Oma's reluctance remained and soon there was no contact between them, and therefore no balance."

When Sibyl paused, Stanley breathed for the first time, exchanging puzzled looks with Lena, who only shrugged.

"There has always been one Keeper, but the gods have decided now to bring forth two—twin souls, if you will. One to keep the traditions, and the other to bring about great change."

Stanley leaned forward. "Are you one of these twin souls?"

Chuckling, Sibyl shook her head. "Luckily, I'm not. But I have been chosen to teach one of them in the ways of the ancients."

"Are you a Keeper?"

"I am. I keep the traditions of the ancients. I remind all those that will hear the old stories handed down from generation to generation, same as the Keeper before me. I have seen the beginning of time, and what is to come. Now that I cannot see with these mortal eyes, I can see in dreams."

Stanley bit his lip. "Are you a time traveler?"

To his surprise, Sibyl raised her hand and shook her head. "Now is not the time."

"But—" Stanley struggled to comprehend. "What does this have to do with me?"

"Not everything is about you, Stanley Becker. Only, you always seem to be in the wrong place at the wrong time. But there is something about you that is very interesting. It appears that you've been chosen to play a part in all this."

The night he had spoken with Future Stanley came back to him, and Stanley shuddered as he remembered his words. He brought out the Time Key to study it. Perhaps there was a reason why Louis had left him the contraption.

"May I see that?"

Stanley handed it to Sibyl, whose blind eyes saw nothing as she fingered the Time Key tenderly.

"You've been through much already, Stanley Becker. And this is how you came here. I had not expected to see this contraption again, not so soon."

"You've seen it before?"

Sibyl's expression turned grave. "The man who used it before you," she asked, "is he well?"

Stanley shook his head and then remembered that she could not see him. "He's being held hostage, or was . . . He's one of the reasons that I'm here."

Handing the Time Key back to Stanley, Sibyl sighed. "Very interesting. And why are *you* here, my dear child?"

Lena jumped in surprise, looking back at Stanley as if he knew how to answer.

"Lena's searching for a way home," he replied. "In the meantime, she's staying with me."

"It's a beautiful name, Lena," Sibyl said, nodding. "I can imagine that you look like your mother Iana. But I have met Sen, and you are your father's daughter."

Lena gave a soft gasp. Stanley saw that her eyes were bright with moisture. As a protective habit, Stanley cuddled her in his hands.

"How do you know all that?" he asked.

But to Stanley's dismay, Sibyl shook her head and waved her hand dismissively. "That's all for tonight, Stanley Becker. Ann will see to it that you get some proper clothes and a place to sleep."

"But my clothes are fine—"

"If you're to stay here, you must blend in," she replied. "You stick out like a turkey in a gaggle."

"How long am I expected to stay?"

"Until your role here is finished."

When Sibyl waved once again, Stanley knew she would not answer any more questions. As he rose, he whispered to Lena, who was holding her arms tightly. She quickly nodded that she was all right and climbed back into his pocket. Stanley's mind spun as he went outside, where Ann waited with a small smile. She nodded for him to follow and took him to a little room across the hall. A dim lamp on a nightstand lit the room. On a modest bed was a bundle of clothes, a towel, and some peculiar shoes. The pregnant woman held the door open for him.

"You may stay here as long as you need to," she said, watching Stanley enter the room with visible unease. "Was Sibyl able to help you?"

"Not quite. I'm afraid I have more questions than before."

The woman smiled, patting the top of her belly. "Sometimes it appears that way. Soon enough you'll find the answers."

"Thank you for your kindness, madam . . ."

"Please, call me Ann," she replied. "You must be exhausted. There's a bathroom there. Please, make yourself at home. I'll have supper ready for you."

Before she left, the woman cast Stanley an odd look, as though she recognized him, or rather, thought she remembered him from a very long time ago.

❧

Stanley looked at himself in the mirror and sighed. He was not used to wearing sweats and a T-shirt, and he thought he looked worse off than the wretches of Whitechapel. He had washed his face and shaken the ash and soot from his hair, erasing the black traces of the night's events. The hollow of his eyes reminded Stanley of all that had happened and the importance of his mission here, but as much as he craved a good night's sleep, he could not will himself to settle down. His thoughts returned to the shadow men. Their sudden appearance in the future had shocked him. He realized that he knew very little about the range of their abilities, and he wondered how much time he had before they tracked him down.

And what of the people he had left behind in the past? Stanley feared for Nuri and Naomi, for the battleground he had fled. Surprisingly, he feared for Louis's well-being, at least for his family's sake. He hoped that Sibyl, despite her insistent secrecy, would tell him how to save the man. At least the shadow men had come with him to the future, leaving those he cared about safely back home. The thought gave him a little peace. However, he wondered how he could ensure Lena's and his own safety here.

When he returned to the bedroom, he saw Lena hugging her legs against her chest, with downcast eyes and clenched fists. She had not said a word since their meeting with Sibyl, and Stanley knew she was thinking about her parents, or at least, about her home.

"What's the matter?" he asked, kneeling in front of the nightstand where she sat, but the girl merely glanced his way. "Was she right about your parents?"

The girl sighed and nodded.

Stanley wished he knew how to help. He also knew he was treading in deep water by pursuing answers from a girl who could set fire to the air around her by the slightest change in mood.

"Why did you run away, Lena?"

The girl looked up suddenly, frowning. "I never said I did," she snapped.

"It was simply a guess."

Lena turned away from him, visibly discomposed. He knew she would say nothing. She would ignore his presence until she calmed herself down, and there was little he could do. But etiquette prevailed, and Stanley had the obligation to thank his hosts properly. He left the room, concerned for Lena, but knowing she would recover on her own.

Stanley felt odd walking down the dimly lit hallway of a futuristic house. The colorful portraits of the family watched from behind their glass frames, as alive as in reality. At the end of the hallway, he saw the girl, boy, and father sitting on the couch with their eyes glued to the loud box with flashing images. At the moment, it revealed two very animated talking fish. Stanley marveled at the moving pictures, wondering how it all worked.

In the kitchen, Ann was putting dishes away for the night. A clock on the wall above the dining table read nine-thirty. It had been one of the most agitated of Christmases that Stanley had ever had, to say the least, but it appeared that in this home it had been a peaceful one. Ann sighed, running a hand over her frizzy hair, slightly tamed by the bun on her head. Stanley realized that her bronze skin and black hair seemed familiar.

"Oh, Mr. Becker!" Ann said, smiling widely as soon as she noticed him. "Please, come sit down. Everyone, say hello to Mr. Becker!"

They all said hello with feigned enthusiasm, eyes glued to the colorful screen.

"Don't mind them," she said, clicking her tongue. "That's my husband Paul, our oldest is Andrew, and the little one's Daisy. You've already met Rosie. She's locked herself up."

"Good to meet you!" Paul called. Daisy bounced on his lap.

Stanley walked into the kitchen. "I only wanted to properly introduce myself," he began, "and to thank you for your hospitality."

Ann waved her hand dismissively. "You hungry, Mr. Becker?"

Stanley smelled the warm dinner that Ann set in front of him and dug in. He felt guilty that Lena would probably be as hungry as he.

"We just had Christmas dinner," Ann said.

Ann placed a basket of rolls and an icy glass of water in front of him as she sat down to finish crocheting a beanie with pink yarn. Stanley controlled the ravenous impulse to gobble down the meal.

"Gotta finish it before the little one gets here," Ann said. "Any day, now."

"Have a feeling it's a girl?"

Ann smiled. "I had a sonogram. I don't like surprises."

Clearly, Stanley didn't understand. "But no one can know for certain what they'll be. I thought my daughter would be a boy before she was born."

Ann, however, gave him a knowing look. "Our technology is quite sophisticated. You're not from our time, are you?"

Stanley hesitated, burying his fork in the potato salad.

"Sibyl doesn't receive many visitors from other times, but they do come once in a while. It's all right to tell us."

Sighing in relief and exhaustion, Stanley replied, "I left the year 1897."

Ann nodded, although she appeared slightly unsettled. "I should have guessed by the clothes. Terribly formal, you people."

"It doesn't surprise you?"

"My husband and I have seen a lot of things living with Sibyl. Our children don't know much. They think it's all fairytales."

"And Rosie—she doesn't know, either. Is she your daughter, as well?"

"My cousin, but she calls me aunt. She hasn't lived with Sibyl for a long time. She doesn't know the things we do." She shrugged, looking over her shoulder. "She's locked herself in her room again. Probably sleeping. Jet lag does that to you."

Stanley wouldn't know, but he nodded politely, glad that at least Ann was considerate enough to answer his questions.

"And Sibyl is your mother?"

"No, only the kids call her Gram," Ann replied. "She's a holy woman, so we do our best to care for her, especially now that she's lost her sight."

"The Roma from my time, they seemed to know her well. How is that possible?"

Unfortunately, Ann was not about to answer that question. Stanley was at another dead end. Somewhat uncomfortable, Ann rubbed a leather wristband she wore as though for reassurance.

"I apologize," Stanley said. "I did not mean—"

"It's all right. That's something only she can explain. It's a sacred matter."

Holding in a yawn, Stanley nodded. "I understand."

"You must be terribly exhausted, Mr. Becker," Ann said. "Why don't you get some rest? I'll have Paul pick out more clothes for you tomorrow."

At Stanley's attempt to help clean, Ann waved him off much like Mrs. Miller would. He retreated, waving goodnight to the TV watchers, who mumbled in response. Stanley glanced at the portraits once again. In his hand he held the roll of bread he had smuggled for Lena. Hearing music from the room to his left, he paused briefly. It was a slow tune, wistful and lovely, but it reminded him of the Roma—*Calé*, as Naomi had explained—and their exotic culture. A thought, brief but present, entered Stanley's mind; he wondered whether Rosie was a descendant of such magnificent people as them. Perhaps there was more to her than Stanley could perceive.

The guest room was quiet. Stanley closed the door behind him.

"Lena, I've brought dinner."

The girl had curled up on the nightstand in the folds of his scarf, breathing peacefully as she slept. Stanley set the roll next to her, turned off the lamp, and sighed. Exhaustion, mixed with traveling sickness, was beginning to weigh down on him, but his mind raced with the events of the night and the worry that he had brought the shadow men to the future. He hoped they would not find him here.

❧

Several hours later, Stanley bolted up in cold sweat from a disturbing nightmare. It was still vivid in his mind as he gasped for air. The pounding in his chest was painful, and he regarded the darkness in confusion. The yellow eyes, the black mist, and the coldness that they brought had all been a dream. Mà de Fusta had had his beefy hands around his neck as Stanley struggled underwater. When Stanley dried his wet forehead, he wondered if it had somehow been real.

He heard sniffing. He listened for a moment, holding his breath, and knew Lena was awake. Through the window behind him came a bit of light that revealed Lena's figure on the nightstand. She held onto her legs tightly, knees bent and shoulders shaking. She was rubbing her wet cheeks.

"Don't be afraid, Lena," Stanley whispered. "This is a strange place for me too."

Lena looked up at last and rose to come near Stanley. He offered his hand and she climbed on.

"Did you have a bad dream?" he asked, leaning back against one of the pillows. Every muscle in his body stiffened and ached. She cuddled against him for warmth, or perhaps comfort, but Stanley knew she craved affection.

"I miss them."

"Your mother and father?"

He saw her nod.

The night life outside was loud and agitated, and while they sat in silence they could hear cars honking, tires screeching, and sirens wailing in the distance. The future was a strange place indeed.

"It isn't fair of me to keep secrets from you," Lena said. "I suppose it's a'right to tell you."

"There's no need, Lena."

"I want to."

Stanley waited as the girl gathered her thoughts.

"I caused too many accidents, you know, with the fire. They said I was cursed. I was never this way, not before my mother's disappearance."

Stanley could see that this was upsetting for the girl, but she was controlling her emotions well, and at least for now he could not smell any smoke.

"No one knew what happened to her," she continued, "but it's not uncommon to be taken by the Tall Folk."

Stanley could not help feel slightly amused. "Is that what you call humans?"

Lena nodded. "My father left to find her. He was gone for a very long time. After three months, he still had not come back. I knew he would never stop looking until he found her, but I was left alone. I wanted to find her too, but he wouldn't let me go with him."

Her fists were tightly clenched, and Stanley remembered the few times he had seen the gesture at the mention of her father.

"The people of my village, they didn't want me. Not with the fire. So I left to find my family."

"But how did you get here?"

"I saw a man in the forest. He was holding your Time Key. He had found a way to cross to this world, but then I felt the shadows coming. The branch under me broke and I fell through. I woke up later in a bottle."

"It was Louis. But . . . how did he cross . . . ?"

Lena shrugged as she fingered the beaded strands in her hair. So Louis had been the reason that Lena and the shadow men were here after all. Their presence in this world had nothing to do with Stanley or his stories. How could he have created shadow men and vaelies, and somehow brought them to life? Lena's account meant that he had not, that they had always existed, and because of the Time Key their worlds had collided.

Lena noticed he was watching her and showed him the beads in her hair. He could hardly see them in the dark.

"It's to remember loved ones that are lost," she explained.

"Your parents?"

She shook her head. "One strand for my mother. Another one for the baby. It was still in my mother's belly."

Stanley noticed her tiny lip quivering.

"I'm so sorry, Lena," he said quietly.

Lena's newly disclosed background made Stanley's heart heavy, but he understood now. He deeply regretted what had happened to her and her family, but he was glad that she had come into his life. The man he had once been would have been doomed to continue through his miserable life, a worthless pistol in one hand and a half empty bottle of brandy in the other. If it hadn't been for Lena, he would have been lost to the mediocrity of his wretched state.

But despite the reawakened instincts and yearnings of fatherhood, present only through the miracle of Lena's appearance, he felt in his gut that their relationship, however precious it was to him, could not continue for much longer. Made clear from her story and her persistent sorrow, the girl missed her world, her home, and her family. Stanley knew that she did not belong here, as much as it pained him to think of it, and his resolve to help her find the way home only grew. He had had the privilege of knowing her, but this little child, such a delicate creature, must return to her world. Although she had brought joy and happiness into his life, the vaelie had to go home.

It was only a matter of time. They would wait for Sibyl's instructions, whenever she was ready to indulge them with the information they sought. By the looks of it, Stanley suspected it would be quite a while longer.

Outside, the streets continued their agitated night life, full of noise and distractions. Lena fell asleep in the concave shape of his hand, resting blissfully, trusting in Stanley's protection. He ran a tender finger over Lena's tiny arm, as though to soothe away the sadness that had befallen such a young child. She stirred, and Stanley placed her on the pillow next to him, using the scarf to cover her. He contemplated her in silence as the moonlight created odd hues on her straw-colored skin, cradling her in sleep. He understood the effort it had taken her to retell her story, entrusting Stanley with such painful memories, and he was glad to at last know about her past, about her family. He was grateful she was safe.

As he fell asleep, he pictured a village in the trees of a secluded and ancient forest. Lena was leading him along, but she was normal sized, or rather, he was a miniature Stanley. He heard singing and music. But there were towering shadows watching all around them.

XXVII

The reality that they were to remain in the future for an indefi-
nite amount of time had not registered fully until the next morning. Stanley awoke to a strange rumbling outside made by numerous
vehicles traveling the road near the house. The incertitude continued
to pester him as he rose, found more neatly folded clothes outside his
door, and retreated to the bathroom to rinse off the layers of filth and
soot that he had failed to wash off the night before. He regarded the
showerhead with fascination, soothed by the warm water that fell on
his bruised and sore body. Stanley had never been fortunate enough to
own a shower himself, partly due to his quickly diminishing wealth, but
deemed it a much desirable luxury. It relaxed him. But once out, staring
at his haggard and battered reflection, he remembered the harsh reality
that there was nothing more for him to do but wait for Sibyl to give him
further instructions all in her own time.

He hardly recognized himself. Who was this poor devil staring back
with hollow eyes, cut lips, and bruised cheekbones? The struggles during
the Christmas night of 1897 had left clear traces on him. He had seen
better days, certainly, and could use a shave. Inside a drawer he found a
razor, similar to the safety razors he knew of his own time, and figured
out quickly how to use it.

The sun was still in its early hours, but Stanley was far too anxious to consider going back to bed. Lena had not yet left the warm
embrace of sleep and Stanley did not want to interrupt her from the rest
she needed. The uncomfortable consequences of being in time would
wear on them, and Stanley worried it would affect the vaelie worse.

Wearing the jeans and long-sleeved shirt that were apparently Paul's, Stanley glanced once more at his refreshed image in the mirror, wondered if he would ever grow accustomed to twenty-first century fashion, and walked into the quiet corridor. From the kitchen drifted a pleasant aroma and the sounds of cooking. The table was set, and Stanley found Ann preparing breakfast with Paul at her heels. Ann greeted Stanley with a smile.

"Good morning, Mr. Becker. Care for some breakfast?"

"Please, call me Stanley," he replied.

Stanley accepted the plateful of crêpes eagerly, thanking her for the meal, and thanked Paul as well for lending him the clothes. He only nodded good-naturedly. Paul was a man of few words, whose manner of speaking had the hint of a foreign accent, but Stanley could not quite pinpoint its origin. His appearance and built reminded Stanley of the shadow man who had come to warn him on the Christmas Eve of 1897. There were obvious similarities. Paul's dark skin and facial features resembled those of an African man, but somehow appeared mixed, a race that Stanley was unfamiliar with.

Stanley did not have the time to think on it further when Daisy jumped up on the chair next to him. She stared fixedly into Stanley's eyes. "Mum told me where you came from," she said.

Stanley gave her an uneasy glance but smiled slightly.

"Is that so?"

Rosie suddenly walked into the kitchen, wearing nearly the same amount of clothing as the day before. Andrew followed.

"Where from?" Rosie asked, sitting across from Stanley.

Daisy stuck out her chin. "He's from the past."

Rosie snorted, and Stanley kept his attention on his plate.

"Of course," Rosie said. "That explains the clothes."

Stanley heard the same mockery that Rosie had shown him the night before but decided to remain quiet. Ann pointed her spatula at Rosie.

"Rosie, don't be rude!"

Rosie shrugged and picked up the guitar she had set down behind her and strummed the strings mindlessly. "I wasn't."

Stanley munched silently, unwilling to provoke any other theories about his clothes and the place he came from. Playing a slow tune, Rosie leaned back in her chair and hummed along.

"Whose car did you drive yesterday?" Paul asked her, setting down a new batch of crêpes.

"Fred's. He came earlier to get it back."

Paul grunted. "Stay away from that boy."

"I like Fred," Daisy put in.

"He's an idiot," Rosie replied. "Hey, Paul, what do you think of this new one?"

And then the dining room was filled with a simple but charming melody, cradled by Rosie's surprisingly gentle voice. It was sweetened with honey when she sang.

Stanley smiled, slowly easing into a more relaxed state in the midst of the family. Their welcoming presence gave Stanley a sense of warmth that he had only felt with Lena, a sense of belonging he had not expected. Suddenly, the future didn't seem so terrifying.

He wondered when he would be allowed to speak to Sibyl again, but Ann informed him that she was not quite ready to see him. At Stanley's disappointment, Rosie proposed to take him to the store to get decent clothes. Stanley consented, surprised by her offer. They were to leave in a few minutes, and Stanley was eager to see more of the future outside the walls of the house.

Back in the room, he placed a few strawberries on a napkin next to a cup filled with milk and whispered to Lena that he would return soon. Still asleep, the girl curled up tightly and grumbled drowsily. Stanley closed the door behind him, feeling his stomach flutter. Wearing Paul's coat, Stanley stepped out into the cold morning where Rosie and Andrew waited inside an old and rusty car. Inside the vehicle it was quite cramped. Stanley took the passenger seat, studying everything around him. In the back, Andrew's eyes were glued to the little object in his hands, but he looked up every so often to study Stanley without a word. After a few tries, Rosie managed to start the engine. They were off.

※

The days of the future seemed as lively as the nights, and although the sun was out and shining there were but a few people strolling about on Boxing Day. There were countless cars, however, all following complicated rules of the road in an orderly fashion. It was fascinating for Stanley to see how much Kingston had changed over the course of a hundred and fifteen years, all the magnificent inventions and commodities created to serve man. His awe must have been clear on his face when Rosie gave a muffled laugh.

"Been a while since you last got out?"

A few streets down, they came upon the market square where Stanley was relieved to see a few familiar sights; at least the monument at the center of the marketplace was intact, a memorial he had so often visited. After parking, they took to the streets. Stanley followed Rosie and Andrew through the crowds, unable to break his stare at the sight of so many people, all of different shapes, sizes, and attires. He was appalled to see many of them covered in markings and piercings, with dyed hair of various hues, but was strangely fascinated by the boldness of their appearance. Clothing also seemed to be as colorful, lively, and daring. It seemed to Stanley that each individual had a voice in the mass of the city, a statement to make, beauty to create, something he was quite unfamiliar with.

They passed various stores, all inviting and exquisitely welcoming. Stanley was glad to see the buildings reflect those he was familiar with. The future had preserved the past and built upon it, linking both in remembrance of its beginnings and the promise of progress.

Rosie appeared interested in a certain pub, where she opened the door and looked back at Andrew and Stanley.

"I'll catch up in a minute," Rosie instructed Andrew, who looked up from under his hood. "Get started on Ann's list and don't let *him* out of your sight."

The boy nodded, shrugging in his hood and glancing at Stanley with slight embarrassment, who was preoccupied in studying the mannequins behind the glass window of a shop.

"Where is she off to?" Stanley asked the boy, who continued ahead, hands stuffed in pockets.

"I dunno."

Stanley followed the boy, eyes wide with childlike thrill that was more than evident. He led them inside a store where he would find his mother's groceries.

I will try my best to sift through what would be common knowledge to the reader as Stanley and Andrew shop for everyday items and ingredients, and although it would be a fascinating occurrence to a man from the nineteenth century to walk through the endless aisles of food and cans and all sorts of items that a person might want or need, it would be a normal part of the reader's everyday life. Stanley could not believe there could be such a wide variety of products in one building, so many tons of boxes and bags storing more and more food. The smells and sights of various types of merchandise were enough to send his mind spinning, but he kept a close distance to Andrew in fear of getting lost in the mass of shoppers. At the bakery, he picked up a cream-filled cake and took a bite.

"You've got to pay for that, you know," Andrew said.

Stanley checked the price and thought it a barbaric cost for the treat, although he was quite taken with the taste. It reminded him of home. He grabbed for his wallet but regretted to find it missing. He then realized that he did not remember the last time he had seen it. Thankfully, Andrew assured him that he had enough to pay, even for new clothes. In that department, Stanley needed more assistance than he cared to admit, but soon enough they were at the register to pay for their items. The woman gave them their total.

"That's outrageous!" Stanley exclaimed.

Sighing, Andrew paid and, ignoring the stares shot at Stanley, led them back to the parked car.

Stanley had not considered the effect of inflation through the period of one hundred years, and he was shocked by the price of the common cost of living. While Stanley voiced his complaints, Andrew returned his attention to his earphones.

Past the current of people flowing against them, Stanley heard arguing ahead. He saw Rosie confronting a young man, who seemed to be begging her for something. Immediately, Stanley approached the pair and tried to appear less breakable than usual. When he reached them, the young man looked up and gave Stanley a measured look. Rosie rolled her eyes.

"*Good-bye*, Fred," she said. She pushed the boy back, who gave a lopsided grin.

"Is everything all right?" Stanley asked, scanning the young man with distrust.

The young man's nose turned up. "Who's this, your bodyguard?"

Rosie pulled Andrew's arm and waved for Stanley to follow. "We're leaving," she muttered.

Stanley retreated unwillingly, turning his back on Fred's mocking grin, and followed Rosie's quick strides back to the car.

"What were you doing with Fred?" Andrew asked.

"Nothing. He was just pestering me."

"Why are we running, then?"

Stanley caught sight of a man standing at a corner, face shadowed by the hood over his head, eyes staring intently. Stanley picked up his pace. It couldn't be. How could they be here, now? They reached the car in a matter of seconds, and Stanley felt fortunate that Rosie was as much in a hurry as he was. They sped off in tense silence. Stanley looked back through the window and was relieved to see that the man was gone. Sighing, he eased back in his seat.

"I don't know why you keep seeing him," Andrew said, stuffing his ears with the white plugs again. "Mum won't like it."

Rosie shrugged, rubbing her nose.

Stanley glanced back at Andrew, who was staring at his little box again.

"Is he hard of hearing?" he asked Rosie.

The girl laughed. "No! He's listening to music. Don't you know what an iPod is?"

Stanley nodded slowly.

"Never seen a plane, don't like music, never seen an iPod . . . Where are you *from*?"

Stanley evaded the question. "Who was that boy?"

"Just an ex who won't get the hint. Did you ever have one of those?"

"I was married," Stanley said hesitantly.

"Where is she now?"

He swallowed. "She's passed on."

Rosie's eyes widened.

"I'm sorry."

Stanley was surprised to find that it was not as painful, but it stung nonetheless. They drove in silence for a while longer before Rosie sighed again.

"I've never met my parents," she said, staring straight ahead. "Gram raised me. We lived in America for a while, until she moved back. Said she was needed here. I was fifteen, then, but I stayed and lived with a friend."

"Why not stay with your grandmother?"

"We don't see eye to eye on some things. I visit often, but I needed to start my own life without her dictating everything I did."

Stanley yawned involuntarily.

"Am I boring you?" she asked with a smile.

He reddened. "I had quite the restless night."

"I know what you mean. I have these dreams that keep me up all night."

Stanley nodded, feeling oddly relaxed.

Her hand pressed the button on the dash. "You don't like The Beatles, then . . . How about The Rolling Stones?"

∞

"Why did you leave me behind?" Lena demanded, stamping her foot obstinately the moment Stanley walked through the door. "You didn't even ask me to come along."

Stanley smiled apologetically. "I'm sorry, love. You were asleep."

"Where did you go?"

"To the marketplace," he replied. "Come. Sibyl wants to see us."

At last they had been granted an audience with Sibyl, and the moment he walked through the beaded curtain, Stanley was struck with the same sense of mystery and apprehension. He saw the woman's silhouette against the window, watching the outside with sightless eyes. There was an air of tranquility. At her sign, Stanley took a seat on the same chair and waited expectantly.

"I am tired," she said softly, petting the purring cat on her lap. "I have seen so much, Stanley Becker, and it is tiresome."

Stanley did not know what to reply.

"I will tell you the second story," she continued. "Take it as you may, but it is part of the history of our world and reality."

Lena trembled slightly as though she sensed a coming danger.

"In a time of turmoil the gods were envious of each other's powers and gifts; each has his or her own responsibility. One in particular rose up against the elder gods, meaning to take the highest of powers for his own. This god, because of his rebellious nature, was cast out to live among mortals. But he was not, could never be, one of them. He would always be rejected by mortality. He lived with the shadows of the night, which lurked among the most sinister parts of the country, preying on people's happiness, hopes, and dreams."

The back of Stanley's neck tingled. Sibyl's words became images in his head of shadows with yellow eyes.

"This god taught the shadows how to shift, how to use a person's soul to take on his shape. This way, they were able to hide among them. The people of that country call them shadow-shifters. They are controlled by the god that was cast out, whose only desire is to return to the Divine Realms and take his place among the highest of them."

Stanley waited, and when Sibyl did not appear to have anything more to say, he demanded, "That's all?"

Sibyl chuckled. "That's all I have for today, Stanley Becker."

"The Lurkers, the shadows—I have seen them, but how does it help—"

Sibyl's hand waved dismissively.

Mouth open and highly disappointed, Stanley obeyed like a rebuked child.

❧

They walked through Kingston marketplace that afternoon, which was only a short distance away from the family's house. Lena shivered against his neck, concealed under Stanley's scarf. He stopped in front of the memorial he knew so well. It had been built at least a decade before the time he had left. Stanley considered the long years that it had waited to see him again. Time was a strange phenomenon indeed.

"What do you think she wanted us to learn from that story, Lena?" Stanley wondered, feeling the exhaustive remains of a long stroll taken out of irritation.

"Maybe she wants to tell us to be wary of them."

Stanley sighed. "As if we didn't know it."

"What do we do, then?"

"We wait, I suppose. It may be much longer than I had expected."

Lena touched his neck with a cold hand. "Do you think she knows how to get me home?"

"Don't fret, Lena. We'll find a way."

Stanley turned back the way they had come, knowing that it wouldn't do any good to complain. Whatever Sibyl wanted them to learn, they would learn eventually, and the answers they needed would be revealed in her chosen time.

As Stanley walked through the bleak day, it occurred to him that the time he had left was temporarily in pause, and in returning to it, he would be able to continue where he had left it. However much time he needed to spend in the future should cause no impact on the past, at least, he suspected as much. His thoughts then turned to the generous family who had so willingly welcomed him into their home. He had had the privilege of conversing with Ann and Paul that morning and found them entirely delightful. Little Daisy was quite taken with him, and even Andrew's quiet presence was calming and comforting. Rosie was a different matter; there was an enchanting influence to her. Stanley knew that there was more to her than what was apparent, and he somehow wanted to see approval beneath her mask of scorn.

Stanley crossed the street at the signal and looked over his shoulder.

"Lena," he whispered. "Do you sense them?"

"Who?"

"The shadows."

The girl poked her head out briefly, but at the sight of other pedestrians traveling briskly past them, she kept herself hidden.

"I don't sense any," she said.

"I thought I saw one this morning."

"Do you think they know where we are?"

Stanley hoped not, but he took it as a good sign that Lena could not sense their presence. At least for the moment, he felt somewhat safe from their pursuers.

⌒∞⌒

The family was gathered in the main room, playing cards and conversing, when Stanley stepped into the warm house. Immediately, Daisy pulled his sleeve and sat him next to her. They all greeted Stanley warmly. He was surprised to see Sibyl sitting on her rocking chair next to the couch.

"We're playing *Go Fish*," Daisy explained, showing him the hand of cards she had. "I'm gonna win."

Stanley sat down slowly, feeling Lena against his neck. He hoped he wouldn't be asked to remove his coat.

"Have a nice walk?" Ann asked Stanley.

"Let's see what Mr. Becker thinks," Rosie interrupted. "We were trying to decide which musical band was the most influential in the twentieth century, and obviously it has to be The Beatles."

"And I said Michael Jackson," Ann remarked.

"*Band.*"

Paul turned to Andrew. "Give me all your threes."

227

"But think about it," Rosie continued. "Who changed the way we viewed our culture, the way we saw everything? They literally changed the world!"

"Go Fish!" Andrew blurted out.

"I really just like his music," Ann added, shrugging.

Paul stroked his chin. "I'd have to disagree," he said. "Bob Marley is irrefutably the most influential of the lot. To this day anyone would recognize any of his songs. Even Daisy knows *Three Little Birds*."

Next to Stanley, Daisy shrugged and whispered in his ear, "They always argue about the same thing."

"I like Queen," Andrew said, turning to Ann. "Give me all your fives."

Sibyl chuckled. "I'd have to agree with Andrew on that one."

Rosie stretched out her legs in an irritated way. "You can't say The Beatles didn't have a greater impact on the world than Queen."

"You forget, my dear. I lived through the seventies."

"He had a nice voice," Ann said good-naturedly. "It's so sad he died so young."

"Michael or Freddie?"

Stanley cleared his throat. "I'm afraid I'm not familiar with their music, although Rosie did show me The Stones . . ."

"The *Rolling* Stones," she corrected. "I'll have to show you what real music is before anyone else here does . . . Oh, and by the way, I got a new gig for tomorrow."

Ann clasped her hands. "Good for you, honey. Is that what you did this morning?"

Paul frowned. "Where?"

"An Irish pub. And don't worry, I won't stay long enough to get drunk."

"Can I come?" Daisy asked.

"No, honey," Ann replied. "It'll be past your bedtime."

"I'm going," Andrew said.

Rosie wrinkled her nose at him, as though she smelled something rotten. "I don't think . . ."

"I'd rather you take him than that boy," Paul said. "I never liked him."

Rosie rolled her eyes, but Stanley stopped listening when he felt Lena wiggle nervously against his neck. He excused himself as he rose.

"I left a plate for you on the table, Stanley," Ann called behind him. He thanked her.

The meal was still warm. Back in the room, Stanley helped Lena out, who was hot and angry. She calmed down at the sight of dinner, thankfully, but Stanley was busy recollecting the events of their first full day in the future. He felt the exhaustion of it weigh on him. His future still seemed excruciatingly uncertain, but he had no power over it at the moment.

❧

That night, Stanley stole out the back of the house to let Lena climb the few trees surrounding the house and leap about to her heart's content. He watched the night in silence, although his surroundings were anything but. Despite the marvels of the future, Stanley missed the calm of the past.

"Needed a breather?"

Stanley turned to see Rosie step out in a large sweater and slippers, rubbing her hands from the cold. She stood by him and stared at the bright night, breathing in the fresh air.

"What do you want from Sibyl?" she wondered. "What has she got to say?"

Stanley did not meet her gaze. "I've questions about my past."

"She always talks about the past like you can just go there," she remarked, slightly cross. "It's frustrating . . . And she wants me to move back here. I'm twenty-one! I visit all the time, but . . . got to start my own life."

Stanley was unsure why she was telling him this, but he supposed that she was in need of some sort of attention, or at least someone who would listen.

"What do you want to do?" he asked.

"Sing, write songs . . ." She sighed and leaned her elbows on the rail. "I perform all the time, but I just need one big break."

Stanley nodded. "Your song was beautiful."

"They're nothing special. But I have a decent voice."

They stood in silence for a long minute, and Stanley worried that Lena had gotten lost in the trees.

"What do you do?" Rosie asked, turning to face him.

"I'm a writer."

"What do you write?"

"Children's stories, although I make a living writing for a magazine."

Rosie nodded. "Does it make good money?"

Stanley smiled. It made enough to live from day to day, although he was fortunate to live in a house that his own grandfather had built. In addition, the money Jane had made from selling paintings to her parents' wealthy friends had kept him comfortable for six years. But he was a humble writer, and he was fortunate to have what he did.

"I'd like to travel, you know," she said. "Meet people. See places. There has to be something more than all this."

From the corner of his eye, Stanley watched the girl. He found her voice soothing when it wasn't filled with scorn. He liked the way her full lips shaped to form a smile.

"It's almost as if the world is full of stories," she continued. "Everyone's got one. I'd like to see all of them."

Stanley looked up at the night sky. "Some may be more incredible than others," he replied.

Rosie turned her head to study him. "What's your story?"

He didn't answer and soon she went inside. Stanley pondered her words, all that he now knew about her, and realized that something about Rosie's story seemed so very familiar.

XXVIII

Things were not heading the direction in which Stanley had hoped, and although he continued to find the future fascinating, his impatience with Sibyl and her stories caused him to dread each visit with the woman. On their second morning in the future, however, Sibyl called for them to make another piece of the puzzle clear. Sitting on the same chair, Stanley waited for Sibyl to gather her thoughts.

"It's important," she began, "what I am about to tell you, Stanley Becker."

Lena made herself comfortable perched on Stanley's shoulder and trembled with eagerness. She loved to hear Sibyl's stories.

"Sibyl has been around since the beginning, and has passed down all her wisdom to the next chosen of the goddess. There have only been three for all time, you see, and now Sibyl is preparing for the next one."

Stanley nodded slowly and muttered a question when Sibyl paused: "What is Sibyl's responsibility?"

At this Sibyl smiled. "To keep the traditions, to watch over the people of the goddess. For this purpose can she travel through time as though it were a sphere, not a timeline, as tangible and reachable as the ground beneath our feet."

"I knew it," Stanley said.

"Sibyl sees time as a whole. She can touch it, she observes it, and she travels to whichever age she is needed. Sibyl has seen many things. She is able to see crucial stirrings in time and space through dreams, and can travel as an observer. She can make no impact on society that would cause an imbalance. She is not allowed to, but at times a change is necessary. It is her duty, above all, to keep the balance."

"She can travel through time like you," Lena whispered excitedly.

Stanley nodded. "That's how the Roma know you. You travel back to see them."

"When I was able to travel on my own, I would visit quite often."

"How does it work? Do you have a Time Key as well?"

"It is a gift granted by the gods, built into my being, and triggered by mere will. Before I knew I was Sibyl, any emotion strong enough could provoke it, whether by intense fear or anger or even joy."

Stanley nodded, seeing that Sibyl's power and Lena's influence over fire were quite similar.

"And to my home," Lena asked. "Can you travel there?"

"When I was young, I was able to cross worlds much easier."

"Do you know how—?"

Sibyl's hand shushed Stanley, and the discussion was over.

✖

Despite the unrelenting effects of being in time, life continued somewhat normally for Stanley and Lena, who were both flustered, yet captivated, by the foreign world they had entered, and even more so by the family that had so kindly welcomed Stanley to their home.

Ann and Paul Taylor were open about their life and seemed willing to answer nearly all of Stanley's questions, but made certain to avoid the subject about their residence with Sibyl and even some matters about their past. When Stanley asked Ann about Paul's slight accent and manner of speaking, she only said he was a foreigner, like her, who had lived in many different countries therefore muddling his speech. Her claim that Andrew and Daisy had been born in England seemed sincere, which explained why they spoke like any regular native, but it left out Ann's and Paul's origins. Ann allegedly had no relation to Sibyl other than as caretaker, but she was Rosie's cousin, and Rosie believed Sibyl was her grandmother. The vague description of the Taylor family tree concerned Stanley; he was unsure whether the branches that grew from it were real and tangible, or merely concealed a distinct truth.

Stanley regretted to keep Lena's existence a secret from their generous hosts. The girl was mostly confined to the guest bedroom, partly as an obvious precaution, but Stanley feared Sibyl's cat. On several occasions, he had found the animal lurking about the hallway, watching Stanley's door with vigilant eyes. Ann assured him that she was a very friendly cat, but Stanley did not trust its intentions. To give Lena the freedom that she yearned, when she wasn't deep in slumber purely from exhaustion, Stanley took the girl on a few long walks each day to nearby parks where she could climb up the tallest trees, leap from branch to branch in careless tranquility as Stanley watched in enchanted silence. On these long walks he would occasionally open the Time Key, ignoring the time traveling functions, and search for foreign energies detected by the longest hand. Besides Lena, the Time Key found no other sources of a similar energy.

Equally confusing, Stanley found, was Rosie's constantly changing attitudes regarding him, which varied from oblivious to his presence to mocking. However, at the end of the day, when Stanley isolated himself in search of a little calm, she would talk to him in an almost tender manner. Stanley could not deny that she was a striking girl and that a part of him felt an attraction, but he suspected that whether her intentions were lustful or otherwise, the girl had no desire to pursue a courtship with him. Stanley was unsure how such matters worked in the twenty-first century, but he could not ignore the obvious gap between their ages. It was not uncommon in the culture that he knew for older men to marry much younger women, but Stanley had always detested the idea. Being fifteen years her senior, Stanley was uncomfortable with the thought of stirring romantic sentiments between them. Frankly, he was still wounded from the past he had visited so often in his own century, and continued to mourn those he had lost.

After a very disappointing meeting with Sibyl, Stanley received an invitation from Rosie to see her gig. Stanley, unfamiliar with the word, supposed she wasn't referring to a horse-drawn carriage, but remembered her mentioning a performance at an Irish pub. As agreed, Andrew came as well, his white earphones plugged in place. Rosie wore a simple orange dress and her guitar strapped to her back. Daisy waved good-bye to them at her mother's side, who called for them to be careful and to come back as soon as it was over. Paul was absent that night, having had to take the night shift at his work. The three drove off into the darkening night, anxious and quiet.

Stanley stiffened in his seat whenever Lena fidgeted beneath his scarf. He wished he could somehow communicate to her that her movements had provoked an irritating itch. Stanley had not been able to dissuade her from coming along; her stubbornness subdued Stanley's logic. He had tried to explain that it would be very crowded and it wouldn't be safe for her, to which she promised to remain hidden. Stanley had then expressed his fear that the discovery of her existence could cause quite a stir, and she quickly retorted that she was not afraid of anything and he would not have to worry because she would stay hidden. Now, riding in the passenger seat, Stanley was unable to relax.

They soon reached their destination, and Stanley met Rosie's gaze.

"Don't be nervous," he told her. "You're brilliant."

Her small smile was grateful. "I'm not. I just . . . I don't want to see Fred here. Not tonight."

"He won't trouble you. I'll see to it that he doesn't."

Rosie's eyes scanned him, as if measuring Stanley's physical potential, and her expression suggested clear doubts. She appreciated the encouragement nonetheless. At the pub, a crowd had queued up to the entrance and Rosie led them to the front where they were immediately allowed inside.

The twenty-first century pub was unlike the taverns Stanley was used to, although it served a similar purpose. There was a relaxed feel to the place, with dimmed lights and warm air. Customers laughed, ate, and drank, having shed any and all problems at the door. To his surprise, there were several families sitting on the tables nearest the stage where a lively band played their music. Perhaps his current sobriety caused Stanley to consider that pubs could serve a higher purpose than merely to tolerate miserable souls like him.

Rosie was called to a back room and, without a glance, left them. Stanley took a seat next to Andrew on an elevated table that overlooked the interior of the pub. Patiently waiting on the tall stool, Stanley ran his eyes over the lively room.

"Have you never been to a pub before?" the boy asked.

Stanley could not tear his eyes away from the multicolored lights above his head.

"Never one quite like this."

Andrew sank back into his regular silence and Stanley tried to keep some composure as Lena squirmed against his neck. Unable to contain his calm, he spotted a restroom and sped off through the crowd. He made sure that the stalls were free of occupants before he removed the scarf from his neck. Lena's wild locks framed an annoyed look.

"You really must stop wiggling," Stanley said as the girl dropped down on his hand. "It's quite irritating."

"But I want to see."

Stanley scratched his neck. "You can see from my pocket."

"I hate it there," she said, folding her arms. "How much longer?"

Before Stanley could answer, the restroom door opened suddenly. In a flurry he slipped Lena into his coat pocket, dropped his head, and stole back out where another group of young men had taken the corner stage. He knew Lena would be angry, which he would have to hear about later, but his fear of someone seeing her exceeded the dread of a reprimand. Andrew had not taken notice of his absence, but had not wasted any time to order food for both of them. Suddenly Stanley felt very hungry. He dug in ravenously.

"When will Rosie perform?"

Staring at the screen on his device, Andrew shrugged. People continued to stream in and out of the pub while performers took the stage. Stanley began to relax, although he felt Lena joggle in the pocket. He slipped a fried chip into it, which she accepted eagerly.

Andrew looked up from his iPod and stared ahead past Stanley. A suspicious wrinkle formed between his eyebrows. Following his gaze, Stanley saw a familiar face emerge from a group of gathered youths. It was Fred with a grin on his conman face. Stanley was about to rise when he saw Andrew had already made his way to the group. Before Stanley could call after him, he heard the interval between music pieces had been broken by a familiar voice.

Rosie's striking image seemed to glow under the dim lights of the pub while her voice flowed through the room in a most breathtaking way. At least for Stanley, her presence was hypnotizing. Her fingers skillfully strummed the guitar with a delicate touch, accentuating the chords to contrast her voice. Stanley could not look away from the ethereal vision of a girl and her guitar.

Few in the audience seemed equally surprised by the influence of her performance, but they were quick to look away and attend to their own matters. Stanley wondered how they could not hold their breath for her, have their hearts stop beating between intervals and speed up at each change of tone, how the mere sight of her could not awaken a craving for more. Her lovely song was done, and the girl scanned her audience with a look of irritation. A few hands clapped when she rose, but Stanley saw a sudden gleam of determination in her eyes. He held his breath the moment Rosie cleared her throat loudly. Using her chair as a footstool, she rested the guitar on her thigh, and her fingers began to strum in a lightning fast speed.

The sound that she created reminded Stanley of Pierre in the Romani camp of 1897, whose music had accompanied Nuri's petite figure as she danced around the fire, and although her song was different to those of the *Calé*, Stanley was struck with a similar sensation of mystery and exotic thrill. This caught the crowd's attention, turning heads among the seated customers, which made Rosie's pursed lips turn up slightly at the corners. This intricate tune she accompanied with a simple rhyme, quick and with beautiful imagery. Her enchanting voice caught those who were within hearing range. It made Stanley smile to see her win over her audience. In minutes, she was done. A roar of applause and cheers followed her performance, and Rosie nodded politely before retreating to the back room. Stanley felt oddly proud of the girl and clapped enthusiastically.

Stanley felt Lena's movements become agitated and he lowered his hand into his pocket. He cried out, causing a few heads to turn. He drew his hand back in more surprise than pain. She had bit him!

Stanley snaked through to the exit and stumbled into the cold night where the streets, thankfully, were empty. He brought Lena out to demand an explanation. Her cheeks were bright red with bile.

"You bit my finger!"

"It's too loud!"

"I told you to stay, Lena."

"I always stay behind!"

"I know, love, and I'm sorry but—"

"Who are you talking to?"

Stanley stiffened. Andrew stood behind him, watching Stanley with distrust. Lena quickly hid inside his pocket again, but Stanley had no reply and stuttered like a boy caught red-handed. Andrew did not take his eyes off him even when Rosie burst through the door and slipped between them in a hurry. Fred called from the door. Stanley followed, hoping the boy would forget the incident.

"What's the matter?" Stanley asked Rosie, whose steps had quickened. "Did that boy—"

"It's fine," she said. "I'm ready to go home."

"You were amazing—"

"Thanks."

In the car, Andrew's eyes would not leave Stanley, whose attention was on Rosie. Lena made no movements in his pocket. They drove off in the same silence that they had come, although Stanley had his mind set on an explanation.

Seeing his attention was on her, Rosie rolled her eyes. "So he came to see me, okay?" she said. "I didn't let him talk to me, but he likes the chase . . ."

"You needn't be afraid of him."

"I'm not afraid of him," she replied. "He annoys me, but I . . . I sort of like the attention."

Stanley didn't understand, but Andrew gave a sigh and remarked, "That's why she's the weird one."

Rosie laughed and the ice weighing on them broke. After a moment, she asked, "Have you not had a girlfriend since your wife?"

Stanley was startled by the question, but he smiled and shook his head.

"It's all right to love, you know. We all need to feel loved."

Stanley leaned back thoughtfully and watched the racing scenery on the other side of the glass. Rosie asked Andrew why he had confronted Fred and if he had lost his mind. Inside his pocket, Lena hugged Stanley's finger and rested her head against it sleepily. With the boy's curious stare fixed on Stanley, they returned home.

That night Stanley lay wide awake, listening to Lena's nearly silent breathing next to him, and feeling a familiar yearning in his chest. He saw Jane on the dark ceiling above him, but he reminded himself that he had already said good-bye.

That it was all right to love.

XXIX

You may have wondered about Stanley and Lena's pursuers, so I regrettably must take your attention to a dark place, an incident which I have visited often, that has brought much despair. They had been waiting for days, disoriented and weakened by the journey they had taken. This world, to them, was exhausting, draining their energies, and they could not shift their shape as effectively as they once could. The influence of Asa was leaving them, and unless they stole fresh energy—however far from satisfying these mortal souls were—they risked withering up in their own shadows to never shift again. They had not hunted since their journey to this future, unwilling to stir unwanted attention in their weakened state, but they had at last found the whereabouts of the man they were after and knew the time had arrived to make their move.

There were three shadow men now, their fourth having fallen in a most unfortunate accident on the road, and had lost yet another during the skirmish with the Roma. Shadow-shifters, as Lena has been known to call them, were not restricted by the aging effects of mortality that inflicted humans, and could live on until killed by one of their own. Of course, there was always the rare occasion when a shadow-shifter would be killed while in their human form, as it was very possible to fall prey in such weakness. Since the time they had crossed to Oma, the pack of shadow-shifters had lost two members and been betrayed by one, as he had refused to follow the wooden-hand man's orders any longer. With their quickly diminishing numbers came the urgency to return to Asa. In their world, their energy could be easily refreshed,

238

but for now, a meager snack from Oma would have to suffice.

The night was a quiet one, a silence that deafened your ears and made you look over your shoulder in fear. The shadow-shifters separated, because hunting for them was not done in packs. It was an individual game against an unsuspecting prey. Number Six—the pack named their members after the numeric order in which they came into it—hid in the shadows of tall buildings in the form of a man that he had hunted in the London of 1897, whose life energy was failing and needed to be replaced most urgently. He, as there were no females among his kind, spotted the lonesome figure of a young man. The figure walked briskly alongside the river Thames, looking behind him as though he could sense a pursuer.

The shadow-shifter's human shape sneered. Their disguises rendered them practically invisible to humans, although a small number of them who were somehow in tune to natural energies were able to sense their presence by a sudden drop in temperature. Some could even see the true color of their eyes. Number Six thought of the man they had been instructed to pursue and wondered about the instincts he possessed. There had always been something odd about the human. He could sense and recognize them, certainly, but there was more to him than the shadow-shifters could understand. They feared what they couldn't explain. The human had no power over them in any physical aspect, but they felt wary of his foreign energy nonetheless.

When the young man ahead sprinted to a run, Number Six awoke from his thoughts and gave chase, allowing his prey a head start in good fun. His human shape caught up easily with a bit of help from his own strength. Number Six tripped the young man to the ground. As he rolled, the boy pulled a pocket knife from his belt and pointed it at his pursuer. The hunter grabbed his wrist and pried the weapon loose. There was anger on the boy's face. This was a brave one. Number Six liked the reckless spirit in him, full of the energy he craved.

"Don't squirm," Number Six muttered. He pressed a knee to the boy's chest to hold him still. "It will be over soon."

When a sudden cry emitted from the boy's throat, Number Six muffled him with a gnarled hand. The boy convulsed in excruciating pain, eyes wide and filled with terror. Like many of his fellow shadow-shifters, Number Six liked to extract a prey's energy slowly, savoring each breath of life from a squirming, fully conscious catch. It elongated the human's suffering, which gave the shadow-shifters an extra boost of energy. From the extraction, Number Six learned the human's name, his age, where he lived, where he was born. He saw memories and felt emotions. He became his prey in more ways than just in shape.

Suddenly, Number Six stopped. He regarded the boy thoughtfully, whose eyes were half shut and was at the verge of unconsciousness. Using the boy's knife, Number Six pierced the boy's neck just below the jaw to bring him back to reality with the shocking sting. The boy gasped for breath.

"Fred." Number Six tasted his name along with the bit of blood he licked from the knife. "You know Stanley Becker, don't you?"

The boy looked up with weak eyes.

"Or perhaps you've only seen him. Who is the girl?"

The boy didn't answer, but Number Six needed only to focus his cluttered thoughts to see what was needed. He saw Rosie Bissett and the house where she was staying. The shadow-shifter had his answers and felt fortunate to have stumbled upon this particular prey. The extraction continued and the boy cried out his last breath with a look of horror on his face. The light went out in his eyes. Feeling renewed, Number Six smiled as he took on his prey's appearance.

He left the corpse where it was and walked away. It would attract attention, but it was a message he wished to send to Stanley Becker. It would only be a matter of time before they went after him next. Number Six sent out the signal through thoughts, their way to communicate with one another, and headed to a specific place in the city. Now that he knew the boy's every memory, they would have a proper place to stay.

They would only need to wait.

XXX

On the third morning since their arrival, Sibyl had no story for them, which provoked obvious irritation that Stanley made little effort to hide.

"I did not come here for stories," he spat. "I came to find answers, to know how to save Louis Vargas, to get Lena home, to stop those shadow-shifters from chasing us—"

"Ah, Louis Vargas," Sibyl interrupted, paying little heed to Stanley's outburst. "You know, his real name is Louis Bissett, but once in Andalusia he changed it to something more common."

Stanley took a deep breath to calm down, apologetic to Lena. Her hard eyes reprimanded him.

"You know him, then?" he asked once he was under control.

"Oh, yes. He's come many times to see me and ask of my wisdom, but that doesn't mean he ever follows my advice." Her chuckle was care-free. "He used to come with that trinket of yours."

Nodding, Stanley began to realize that the events of his past had always correlated with Sibyl and all that she knew. "Is that how he seemed to know me? Did you tell him about me?"

Sibyl's clouded eyes were warm but secretive. "I told him a man would intervene who could be trusted."

"And how did—"

"That's all for today."

"But I need to know—"

Lena's gentle touch calmed him enough to abandon his efforts. They left in silence with the burden of yet another day with unanswered questions. To air Stanley's touchy mood, they found themselves strolling about Canbury Gardens through familiar sceneries, though aged and foreign in detail, overlooking the river Thames. As the only visitor that morning, Stanley walked through a paved trail beneath canopies of bare branches. Lena did not seem to have the energy or desire to climb that day, and remained cuddled in Stanley's scarf to watch the world from his protection.

After several minutes of silence, Lena interrupted Stanley's thoughts. "I knew someone who called himself Bissett," she said. "Raoul Bissett."

"A vaelie like you?"

"No, he was human. A *cursed* human."

Stanley could not help grimace at the word, which Lena used to describe many unfortunate conditions, as though being cursed was merely a common illness. Stanley's mind could not understand how a curse could be a real affliction, but he reminded himself to keep an open mind when discussing such things with a five-inch-tall girl.

"What do you mean cursed?"

When Lena sighed, Stanley knew it would be a lengthy explanation.

"My father," she began, "has a cousin named Lamaika Ema. But I call her Maika. A long time ago, when she was young, she was lost during the Scattering. The vaelies call it the Scattering when the humans came to disrupt our way of life. Well, Maika was lost, and for almost three years she wandered about trying to find the vaelies that had run off. One day she met a human who saved her life. But he was cursed!"

"How was he cursed?"

"They say he angered a witch, I think. She cursed him to have the body of a vaelie. But that's silly. How can being a vaelie be a curse?"

Stanley chuckled. "It can be if you're used to being my size."

"Well, they traveled all around to find a cure, because Maika felt pity for him. They say they found an ancient stone that cured him, but that doesn't make sense. How could a stone cure anything?"

"Seems that you don't believe the story yourself."

Lena scoffed. "I know it's true, only I think that it's a little exaggerated."

"And you knew this man?"

"Maika lives in my village, so he comes to visit her. He knows my father too. Raoul taught me to speak your language."

"That's quite a story."

"You don't believe me?"

Stanley laughed. "I must confess that it sounds quite extraordinary. But I do believe you, Lena."

While Lena chattered on, Stanley's thoughts strayed. If her story about curses and shrunk men was true, and if this Raoul Bissett really did exist, what sort of connection did he have to Louis? Perhaps the fact that at one point they had both been in the same world, the world that Lena came from, meant that a link was not unlikely. Or perhaps it was merely a coincidence.

∞

Rosie was leaning back against the car when Stanley returned home. Her eyes had dark shadows and her smile was tired. She and Andrew were headed to the marketplace again and Stanley was invited to come along. He passed Andrew on his way inside, who eyed him under furrowed brows. Ever since the boy had nearly caught him talking to Lena the night before, Stanley was always under his unwavering scrutiny.

Stanley closed the door to the room before he let Lena out. Her big eyes were disappointed, but she did not ask to come along. She was tired, anyway. Stanley could see that for the vaelie, being in time for so long was wearing on her, but Lena never once complained. Suspecting that she was still upset about the night before, Stanley promised he would return shortly.

On the drive, Stanley tried his best to ignore Andrew's scowl, and Rosie yawned at the wheel.

"Want me to drive?" Andrew asked her without much humor.

"Right . . . you're only thirteen," she replied. "I just couldn't sleep. I had weird dreams all night."

A hazy memory tried to resurface in Stanley's mind, but he couldn't fish it out to remember it.

"Don't tell me you're afraid of the bogeyman," Andrew said with a smirk.

"It was about Fred," Rosie continued, as though vocalizing it would help her forget the dream. "And there was someone following him. It seemed like all these shadows were after him."

Stanley swallowed, hearing little Maisie's voice in his head about the shadows chasing her, and tried to shake off the cold feeling that the thought brought. Rosie shrugged it off and pointed out yet again that it had only been a dream. Andrew smiled in the backseat with amusement.

Within minutes they had reached the same market that Stanley and Andrew had entered on Boxing Day. Inside, Stanley automatically followed Andrew to find the ingredients on Ann's list. It was a relaxed Friday, and few people were out shopping that morning, but Stanley sensed that something was off with the peaceful impression of the market. He felt all eyes on him as he walked.

"Will you relax?" Andrew said, eyeing him. "We're not robbing a bank."

Stanley didn't answer but noticed that Rosie had strayed from his view.

"Where's Rosie?"

"I dunno."

It was probably nothing, but the feeling remained. It reached an unexpected intensity the moment he saw the front door open and a familiar figure entered. The boy who persisted in bothering Rosie stood with his back to them, turning his head slowly, studying the interior of the market. Stanley took a step forward and looked wildly around to find Rosie before Fred did.

"Where are you going?" Andrew asked.

"It's Fred—"

Fred's head turned and looked directly into Stanley's eyes, penetratingly bitter and intense. Taking a sharp breath, Stanley staggered back into Andrew, who pushed him away angrily. Fred took a step toward them, yellow eyes fierce. Stanley grabbed Andrew's arm and dragged the boy behind him to the next aisle.

"What are you doing?" he demanded. "Let go!"

"Hush!"

Stanley could hear Fred's quickly approaching steps and he scrambled to spot Rosie.

"I'll find Rosie." Stanley pushed the boy forward. "We'll meet you in the car."

"What's happening?"

"There's no time, Andrew!"

While Andrew dashed away to the next aisle, Stanley headed in the opposite direction. Fred spotted him. Stanley snaked through customers as quickly as he was able with Fred at his heels. Through the dairy products he took off in a dead run to lose him behind several stacks of boxes, but Fred caught up easily. By the milk, Stanley spotted Rosie, who looked up in bewilderment. Stanley grabbed her arm and pulled her behind him.

"What the—"

"We must leave!"

"What's going on?"

Fred was catching up to them. People cried out in surprise and evaded the runners. At the exit, Andrew held the door open for them. Grasping Rosie's arm, Stanley led them back to the car. In a matter of seconds they were inside.

"Drive!" Stanley cried out when Fred approached the car, followed by two other men with hoods pulled over their eyes. Rosie obeyed, pushed the gas pedal, and the car sped off into the fast traffic. Stanley looked back at the three figures standing motionless in the street, watching their retreat with yellow eyes filled with hunger. He didn't feel the relief he expected. It had been too easy to escape them.

It wasn't until they passed three green lights that Stanley faced forward once again and breathed.

"What," Rosie said with gritted teeth, "just happened?"

Andrew was staring at Stanley with uncertainty, but said nothing.

"We were in danger."

"That was Fred," Rosie remarked. "He might be stubborn, but he's not dangerous."

"Take a different route home. They'll be watching us."

"Who?"

Stanley rubbed his temples. "If I tell you, you must promise to remain calm. And do not slow the vehicle."

"What is going on?"

"There are people after me."

Rosie glanced at him. "What are you, some kind of criminal?"

Andrew's eyes were fixed on the hand that Stanley brought out from his pocket. The bronze surface of the contraption gleamed brightly when the light of the sun shone on it. Stanley gripped the chain of the Time Key.

"What is that?" Rosie asked.

Stanley took a deep breath. "I am not from here. You two already know that, but not in the way you imagine."

Andrew's eyes narrowed.

"I am from the past."

Rosie rolled her eyes. "Are you high?"

Stanley continued, opening the Time Key to show them. "I come from the year 1897. This contraption allows me to travel through time."

After a long pause, Rosie broke it with a mocking tone of voice that Stanley had not heard in a good while. "Like a time machine?"

"Yes, and there are people—*creatures* chasing me."

"Do they come from the past too?"

Stanley sighed. He knew that she didn't believe him. Andrew continued to study him with unwavering eyes.

"I came to see Sibyl because she knows about the events that are happening in my time. She has been there herself. I know all this sounds insane, but you must listen—"

Rosie's nostrils flared. "No, I don't! I don't know who you are, or where you think you come from, but I am not an idiot!"

Stanley hung his head and slipped the Time Key back in his pocket. They reached the house in a matter of minutes. As soon as Rosie parked, she burst out of the car and stormed into the house. With Andrew at his heels, Stanley ran after the girl who was cursing in anger.

"Okay!" she cried. "What is going on? Someone tell me why I've been driving around with a *madman*—"

Her voice choked. Stanley arrived in time to see the girl freeze in the middle of the room. She faced the kitchen table where Ann and Daisy sat, who seemed shocked by Rosie's sudden outburst. He was startled to see that on the table was Lena, sitting cross-legged and wide-eyed, and was the obvious reason for Rosie's sudden silence.

Rosie's eyes rolled to the back of her head.

～✤～

Lena's entire body quivered as she cuddled against Stanley's hands that formed a wall around her protectively. He could not blame her for the fear she obviously felt, as it mirrored Stanley's uncertainty about what would happen now. Rosie was recovering on the couch, Ann and Daisy attended to her, and Andrew had retreated back outside. Stanley's attention returned to Lena, who looked up at him with big eyes.

"Did I kill her?"

Stanley shook his head, unable to hide the smile on his lips. He understood Rosie's reaction, even expected it, but Ann's calmness was odd. It led him to suspect that she was not unfamiliar with the idea of someone like Lena. Perhaps, among all the oddities she and Paul had seen while living with Sibyl, a vaelie was the least shocking of them all.

On the couch, Rosie mumbled bitterly when Ann remarked that there were things they needed to discuss. Within seconds, the girl's surly temper returned.

"Can someone explain to me what is going on?"

Ahead, Stanley saw Sibyl's wobbling figure emerge from the dark hallway. Without seeing, she regarded the scene with stern patience. The moment Rosie saw her, she confronted the old woman.

"Did you know about all this?"

"Come, Rosie," Sibyl said. "We need to talk."

"You know that I've been driving around a time-traveling maniac, and no one bothered to tell me—"

"Rosie!"

"You told me it was all in my head, Gram! I thought I was insane!"

"Come. Now."

Rosie obeyed reluctantly and followed Sibyl to the back room, casting Stanley and Lena an unsettled look that gave away sudden dread for things that she did not understand. Lena ducked behind Stanley's hands. They could still hear their agitated voices when Ann returned to the kitchen and smiled sweetly at them to appease the mood. She asked Stanley why he had never introduced Lena to them. Stanley had no reply, and Lena accepted her offer to make cookies with them. Struck with amazement that Lena seemed so comfortable with Ann and Daisy, Stanley rose uncertainly.

"What will Sibyl tell Rosie?"

Ann cast him a sideways glance. "It's about our family."

"Will she give us an audience?"

Ann didn't answer, and there was nothing more to do than wait.

❧

They hadn't had the chance to taste any cookies before Rosie ran down the hallway. With blushed and tear-stained cheeks, she raced for the front door without even a glance and stormed out. She left a trail of tension. Andrew stood at the door, having spent the entire time shooting his basketball outside, and cast his mother a concerned look. Ann hurried to Sibyl's room, but came back almost immediately to wave Stanley in.

"She wants to see you."

Lena rose, but Stanley instructed her to stay with Ann and Daisy.

While crossing the hall, his feet were heavy. The beaded curtain brushed against his arms, parting for him to enter. Sibyl's figure stooped in her rocking chair, and although she didn't speak for a few minutes, Stanley knew that her energy was spent and she was attempting to recover before she finally directed her attention to him. Stanley was desperate to know what had happened, what she had told Rosie, and what it had to do with him, if it did. He suspected that he knew who Rosie really was.

"I don't have much time," Sibyl said. Her hand trembled as she stroked her cheek thoughtfully.

Stanley waited.

"She isn't ready."

At last, Stanley armed himself with enough courage to say, "All the stories, all that you've told me, it was all for her. *She* is the next Sibyl."

Sibyl nodded, and for once, her lips did not curve up into a smile.

"She is one of these twin souls. But who is the other twin?"

"I will tell you another story, and this one you will recognize." Her pause lasted over a minute, and finally she gave a sigh to continue.

"A man was born unto Asa who fell in love with a daughter of Oma. It was against tradition to even have contact with someone of the other world, but still the man crossed the boundary to be with his beloved. They were married and soon had a child. Because Oma did not approve of the union, the child was born with a curse."

Stanley took a deep breath. Naomi had told him part of this story, except she had substituted the word curse with demon.

"They tried everything to cleanse the child of the curse, but all failed. The man sought the wisdom of Sibyl when she visited their people. But there was nothing she could do. They were told to wait. A short time later, the man and woman had a second child. On the day of the birth, the cursed child disappeared, and the newborn was blamed to have brought bad luck. They searched for the child for many days, but she was never found. One day Sibyl came to them and assured them that the child was safe but could not come back to them. She promised them that she would look after their lost child. Sibyl was the only one who would be able to control the curse until the child was old enough to control it herself. The man and woman didn't see their child again.

"But their second child had also a curse, and there was no Sibyl to give them counsel. The man sought the help of a man whom he knew possessed the ability to travel from world to world, and through time.

Having lost the knowledge of how to return to Asa, the man needed the aid of this traveler who had such knowledge. He made an agreement with the traveler to be given a special key that would take him to that which he most desired, in exchange for something very powerful. The traveler sought the mythical Fountain that was said to posses the Tears of the gods. The man was to bring them back to the traveler. In his desperation, the man agreed. With the key given him, the man sought out the wisdom of Sibyl but also to see his child that was lost."

Stanley's head spun. He had seen this revelation of truth coming before he had heard it from Sibyl's own mouth. "Rosie is Dione," he stuttered. "Louis and Naomi's lost daughter."

"Louis hoped that with the Time Key he would find his daughter. But it did not prepare him for the reality that she'd grown up without any knowledge of him. She knew nothing of her past, of her family. Louis was devastated. Sibyl counseled him that there was nothing he could do about Dione, but that he still had another daughter who depended on him. She warned him of the dangers in his path, of the shadows that loomed near. But Louis's mind was set. He crossed over to find the Fountain—to cure both his daughters' curses. He knew that the water from the Fountain could not only cure any illness and elongate life, but it also had the power to break curses."

"And he found it but brought the shadows with him," Stanley said.

"The shadows are mere puppets, but they serve no mortal. They have no choice but to do the bidding of the god who was cast out. What Louis didn't understand was that Rosie's curse is a gift. She will carry out my work. Her sister was born with an even greater gift, used to bring about change. It has already started, and there's nothing that can stop this from happening. The universe is attempting to restore balance. It was no accident that your attempt to take your own life failed, Stanley Becker. Someone is watching you and has guided you to this path. There is something you must do to carry on the chain of events that will lead on the change."

"What am I meant to do?"

"The goddess has already visited you, has she not? Only she can tell you what to do, but know that the role you play is a crucial one."

"In my dreams—she tells me that I need to restore the balance. How?"

Sibyl shook her head. "I cannot tell you how."

"If Rosie is meant to be Sibyl," Stanley asked slowly. "Does she have all your abilities?"

Sibyl nodded. "She has always been able to do what I can; that is how she came to me when she was merely a child. I caused her gift to remain dormant until she was ready to use it, but it can only be triggered when she accepts the responsibility."

"How can it be triggered?"

"Do you remember the second story?"

"I do."

"Remember how my gift was triggered—it will be the same for Rosie. Perhaps that is why you came here, Stanley Becker. To help Rosie reawaken her gifts."

Stanley allowed Sibyl's words to sink in. He had been chosen for this—whether by a Creator or the universe itself. Maybe he was simply following a trail fate had designed for him. He felt uneasy by the idea.

Hesitantly, he asked, "Why did Louis leave me the Time Key?"

Still, Sibyl's lips did not shape into her usual warm smile. "He feared being found. He knew you would need it to find me, if anything went wrong."

Stanley nodded. "And Lena . . ."

He paused. He couldn't find the words.

There was a sad light in Sibyl's eye.

"Why was she left to me? Would . . . would Louis have . . . ?"

"No," she said. "Perhaps he feared her influence over fire. Such energy would have no doubt attracted the shadows."

"And did . . . I create her?"

To his surprise, the old woman chuckled. The cat by her feet looked fixedly at Stanley. "I don't believe anyone could have such power, besides the gods themselves, of course. But I do wonder, Stanley Becker. There's something about you that is quite interesting. Your energy is . . . well, nothing I've ever come across."

Stanley frowned and leaned back in his chair. "What do you mean?"

Sibyl waved her hand. "Oh, never mind that. Perhaps one day you'll figure it out yourself. Like Lena, you have a certain influence, a gift you do not understand. You couldn't have created her, or anyone like her. But you have a certain eye for such things. Perhaps you received a *glimpse* of her. A glimpse into the other world."

"A glimpse . . ."

Sibyl chuckled to herself. "There's more to you than meets the eye, isn't there?"

Stanley had no words to answer her.

XXXI

In the early hours of New Year's Eve, Stanley rose from his bed, unable to pretend to sleep any longer. On the pillow next to him, Lena slept peacefully and untroubled. He had tossed about uneasily all night (careful not to bother Lena, of course), pestered by thoughts and questions, and tortured by the events of the last two days.

The slumbering house didn't stir. Outside, he found the day bleak. Breathing the cold air of the still dark morning, Stanley recalled all that had happened.

❧

After Rosie's outburst, the girl had driven off in her car without a hint or warning that she did not intend to come back. By the time Paul returned home, Ann was in a panic. She was ready to go after Rosie, despite Sibyl's instructions to leave the girl alone. Rosie would return in her own time. Stanley wasn't so sure. Ann wanted to inform the authorities, but Paul dissuaded her from the idea. They would wait until tomorrow to act, to give her the space she needed.

The next day came and went, and there was still no sign of Rosie. On the night of the 30th, Paul drove around to find her. He had hoped she had gone to Fred's flat. Ann paced the living room nervously, and on the couch sat Andrew, ears plugged and head down. In the kitchen, Stanley sat with Daisy and Lena on the table playing *Go Fish*. Stanley held the cards for Lena, lost in thought, and Lena had to tap his hand when her turn came again.

Ann entered the kitchen to grab a drink. Stanley noticed that the usual leather bracelet she wore was gone, and he saw her right wrist was tattooed with strange symbols. She immediately pulled down her sleeve when she saw Stanley looking at it.

"Where could she have gone?" Stanley asked.

But Ann didn't answer him. She patted her belly and stared at the television in silence. Just then Paul came through the door, claiming that Fred had not been home when he knocked on his door. Ann didn't seem to hear him, either.

She suddenly muffled a scream. Stanley rose automatically. The television flashed with three images: the portraits of three victims from the weekend's unexplainable murders. The authorities had no leads on a suspect and any information would be greatly appreciated.

Stanley recognized the pale face of the first victim, whose eyes were dark and lifeless, wearing an expression of terror brought on by his last moments of life.

Fred had been murdered.

∞

Stanley knew all too well what was responsible for such horrifying crimes, as the same murderers had lurked the streets of London in 1897. He should have expected the shadow-shifters would terrorize this future.

Shaking away the memories, Stanley returned to the present moment, the morning of New Year's Eve. As he gazed at the dark sky stretching on endlessly, Stanley felt a stirring in his chest. Even though Sibyl had not allowed for any of them to go after her, for their own safety, Stanley could not wait any longer. Rosie could be in danger. There was no more time to waste, and Stanley knew where he would find Rosie.

He returned inside, climbed the stairs silently, and stole into Andrew's bedroom. He placed his hand over the boy's mouth and shook his shoulder. Startled, Andrew jerked up, eyes wide.

"I need you to drive," Stanley whispered, glancing at Daisy's motionless figure. "It's urgent."

When the boy calmed down, he sat up hesitantly and scowled, resentful of his interrupted sleep.

"Where are we going?"

"Fred's."

On the drive, Andrew sat on a cushion and did his best to appear larger than he was. Stanley hadn't said a word since they had left the house, and Andrew cast him a curious look.

"Why can't you drive?" he said, swallowing uneasily. "I might get in trouble."

"I don't know how."

"You think Rosie's been staying at Fred's? But you saw . . . the news . . ."

Stanley didn't give him an answer. What could he say? That he suspected he knew who had murdered Fred and had probably kidnapped Rosie? The poor boy didn't need to know the gory details of the situation, especially since he had been terribly shaken by the mere sight of Lena. He probably could not even grasp the unbelievable fact that Stanley was a time traveler. Stanley sympathized with the boy. There were too many unbelievable details to swallow without difficulty.

After a moment, Andrew glanced at him again. "You're really from the past," he mumbled. "Aren't you?"

Stanley nodded.

"And Lena is from another world?"

"She is."

Andrew seemed relieved, as though the questions had been weighing on him. "And the people chasing you," he continued. "What about them?"

"They came from the same world. They are very dangerous."

"Why are they after you?"

Stanley didn't answer.

As Stanley instructed him, Andrew parked the car a considerable distance away from Fred's flat and left the engine running. Stanley told Andrew to wait. If he didn't return in ten minutes, Andrew must go home and tell his parents what had happened. Sibyl would know what to do, surely. Andrew was unwilling to let Stanley go on his own, but he understood that it was imperative for him to do as he was told.

Following Andrew's directions, Stanley walked briskly to Fred's flat, dashed up the stairs, and braced himself as the cold fingers of the shadow-shifters' influence touched him. Facing the door that read 7C, Stanley reached out to knock but stopped himself. He had suddenly seen Lena in his mind and feared he wouldn't live to see her again. He deeply regretted having left without saying good-bye.

The door opened, and Fred's sinister figure smiled at him mockingly.

"Where's Rosie?" Stanley demanded.

Fred only sneered. From behind Stanley, two burly men appeared and grabbed his arms to restrain him. Stanley fought his oppressors, but was no match against their strength. After several beatings and a hit to the head, Stanley succumbed to the dark that lured him into unconsciousness.

Every inch of his body ached and throbbed. What had he expected would happen? His slight frame and childlike physical strength had proved yet again to be unprepared for such confrontations. Blinking painfully as a drop of blood ran down his forehead, Stanley struggled to study the dark room in which he found himself. Somewhere across from him, he heard sobbing.

"Rosie, is that you?"

The sobbing stopped and a figure crawled to his side. Her tear-stained face was blurry above him.

"You're okay!" the girl whispered, more relieved than surprised, and hugged him. Stanley groaned. "They hurt you!"

"Not badly," he replied with a shrug that sent an electrifying sting down his spine. "And you?"

"No."

Stanley sat up slowly and leaned against the wall. He noticed that they had taken off his coat. They had probably searched every inch of him, and unfortunately, had found the Time Key in his pocket. He cursed.

Rosie sat next to him, hugging her legs to her chest. "I thought he was Fred, but it just didn't feel like him. Then they all grabbed me and I felt so cold . . . I guess they must have knocked me out . . ."

"That isn't Fred. They're called shadow-shifters. Shadows that can look like the people they've killed."

Rosie's eyes were wide as she understood. "You mean . . . Fred?"

Nodding, Stanley knew it wouldn't do any good to massage the truth. The girl burst out in new tears. She was frightened. Terrified. Stanley held her shaking body against him.

"What do they want with us?"

Stanley could not say for certain, but he realized that they were not important at the moment. Everything depended on Rosie now, and he had to find a way for her to realize it.

"What did Sibyl tell you, Rosie?"

After a pause, the girl replied, "That . . . that I have a gift . . . that I can do what she can—that I'm a chosen of the gods."

"That's right. You can get us out of here."

Her shoulders tensed. "W-what?"

Stanley licked his bleeding lip thoughtfully. "Sibyl can travel through time," he explained. "I can travel with the help of the contraption that I showed you. But she can do it by mere will. So can you."

"I-I don't know how it works."

"Sibyl mentioned that it can be triggered by a very strong emotion."

She felt overwhelmed. "And what? I'll go back in time?"

"It's a way out."

She turned her head away and made her hands into fists. Perhaps she still did not believe in her abilities, what she had always been able to do. Stanley's thoughts raced with possible ways that he could convince her, not only because this was the role he was meant to play, but also for her safety.

"She said," Rosie said after a moment. "She said it works like gravity. I'll end up where I am attracted to—where I'm most needed."

"Try."

"But I can't—I don't know how!"

He knew it must be provoked by a strong enough emotion to light the dormant spark of her gift. Stanley's mind wandered to Lena. Stanley had seen her unknowingly influence fire several times, but on the first occasion, in Gilmore's library, he remembered her look of terror. Fear had controlled fire.

Fear must be a strong enough emotion.

Stanley's head spun and he truly regretted the pain he imagined he was about to experience for Rosie. But he *must* do it, for her.

Stanley groaned as he rose suddenly. With gritted teeth, he thumped the walls that held them captive. Kicking and yelling, Stanley's adrenaline began to rush through him. Rosie gaped, unable to understand what he was doing.

She gasped when the door opened. The three men entered and wasted no time to pummel Stanley to the ground. They seemed to enjoy the bustle that beating this weak human granted them away from boredom. Stanley tried his best to put up a fight. Rosie screamed and cried behind him. He was doing this for her, for her safety, but oh, how it hurt. Through the sweat and blood, Stanley found Fred and lunged at him. But then something stopped him. Something unnatural. It pierced him with a most shocking sting. Stanley couldn't breathe. When he looked down, Stanley could see Fred's fist gripped a knife. It was stuck in Stanley's belly.

Fred sneered, inches away from Stanley's face. He pushed a little deeper. Stanley gagged.

Rosie realized what Fred had done just as it happened. Her scream sounded muffled and far away in Stanley's ears. He turned his head, but she was gone. It was as though she had never been there. The remnants of her scream resonated against the bare walls of the room.

Fred cursed and pulled the knife out. He kicked Stanley to the ground. Stanley lay in shock, unable to feel or understand.

"Where is she?"

"She's disappeared."

"Smells like the same energy this man used to travel."

"We can trace it."

"But we have not much energy. It isn't wise to travel again."

"We won't be able to shift."

"Find her. The wooden-hand man will want to see her."

The shadows vanished, leaving traces of their black mist behind that drifted and touched Stanley with cold fingers. But there was one left, who stood over him with a look of contempt. Fred raised his knife to his lips and licked the drops of blood from the blade.

"Number Two was right about you," he said. He seemed to enjoy the last moments of Stanley's life that were slipping away from him too quickly. "I can sense the strange energy from within you, and I wonder what it will taste like. You're only a man—a reckless, delicate man. I can finish you off with this knife. It won't be painless, and it will be very slow."

The knife was inches away from Stanley's face. He could see the sticky blood dripping as it lowered down. It was warm against his neck. It didn't matter what would happen. Stanley was close to death, and somehow, he didn't fear it. Hadn't he been hoping for this very thing as he had stood over the frozen waters of the Thames? Pity he hadn't said good-bye to Lena.

Stanley heard a *clunk* and glass shattered. Broken shards rained on him. Stanley heard the knife clatter next to his head, and through his darkening vision, he grabbed for it. Shaking, he rose to his knees. Fred had fallen beside him, clutching the back of his head in shocked pain. Stanley saw Andrew a few steps behind Fred with the broken neck of a glass bottle of scotch. Where he had found it, Stanley did not waste any time to ask.

With the knife in his fist, Stanley threw himself on Fred and struck down as hard as his failing strength allowed. Fred gasped and stared up in disbelief, unable to comprehend how roles had switched so quickly. Stanley struggled to keep awake. He gripped the knife that he had stuck in Fred's chest.

"You're only a man now," Stanley said. He heard poison in his own voice. "You can't shift to save yourself."

Fred's eyes were yellow and terrified. He gurgled.

"W-what are you?"

"You should have left Rosie alone."

Stanley couldn't hold himself up. He dropped down and inched away from Fred, who was choking in his own blood. Black mist emanated from him. The dying shape that Number Six was bound to didn't allow him to shift, until gradually his figure vanished entirely. Stanley had killed a shadow.

Andrew went to Stanley's side and looked so frightened. Stanley regretted that the boy had witnessed the gory scene.

"You didn't stay in the car," he wheezed with effort.

Andrew's lip quivered. "Are you okay?"

Stanley struggled to smile.

"P-please, you have to hang on. Help is coming."

Stanley sighed. "Rosie," he said with gritted teeth. His vision was dark. "Rosie—she traveled. Tell Sibyl."

"Okay."

"A-and Lena . . . must get home."

He could hardly hear his own voice, much less the boy's.

"Don't say that. Help is coming."

Stanley's eyes closed.

"Maisie . . . Janey . . ."

He was going home.

Part Three

XXXII

It was a chaotic jungle of men and women in scrubs rushing about, transporting patients, yelling out commands, and running through halls. Among the mass of moving bodies, a single man stepped out of an equipment closet nervously, dusting the scrubs he wore and looking uncomfortable in them. He kept his gaze lowered as a group of nurses passed him. Uneasily, the man ran a hand over his dark, short-cropped hair and turned his attention to a sudden commotion at the entrance to the Accident and Emergency department. He had arrived just in time.

If I may take a brief moment to clarify to the reader that the man who we are currently following we have previously met as Future Stanley, who had the sudden impulse to return to this specific time, for reasons unknown, and witness the distressful events following Stanley's stabbing. You may be relieved to know that, despite being badly injured and under the influence of quite a traumatic shock, Stanley survived his encounter with the shadow-shifters and, thanks to Andrew, was taken to the hospital for treatment.

For now, Future Stanley stared somberly as a group of nurses and paramedics rolled Stanley past him. His face was sickly, having lost a considerable amount of blood. Future Stanley stood back and watched his past self disappear through a set of doors that led away from the tumult. The memory of Fred jabbing the blade into his belly was still vivid in his mind, and the wound still tender. Coming back here stirred familiar feelings of anxiety, to know that this was only a quick visit, that there were more crucial matters awaiting his return to his present. But he had not come here for himself. There was someone he had come to see and offer a small ounce of hope.

He paced around the various sections of the hall, surrounded by sickly patients, each separated by curtains. He found Andrew being inspected by a nurse, his face pale and distressed. Two officials in uniform asked him questions about the events of that morning, and the boy did his best to explain what he knew. The police had found traces of a struggle at the site which suggested there had been more than just one assailant and one victim, but having no tracks to lead them to Stanley's attackers, they were baffled by the entire scene. Andrew only told them what he knew, omitting that he had seen Fred die and dissolve into black mist. He claimed to assume that the attacker had fled.

Finding no further answers, the officials left, and Future Stanley turned away to avoid being recognized. Just then, Paul came running when he spotted Andrew, and threw his arms around the boy. Future Stanley watched the scene hesitantly, waiting, until he saw a tiny head peer out from Paul's pocket. Future Stanley smiled. He hoped that she would see him and know he was all right.

∞

He carried a tray with two bowls of steaming soup. Wearing a confident, businesslike expression, Future Stanley headed for the room where they kept Stanley, who, after two days, still refused to wake up. Future Stanley had traveled forward to the third day at the hospital where they had strictly monitored his vitals and kept under close scrutiny, practicing what they called "watchful waiting." Apparently they suspected that his wounds were not serious enough to be fatal and anticipated that he would soon recover from the shock. Future Stanley knew very little about medicine to understand all the details about his condition. It occurred to him that in his position, Russell Gilmore would be fascinated by all the medical advances of the twenty-first century.

In reaching the room, Future Stanley opened the door and shut it gently behind him. There he was next to the window, deep in restless sleep. There were dark shadows around his eyes and large bruises splattered on his face, more pitiful than he had ever looked. Future Stanley set down the tray and studied his mirrored self. He couldn't help feel sorry for the man, for himself. Things had not been easy since all this had started, certainly, but Future Stanley knew he would not change a thing.

"You poor devil," he mumbled.

"Stanley?"

He turned to find, to his relief, the person he had come to see.

☙

Stanley Becker was aware of very little. Above the soundless depths of his subconscious, Stanley would occasionally identify faint voices, hazy in his mind. He was often in a cloudless sky, floating weightlessly, and waiting for the light to lead him to the next life. Was there a next life? Was this what death meant—circulating a meaningless trail of bliss? It certainly felt far from bliss as he kept seeing vivid memories of the most recent events of his life, and felt the excruciating regret of leaving Lena so suddenly. She had been the only person that could delay the coming end of his life, and now that he had finally reached it, he was angry to have left.

There were dreams of gods and faraway lands, of shadows and bright-eyed beasts, of vaelies in trees. He saw endless blue oceans, ancient forests, and magnificent cities of gold. The goddess came to him at times, to rebuke him for his negligence to finish his task. As her image faded, he saw Jane holding onto Maisie's little hand. They called to him, wondering when he would come home. Stanley had no answer to give them, and as quickly as they had appeared they vanished in the mist.

He walked through thick fog to find that he was on the bridge, looking down at the black waters of the Thames. There was a pistol in his hand which he pointed to his head. He couldn't control his muscles when he wanted to lower his arm. His finger squeezed the trigger. The bang resonated in his ears, but the pain stung under his ribs like a sharp knife. He fell into the black waters and floated down the current, eyes closed. He was dead, certainly, but outside of him he felt someone touch his arm. Many hands pulled him, hoisted him in the air, and dragged him out of the water.

He drifted along without a clue where the mist would take him. Eventually his vision grew dark and he was bound inside his body once more. He couldn't move. Through muddled thoughts, he tried to understand what had happened to him, why he hurt so badly, which led him to suspect that he must not have died. The visions he had had must have been dreams. With the pain from the stab wound came other senses. The smells seemed foreign, and he was sightless. He heard the occasional voice jumbled in his mind. But he could feel. A few hands touched him, comforting. Sometimes, a pair of tiny ones would rest on his cheek. It was Lena, he knew. He wished he could tell her that he was all right, but his voice did not work. It would have to be enough to know that she was safe, curled up in his limp hand.

Time was uncertain in the endless oblivion where he felt trapped, and days seemed to go by before he began to regain his muddled senses. His vision was blurred, but he could hear hushed voices near him when he tried to open his eyes. A very nimble body climbed up his arm.

"Stanley!" Lena's voice cried desperately.

At last, Stanley found his own voice. It sounded dry and raspy.

". . . Lena."

"You're a'right!"

Stanley's laugh was hoarse and weak; her familiar phrase came as a relief. He had not left her, as he had feared. And she was all right. He felt overjoyed by her sweet presence. Blinking, he could just make out the girl climbing onto the armrest next to him and was unable to contain his broad, pained grin.

Before he could speak, Stanley tried to move his arms but found that his right arm was restrained by tubes.

"I'd be careful of that," a male voice said. "They stuck a needle in you."

Stanley turned his head to see his future duplicate sitting with his legs crossed, wearing a relieved grin on his lips.

Stanley cursed between gritted teeth. "It's you."

Future Stanley chuckled. "Pleasure to see you, too."

Lena now stood on the food tray to his right, hands on hips, but unable to hide her smile.

"He came to see you," she said.

It was difficult to focus through the drowsiness and the sudden stinging in his torso.

"What in blazes are you wearing?" he asked, squinting at Future Stanley's clothes.

"A disguise," he replied, unmoved by his irritation. "Actually, I came to see Lena while you were sleeping. But also to bring you this."

He set a leather coin purse on the tray and its contents clinked. There seemed to be a great amount of currency in the bag.

"For the Taylor family."

"Where did you get that money?" Stanley demanded.

But Future Stanley shrugged. "Father left another generous check. They need it more than we do."

"But our monetary system is different. It will be worth nothing here."

"Not when 1890's currency is in such good condition. Who knows? Perhaps the coins will be worth more than you expect."

There was a sad gleam in Future Stanley's eye. Stanley briefly considered asking him about his current present, what awaited him in his return to the future, but the uneasiness of knowing what Stanley could not see stopped him.

"Where are we?" Stanley asked, noticing his surroundings for the first time.

"The hospital. In case you don't remember, you've been stabbed."

Stanley didn't appreciate his future self's sarcasm but didn't get the chance to reply when the shooting pain attacked his side once again. "What's happened?" he said, gasping. "The shadows—and Andrew, is he safe? Rosie?"

Lena's eyes were wide, but Future Stanley shrugged dismissively as he said, "Fret not, Stanley. They're quite all right. Lena will explain."

Stanley leaned back against his pillow. "I suppose I should thank you, for looking after us."

The identical man rose. "My pleasure. I really must go."

Stanley felt slightly relieved, although he was glad to have been visited by Future Stanley. It gave him a sort of reassurance that somewhere in his immediate future he was still alive for Lena. The man from the future smiled and touched Lena's extended hand.

He whispered, "Take care of that poor wretch for me."

Lena nodded. At the door, Future Stanley hesitated. He seemed to be saying a different sort of good-bye.

"You've done well, Stanley," he said before slipping past a nurse, who cast him a curious glance.

⚯

"How do you feel, Stanley?"

Slightly alarmed when called by his first name by a complete stranger, Stanley tried to sit up, but the nurse patted his arm. She had been checking things on the monitor next to Stanley before she turned to his wrist. A little tube was taped to the inside of his arm, connecting him to a bag hanging by a pole.

He hesitantly answered the nurse's question: "As though I've been stabbed."

Smiling, the nurse apparently took it as good humor. She placed a cup filled with pills on the tray where Lena had been minutes ago. Stanley had not seen where she hid.

"Take it easy for now," she said. "We're monitoring your recovery closely. It's really a miracle you didn't have any complications. The knife seemed to strike in just the right place to miss all the vital organs, although it did cause you to bleed quite a bit."

The nurse seemed to like to chat with her patients, and there was hardly a break in the conversation as she pulled up Stanley's covers to inspect the wound, who reddened by her indifference.

"There's some damage to the muscle tissue," she continued, removing his heavily saturated bandages, "but by the looks of it, it's healing quite well. There must be someone up there looking out for you . . . Take those pills after you eat. They'll help with the pain."

He didn't say a word while the nurse exchanged the bandages for new ones and assured him that he was under good care. It was understandable for a man of the nineteenth century to wake up in a hospital, an institution intended to house a cesspool of sickness, and be uncomfortable. But he felt at ease to know that he at least was confined to his own chamber. While the nurse finished checking the monitor, Stanley ran a hand over the wound, feeling the damage of the stab, beneath his ribs on the left side. Although it was not quite as serious, the wound reminded him of Lena's accident and the jagged glass that had pierced her body.

When the door closed, Lena emerged from her hideout and sat at the edge of the little table next to Stanley. There was clear relief on her face, mingled with delight to finally see him awake. Stanley inspected the food-filled tray on the table and offered her some of the soup. She ate ravenously, rebuking him between mouthfuls for having left her behind without a warning on New Year's Eve morning. Apparently, Future Stanley had explained to the best of his ability the logic behind such a drastic decision, but the mere fact that she had not been involved for her own safety did little to change her reasoning, as was normal for her character. To hear her bickering only made Stanley smile; he had missed her.

Stanley picked up the cup of pills and swallowed them with icy water. Lena finished off the rest of the soup by dipping pieces of bread, and looked up when he sighed painfully.

"How long have I been here, Lena?"

"This is the third day."

"And you've been here the entire time?"

The girl nodded.

"You shouldn't have."

Her nose wrinkled.

"And you shouldn't have left."

"Do you know what happened to Rosie?"

The morning of the stabbing, as Lena briefed Stanley, Andrew had called Paul and told him what had happened. Lena, worried sick for Stanley, had waited in the living room with Daisy. She had demanded to be allowed to find Stanley. The family had been in a panic that morning, and while Ann insisted for Lena to remain in the house, Paul scavenged for a neighbor's car, having no access to his own or Rosie's. No one had expected to hear a sudden scream. At the center of the room, Rosie's figure had materialized out of thin air. She had fallen down in a heap, body bare, shivering, and unconscious.

During the confusion, Lena had convinced Paul to take her to the hospital while Ann and Sibyl attended Rosie. On the drive, the poor girl feared the worst when no one could explain what had happened to Stanley. The sight of him stretched out and bloody had wrenched her little heart. Andrew had told her all he knew: Stanley had killed off the shadow-shifter who had stabbed him, only to pass out from shock.

With Stanley at last, Lena had not left his side. She had waited, pleaded, for him to wake up. The Taylor family had been sure to visit frequently, but Stanley had remained unconscious through the New Year. Even when Rosie came to visit, there had been no response from him. Stanley regretted to have caused so much distress, but he found it rather endearing that Lena had been so furious and worried all at once. When she noticed him grinning, she crossed her arms.

"What's so funny?"

Stanley shook his head. "You were concerned about me," he said. "I find it very . . . sweet."

While Lena grumbled in her foreign little language, Stanley's thoughts drifted to the urgent impulse of seeing Sibyl again. He had completed his role here, but there were still questions pending to be answered. Without much thought, and gritting his teeth as his wound stung him, Stanley swung his legs over the bed and stood on unstable feet. Lena rose as well.

"Where are you going?"

"We must leave," he said, inspecting the tubes attached to his wrist. "I need to speak with Sibyl."

"How will we get there?" she asked. "It's cold, and you have no clothes."

Stanley frowned at the gown that draped loosely over him, but he grabbed the IV pole and offered Lena his hand.

"Someone's bound to help us," he said, opening the door and dragging the pole behind him.

In a little pocket over his chest, Lena called up, "I think we should wait."

"Nonsense," he replied, stepping into the hallway.

The corridors were eerily empty. He was unsure where to find an exit. The long hallway outside his room was silent and still, but for muffled voices coming from another part of the hospital. The patter of his bare feet echoed down the hall as he headed for the two doors south of his room. Soon he heard running.

"Stanley!"

"You're awake!"

Stanley was surprised to see Daisy's and Andrew's smiling faces as they came through the doors, who had not expected to see him walking about after three days of unconsciousness. He bent down rather painfully to return Daisy's embrace.

"How long have you been awake?" Andrew asked, letting down his guise of apathy for once to show his relief.

"Not long."

"Mum's having her baby," Daisy said.

"Is she now?"

The children were thrilled by the prospect of a new baby sister, and it shocked Stanley to hear that, besides seeing them inside a hospital filled with sick people, their mother was giving birth in the same building. This was foreign to Stanley, whose knowledge of childbirth was limited to what his wife had experienced, but even he knew that labor assisted by a midwife or doctor was done in one's own home. Only in the most serious of cases would a woman go to the hospital, but it was never encouraged. Apparently, in the twenty-first century such attitudes toward hospitals had changed considerably.

He was allowed to go up, although the nurses that tended him did not like the idea of Stanley wearing himself out, but it was a clear relief that he was healing quickly. The maternity suite was above his room, and it was quite hectic. Sounds of pain and distress filled the busy hallways as they walked past stern-faced nurses and perturbed husbands. The children led Stanley, with Lena watching from his pocket, to the room where a few nurses rushed Paul outside. Stanley could taste the tense air and read it on Paul's furrowed brows. In minutes, they had rushed Ann to another room. She was at the verge of unconsciousness.

"Complications," Paul muttered as he took a seat.

"What are they doing?" Andrew asked.

"C-section."

∞

Stanley had heard of cesarean sections from Gilmore, whose fascination with the operation had led him to believe in the potential of such procedures and what it would one day offer the world. Stanley could not imagine how cutting open a woman could ever be successful without endangering both the mother and the child. He remembered well the anguish he had felt the day of Maisie's birth, waiting in a separate room, unable to help his suffering wife, and he could only imagine what Paul would be feeling knowing that they were about to cut his wife's abdomen to remove the child surgically. Obviously, an ordinary man of the nineteenth century could not possibly imagine such an operation, but Stanley believed that this world, one hundred years ahead of his own, could manage impossible things.

Paul expressed his relief to see him well, but Stanley noted the man's exhaustion and worry. There was nothing more to say. The four sat and waited, and Stanley felt Lena wiggle in the pocket. She didn't venture out. Rosie came minutes later and froze when she saw Stanley, who in turn was robbed of words. It was as though he had expected to see her differently, changed, perhaps. But this was the same girl, relieved to see him. When she gave him a hesitant smile, Stanley could see gratitude mingled with a bit of excitement, as though they shared an important secret. He found the gesture comforting.

Less than an hour had passed when a nurse delivered the good news that the procedure had been successful and they were allowed to see the baby while the mother recovered. It came as a breath of fresh air after holding it underwater, and as they resurfaced the parted water revealed a tiny being filled with new life. Stanley was struck with the innocence of it all. Seeing this infant, taking its peaceful first breaths of life, he realized that life really was a marvelous thing and all the difficulties it brought. It was beautiful and wondrous. This newborn was the proof of it.

In his pocket, Lena whispered for Stanley to get closer. He tapped the glass that separated them from the infant, whose eyes opened slightly.

"What is her name?" Stanley asked.

Paul smiled. "Saira."

Stanley wondered, picturing a black-haired Romani girl with color-changing eyes, if Paul and Ann knew about Saira Nuri Vargas.

∞

It wasn't long before Ann awoke to reunite with her family and her healthy newborn daughter. Stanley gave them the privacy they needed and returned to his room, where, in exhaustion, he collapsed on the bed. The first day of consciousness had been a tiring one, and he was grateful to know that everything was in order. Even Rosie seemed well, despite everything.

"They brought you the Time Key," Lena told him, pointing behind him, "while you were sleeping. They put it under the pillow."

Stanley had forgotten that the shadow-shifters had taken it from him. Lena saw his confusion.

"Andrew said he found it when the shadow-shifter died. The one you . . ."

Stanley nodded, understanding Lena's uneasiness. As a comforting ritual, he opened the contraption, cold in his palm. The big hand pointed at Lena and the little one spun out of control.

"We should be home," he muttered. "We should be looking for the vial."

Lena dangled her feet in the air and watched him from the tray, but she didn't say a word. Stanley knew that things were about to become quite difficult for them, and the urgency of the approaching events caused him to fear for the unknown. But he was grateful to be alive. He was grateful, above all, that he had been able to see Lena again, safe and with him.

XXXIII

With the end of the fourth day came the release from the hospital. Much to Stanley's relief and to the amazement of the doctors and nurses, he was healing quickly and there was little for them to do. Stanley had visits from the authorities as well. He told them all he knew, but omitted the unnecessary parts of the truth to avoid questions he was unable to answer.

By the time he was dispatched, Stanley was relieved to change into somewhat decent clothes (of the twenty-first century, of course). He followed Rosie outside into the cold haze with Lena nestled under his scarf. Rosie held Stanley's arm for support as he limped his way to the car. The wound stung his side at each step.

During the drive, Rosie remained quiet while Stanley and Lena conversed in whispers. Stanley could understand her unease. Like him, she had been introduced to unexpected oddities she had never thought belonged outside of fairytales, and now there was no way to reject or forget them. Lena was only a small part of what was to come.

"Thank you," Rosie said.

Stanley and Lena looked up.

"For what you did for me."

Stanley shook his head. "I had nothing—"

"You saved my life and helped me find my gift. I'll never be able to repay you."

He couldn't take credit for something he had had no control over, but he acknowledged her gratitude with a nod. In thirty minutes they had reached the house, which welcomed the three inside its warm walls, and Stanley realized that he felt comfort in this humble place. Rosie was visibly exhausted, and with a small grin, she retired to her room.

Stanley was not about to waste any time. Down the dimly lit corridor, he approached Sibyl's room and limped through the beaded curtain. He had not seen Sibyl since before the incident, and he was a bit nervous to come to her.

The towers of books, the statues and figurines, the woven baskets, and all the trinkets and objects from other lands and cultures appeared welcoming as Stanley ghosted through silently, almost reverently. At last he saw Sibyl's figure in the rocking chair, looking out the window but seeing nothing through her eyes. He took his regular seat on the chair. Her lips turned up in a smile.

"You've played your part well, Stanley Becker," she said. Her voice was soothing.

"It isn't over."

"I'm afraid it isn't."

"I see Rosie made it back safely."

Sibyl nodded. "It seems that what you did caused enough fear in her to trigger it. She traveled, as you know."

"Where did she go?"

"It's not important. She is on the right path now. I have begun her training, and she has a much higher control than I ever had at her age. She will be ready when I pass." Sibyl smiled again. "But you're here for answers, are you not? You are here because you wish to free Louis Vargas."

Stanley exchanged a hopeful look with Lena. "I suppose we must find the water and trade it for his freedom."

"I assume you know the risk of taking such a gamble," she said in a disapproving tone. "Even if that were the case, Mà de Fusta is not one to keep his word."

"Then what must we do?"

"That is for you to decide. It will not be simple, as you know."

Stanley was growing impatient. "And what of the shadow-shifters?"

"There is one whose allegiance lies elsewhere, who can be trusted to deceive Mà de Fusta. The other two are scattered and confused. They only desire to return home."

"Louis's daughter said as much," Stanley said. "They agreed to help Mà de Fusta in exchange for a way to cross. How do they expect this will happen?"

Sibyl tapped her lip thoughtfully. "They say," she began, "that all the rivers are attracted to the lowest point of gravity, but through the journey there are places where gravity is uncertain. It causes holes, glimpses into other energies. These uncertainties, if found, allow one to step into other worlds. And because Asa is constantly trying to get closer to Oma, the boundaries to her world are the most accessible, although they are always shifting."

"How can one know where these holes exist?"

Sibyl's hand patted her ginger cat. "By the energies they give off. At times, they are nearly palpable."

"Of course . . . ," Stanley understood as he whispered, "the Time Key."

"That contraption may detect those energies influenced by Asa. Perhaps with it you may find a way to cross."

Stanley had suspected that he would be capable of finding these energies with the Time Key, but he never expected they would lead him to another world. He looked down at Lena, whose body emitted a type of energy that caused the Time Key to spin out of control, and wondered if her abilities with fire were energies from Asa. Lena gleamed with hope.

"And Lena's curse, so to speak," he began, grimacing at the word. "I've been meaning to ask—"

"The nature of your curse, Lena," Sibyl interrupted, "is a hidden gift that can be easily controlled. You needn't fear it, for fear feeds it, but control requires patience and acceptance. You can do great things with it if you learn to harness it. Otherwise, it can cause great damage, as you know."

The girl pondered Sibyl's words and Stanley opened his mouth to demand a clearer explanation. Sibyl's nod silenced him, and her extended hand asked for Lena. Stanley urged her to go with Sibyl. Hesitantly, Lena climbed onto her steady palm and waited patiently when Sibyl closed her eyes in deep concentration. Stanley wasn't certain what she would say to the vaelie, and was startled when the old woman suddenly began to speak in a strange language, very somber and urgent. It was quite unlike her usual relaxed manner, and her voice was filled with intensity. Lena hugged herself, eyes wide. Sibyl concluded her message to the vaelie and handed her back to Stanley. Lena trembled in his hold.

Before Stanley could ask her if she was all right, Sibyl's hand clutched his arm.

Her blind eyes seemed to stare into his as she spoke in a grave tone. "Time is of the essence."

Stanley's vision blurred. In a panic, he pulled away from the old woman. Lena scurried into his coat pocket.

"What are you doing?"

Sibyl shook her head. "If you want to see your future, you must trust me."

The word brought dread. Stanley did not want to know his future; the thought of it made him lose his breath. He was afraid to know what it held for him. However, something within warned him that if he chose not to see it, he would certainly regret it. Consenting, he took a deep breath, and Sibyl's hand grabbed him tightly by the arm.

Stanley's vision vanished into an endless white, submerged from reality, drifting into his future.

XXXIV

It was the same misty white from the night that Stanley had seen the woman who had commanded him to restore the balance, but it was far from soothing as the mist rushed past him, thin tears of water stinging his skin as he or the space around him traveled at high speeds. It was quite nauseating to feel his body flying by some unseen force to no apparent destination. Time travel with the Time Key took only a moment for Stanley's molecules to disperse into the air and quickly regenerate back into his body; but this, traveling under Sibyl's control, felt as though he was not an existing being, that he was merely a thought, a memory, intangible to time and space. He was an observer that could not influence the space he so badly wished to occupy. Such is Sibyl's power, I found, at least through her dreams. I am allowed to travel through space and time physically, but I am not permitted to change events or consequences without necessity. At least through my dreams, I can observe the subjects of time without making a wrinkle in the fabric of reality. What Stanley was allowed to experience through Sibyl's mind was merely a glimpse at the range of her power, and although he imagined it was a physical journey, it was only an illusion.

Stanley may have traveled for the space of an hour, or perhaps only a few minutes, before the whiteness dissolved to make way for color. When his head stopped spinning, Stanley immediately recognized the dark interior of his library. Here he felt comfort. The lingering traces of his misty journey vanished, and Stanley saw a man sprawled on the floor by his feet, unconscious. Beneath his ragged appearance, Stanley recognized his past self. He had fainted. The open window to his right suggested that this had been the night that Louis had broken into his house, had retrieved the vial, and had left Lena in a bottle. Looking closer, Stanley saw the shadowed outline of the glass bottle on the desk rolling toward the window.

"No, Lena!" Stanley called as he rushed to the desk. "You'll fall!"

The frightened vaelie didn't seem to hear him, but already Stanley's vision was blurring once again. The room vanished and he traveled through the mist.

It wasn't long before he found himself in the gardens occupied by caravans and tents. Busy men and women ran to and fro, and Stanley knew, still unsettled by the previous vision, that he was in the Romani camp. He spotted Past Stanley, snuggled in his coat. Toma led him through the crowds to Naomi and Nuri's tent. It struck Stanley that he appeared quite young, untouched by the events ahead of him, unconcerned by what was to come. Stanley wished he could step inside the tent and tell Naomi that he had found her daughter, that she was safe, but soon he was gone again.

In a lonely street, Stanley heard running behind him and the cold air smelled familiar. When he turned he saw a figure enter a nearly empty pub. Stanley tasted beer like a lost memory. He approached the window to see himself fingering the Time Key with an almost hungry look, thrilled for what he was about to do. His past self pressed the crown and disappeared. A few men noticed his sudden absence, but Stanley turned away when he heard arguing voices behind him. Nuri and Pierre entered the pub, walking right through him, to witness the sudden appearance of a man covered in ashes and reeking of smoke. Stanley looked down at himself, wondering if he was a ghost, if Sibyl's promise to show him the future had meant his immediate death. But the mist took him up in its wet embrace.

An abandoned house loomed before him. Stanley had the impulse to walk through the slightly open door. Inside it was musty and infested with cobwebs, and up the stairs nothing creaked as he had expected. At the top there were three doors, two of which were closed. Hesitantly, Stanley walked through the middle door across from him. To his surprise, he saw Louis's worn figure shivering in a corner, muttering curses in his sleep. Louis whispered his daughter's name. After a pause, he said Rosie's given name.

Dione.

Several hours seemed to pass by as he traveled through the mist. It saturated his face, but when he wiped it, his hand was dry. With thoughts racing about what he had seen, he hardly noticed when the mist lifted to reveal bare trees, dry from winter. It was peaceful, at least, as Stanley walked through the grove soundlessly. Perhaps it was over. He hoped he had been deposited into a serene heaven to rest.

The branches swayed with the breeze, and above him he heard the soft laughter of a vaelie girl leaping from tree to tree. He smiled, but he knew she wouldn't see him.

Almost instantly, the trees dissolved to reveal the Bird Room where the ceiling was covered in green vines and birdhouses. Stanley saw his past self standing by the window as his body shimmered and vanished. In a partly painted birdhouse, Lena stared at the place where Past Stanley had been, solemn and disappointed. Stanley leaned down to meet her gaze, but the girl retreated inside.

"I'm so sorry, Lena."

She didn't hear him.

∞

Past Stanley was in Maisie's room, cuddled next to her under the covers, telling stories that made her giggle. Stanley stood at the foot of the bed and listened to his daughter's voice.

Next, he stood behind Past Stanley as he retold the same stories to Lena. Her eyes were round and awed.

∞

He heard Jane and Maisie singing in the garden, whistling like the birds, and laughing. He wanted to sit behind them and sing along.

In the Bird Room, Lena sat on top of her birdhouse to watch the outside world with longing.

∞

"I don't wish to see the past!" he yelled to the white mist. The thick clouds muffled his voice. Stanley knew he had no control over what was happening; seeing the past that pained him, the mistakes he had made, the memories he wished to erase. If Sibyl could hear him, he wanted to be sure she knew he was greatly irritated.

Days had drifted by now, or only seconds, but the next scene was scorching hot as the flames of his burning house jumped out in front of him, stretching its eager fingers to touch him. It was a cleansing fire, a way that the universe wanted to communicate to him that soon it would all be over and he was obligated to move on. It was a sign of rebirth. But something in him knew that it would all have to come to an end. Stanley stood back, throat tight, to watch his house engulfed in flames. It distressed him to think that Lena could be in there now, frightened by the deadly fire she could not control, that she could not harness.

It was a relief when he saw Past Stanley emerge from the burning house and run toward the carriage, followed by Gilmore and the Millers. The doctor looked back once before he instructed his coachman to take them away. The scene dissolved before Stanley's eyes.

He was suddenly in a small room he recognized as Mark's. Toys were scattered on the floor, among them a red yo-yo. Stanley approached the bed where Gilmore sat holding his young son. The boy's eyes were closed, chapped lips were parted, and his hold around a stuffed bear was limp. Stanley choked. It could not be.

Gilmore kissed his son's head, rocked back and forth, and hummed soothingly, but there was no movement from Mark. The sickness had taken him and there was nothing anyone could do, not even his father.

Before the white mist came, Stanley turned away. Tears blurred his vision.

❧

He didn't want to see any more, but he was powerless.

The whiteness showed him a foreign place where barren plains were home to colorful caravans and tents. Stanley suspected this valley was the place where the *Calé* Travelers had come from. He walked through the thorny bushes where haggard sheep feasted and approached a little girl who seemed to be alone. Her brown hair fell in waves over her shoulders in a familiar way, and when her hazel eyes looked up, Stanley saw that it was Rosie as a young child. The girl's attention was not on him, however, but on an approaching figure behind him.

The sudden rage that Stanley felt was useless. He could do nothing when the bald man took Rosie's hand and led her away, talking in a syrupy voice. Stanley followed closely until they reached a sort of ditch in their path. Suddenly, Rosie's two-year-old voice began to scream as she tried to pull away from the bald man. There was no one to hear her, only the ghost of a man she would meet many years later, an observer who could do nothing to help her. The girl screamed and struggled, until suddenly they both vanished. Stanley stood back, knowing that she had traveled, and Mà de Fusta had gone with her.

The mist took him to the same place a few days later, where he saw a man appear out of thin air and fall into the ditch. His bloodcurdling scream was penetrating. Stanley felt satisfied at the sight of the bald man in pain, holding onto his handless arm. Somewhere during the travel he had been left behind, separated from his hand, still holding onto Rosie.

❦

He was in the year 2012 when Rosie stormed out of the house. Tears smeared her cheeks. She rushed past him, determined to find comfort in the only place she knew. She would only find shadows and fear.

❦

Stanley saw Fred jab a knife into him. Past Stanley's eyes glazed over in shock.

❦

He was in the Kingston he knew of 1897, standing on the bridge where he had once tried to take his life. He saw a girl suddenly appear and stumble into the cold night. A few carriages rushed past her, a coachman yelled for her to get out of the way, and the girl ran to avoid getting trampled by snorting horses. Stanley wished he could help Rosie, who was understandably overwhelmed. Shadowed figures, stumbling behind her, gave chase. Rosie closed her eyes and vanished once again. Stanley was relieved to see that the shadow men stopped in the place where she had been moments before; they stared down at the clothes she had left behind, but made no attempt to pursue her.

❦

Stanley saw himself appear by his burning house, who didn't waste any time to acknowledge it as he ran toward the Millers' home.

Stanley had little time to understand the scene that had not yet occurred when he was suddenly on Kingston Bridge. A group of men gathered in the middle of the bridge. A bald-headed figure pointed a pistol at another man who stood motionless in the night, when a sudden *bang* cracked the silence. Stanley heard his own voice choke as a bullet hit the man, and he recognized himself. His future self fell on his back. Two shadow men stood over him.

In the dark street, Stanley heard running. A lone figure approached him, gasping for breath. Stanley gritted his teeth when he recognized Louis, who looked back at the scene he had just escaped.

"They shot me!" Stanley cried, but Louis didn't hear him. "They shot me and you ran off, you spineless cur!"

The shadow men dragged his unconscious future self behind Mà de Fusta, who fingered a little glass vial in his hand, wearing a smile of satisfaction. Stanley ran to catch up to the group who had reached the river and trailed down to the shore. To Stanley's bewilderment, they suddenly vanished as though they had walked through an invisible doorway.

⚶

The mist lifted and Stanley saw the scorching sun above his head shine down on a group of sun-burnt wretches sprawled on the ground, all chained to a caravan. They stared with hollow eyes into the distance. Stanley walked around them and spotted himself leaning against the caravan, still unconscious. A thick collar around his neck had a chain attached to his cuffed hands. They had stripped him of his clothes, and the rags he wore hardly covered a bloodied bandage around his chest and shoulder where it was obvious he had been shot. Apparently, he wasn't dead quite yet.

"Let us go!" an angry voice shouted. Stanley looked up to see Lena gripping the bars of a cage, yelling out as loud as her voice would allow. When no one took notice of her, she stuck her arm through the bars and reached for Future Stanley, who was wheezing for air.

"Stanley?" she pleaded. "Wake up."

"I'm here," Stanley said. He reached up to touch her hand, but it went through her. He was not there.

The scene changed once again and he saw foreign places. He saw caravans pulled by strange beasts; files of countless men and women followed behind with collars around their necks and chains on their wrists. He spotted Future Stanley and ran to catch up. He was walking alongside the caravan, eyes half closed, back bent in submission and decorated by several fresh whip marks. Above his head was the cage. Inside, Lena was curled up, motionless. She held her arm out through the bars. Stanley clenched his fists and gritted his teeth.

"What's happened, Lena?" he asked, eyeing Future Stanley with disdain. Why did he not help her? Before he could reach up once again, Stanley's vision blurred as the white mist returned.

"Lena!" he cried. "Lena!"

Her image was gone.

"It's all an illusion, Stanley."

Stanley spun around to find the speaker and saw he was back in his library. The strange visions were over, but the remaining influence

281

of a terrible future still had a grip on him. Stanley couldn't find air as he gasped and clutched at his shirt. He was wearing regular nineteenth century clothing. Looking out the window, in the armchair across the room, was a future version of Stanley, who turned and contemplated him knowingly. Stanley remained motionless as he studied the man. His wrinkles and graying hair betrayed the hard years that had worn him down.

"Sit down," Future Stanley said, gesturing to the chair facing him.

"What happened to Lena?" Stanley demanded. "To us?"

Future Stanley looked down at his hands wearily. There were tattoos around his right wrist, and Stanley realized that he had seen similar markings on Ann.

"That doesn't matter," he replied. "You did well to see all this. I was not so courageous."

Stanley sat down, but his eyes drilled into the other man. "Tell me what happened."

Future Stanley sighed. "After Mà de Fusta shot me, we crossed into the other world. He branded me a slave and tossed Lena in a cage. He sold us to the slave market, but on the way there, Lena didn't— she . . . she was so young. It-it was too much for a child . . ."

The tightening in his throat choked Stanley. "Sh-she didn't make it home?" he asked, hoping that the answer would be different.

Through the tears in his eyes, he saw Future Stanley wipe his own. "There was nothing I could do," he explained. "I tried to free her so many times, until eventually they took her away. Days later, I saw her . . ."

Stanley knew what Future Stanley couldn't bring himself to say, and the rage made Stanley shake. "And . . . what happened to you?"

"I was a slave. I had many masters, and many tasks." He showed Stanley the symbols on his wrist. "One for each owner. I was useless, as you can imagine, for hard labor. But they beat you to do the work. Eventually, I was sold off again and put in a ship to cross the sea into the country they call Kor. On the way there we were ambushed by pirates, absurdly enough, and the ship sank. A handful of us were able to escape and float on the remnants of the ship to shore. I won't bore you with the details, but after months of traveling, I was able to find a safe place, a country where they speak our language. That's where I am now."

Stanley studied the man pensively, and gestured to his wrist. "Ann had the same tattoos," he said. "Does that mean—?"

Future Stanley shook his head impatiently. "You've not figured it out?"

"What?"

"Ann is Ann *Marie*," he said. "The little girl from the Romani camp. She is Pierre's sister."

"How can that be? She could not live so long . . ."

Future Stanley's eyes softened, as though thinking of a simple way to explain it to a child.

"The Roma crossed over. I don't know the details, but Ann was a slave, like me."

"And Paul?"

"He comes from the other world."

"How did they come to live with Sibyl, then?"

"I don't know."

Stanley abandoned his need to know about Ann and Paul, and nodded to Future Stanley.

"How are we here?"

"Sibyl can communicate through dreams, and since this is what is familiar to us both, it appears real."

"This is all a dream?"

"It's all an illusion," Future Stanley repeated.

Stanley shook his head impatiently. "I can't stop any of it from happening . . ."

Future Stanley regarded him for a moment, the gears in his head working to find a solution.

"I can't change my past, as you know. But you can dictate your future. Perhaps it can be mended."

"How will I know what to do?" Stanley asked.

"I made the mistake of trading the Divine Tears for Louis's freedom, and was shot. You cannot let him have the water."

"What will he do with it?"

"Mà de Fusta is not the one you need to worry about. It's the shadows. They have been after the vial since the beginning. That's why they tracked Louis down."

Stanley nodded, remembering Sibyl's story about the god who was cast out and could somehow control the shadow-shifters.

Future Stanley continued, "I suppose that if you succeed in hiding the water, things will change here. Perhaps not. But we are connected, you and I. Sometimes, I see fragments of what must be your memories. It's all an illusion, really—time. It's a mirror that warps what you see, and no matter how hard you may try, you will never make heads or tails of what it's showing you. Perhaps . . . I'm the way that the gods chose to mend the past . . . a warning. Perhaps I exist only to see you through your journey."

Stanley sighed as the heaviness of a predestined responsibility weighed down on his shoulders.

"I'll do my best," he muttered.

"If you don't succeed, well, know that this place is magnificent. It's all that we ever could imagine—*more*, even. I'm quite content here."

Stanley nodded thoughtfully, but the visions of Lena troubled him deeply, hacking away at the mangled pieces of his heart.

"And Lena's family?"

Future Stanley's face showed traces of long years of remorse. "I haven't found any vaelies. They're out here, but it's been difficult to locate where they live. Do you remember the story Lena told us, about the man named Raoul Bissett? I've managed to track him down. Turns out he's Louis's brother. I suppose that when I find him, he can take me to Lena's village."

Stanley's head spun as he tried to understand what it all meant.

Future Stanley nodded to himself.

"It'll all come together."

For a moment, Stanley realized that despite all the turmoil and sorrow that had tainted Future Stanley's life, the man seemed happy, and his tranquility gave Stanley comfort. Perhaps he had found peace at last. Perhaps his future would not be so bad. As they both sat in silence, Stanley's vision began to blur.

"Wait—where is the water?"

Future Stanley's voice reached him like an echo.

"Beneath the ashes!"

XXXV

It was dark, and for a moment Stanley wondered if he had gone blind. He gasped for breath, feeling his spirit return to his body. A cold drop of sweat ran down his temple. He lay motionless for several minutes, listening to the sounds of the night and thanking whatever being had watched over him for his safe return. Beside him, curled up in a ball on the pillow, Lena slept blissfully unaware of the future that Stanley had seen.

Stanley studied the girl for a long while. He had mixed emotions about returning to a reality where both their fates were still undetermined, where a coming danger threatened their very lives. His chest pounded, and his throat tightened once again. What he had learned about her future made him tremble with dread. He could not let it happen. He would not let her die.

It was early in the morning, and to avoid disturbing Lena's peaceful sleep, Stanley stole into the hallway. He limped his way to the front door, where he was surprised to find Rosie on the other side, sitting on the porch with her guitar. Without opening the door, he listened to her song. Reassuring warmth accompanied her voice.

> *He came from a land where rivers run bold,*
> *The trees stand tall, with cities of gold.*
> *Traveling's his trade, and then came a day*
> *That his wings took him to the land of gray.*
> *He was a swift bird, and she a shy doe.*
> *Hold tight on his heart; she never let go.*
> *My mother the doe, my father's a bird.*
> *My trade is a song, but a soundless word.*
> *I see many stories while still at my post,*
> *And although I travel I'm only a ghost.*

Stanley smiled as he opened the door and stepped outside. Rosie looked up but continued strumming mindlessly. She blushed faintly when Stanley took a seat next to her.

"Another beautiful song," he said.

Rosie put down her guitar and smiled gratefully. "Needs work," she replied. "You feel okay?"

He nodded, touching his tender side. "How long was I asleep?"

"Just for the night," she said. "Paul came to drop off the kids, so he and I took you to bed. What did Sibyl show you?"

Stanley shook his head. He didn't want to share the burden of what he had seen with Rosie, who had difficulties of her own.

"She says I have good control," Rosie said with a dismissive shrug. "While you were in the hospital she helped me travel. I know how to do it well, but without her I don't think I can . . . She says I'm the next Sibyl, but I don't know how to be one."

Stanley nodded. It was unsettling to know that one's life was at times manipulated by forces beyond one's control.

"I wouldn't worry. You'll be a great Sibyl."

Rosie brushed her fingertips over the guitar strings. "I guess you know more about time travel than I do."

"It isn't very difficult. Only, I have limitations . . . unlike you."

Rosie nodded.

"Rosie," he began, slowly. "I have a favor to ask of you, but only if you're willing."

She listened intently to Stanley's plan.

❧

Stanley set the Time Key to the amount of years and days he needed to travel back, and handed the contraption to Rosie, who handled it with caution. They stood in the backyard behind some bushes to avoid being seen by unwanted witnesses. Stanley had felt the need to travel to his past, to fulfill a promise he had made to his future self, and learning that Rosie was capable of traveling to whatever time and place she wished, he couldn't pass up the opportunity. Rosie was more than willing to practice her wondrous talent and immediately agreed to take him where he needed.

"Can you see when we need to go?" Stanley asked Rosie while she studied the hands of the Time Key.

Rosie nodded, but she suddenly grabbed his hand. "I only need to see your memories," she said, closing her eyes. "They'll take me there."

Stanley wasn't certain how it would work, but he waited patiently, finding that her touch was tender. His hand began to tingle. It spread through his veins and tendons, all over his body, until he was overtaken by a soothing sensation. He was intangible, and along with Rosie, he vanished into white light.

Several seconds passed before Stanley surfaced into reality to see that they stood facing his house. There was no trace of the fire that would consume it. He gave a long sigh and looked down at Rosie, who hugged him tightly, panting.

"It's all right," he whispered, holding onto her unsteady body. "You were brilliant."

The girl blinked. "Is this your house?"

Stanley nodded and led her to the back side of the house, where they entered through the rear door. Every step felt secure, familiar, and the smells that hit them once inside cradled Stanley in welcoming comfort. The house was silent. Stanley suspected that his past self had probably traveled to the past with Lena to find Louis, and would not return until morning. Rosie followed him to his room. Stanley found a velvet cloak that had belonged to Jane and handed it to her.

"This will help you blend in," he said and returned inside to change into some proper attire.

Rosie waited patiently in the corridor, and her eyebrows rose when she saw Stanley wearing his suit and hat. He hurried to the kitchen where he saw what he had been hoping to find: his father's Christmas check.

"Where to now?" Rosie asked once they were outside.

"I need to give Past Stanley some advice."

Rosie took them to the village of Woking six years back, to the night of the accident that would never occur, where they found a cab. Stanley held the door open for the girl, who shook her head.

"I think I'll stay here," she said, eyeing him uneasily. "I promise to wait."

Rosie seemed spent, and Stanley consented. It was probably best, since it would surely cause confusion to bring her to speak with himself. Frankly, he wasn't sure what he would find in this version of the past, where there had been no accident to go back to, where there was no reason for Past Stanley to visit this night, but it was the mere thrill of traveling that had urged him to come. He gave the coachman instructions, and within minutes had reached his house. He saw a shivering man without shoes walking alongside the street. Stanley parted the curtains to speak to him. Past Stanley's expression was one of pure shock, but Stanley had expected it.

It was as though he was playing a role that he knew well, although at times the déjà vu seemed slightly distorted. He didn't have brandy to drink or to offer, and their conversation was quite different. Past Stanley didn't know about the accident and had been wandering mindlessly during this night only because he had suspected to find the source of Maisie's illness the night she had first shown signs. Stanley didn't want to confuse or distress his past self, therefore omitted the fact that they had been victims to another fate. The time traveling knowledge that Past Stanley had was limited; Stanley had to remember to be patient.

Before their meeting came to a close, Stanley reminded him to care for Lena as he would Maisie, and was relieved to see that this version of him was growing to love the girl as much as he did. It was strange to be the guide, to be the future of his past self, but he knew he had done right to come.

Stanley reflected on Future Stanley's words during his visions of the night before. If time was merely an illusion, then perhaps this was all for naught. If he hadn't really traveled through time, how had he been able to create a different timeline, a different version of himself, and even spoken to a Future Stanley? If the Time Key only created the illusion of traveling through time, how would any of this matter, any of it be tangible? Perhaps Future Stanley had been correct to assume that powers beyond his own dictated events in his life only to lead him on the right path, to change the possible future that could trigger catastrophic consequences. Stanley brushed aside the weak sensation that the thought brought him. He was his own person, making his own choices. If time was merely an illusion, then it was quite a convincing one.

By the time the cab returned to the village, Rosie was in the same spot he had left her, shivering in Jane's cloak. She willingly climbed inside to warm up as they headed for Kingston. Rosie's eyes were heavy, and Stanley caught himself smiling when she leaned her head on his shoulder.

"I like where you come from," she said, listening to the *clip-clop* of horses pulling carriages in the busy streets. "It's peaceful."

Stanley leaned back. The sound of Rosie's voice was calming.

"I remember my mother, you know," she said after a long pause. "And my father, if I think very hard. I know I've seen them in dreams."

Stanley listened in silence.

"I've seen what I think is my father always in a dark room, in my dream. He looks all beat up, but I don't know what it could mean."

"Hasn't Sibyl told you about your family?"

"When I was little she would tell me that they were very far away, until I stopped asking altogether. She'd say that the dreams I had about them were only my wishes, but when they kept getting worse . . . more real . . . I thought I was going insane. And it wasn't only about my parents. There were times when I could swear I had gone back in time, or gone forward. I saw terrible things. I've been in school shootings, I've drowned in tsunamis, I've been in planes just before they crash, I've . . . seen children starving, dying . . . I . . ." Her voice choked, remembering, and Stanley wrapped his arm around her shoulders. "I've seen so many terrible things, and I always thought I was insane."

Stanley could only imagine what Rosie felt.

"She never once explained what I was. I think that I couldn't travel by will when I didn't know that I could. It was a way of protecting me, I guess. And when I first traveled, when you helped me, I went to the time where I most yearned to be. The time when my parents lived—where you came from."

Stanley nodded, and when she remained silent, he remarked, "I've met your mother and father, Rosie."

Rosie sat up and frowned.

"I know your mother better than your father. They miss you."

She didn't seem entirely convinced, but asked, "I have a sister too. Don't I?"

"Yes."

"I have dreams about her," Rosie said, resting her head against him once again. "Do you think they know what happened to me?"

"I think they do."

"I'd like to meet them." Rosie closed her eyes. "What's my mother's name?"

"Naomi. Your father is called Louis . . . you look like him. And your sister is Nuri."

"Nuri," she mumbled softly, drifting off in her own thoughts, cradled by the gentle rocking of the carriage and the sound of horses' hooves. Stanley rubbed her cold hand as she fell asleep.

❧

They went forward six years for Stanley to claim the check that his father had written, and once he had a purse filled with coins and banknotes, Rosie took them to the Kingston hospital in the year 2012. Stanley stole into an equipment closet to change his clothes again. Blending in with the nurses around him, he saw Past Stanley being wheeled by a group of paramedics. He used the Time Key to travel forward a few days to deliver the money, where he met with Lena and explained as well as he could what had happened to her Stanley. Lena was uncharacteristically timid with him, and Stanley supposed that it was difficult for her to understand that he had come from the future. She was relieved to know that he was *a'right*, and Stanley was glad to be able to offer her some comfort. But he felt that he was also there to say good-bye, and the reality of his own future began to sink in.

Stanley returned to the time and place where Rosie waited for him patiently, but her tired eyes demanded rest.

"Let's go home," he said, also feeling the effects of time travel, and she nodded.

They arrived just a few seconds before they left the first time, and watched from inside the house as Past Stanley's figure, waiting alone in the backyard, vanished into the future. Shocked, Stanley looked to Rosie for an explanation.

"W-what—how?"

Rosie gave a sad smile. "I'm only a memory."

"But you came with me . . ."

"I am real," she replied, as though trying to convince herself. "But I'm not allowed to change things, so you not might see me. Some people can. If I have to, I can change things, but I shouldn't. I'm supposed to only watch."

It seemed that she wasn't certain of it herself.

Stanley was uneasy at the thought. He realized how alone Rosie was and would be as Sibyl.

"You're going to leave now, aren't you?"

"I must."

Rosie was downcast for a moment. "I can take you where you need to be."

Stanley returned to his room where Lena slept on even as the morning light shined on her curled figure. He changed into his old clothes, singed and covered in ash. He found a pen and paper, which he set on the nightstand, and sat on the bed next to Lena. His gentle touch woke her, and her sleepy smile made Stanley chuckle.

"Time to wake up."

∽

Lena munched on a slice of apple while he scribbled on paper. Stanley had intended to do this before, but time had caught up to him and he regretted the need to rush. He must to tell Gilmore everything that had happened, all that was happening, and the dangerous possibilities of his uncertain future. He had thought hard about leaving Lena with Gilmore when he delivered the letter, but something told him she needed to come along. Stanley didn't intend to have her in harm's way, but he suspected that they would find a way home for her before long. He expressed his fears in the letter, and hoped his brother-in-law would understand the reasoning behind what he was about to do.

Lena couldn't make heads or tails of what Stanley's scribbles meant, and her expression made him chuckle.

"Can't you read?" he asked playfully.

Her nose wrinkled obstinately. "Of course I can. But not your language."

At her bidding, Stanley handed her the pen, which she held awkwardly in her hands as she wrote down a few foreign characters at the bottom of the page. They were simple strokes that formed a language distinct from any that Stanley had ever seen.

"What does it say?"

Lena grinned triumphantly. "It's my name."

"Beautiful."

It was time to leave. Wearing his old clothes, Stanley checked the pocket for a pistol that he wouldn't need to use, and found the empty flask in the other. He brought it out and examined it with slight disgust.

"What is that?" Lena wondered, perched on his shoulder.

"Something I may use shortly," he replied, returning the flask to his pocket.

Stanley left the coin purse on the bed with a simple letter of gratitude signed by both Lena and him, and hoped it would be enough for all the kindness the family had shown them. He regretted to leave before

Ann and Paul returned from the hospital, and was unwilling to wake Daisy and Andrew to say good-bye. Stanley was useless at it.

Passing by Sibyl's room, Stanley hesitated. He didn't want to disturb the old woman. He considered last night's conversation to be enough of a farewell, and dreaded to be reminded of the troubling visions she had shown him. No, there was nothing more to say.

During the drive, Rosie didn't say a word. Lena sat on Stanley's shoulder to watch the world outside dash past them. The somber mood was contagious, and Stanley knew that Lena was thinking about Sibyl's message to her the night before. Whether it had been good or bad news, Stanley couldn't be sure, but he didn't want to risk upsetting the girl by asking. Rosie was as difficult to read as ever, and Stanley could only guess that her thoughts were busy recounting all the things she knew now, about the past, present, and her uncertain future. Stanley imagined she would have difficulty accepting the heavy responsibility of being the next Sibyl. As for his own scattered thoughts, Stanley was unsure how to organize them. One thing was certain, however: the fast approaching future that he suspected might happen filled him with dread.

"You're worried," Lena said quietly. "Is it something that Sibyl showed you?"

"I'm all right."

"When we go home," she continued, "what will happen?"

"We must find the water."

"Do you know where it is?"

Stanley had given it a lot of thought, and the memories that replayed in his mind stirred confused emotions of irritation and relief. His stare was grave when he answered.

"It was under my nose the entire time."

❧

The Becker home was nothing more than an abandoned warehouse in the twenty-first century, and the tragic state of what now stood there made Stanley's throat tighten. From it he gathered that the house had burned to the ground not long after he had left for the future, and in his absence, no one had rebuilt it. His parents had probably thought him dead and sold off the property. The thought that all his belongings, the memories, had been devoured by the fire and could never be restored was quite painful. Stanley had avoided such worries during his stay in the future, but now the revelation of what had really happened in 1897 troubled him.

As he stood in the cold facing the warehouse with vandalized walls, Stanley felt Lena tremble in his collar and give a sniff. He raised his hand to her.

"What's wrong?"

"It's your house," she said. "I burnt it down."

"It wasn't your fault, love. You didn't cause it."

The girl didn't reply. Stanley approached the building, followed by Rosie, who had still not said a word. Bringing out the Time Key, Stanley set all the hands to the neutral markers, his way back home. He turned to thank the girl, who looked up timidly and embraced him. The gesture took Stanley by surprise, but he wrapped his arms around her in return.

"Thank you," she said, her voice muffled in his shirt, "for everything."

"I—" Stanley could find no words.

Rosie let go, gave him a familiar smile of amusement, and retreated to her car. From there, she watched gravely as Stanley prepared to travel. She waved once.

"Hold on to me, Lena," Stanley said, needlessly, and pressed the crown of the Time Key.

XXXVI

The sickness was more overwhelming than Stanley had expected. It sent him straight to the ground in dizziness. Stanley didn't dare open his eyes as he grasped the dead grass in shaking fists, but he could feel the heat scorching his exposed skin and heard the crackling of flames devouring his house. He braced himself as another wave of nausea overcame his body and was afraid he would be sick, when he heard Lena groan in his collar.

"Are you all right, Lena?" he asked, straightening up when he realized she was having difficulty holding on.

"I'm a'right," she said in a small voice.

The sickness seemed to be worse because of the greater distance in time that they had traveled, but Stanley knew there was no time to waste.

Stanley squinted to see a figure running ahead toward the house, covering his face with a scarf before breaking inside. They had returned moments before they had even left. Past Stanley had just escaped the massacre at the Romani camp and was about to rescue Lena from the fire, which didn't give them much time. His legs trembled as he rose, but he suddenly felt a hand clutch his arm. Stanley whipped his head to see Mr. Miller wearing a bewildered look.

"Mr. Becker," he began slowly. "You just went inside—"

Stanley gritted his teeth and held onto the coachman as he took a step toward the little house where he and Mrs. Miller lived. The roof had just caught on fire.

"I don't have much time, Tom," he muttered, trudging on with the help of Mr. Miller. He was glad to see him again after so long.

Without another word, the coachman helped Stanley reach the front door to the Millers' little home, but before Mr. Miller could stop him from entering, two voices called them from behind. Stanley turned to see Mrs. Miller running, holding onto Brutus, behind Russell Gilmore. Both were visibly concerned, and Stanley couldn't conceal the relief that overcame him in seeing them. Gilmore confronted Stanley and grabbed his arm desperately.

"What in blazes is going on? I saw the fire from my house—"

What Stanley placed in Gilmore's hand silenced him immediately, and the doctor cuddled the shivering vaelie, who looked up in confusion. Before Gilmore could demand an explanation, Stanley had disappeared inside the Millers' house. He had no time to conceal Lena from the Millers. Their eyes were wide in disbelief. Mrs. Miller dropped Brutus. The cat spat and hissed as he disappeared into the bushes.

Stanley wrapped the scarf over his mouth and nose, and although the fire had not entirely consumed this part of the house, he still had difficulty seeing through the smoke. He found their bedroom. Stanley stepped through the ashes that were quickly gathering on the floor, and heard Future Stanley's words in his head.

Beneath the ashes.

Sibyl had shown him a future where he had appeared and had run to the Millers' home. Stanley had had no idea what it meant before speaking to Future Stanley.

Stanley approached the bed. The memory was hazy, but Stanley recalled the day he had first traveled. He had looked out from the library window and seen Mr. Miller retrieve something from the ground. What the coachman had found on the street near the gates, Stanley had never thought could have been the cause of so much trouble. Stanley and Lena had traveled to find Louis, and had only witnessed the shadow-shifters overtake Louis in the street. The man had fallen near the gates, and Stanley had not been able to find the very valuable item that must have fallen from his pocket . . .

Breathing in the smoke that only worsened his dizziness, Stanley crouched and fingered the floorboards underneath the bed.

"Where do you keep your treasures?" Stanley mumbled.

He found a hole in the crack. With his finger he lifted the loose floorboard and found the small compartment that contained documents and small pieces of jewelry. He rummaged through the stuff, feeling guilty for the intrusion. He saw a rusted tin box and lifted it out. When he opened the top, Stanley breathed again. Shakily, he reached inside the box and, pinched between his fingers, pulled out a little glass vial.

⚬

"What's happened?" Gilmore asked Lena, who was holding her head dizzily. "Is Stanley in some sort of trouble?"

"We came back from the future," she replied, peering at Mrs. Miller on the grass as Mr. Miller waved his hand over the housekeeper's pale face. "Stanley knows where the water is—the shadow-shifters are after it."

"You found it by going to the future?"

Lena nodded and pointed at the housekeeper. "Is she a'right?"

Mr. Miller muttered softly to Mrs. Miller while fanning her face, "Now, keep the head, Norah."

Mrs. Miller shot him a crazed look. "Ma heid?" she cried. "I'm aff my blooming heid!"

Suddenly, they heard a gunshot from inside the main house just as Stanley emerged from the Millers' home, coughing convulsively. Gilmore approached him, wondering who could possibly be inside the main house.

Gilmore grabbed Stanley. Lena leapt from his hold and scurried up Stanley's arm.

"Stanley, could you please explain—"

"I don't have much time, Russell," Stanley said between coughs. He grabbed Gilmore's hand and placed a whiskey flask inside it. "This is for Mark. Have him drink from it."

"W-what?"

Stanley grabbed a folded note from his pocket and handed it to Gilmore. "Read this. It will explain everything."

Stanley embraced his speechless brother-in-law, who was staring at the flask in his hand, and then knelt next to Mr. Miller to shake his hand. There were so many things he wished he could say, but there just was no time. The coachman met his gaze and gave a simple nod. Stanley held Norah's hand, gave it a squeeze, and rose to leave without a word. His past self was probably making his way downstairs. He ran to the gates, leaving the Millers and Gilmore in confused silence.

Stanley hopped into the carriage that Past Stanley would shortly use to get away from the shadow-shifters. Closing the door, Stanley saw the shadows emerge from the house behind Past Stanley. To the right he saw a dark-skinned man, the only one among the crowd who had noticed him climb into the carriage. The shadow man's yellow eyes flashed apprehensively.

Lena trembled in his collar. Stanley sank into the dark interior of the coach the moment that Past Stanley jumped onto the perch of the carriage and whipped the horses to a run. Stanley cast one look at his burning house. All the treasures, the memories in it, were in flames. Stanley's throat stiffened. The Bird Room with Jane's birdhouses, Maisie's drawings, the canopy of vines, and Lena's little floating homes would be left undiscovered to be devoured by the fire. Her existence, along with Stanley's memories, would be forgotten.

As the carriage shook and rattled them, Stanley held on to whatever he could. From his collar, Lena poked out.

"I can sense them!" she cried.

"They won't see us. They don't know we're here."

"I can scare them!"

Stanley felt her climb down his arm. He picked her up and shot her a questioning look.

"Sibyl said I can control the fire!"

"What are you suggesting?"

Lena pointed to the window, a fierce light in her eyes that Stanley had never seen before. She instructed him to hold her out the window. Stanley shook his head sternly, but she would not be dissuaded.

"But don't drop me!" she called back as Stanley carefully extended his arm out.

The cold air whipped against Lena furiously. The girl closed her eyes and held onto him tightly. He saw Past Stanley's figure driving the carriage and ducked when the man looked back at the shadows that slithered close at their heels. Just then, an explosion shook the carriage from behind and a tree caught fire. Sparks sprinkled down over their heads. Stanley looked at Lena, who was clenching her little fists and trembling, deep in concentration.

Stanley had believed that Lena's fear had caused the spontaneous combustions, but now he realized that their future had always been inside the carriage, looking out for them. He had not known that a

297

future version of Lena, courageous enough to harness the energy in her, had been the one to delay the beasts chasing them.

Another explosion crackled. This time it hit the road behind them. The shadow-shifters shrieked and dispersed. Stanley brought Lena inside the carriage, who hung limply, her eyes heavy. He warmly cradled her, whispering as she blinked wearily.

"You were brilliant, love."

Her smile was weak. "I did it?"

"You scared the bloody beasts."

She gave a long sigh.

Stanley knew that their past selves were preparing to jump. He peered out to see Past Stanley standing on the perch and look behind him. There was surprise on his face when their eyes locked, but Stanley nodded and his past self acknowledged him. Before turning to drop down, Past Stanley tied the reins to the carriage. As he disappeared, Stanley secured Lena under his scarf and climbed out. It made him feel weak at the knees to see the racing ground beneath him, but he hung on tightly and looked ahead as he inched his way to the front of the carriage. Despite the violent shaking, he was able to climb onto the perch, sighing in gratitude.

"Where are we going now?" Lena asked as loudly as she could.

Stanley slowed the horses to turn them around, to which they snorted and tossed their heads in refusal.

"To Kingston Bridge," Stanley said as he whipped the horses.

"How did you know where to find the water?"

"I had seen it, Lena. The first day that I traveled, I saw Mr. Miller find the vial in the street, although I didn't realize it before."

"You'll trade it for Louis's life?"

"I hope that I can."

∞

It was a silent night, and very few people were out on Christmas, although the few carriages that they could hear *clip-clopped* loudly through the streets of Kingston. In the distance, Stanley heard the echo of voices singing carols. It didn't seem as though it would snow, unfortunately, to embellish the quiet Christmas night with the pure white of winter, and Stanley was glad of it. His hands were numb when they reached the bridge over an hour later, but it was merely a nuisance compared to the droning sickness he had had to endure for so long. Now, he could breathe freely at last.

He steered the horses off the road toward the river shore where the black waters of the Thames slothfully flowed by. He felt Lena stir against his neck, moving for the first time since she had fallen asleep. He breathed in deeply, feeling his chest tighten with sadness that suddenly overtook him as he allowed the reality of what was about to happen to sink in.

The horses slowed to a walk, and when they reached a secluded area untouched by streetlights, Stanley made them stop to rest. The streets were mostly empty, and there was no sign of Mà de Fusta or the shadows, yet. He climbed down slowly, feeling every muscle, every bone, groan in refusal, straining without the adrenaline that had flowed through him not long ago. His side stung when his torso stretched. Wincing, he stepped down. Lena moved again, and he imagined her stretching her arms sleepily under his scarf.

"Does it hurt you?" she asked with a yawn. "The cut, I mean."

"Not badly."

"My cut hurt me a lot," she replied, sounding refreshed and full of energy. "But vaelies heal faster than Tall Folk."

Stanley smiled at the name. The dead leaves on the frozen ground crunched under his shoes. He brought out the Time Key to open it, looking snug in his palm. All the hands aimed north. The longest hand pointed to Stanley, indicating Lena's strong energy. As he walked, he watched for the slightest change.

Lena poked her head out from the scarf. "I thought Sibyl said that you couldn't trade the water. That the bad man couldn't be trusted to keep his word."

"It's all about misdirection, love."

The girl pondered his words.

"Lena, what did Sibyl tell you?"

Lena knew to what he was referring, but she paused to recollect her thoughts.

"She spoke to me in my language," she replied. "She said that—that if I don't return home . . . my father will be . . . killed."

Stanley bit his lip, feeling inadequate to tell her that it would be all right, when he couldn't be sure that it would be.

The longest hand of the Time Key twitched slightly.

"But she never said how to get me home," she muttered. "Do you think we'll ever find a way? I do like living here with you, but I want to see my family . . ."

"I understand, love."

"And if we do find a way, you must come with me. I think you would like it there. It would only be to visit, though . . . I know this is *your* home . . . but I would like it very much if you came to visit me."

"I would like that, Lena."

Stanley stopped in his tracks, watching the hand point toward the shore. The tiny arrow spun quickly to indicate that whatever it was sensing was very close. Lena noticed as well and leaned forward as Stanley followed the arrow, crushing through the undergrowth. He stopped at a cleared spot where he supposed the energy was coming from. Stanley could feel it, as though there was a strange wrinkle in the air, a pocket giving off a different pulse that made the hair on the back of his neck stand on end. Stanley crouched low on the icy ground to inspect the unseen space in front of him.

With a gentle hold, Stanley picked up Lena from his collar. The girl looked up expectantly as he lowered her to the ground, where she stood and appeared so small.

"Lena," he began, but his tongue was heavy and his throat stiff. "This is your way home. Can you feel it?"

The girl perked up with interest. She sniffed the air like a hound, turning this way and that, growing excited and impatient. She faced the pocket of energy that the Time Key had indicated and suddenly crouched in alarm. Looking back at Stanley with a wide smile on her face, the girl nodded enthusiastically and pointed to it.

"I can feel it!" she cried. "It smells like home!"

Stanley's chest pounded. He wanted to remember her image, to carve it into his mind, but his vision blurred.

"That's the way."

A dark thought entered Stanley's mind. Could he really change the future? Had fate designed an unchangeable ending for them both, one that Stanley could never hope to alter? It suddenly frightened Stanley that he didn't know what awaited Lena on the other side. What had fate written as her ending? Would she need Stanley after she crossed?

Clasping her hands in delight, the girl bounced on her toes. Hesitating for a moment, she glanced back.

"But you'll come with me?"

Stanley did his best to sound natural. His throat was so choked up that it was difficult to speak. He reached down shakily, and Lena touched his finger.

"I'll be right behind you."

She grinned and bounced wildly. "I can take you to my village and show you all my favorite places! And you can meet my father and mother and the new baby . . . I'm sure my father's already found them by now . . . They won't like you at first, because you're a Tall Folk, but they like Raoul so I think—"

Stanley blinked once, then twice in disbelief. The girl had vanished.

He almost expected her to pop out from behind a rock, or to hear her giggling above him in the trees. But she wasn't there.

"Lena?" he whispered.

Her answer never came.

Stanley felt empty.

He waved his hand through the air in front of him, hoping to feel the passageway that she had taken to a world he could not see. He wished he could keep his promise. He had broken so many of them, and the one he desperately wanted to keep was impossible. His fingers fumbled for the Time Key, reaching for a faint hope. Perhaps the unseen passage was large enough for him to cross after her. But the Time Key's arrow had resumed its constant spinning. The passageway was gone.

Her absence was heavy in Stanley's chest. It cut a hole in him, as deep as the one Jane and Maisie's deaths had created. The small stitches that had repaired his broken heart, the fragments of happiness that had grown and mended it, had been pulled out. It was left raw and bleeding. He had not had time to prepare for this. Lena was finally home, but why did it hurt so badly?

He regarded the silence of the night, remembering the girl who had changed his life. He buckled over and his vision blurred. Lena—as unexpectedly as she had come into his life, in the same manner had she left it.

Stanley sat in the silence and allowed himself to sob.

◆◇◆

Despite everything, he must continue.

It wasn't long before he saw the figures on the bridge, trudging briskly to the center where an occasional carriage passed through, but nothing seemed out of the ordinary. Stanley regained enough composure to wipe the tears on his cheeks and return to his own carriage, feeling each step heavier than the last. Before he climbed on, he grasped the rail and struggled to breathe. His sagging shoulders shook slightly, and he wished he could tear out the heart in his chest that drummed so loudly. With one final look at the place he had last seen Lena, Stanley armed himself with the little courage he had left and climbed on the carriage.

He urged the horses to a trot and headed for the bridge where he counted five figures against the dark horizon, a brooding foreshadow of his coming fate.

Stanley recognized the two shadow-shifters who had chased after Rosie, still in the same shape that he had seen them in the future. They walked behind a man wearing an overcoat. Stanley guessed it must be Louis. Mà de Fusta was the leader of the group, his bald head shining under the streetlamps. The dark-skinned man followed several steps behind the two shadow men, his yellow eyes watching the scene intently. The fog that had risen during Stanley's wait drenched him. It reminded him of the visions Sibyl had shown him where white mist had always been present. He steered the horses onward. Mà de Fusta's sneer was clearly visible when he recognized the driver.

"Took less time than I had anticipated," Mà de Fusta said when Stanley climbed down from his perch to face the group, keeping close to the stone wall where he could easily see the drifting black waters of the river.

Stanley saw Mà de Fusta's gaze shift for a moment to look past Stanley's coach. A line of a half dozen people had gathered at the end of the bridge where Stanley had come from. At the front of the group, Stanley recognized Nuri's bold figure in the distance.

"I have what you want," Stanley said.

He stepped closer to Mà de Fusta, his back to the wall of the bridge that overlooked the river Thames. Stanley had stood there once, hoping to end his life. He could think of nothing more poetic than returning to the same place.

"Let him go."

Mà de Fusta's lips parted with visible disgust. "You really think me stupid enough to fall for that again?"

Stanley's gaze shifted to Louis. The man looked up intently, as though to read Stanley's thoughts. There he was, battered and helpless. The man who had started all this would be present in the end. Stanley felt a mixture of contempt and gratitude. Louis had made it possible for him to travel through time, to see many marvels, and had allowed Stanley to be a father again.

In answer to Mà de Fusta's question, Stanley stepped back and stretched out his arm. He gripped the chain of the Time Key over the river. It dangled freely in the chilled air, swaying enchantingly over the frozen waters. He looked back to see the dark-skinned shadow man watching calmly. Mà de Fusta grew serious.

"How can I trust you?" the bald man asked.

Stanley scoffed. The feigned innocence in the man's voice rendered him as the one in jeopardy, the one who had much to lose. The bald man took a step forward and Stanley another step back.

"Set Louis free," Stanley instructed slowly.

Mà de Fusta showed his golden teeth. "I believe you're lying."

He regarded Stanley for a few seconds. From the right corner of his eye, Stanley saw Nuri and the Roma watching the scene, motionless. Suddenly, Mà de Fusta brought out a pistol and backtracked to where Louis stood. The shadow-shifters shoved him to his knees and Mà de Fusta pointed the pistol at his forehead. Nuri muffled a cry in the distance. With wrists tied behind his back, Louis stared fiercely at the barrel.

"Maybe I should just shoot him," Mà de Fusta said, "and have the shadows tear you limb from limb. I'll take the Time Key from your cold fingers."

Stanley lowered his arm.

"Hand it here," Mà de Fusta repeated.

Stanley gripped the Time Key in his hand. He saw memories flash across his mind's eye of foreign lands and slave caravans. Lena wouldn't be part of it. With the same gentleness that his fingers had always handled the tiny vaelie, he pulled a little knob in the Time Key. A small compartment opened. Mà de Fusta approached. His eyes squinted. Stanley held up the Time Key. Inside it was a little vial fastened for safety, snug in the compartment.

"It can't be," Mà de Fusta muttered, walking toward Stanley, who suddenly held the contraption over the river again. "Wait!"

With a nod, Mà de Fusta dismissed the shadow-shifters, who shoved

Louis forward onto the wet cobblestones. Louis shot Stanley a look of dread. The dark-skinned man grabbed Louis by the arm and pulled him away from the scene.

"Are you mad?" Louis cried in panic. "Throw it in the river!"

Mà de Fusta was a few feet away. He stretched out his wooden hand eagerly.

"That's it, now. Hand it here."

Stanley saw Mà de Fusta's good hand clench the handle of his pistol, finger pressed to the trigger. Stanley swallowed. He clutched the chain of the Time Key. The shadow-shifters were motionless behind Mà de Fusta. The dark-skinned one met Stanley's eyes as he pushed Louis away. The bald man took another step. The barrel of the gun pointed straight at Stanley. Mà de Fusta's grimace was all Stanley could see when he heard the pistol fire.

Mà de Fusta had hoped to stop Stanley's clear intentions before the Time Key was lost to the black waters of the Thames. An intense force shoved Stanley backward. His spine hit the stone wall. Excruciating fire burned his shoulder and spread through him. It numbed him. Stanley supposed that his hand still held the Time Key, clenched between his fingers.

Mà de Fusta lunged forward to grab it. The pistol clattered on the cobblestones.

Stanley glanced down at the black waters and remembered his dream while unconscious in a hospital of the future. He had fallen, and it had been peaceful. When he looked up, Mà de Fusta was on him. The meaty fingers reached for the Time Key. The man still believed it held the Divine Tears, a story that a certain Romani girl had told Stanley only that morning. It seemed so long ago.

Stanley noticed Nuri running toward him. Terror distorted her stunning features. He wished he could tell her not to worry. Her father was free at last.

Stanley took a deep breath and felt a sticky pool of thick blood soak through his shirt. He dropped the Time Key behind him just as Mà de Fusta cried out in rage. Now it was Stanley's turn to sneer when he grabbed onto the bald man's coat. Aided by a surge of energy not his own, Stanley pulled with all his might and flung them both over the stone wall.

Above the rushing adrenaline, a clearness of mind allowed Stanley to collect a variety of details, feelings, and sensations that surrounded the last seconds of his life. The night was peaceful, and he wished he could have had the understanding of this moment, before all of it had happened, to have been able to enjoy more of them like it. Life had been simple; lonely, but serene. Sorrow had been crudely mended, re-stitched by Lena's loving presence, torn up by his own mistakes, and at last pieced together by his accomplished task. Everyone who had depended on him was safe. Regret, like a jab to his mangled heart, pulled at him relentlessly, but he knew it was over. Whatever he had been unable to fix would be left undone. He only wished he could see what followed the end.

On the opposite side of the bridge, Stanley caught a glimpse of girl in a velvet cloak observing from the shadows, face framed by wavy locks, hazel eyes bright with tears. She concealed her quivering lips with her hand. Her image flashed in Stanley's mind, and he suddenly realized that she had always been there, watching every moment of his life. He had not noticed her presence until the arriving end of it. Stanley gave a sigh as her image disappeared from his view.

He closed his eyes. He heard Mà de Fusta's cry of terror falling with him. He felt the rushing air embrace him, cradle him. He saw Lena perched on a tree, smiling down sweetly. He saw Jane and Maisie, and they waved to him.

His back cracked the ice and the shocking water robbed him of air. The black waters swallowed him and drowned out Mà de Fusta's scream.

He had played his part, but it was over, now. The story was done.

XXXVII

The funeral had been short, simple. Those of higher classes, acquaintances of Frank and Edna, had had little to say about Stanley Becker and the events of his life. It had been drowned out by much drinking and self-pity, the consequence of a love too strong and too fragile, and it concealed the truth that Russell Gilmore knew about his former brother-in-law. There had been others present that had known Stanley Becker in his last days, the best days, and were regrettably looked down on below upturned noses as if they were inflicted by a plague. The *Calé* had come to pay their respects to the man who had sacrificed his life for a mere stranger.

Gilmore had spoken with them, had met Nuri and Naomi, shaken hands with Louis, and laughed with a little dirty-faced girl with frizzy hair named Ann Marie. Many of the incredible people that Stanley had known had been present at the funeral. All had wept, all had remembered. This had caused quite a stir, obviously, and Frank and Edna had not known what to think when approached by the group of Roma offering sympathy in their time of mourning.

Not much time had passed since Gilmore had left the funeral. The doctor's figure shrugged inside his coat, burrowed in his own sorrow, as he walked alongside the river that had taken Stanley's life. He looked toward the bridge where it had all happened. Gilmore's hand held the letter, which he had read over and over again, trying to understand what it revealed about his late brother-in-law and the events that had shaped the last days of his life. He unfolded the wrinkled paper to reread the scrawled handwriting.

I'm not quite certain how to begin this message to you, my dear brother and friend, when I know that the end broods near my horizon. Although the thought causes me to tremble like a frightened boy, it brings a sort of peace that I cannot explain. Even as I now write, things are happening quickly and I know I must act without delay. I will be brief in explaining where I've been, where I am, and where I will be.

As I mentioned to you on our last meeting, I was expected to arrive at the Romani camp on Christmas night where Mà de Fusta found me. Through a series of devastating events, I found myself fleeing from my burning house and the Lurkers, or shadow-shifters as Lena calls them, close behind me. I had no other option. Lena and I traveled to the future to escape our pursuers, although I soon found that they were able to follow us through time.

I won't say much about the future, only that it is a magnificent time. You would appreciate it more than I did. Worried as I was for the risk we were taking in being there, I'm afraid I was ignorant to the incredible time I was visiting. The leaps that humanity has achieved in technology will astound you. In the field of medicine they can do miracles, Russell.

I suddenly find myself short of words. My thoughts are quite scattered. I think I have found a way to get Lena home before I must face Mà de Fusta, and the thought tears my heart to shreds. I suppose that if we don't succeed, she will be by the river waiting for you. If you do not find her in the trees, then perhaps she is home.

I will take the vial with the Divine Tears to Mà de Fusta, who will expect it to be inside the Time Key. I won't allow him to have it. If you are reading this, then I suppose you may be wondering why I have given you the flask. The Tears are inside. They come from a land where incredible things are possible, and this water will cure any ailment. It's for Mark. Send him and his sisters my love. He will be better soon, you will see.

There is a young woman, Russell, whom you may see here and there. She is a dear friend. It may be difficult to understand, but she is an Observer of Time, a Traveler by mere will. If you ever see her, send her my thanks. I do wish the best for her and her family.

There isn't much left to say. I hope to see you soon, if fate allows, but know that what I've done is for a greater purpose, higher than all of us. And if I succeed, I would prove that not only could I change the past, but I dictated my own future.

At the bottom of the note was his scribbled signature beside a different set of markings, shaping a language Gilmore had never seen before.

He ventured to guess that they had been made by Lena. Her unbelievable existence, which remained only in memory, still brought a smile to his lips. Gilmore had reached the trees by the river shore, and yet he heard nothing as he stood beneath them, waiting for Lena's voice to call him. He had come on the night it had happened, but she had not been there either. Perhaps she had gone home.

There had been no body to bury, but the simple headstones of an unfortunate family—daughter, mother, and father—rested together in peace at last. Gilmore gazed out at the Thames expectantly, as though hoping that he would see Stanley surface from beneath the chunks of ice and swim to shore with that boyish grin on his face. Gilmore missed Stanley dearly. He had explained all that he knew to the Millers, had even read the letter to them, yet he still found it difficult to swallow the truth of Stanley Becker's incredible life. Gilmore had struggled with all that Stanley had told him, had chosen to believe it, and now saw that it had always been directing Stanley to the end of his life.

Gilmore stood near the river as it washed up on shore, lazily bringing in debris from its waters. Something drew his eye, a shiny object caught between two stones. When he bent down to grab it, he was surprised to see that it was the Time Key. He snatched it from the frozen waters and dried it as well as he could. He opened the contraption in hopes that it would still work. Three hands pointed north, while the longest hand spun counterclockwise in a constant manner. Gilmore supposed that its functions might still be intact. He regarded it with wonder, looked out across the river once again, and tipped his hat to the silence. He wondered what else the cold river had witnessed.

This was his good-bye to the man who had saved his son's life, who had done so much in a short time, incredible things, and no one knew about them but a handful of individuals who recognized the man's courage and strength in his last days.

Gilmore walked toward the carriage that awaited him a few yards away. He was eager to return to little Mark. Since he had drunk from Stanley's flask, the boy had shown no signs of the sickness that had nearly taken his life. Gilmore nodded to Tom on his perch. The coachman looked out at the river in a similar way, missing Stanley Becker and the man he had become.

Inside the carriage, Mrs. Miller wiped stray tears with a handkerchief and Gilmore took her hand.

"My wee scunner," she whimpered.

Gilmore attempted a smile. "He's all right, now, Norah. He's with them."

❧

As I watch them, I take the image to heart. Those who loved him would never forget him. The first time that I saw Stanley Becker, he appeared to be nothing more than a man lost, whether in time or in himself. Now I see that if it were not for him, I would probably be lost as well. I walk the streets where he walked; I watch all he did, all he experienced. When I am tired and feeling alone, I think of him and his story. He was a man who found acceptance, who found love. He was a father and a friend, a husband and son. He was a traveler and observer, who only wanted to find that little bit of love he had lost, who broke the rules and found pain, who at last found happiness where he had least expected it.

I visit the *Calé* as is my obligation, and when I see my mother, I think of him. I stood back at his funeral, away from the crowd, and she spotted me from a long distance. Our eyes met and I knew that she knew me. The man next to her with waves of hair that framed sparkling eyes smiled when he saw me, and I recognized him from my dreams. The girl next to my mother, Nuri, didn't know me. But I know her, and her involvement in all this is not quite finished. Her story is one that intertwines with mine.

A nagging thought never leaves my mind, and I often wonder what Mà de Fusta wanted with me and my sister. I know we are fortunate to be far from his controlling grasp. At least, I hope that we will be safe for now, even though I cannot imagine the conspiring intentions of the man. Something tells me it won't be long before it all circles back.

As for the shadow-shifters, the Dream Lurkers of Stanley's stories, they fled the moment they knew that their only way home had been washed away by the river. That night I had stood in the shadows of the city, witnessing the terrible events of Stanley Becker's last hour, unable to change a thing, and saw that there had been a third shadow-shifter who had not been a threat. He had escorted Louis to safety, away from Mà de Fusta's rage, and had disappeared soon after both men's deaths. I don't know where the shadows are, or whether they found a way to cross, but with their weakening strength it would not surprise me that they have remained in their human shapes to live out the rest of their lives among us, unable to return to the place where they belong. The one whose human shape was that of a dark-skinned man, whom they called Number Two, had locked eyes with me, and I saw beneath the yellow eyes of a monster. There was a glimpse of humanity in them, and I wondered if the shadows could feel.

Still, I struggle with what I am meant to do. I am merely an observer, sifting here and there as though I were a memory—a thought, a wrinkle in reality. Through dreams I am intangible, but awake I can be seen by some, and I quickly realized that Stanley was one of those few. He found me in the streets, watching, pursuing him. He merely glanced my way from behind his beer glass at the many pubs he visited. At one point my hand grazed his cold one and he noticed me in the crowd, but the eyes of the drunkard didn't recognize me. He wouldn't meet me for a very long time.

When I revisit Stanley, I remain hidden in the shadows to conceal my existence, but at times my humanity resurfaces and I make mistakes. I am reckless. I'm not allowed to intervene, but sometimes I do. Sometimes rules should exist to be broken. So I exist to ensure that time is kept in order, that events follow the direction the gods have intended.

So, I exist.

At times, during my travels and wanderings, particularly when I see Stanley Becker in the street, inside his house, or drunk in a pub, I wonder if I will ever see Lena and her people, the world she came from. I like to think that after she crossed, she found a way home to see her family again. I can imagine that she would miss Stanley, as much as I do.

Stanley's strange yet powerful influence must have remained as a strong connection to me, because whenever I am overwhelmed with longing, I find myself in his life, seeing all the events that shaped it, soaking myself in him. I can sense what the shadow-shifters felt emanating from the man, a sort of foreign energy that they did not understand. But it never makes me fearful. It gives me reassurance. There was something quite special about Stanley Becker that surfaced the misery and gave way to the father he was always meant to be, the loyal friend that he was, and the man who allowed fate to guide him even to the end. Sometimes I imagine that he is looking down at me from wherever he is, smiling, because at last he is peaceful. At last he is with his family; he is home.

I suppose it is my time to move on, and seeing a little boy with a red yo-yo and a stuffed bear given him by his dear uncle, I know I am called elsewhere. I have only to wait and see the chain of events triggered by Stanley Becker's story.

Epilogue

The waters of the once-black Thames turned a peaceful blue, surrounded and cradled by tall yellow grass. Under the scorching sun, the waves winked and revealed a limp figure that had washed up on shore not long ago, pushing the unmoving legs as though to stir the unconscious man to life. A soothing wind from the east blew on his face, swaying the dark hair on his head back and forth in an enchanting rhythm. The sand beneath him soaked up the blood that gushed from the wound on his shoulder.

When a wave jumped to lap against him, the salt water stung the open wound and the man opened his blue eyes, fixed on the foreign sky above him as he gasped for air.

Acknowledgments

Any piece of writing has its faults, its holes, its could-be-better parts, and a book this large has a lot of demons. I wish to thank everyone from Cedar Fort who worked tirelessly to make this project what it is. Thanks to Emma Parker and Deborah Spencer, whose suggestions massively helped strengthen the story, and to Justin Greer for catching all my silly errors. Also, big thanks to Michelle Ledezma for the beautiful cover and her guidance through this whole process.

I greatly appreciate the following people for their contributions and their selfless help in creating this book: Joselyn Zegarra, Haylee Frolich, Candace Bateman, Miguel and Daniel Morales. Thank you to Brett Jensen, Cameron Sutter, Kevin Scholz, and Erin Nelson for your kind words and support. A huge thanks to those I didn't mention for your snarky remarks and loving words that kept me sane.

Thanks to my husband—who makes me feel like the coolest person in the world—for his love and support from the moment I showed him the few chapters I had written, and to my children, whose innocence breathed life into the children of this story. Lastly, thanks to my parents, who always believed that I could create beautiful things in the world.

About the Author

Melanie Bateman is a freelance illustrator whose passion for nature and pretty pictures will sometimes translate into written stories. When she isn't daydreaming, she enjoys being a mom. *The Time Key* is her first novel.

0 26575 18564 5